Also by Shirley Streshinsky

A Time Between

Hers the Kingdom

And I Alone Survived
(with Lauren Elder)

Gift of the Golden Mountain

Gift of the
Golden Mountain

Shirley Streshinsky

Villard Books

New York
1988

Library of Congress Cataloging-in-Publication Data
Streshinsky, Shirley.
Gift of the golden mountain / by Shirley Streshinsky.
p.   cm.
ISBN 0-394-55064-1 : $18.95
I. Title.
PS3569.T6928G5 1988
813'.54—dc19

Manufactured in the United States of America

24689753

First Edition

For Mark
son, critic, friend

Gift of the
Golden Mountain

PROLOGUE

— ◻ ◻ ◻ —

May is missing. She is somewhere in Southeast Asia, possibly she made it into Saigon on one of the last flights, we can't be sure.

Strange, how I put off turning on the lights. Sometimes I let the dusk gather so that I can scarcely make out the corner of mother's old cherrywood sideboard, and go banging into it with my wheelchair. I have been holding on to the fading light, trying to deny the darkness. I know it is a futile thing to do. At my age, I know.

All day long I've been listening to the radio reports from Saigon. I switched to the television for the five o'clock news. The first films were being shown, flickering images of crowds pressing against the gates of the American Embassy, of helicopters landing on the roof of the building, creating dust swirls lit by arc lights, lifting the last Americans out.

I am transfixed by the scene, the exodus: the fall of Saigon, the true and vainglorious end of the war in Vietnam, as confused and chaotic and humiliating as everything else we have done in that poor, sad country. It is dark now; only the television lights my parlor, sending flickers and flashes and shards of color into the dark corners. I don't think I could bear to see it in full light.

. . .

May is missing. That was the message. *We think she got into Saigon, we can't be sure.*

And I think I saw her, in one of the news films. It was only for an instant, she was in the surging crowd outside the American Embassy, her arms were raised, she seemed to be reaching for one of the marine guards. I only had a glimpse but I think it was May. Now I am watching every program, hoping to see her again. After the eleven o'clock news there is going to be a special on the events of the past days in Saigon, and if they show the film, maybe I can tell for sure.

Two men came to my door late this afternoon. One flapped an official-looking identification card from the U.S. State Department at me and said they wanted to ask a few questions about May. A routine background check, "nothing ominous," he added, with a condescending smile that was supposed to reassure me. They would appreciate my help, he said.

I have had some experience with these men with their empty eyes and practiced silences, enough to know that it is best to volunteer as little as possible. I was not in a mood to tell them about May, I wanted to stay close to the coverage of this last, big story out of Vietnam. But I knew, too, that they would not easily be turned away, so I motioned them into my parlor but made no move to turn off the television.

"We would like to ask you a few questions," the older of the two repeated politely.

"Shoot," I came back, feigning a feistiness that I did not feel, my eyes on the television.

"I believe you are a sort of historian to the Reade family . . ."

"Not *sort of,*" I corrected him, "I am the archivist for the Sara Hunt Trust, with responsibility for all of the documents and personal papers of the Hunt and Reade families, two old California clans."

He cleared his throat, trying, I suppose, to decide how best to approach an old woman who shows signs of not cooperating. He was about to say something when I held up my hand for silence. The commercial had ended and the television had returned to Saigon; lights flared, you could hear the dull sounds of artillery in the background, the reporter was breathless. *The ambassador will be leaving soon . . . The compound is filled with Vietnamese, desperate to get out . . . The American*

4

fleet is offshore, waiting . . . The Viet Cong are at the gates of Saigon, closing in . . .

"Are you associated with the California Historical Society?" the man asked.

"No," I answered absently, stung by the panic in the Vietnamese faces caught pressed against the bars of the Embassy, "I am employed by the Hunt Trust, though we do cooperate with the Society. Sara Hunt was one of its benefactors."

"I see," he said, though plainly he didn't. As CBS turned its attention to some other part of the world, I turned mine to the men sitting in my parlor. The older of the two was, perhaps, thirty-five and beginning to bald. His face was curiously nondescript; it might have been handsome, had it any animation. He was wearing a suit and a drip-dry shirt which had not been pressed. I could imagine him solemnly washing it in a basin and hanging it to dry over the bathtub. The other was younger, not more than twenty-five, I think, and his hair was shorter than any of the young men I knew. Even the residents out at the Medical Center wear ponytails and dress in jeans. I wondered if he knew how clearly his appearance marked him.

"Why exactly are you investigating May?" I asked, to see how they would evade the question.

"We thought you would be the best person to give us a rundown on her family history—her grandparents, that sort of thing," the older one countered.

"I suppose I might be," I answered, and left it at that, knowing he expected me to play the garrulous old woman and give him what he wanted for the asking.

Instead I turned back to the television. Walter Cronkite was intoning the benediction for CBS: "This is a night that history will long remember . . . the last American Marine has left Saigon." And then they showed it again: A woman, tall with long dark hair, her arms raised. May, it could be May.

"Will you tell us?" the younger of the two, grown impatient, finally asked, causing the older man to frown.

"Tell you?" I repeated, for a minute thinking they had read my mind, thinking they knew it was May I was straining to see.

"About the Reade family tree," he said.

The older man cut in, "Perhaps you could begin by telling us why she uses the professional name of Dr. Wing Mei-jin."

I laughed out loud, I couldn't help it. They looked at me peculiarly, as if laughter was the last thing they expected. "She calls herself that because it's her name," I told them. "If you don't believe me, check her birth certificate—though you won't find the 'doctor,' of course."

He scarcely took time to smile at my small joke. "Then why did she go by the name 'May Reade' for so many years?"

"I don't really know," I lied, then added a grain of truth: "Maybe she just wanted to sound more American."

"But she is American," the younger man said. Suddenly I was weary of the banter; best to give them the information that was on the record and be rid of them.

"May's father, Porter Reade, grew up on the family ranch in southern California," I began, turning off the sound but keeping my eyes on the television. "Willa and Owen Reade had come to California in the late 1880s. Unfortunately, Owen died before Porter and Katherine were born in 1904. Katherine is now Mrs. Katherine McCord." I was on thin ice here, I had to choose my words carefully not to lie outright, while keeping the family secrets. "The children . . ."

"Porter and Katherine were twins . . ."

It was a statement, I didn't have to answer. "The children were raised by Mrs. Reade's younger sister, Lena Kerr. In those days she was called a spinster, and she lived with the Reades."

"Why was that?" the younger man asked.

"Oh it wasn't so unusual for the times," I told him. "After her husband's death, Mrs. Reade was busy running the ranch, an occupation she was good at, and one she enjoyed. Her sister had a natural affinity for children, and they for her. In fact, Lena reared all the Reade children—there were two older boys. It was an arrangement that seemed to satisfy everyone." I turned up the sound on the television slightly, hoping it might get them off the subject. Dear Lena is not in the public domain. Few people now living know that Porter was her child, that Kit was not his twin but his cousin.

"What about Porter Reade as a labor organizer?"

I nodded, relieved to be off the subject of Porter's parents. "In the thirties he was active in the labor struggles on the San Francisco docks. And he was in the thick of things during the General Strike and riots in the 1930s. But all of that information is detailed in the files of the House Un-American Activities Committee. If you don't have access to those files," I said, more sarcastically than I had meant, "just read Porter's book, *Notes from the Waterfront*. You can get it at

Moe's bookstore in Berkeley—it was reissued in paperback a year or two ago. Or if you want to know what happened to him as a war correspondent, read *Dispatches from the Burma Road.* Unfortunately, he didn't get to write about his trials with Joe McCarthy and those characters on the House Un-American Activities Committee who were so certain he was a Communist."

"That's been pretty well documented," the older man said, "It looks as if Reade is in the process of being historically vindicated." I was disarmed by this sudden breach in intelligence practice. He threw me off guard. Defending Porter had become almost second nature, it felt strange not to have to. I turned back to the silent television and for a few moments stared at a tap dancing peanut. When the young man started to prod me, the older one stopped him. He was going to give me time.

I cleared my throat, and resumed in what I thought of as my archivist's voice: "May was born in San Francisco on Valentine's Day, 1943. Her father was a correspondent in the China-Burma-India theater, attached to General Stilwell's staff. Her mother was Chinese, a medical doctor and a member of a distinguished Shanghai family. Liao Ch'ing-Ling." I paused a moment and thought about Ch'ing-Ling. Many of the faces from my past are lost to memory now, but not hers. Never hers. I can close my eyes and see her as she looked the day May was born, her jet black hair fanned out against the white of the pillow, that beautiful, porcelain mask of a face, perfectly still, those great black eyes, anguished and determined. I knew then that she would not stay. I believe the others saw it in her face as well, and were helpless against it. I shook myself to continue. "She was working in a hospital in Honolulu when war broke out; it was a rushed, wartime marriage. Porter sent his wife to this country to await the birth of their child. The baby was named Mei-jin. We called her 'Mei.'

"One month after the birth, Ch'ing-Ling chose to leave the country, giving the child to the care of Katherine Reade McCord and Lena Kerr. We know that May's mother returned to Mainland China, but there has been no trace of her since. May was cared for by Mrs. McCord, Lena Kerr and a devoted friend, Sara Hunt, in Mrs. Hunt's San Francisco home, until Porter Reade returned from the war, at which time he took complete and loving charge of his daughter.

"Lena Kerr died not long after Porter's return from the war. Sara Hunt—to whom May was especially attached—died when May was eleven. May and her father were inseparable, though he was embroiled in controversy and was spending most of his time and energy appearing before government committees. May was his constant companion. The two were in a Los Angeles hotel room, waiting to make a court appearance when Porter Reade suffered a fatal heart attack. He died in her arms. She was thirteen years old."

"Tough break," the younger man blurted, and the phrase hung in the air, awkwardly, until the other banished it with a let's-get-on-with-it question: "What can you tell us about her early schooling?"

"She went east to boarding school—the Colworth School in Colworth, Maine, where my daughter teaches. May lived with my daughter and her family in town. Then she went on to Mount Holyoke, and graduate school . . ."

"Yes," he interrupted, as if he knew all that, "I wonder if you could tell us something about her professional career?"

"Tell you?" I repeated, not quite understanding what it was he wanted to know. "Oh well, she is a geologist, surely you know that. A geologist needs to understand those events which can seldom be directly observed, which are buried in the vast depths of the earth. Her task is to search out secrets which predate human history." I looked into the eyes of the young agent and saw a flicker of confusion. I thought, he does not know if I am rambling or if there is a point to what I say, if I am shrewd or if I am slightly senile. "Geology," I went on, as if warming to my subject, "is the study of indirect evidence—of fault lines and alluvial plains, of glacial scour and eolian deposits . . . the geologist must work out all of the possible combinations of events that occurred ages ago. In short," I said, as pedantically as I dared, "geology probes far beneath the surface, looks to times beyond memory. To do this, a geologist must go into the field, must know where to look for the clues. May's particular field of study is volcanoes."

I did not tell him that it was not surprising that May should have become a geologist. I did not say that the whole of her life has been a probing for answers buried deep in the bedrock of her past, that all this while she has been searching to discover something about the pressures which caused the slip-fault that occurred before her birth, an event which profoundly shaped the contours of her life.

The older agent shifted gears. "Can you tell me if her politics are similar to her father's?"

I wanted to sigh, instead I did the expected and bristled noticeably, making no attempt to hide my annoyance. "May is a geologist, as I told you. She is not political. She is interested in rocks and volcanoes, and that is all I have to say."

"Is there . . ." he began.

"No," I answered, "there is nothing more I can tell you."

It was not true. I could have told him a great deal more. I could have said I was there that Valentine's Day, with Lena and Sara and Kit. My Emilie was in her junior year at Mills College that spring, and she joined us at the hospital. It was wartime, and we were a company of women, closing ranks. It seems to me now that in those dark early years of the war, Ch'ing-Ling's baby became for each of us all the hope that was left in the world. We were determined to make a warm, safe place for this exquisite child, nestled that day in the arms of a mother who had, even then, decided to abandon her.

I could have told them that it was Porter who decided she should be called "Mei-jin," which means "Beautiful Pearl." He wanted his child to be proud of her Chinese heritage. I could have told them so much more, but I would not. I wanted to concentrate on the new film clips coming out of Saigon, so I could try to catch a glimpse of May in the frantic crowds that were clamoring to escape that lost country.

Most days are lost in the mists of memory, but the day of Sara Hunt's last visit is not. It was a Thursday in May of 1954, and it stands clear in my mind, all details perfectly intact. I had positioned myself that morning on the daybed on the sunporch so I could look out to the garden and see down the hall as well, to the frosted glass of the front door of the cottage. If I had to stay in bed, as the doctor seemed determined I should, I wanted to be where I could at least see something. Repose is not a natural attitude for me; I think of myself as being in motion. Folded hands please me in others—I once had a show of photographs called "Hands"—but my own require occupation. I shifted the heavy cast that encompassed one leg and attempted a more comfortable position.

I thought about taking a photograph of a tall ladder in an empty room, captioning it "On the Humpty-Dumpty front, this is the ladder from which Faith had a great fall . . ." and sending it to friends and clients, to let them know I was going to be out of commission for a time with a shattered leg.

Looking out the window gave me no pleasure, untended as my garden was these past weeks. It turned out not to be a bright day, as promised, and I was glad. The sun had been erased by a fine white fog that washed in about midmorning, first in quiet reconnoitering puffs, then in strong invading gusts. In the sunlight, the bougainvillaea glowed a garish purple against the white glare of the DeLuccis' garage, but in the fog it became a soft, pastel pink. Sara would appreciate the fog. Her eyes had become sensitive to light these past few years.

Sara. How long had it been since she was here? Almost a year, nine months at least, since she had been well enough to venture out of her house on California Street. Which meant that this trip, even if it was a relatively short distance, would have a purpose. That was what troubled me. I shifted again, determined not to let myself get lost in the vagaries of what Sara might be thinking, or why Sara was coming that morning.

I had lived in the cottage long enough to know all of its sounds, and I knew how to filter certain of them: the mad whir as the refrigerator switched on, the methodical ticking of the gas heater as it gained momentum, children's laughter lifting from the schoolyard down the hill. If I couldn't move about, I could at least listen to the world outside. I switched on the radio. Static crackled, then an apocalyptic voice from some far place intoned: *On this day in a little known corner of the world once called French Indochina, the French army has been defeated by the Vietminh forces of Ho Chi Minh at the Battle of Dien Bien Phu.* Silence then, until suddenly calypso music blasted out and I switched the radio off.

I heard the Cadillac as it turned the corner and began the laborious climb up the hill, its great engine grinding and complaining. The auto, like the small woman who would be perched on its rear seat, her gloved hand grasping the chromium handle, was of good, prewar stuff; both had been well tended over the years; each was, quite simply, old.

The car and the woman and the driver had been coming to my cottage for more than thirty years, long enough to have developed a ritual. I considered trying to get up to go to the door, to be there when Sara arrived as I always was. I actually went so far as to move one leg—the good one—before giving up. Sara was ill and I was only mending, but it didn't matter. I couldn't move. Annoyed with the intransigence of my body, I leaned back on the pillows and tried to be content with imagining a scene I knew by heart.

I listened as the car pulled up to the cottage, noted the full roar of the engine as Henry shifted into reverse to curb the wheels on the steep hill. Henry had been hired when Sara purchased her first "machine," as she called them, a Pierce-Arrow. A slow three-count and there was the solid thud of the driver's door closing; another six-count and he would have gone round to help Sara out of the back, holding her firmly with one hand while he closed the door behind her. Once, not all that long ago, Sara would have been out and up the steps before Henry could come around to open the door. I could not remember when Sara had started to wait for his help. Now I could hear them on the stair, and the soft, fussing sounds they made to each other. "Watch it here, Miss," Henry scolded, and Sara muttered something about him watching out for himself.

And so they came: slowly, Sara's age and the heart condition she would not admit to, impeding their progress.

"Faith?" Sara called out.

"Back here, on the sunporch," I answered, shaken by a new weariness in her voice.

Sara appeared in the doorway to the little sunporch, flushed from the exertion of climbing the cottage steps, looking so fragile it seemed a small puff might blow her away.

"What's going on here?" she asked, her eyes scanning the leg cast.

"My tap dancing debut has had to be canceled," I answered, determined to make light of it, then ruining the effect by blurting, "You shouldn't have come, Sara darling—but I'm so glad that you did."

She grasped her cane with both hands and lowered herself into the chair beside the daybed. Then she held hard to my hand and said nothing. Catching her breath, she looked out to the garden.

"Weeds are taking over," she offered with what sounded like a sigh of acceptance. "It used to be such a pretty place."

Alarmed, and feeling a need to reassure her I said, "It will be again, Sara. It's not as tangled as it looks. You know my theory on gardens— planned disorganization. I'll have it set right in a few days, just as soon as I get back on my feet."

"Yes," Sara said briskly, as if she had turned away from the business at hand and was now turning back, "and how soon will that be?"

"The doctor says six weeks, maybe a bit more—it seems to have been a rather complicated fracture—before I can get around."

"What does he mean by 'get around'?"

I knew Sara in this mood; it was no good to put her off. "I think he means get around enough to do for myself. As far as my going back to the studio, that will be a while."

"How much of a while?" Sara could be relentless.

"Six months, probably." I coughed nervously, but made myself add what the doctor had said was more likely: "Maybe longer."

"Then we have to find you a gardener, don't we?"

I laughed, relieved. Sara had not given up, after all. I touched her face, and for an instant she seemed herself again: not old, not ill, but filled with plans. For a long moment we looked at each other, remembering.

Sara allowed a contented silence to gather before proceeding. "How old are you, Faith?"

"How old?" I repeated, as if it was the question I didn't understand and not the reason for it.

"Sixty-one," I answered.

"Sixty-one," Sara repeated with a small lament of a sigh and then, catching herself, she added, "Oh to be that young again!"

I relaxed. We were on familiar ground now, having bridged the gap of time and events that had separated us for so many of the past months—Sara's heart trouble, my fall.

"I came for a reason," Sara offered, holding to my hand, "I need to ask a very large favor of you."

I nodded but said nothing, knowing that whatever she had in mind would be couched in terms of a favor to her. It was Sara's way.

"Before she died," Sara began, "My dear Lena left all of her journals and her correspondence as well, in my care. There is quite a volume—letters she received from others, notably Porter and his father, and letters she wrote to them. Some are copies she made herself, others Porter gave me when he came back from the war, along with his papers." She paused, frowned. "He gave them to me for safekeeping, you see. Porter's the one who suggested I collect all the papers in what he calls 'the family archive.'"

Suddenly, Sara's voice grew weak. Wanting to give her time to recover, I broke in: "I can still see Lena sitting at the little desk in your library during the war, the morning light flooding in from the east window . . . a perfect Matisse subject!"

Sara smiled, reviving to the thought of Lena. "She did write wonderful letters," she said, braced by the memory. "She always chided me so for preferring the telephone."

"So," she went on, "I have six boxes filled with all sorts of letters and papers and journals, and I must see to their safekeeping. Some are of historical significance, at least in California. Kit's father, you know, was a classmate of Teddy Roosevelt. They corresponded, and there are pictures of him at the ranch. In fact, there are at least six more boxes of photographs . . . the Reades were great picture-takers, and you have been photographing all of us for years now. They knew all sorts of famous and semi-famous people, and even a few who were infamous, as you will see from the papers.

"Someday, perhaps, the descendants will decide to make them public, but I think that will not be for some time. Current history has made Father Hunt something of a heroic figure as one of the great railway barons of the West." Her eyes lit wickedly for a split second. "With this new material the historians should have some fun revising Father's reputation—I'm sorry I won't be around to cheer them on.

"So," she said, "I have first to convince you to take on the job of keeper of these archives, and then we will have to settle on how this trove is to be managed."

I could only stare at her. "I knew you had something in mind," I told her, "but I must say you've taken me by surprise. Have you spoken to Kit and Porter about this? Wouldn't one of them want to handle the family papers?"

"I've spoken to both, of course. Porter has his hands and his mind full with all of the charges brought against him, and Kit is working so hard to help him—at the same time handling her own business interests—that she hasn't the time to do it, or the inclination either. To answer your question—both agree with me that you are one of the very few people in this world we could even consider asking to take on what is certainly a delicate job. They trust you implicitly, and so do I. You know that."

"Then of course I'll do it, Sara," I answered, my mind racing, one question pushing out another. "The photographic file I can handle, but I wish I had some training as a librarian. I do have a friend at the Historical Society who is discreet and will help me." Then it dawned on me: "Could any of the papers in the archive be used against Porter?"

Sara was blunt: "Certainly. That's why the papers must be hidden. Only Kit, Porter, I and now you know about them. That won't be forever, of course. There are some family secrets which need to be kept a while longer. But to be honest it is May I'm thinking about. And something more I need to ask of you. Something quite . . . momentous."

Suddenly I understood. For all of her long, good life Sara had been a gentle guardian to those she loved. And she loved Lena's granddaughter.

"I don't know if you realize how strained things are between May and Kit," she said.

I had noticed, and said I was at a loss to understand the rift. Sara told me, "It seems to me it started at about the same time that the child insisted she be called 'May Reade.' That was what—about a year ago, when Porter started taking her to the hearings with him. At the time I thought it was because she wanted to have the same name as her father. Now I think it is something else."

"What?" I asked.

Sara, tiring, sighed. "She is such an intense little thing. Sometimes I look at her and see Lena. There is something in her that is so like her grandmother—the great sweetness, a quality of *knowing*. What troubles me is the anger I feel in the child, the resentment. I believe it has to do with her mother, I think it might be a rejection of that part of her that is Chinese . . . something like that."

I patted her heavily veined old hand. "Does she ever ask about her mother?"

"Never," Sara said, "not even when I try to move her in that direction. And that troubles me. Porter brags that she is ten going on thirty, and that bothers me, too. She shouldn't have to be so grown up. She is just a little girl."

"You really have become May's grandmother, Sara," I said, moved by the affection and the pain in her voice.

"I know that," she answered, picking up the photo I keep of Emilie's twins by the bed. "Your grandchildren are what—two now?" Before I could answer she went on, "I know that May is going to need me—perhaps next year, perhaps ten years from now—and I'm not going to be here. There are questions she has to ask, Faith. No matter how much the rest of us love the child, she is going to need to know why the woman who gave her birth left her behind. When she is ready, the answers are in the papers. They may not be the ones she wants. That is where you come in. May thinks of you as one of the family . . ." She gave me a searching look; her hand, grasping

14

mine, began to tremble. "Do you see what I am asking?" she finished, in a weak voice.

I did see, and it took my breath, the enormity of it. "I wonder if I am up to it," I said, weakly.

She touched my face. "About that I have no doubts at all."

We sat for a time, thinking our own thoughts, my mind reeling at the idea of even attempting to take Sara Hunt's place as May's friend and protector.

Sara cleared her throat, "I had in mind a professional arrangement, to make everything legal and such."

"I thought as much," I answered, teasing.

Sara did not smile, but said quite deliberately, "I know you thought I was coming to offer you some kind of make-work job to keep you busy while you convalesce, and I know you were thinking it would be an excuse to make you take some of my money—of which I have far too much, thanks to my robber baron of a father— and you far too little."

I tried to break in but she wouldn't let me. "Hush and let me talk while I've got the strength," she said. "I think you can see that I'm asking you to take on a task that goes far beyond money, and to be honest I don't know what I will do if you turn me down. There's no one else I can trust to do what is going to need doing. Lena's family is precious to me, Faith. I never had a family until Lena made me part of hers. And now May . . ." her voice broke and a small sob escaped, ". . . if she were close to Kit I wouldn't be so afraid for her, but she will have nothing to do with Kit." She had to stop to blot her tears.

I started talking, to give her time. "I keep thinking of how Kit looked, the day May was born. It was so strange . . . she's always been so small and trim and stylish, but in those weeks she seemed to fill out, to be all pink and glowing, almost as if she were the one giving birth. And when Ch'ing-Ling left, I remember thinking that Kit was going to get a chance to be a mother after all. That seemed almost, well, somehow fair . . . she was so young when she was widowed, and she and Porter had always been so close. I really felt that if this had to happen—if all our pleas to Ch'ing-Ling could not change her mind—then at least May was going to have the very best substitute mother in the world."

Sara nodded, dabbing her nose with a lace-trimmed, linen hand- kerchief. "Yes. It was what we all thought, Kit too. Dear Kit, this pains her terribly. But something went awry, and Porter hasn't been much of a help. He sloughs it off by saying it is just a phase, and then he drags the child to the hearings with him—she has to run that gauntlet of photographers. . . ." She shuddered.

"Have you been watching that man McCarthy on the television?" I asked, wanting to distract her.

Sara would not be distracted that day. She continued: "Porter has never wanted an inheritance, you know. Lena left him what she had, and Kit is taking care of his defense. So I am leaving the bulk of my estate to May. She will receive a yearly stipend until her twenty-fifth birthday, then she will have it all to do with as she wishes. By then I hope that—with your help—she will have come to terms with her past. If that happens, I believe she will also be able to come to terms with Kit."

She was having difficulty breathing now, and I wanted to stop her, to make her rest, but she wouldn't. "My lawyers tell me we can set up an archive with you as administrator, with complete control. You will receive a salary. You've always been so stubborn about taking money from me, but surely you won't object now, knowing that I couldn't possibly pay you enough to do what I am asking of you."

I pulled myself up on the bed, ignoring the shooting pains that shimmered up my leg, feeling nothing but a great warmth for this tiny woman. I wrapped my arms around Sara Hunt and held her close. "Yes," I whispered into her hair, and then I repeated it, softly, "Yes, Sara, I will. Never as well as you, but I will do my best."

Sara Hunt died two months later on the afternoon of the Fourth of July. That night I watched the fireworks exploding over the dark waters of San Francisco Bay and told myself they were a fitting tribute to the dearest of women, the best of friends, and then I shifted under the weight of the mantle she had left me.

1

August 1965

It doesn't matter, I don't care. She rested her head on the back of the chair, turning her face so that she was looking out of the window and over the wing to the wisps of clouds flashing by, and repeated the words to herself, over and over again as a distraction, a litany to occupy her mind, to keep from thinking. *It doesn't matter, I don't care.* She could not have said what it was that didn't matter, or why she didn't care, and at that moment in the sky over Chicago, she would not have recognized those words as residuum of her childhood, would not have remembered the nights when she would bury her face in her pillow and tell herself that it didn't matter and that she didn't care.

The big plane banked and turned, lurching as it lowered itself clumsily through the layers of summer storm clouds that billowed over Lake Michigan. She looked out the window and caught glimpses of the city sprawling below through breaks in the clouds.

A steward intoned: "For those of you who are continuing with us to San Francisco today, we will be on the ground at O'Hare for fifty minutes."

She rummaged through the pocket of the chair in front of her, found an OCCUPIED sign and put it on her seat, then she made her way to the end of the line. She would go into the terminal, buy a newspa-

SHIRLEY STRESHINSKY

per, a magazine. A young woman pushed in line behind her. "Looks like rain," she offered in a twanging, midwestern accent.

Suddenly, the plane seemed close, the air hot and thin. The girl behind her in line chattered on. "These can be something, these August storms. Real honest-to-God cloudbursts where it rains little frogs." The girl laughed and asked if she was from around here.

"No," she answered, attempting a smile, and then she excused herself and pushed her way back to her seat.

The door was open now and the line began to move out of the plane. She had to tug to get her carry-on bag from under the chair; it came free and she made her way out to the boarding lounge. Then she was walking, walking fast and in long strides, though impeded somewhat by the straight cut of her linen dress, her shoulder bag bumping against her hip in the hurry. She made her way around clusters of travelers, who turned sideways to let her push by. Their eyes followed her. She was someone to watch in an airport—elegant in an unstudied way, the thrust of her body, the straightness of her spine, the mix of grace and determination. Her hair, long and dark and perfectly straight, rested precisely on the shoulders of the yellow dress, and stirred slightly in the breeze she made. Those who make a habit of watching people in airports might have concluded that she was late, that there was some kind of emergency. They might have thought she was meeting a man, or that she had decided not to, or that she was trying desperately to extricate herself from some romantic entanglement. She had a look about her that was almost mysterious, exotic yet efficient, too. Softly shaped eyes lined in kohl, the only makeup she used, prominent cheekbones, skin clear and smooth. A face that was hard to figure, a face that required study.

She stopped at a bank of telephones, dropped the bag to the floor and began rummaging in her purse.

The phone rang five times, six. She closed her eyes and tried not to think.

"Yes?" a man's voice answered.

"Karin," she said tentatively, then, "Is Karin Rolofsen there?"

Karin came on the line before he could answer, her voice filled with alarm. "May? Where are you? What's happened?"

She exhaled, steadied by Karin's voice. "Nothing has happened. I'm in Chicago, I just got in. Listen, I'm going to stop over . . ."

"No," Karin interrupted, "No you aren't, May. Don't do this, not now. You were supposed to be here last week, now finally you're on your way and you tell me you are stopping in Chicago. May—this is insane . . . Why didn't you get a nonstop? Why . . ."

"Calm down, Karin," she said, trying to sound in control. "Listen to me. I promised a man I met in Paris—a physicist—that I would stop over and see him on my way to San Francisco. He's in a place called Batavia, a little town just west of Chicago, on a project of some kind and . . ."

Karin cut in, "Don't tell me stories. There's no French physicist or you would have told me about him. You're making it up, it's just another excuse. God."

"I'm not making it up. I didn't say he was French, I said he was a physicist I met in Paris. He's American, and I don't tell you everything. Which reminds me, who answered the phone?"

Karin was not going to change the subject. "Listen, May, you've got to come on tonight. Everything's planned. Oh God, I should never have let you talk me into coming on ahead."

"Have you found an apartment yet?" May cut in.

"Yes!" Karin said, suddenly willing to shift subjects, "That's another reason you have to come now. It's not an apartment, it's a house. The couple who owns it are being transferred to Cleveland, and they've decided to rent it out. It's more than I budgeted, but there is something they call a mother-in-law cottage in the back that we can rent out, and that makes it just about the same as an apartment would be. You have to see it, May. It's beautiful—all wood inside, and beamed ceilings, a fireplace and window seats and a view of the Bay and within walking distance of the campus. But they won't hold it, they have to know and I said we would tell them for sure tomorrow."

"Take it. If you like it, I will. You know that."

"But I don't want to do it that way. I want you to come and look at it with me and decide together, if we're going to live here together. That was the deal."

"Karin, take it. Call the people now and tell them. It sounds wonderful, it sounds perfect."

Karin allowed a silence to grow. May waited; she knew Karin would break it.

"You know what you're doing, don't you?" Karin finally said.

"What is she doing?" the male voice called out from the background.

"Who is that?" May asked again, insinuating a sternness she did not feel.

"You're delaying, May, and you can't. Not any longer. It's time now, time for you to come home. I'm here. I promise, I'll be at the airport to meet you."

May closed her eyes and tried for the right tone. "I suppose that person who keeps yelling in the phone will be with you?" But it was too arch, too obviously provoking.

Karin's voice was gentle. "Don't do that, don't try to pick a fight with me. He's a guy who offered to drive me out to the airport to get you, that's all."

"Does he have a name?"

Karin was speaking carefully now, holding in, trying hard. May knew she would be twisting the small gold heart on the chain around her neck. She could see her hands, small and plump, fingernails bitten to the quick. (Bitten in her sleep, May knew that too. In school they had put Band-Aids on Karin's fingers at night, to keep her from biting them, and she had bitten through the Band-Aids.)

"His name is Sam Nakamura," Karin said. "He's a graduate student in chemistry. He's been very helpful."

"I'll just bet," May said.

Karin sighed.

"I'm sorry," May answered, and she was, but she couldn't get back on the plane. "Look, K, I'll call you tomorrow. I promise. I won't stay more than a day, two at the most . . ."

"There's a big welcome home party for you tonight," Karin put in, her voice pleading now, "at Kit's."

"Poor Kit," she answered, "maybe she should have informed the guest of honor."

Karin's voice was full of reproach. "It was supposed to be a surprise party, May. The twins are here visiting Faith, and it was their idea. They've been decorating all day, and it's going to be an awful disappointment. . . ."

Faith and Annie and Amos and Karin—all of them waiting for her. She bit her lip. "Listen, K—I can't talk anymore, there's a line of people waiting for this phone. I'll call you tomorrow, I promise." And she hung up.

No one was waiting in line, she was all alone in the glaring white corridor, her stomach churning and her eyes blurred with tears, feeling sick as the clouds gathered outside the big plate-glass corridor.

She was, she thought, being suffocated: the plane, the air-conditioned airport lounge, the corridor. She stood for a minute, looking at the dark clouds closing in, and she knew she had to get out and into the open.

She made her way to the airline counter to ask that her luggage be held in San Francisco, then she found the car rental desk and calmed herself with the ritual filling out of forms.

The girl at the counter had brightly lacquered fingernails which she flashed ostentatiously, lingering over the small x's where you signed on the line.

"Destination?" she asked.

May had to think a minute. "Batavia," she finally told her, "I think that's west of Chicago."

"Here," the girl said, stabbing the map with a red forefinger, then drawing a few quick, deft lines with a green marking pen.

"We have a brand-new Mustang for you today, Mr. Ford just sent it over, a bright shiny new red Mustang. Here," she went on, fingernails flashing over the map, "you are here, your car is here, make a left and a left and a right, keeping to the right, and that will take you onto 294 south. Here." She made a mark on the map. "Then you want to watch out for Highway 38, Roosevelt Road, west."

May pushed hard on the doors and a tidal wave of heat washed over her, thick and choking and heavy, filling her lungs. A hot wind caressed her, moving up her skirt. She opened the car door and rolled down the window and waited for the heat to escape. Settling herself in the driver's seat, she pulled up her skirt, exposing long, slender brown legs. She rummaged in her purse until she found an elastic and caught up the mass of her hair, thick and jet black in the pale light. For an instant she smoothed her hands over her stomach, as if to allay the churning inside her.

The slow throb of the motor steadied her. She needed to be behind the wheel, moving, traveling, in control. She could not sit, not wait in the heat. She swung around the turn, left and left again? She didn't remember but it didn't matter, she could see the highway, she could follow her instinct, feel her way.

Driving helped, feeling the slow power of the engine beneath her helped, moving along a strange highway in an alien city helped; the windows were down and the wind was blowing, the clouds moved dark and ominous above and all of it helped.

She turned on the radio but all she could get was static, so she turned it off again. She didn't need that sound, the wind blowing warm against her face was enough.

The sign said Highway 38 and she turned, hoping she was turning west. She was moving now through small towns, one after another, all of them connected: Elmhurst and Villa Park and Lombard and Glen Ellyn, yellow and red flags snapping in the wind at used car dealers, a long cluttered stretch of A&W Root Beer stands, laundromats, auto parts stores. Then a sign for a town called Wheaton, and suddenly wide streets and great trees and houses set in an expanse of green, with porches all around, houses lived in for a hundred years, old houses from another time.

She slowed and tried to think what it would have been to grow up in a town like this, on a hot afternoon in August, sitting on a front porch in white shorts, barefoot, with a hot wind rising. At the edge of town she stopped to let a tall boy cross the road. He loped along, not to hold her up, raising his hand in a small gesture of thanks.

She should probably stop and call ahead. He could be away, be out of town, it could be a bad time for her to show up. She didn't stop because she knew it didn't matter if he was there or not. She had a name and an address and a phone number, she had an excuse, and it was all she needed.

Then she was out of town and there was nothing but cornfields and an expanse of country that stretched out flat and forever, a country so wide that even the occasional farmhouse seemed only to emphasize its great emptiness.

Road signs loomed, a light flashed a detour. She followed the arrows, swinging onto a narrow blacktop lane that cut straight into the wide green heart of the August land, a road narrow and slick and rimmed with cornfields rustling high, the earth plowed to the very lip of the roadway. There was no end to it, none at all, as far as she could see. She was alone in a red Mustang riding a country road into the heart of nowhere. She stepped hard on the gas, gulping in the air. It didn't matter how fast she went, she knew that she was never going to get there, never going to reach the other side.

She glanced at her watch. It was one in the afternoon and suddenly it was dark. The clouds that had been threatening closed in, the wind was rising, blowing, she could feel it coming . . . something was coming. She slowed the car, waiting, listening as the wind raced flat and hard through the dry cornstalks, the sound a hollow rasping that echoed into the clouds and expanded, like the swelling song of some infernal choir.

A crack of lightning shattered the sky and then the sound hit her full force, thunderous and bone-rocking, and she shook with the shuddering blow of it. The wind rattled through the cornstalks, seven feet high all around her, reaching a crescendo, but all she could see was the straight path of the road ahead. She felt the first drops on her arm, heard them as they hit the roof and splattered. She reached across the passenger's seat to close the window, just as a second flash of lightning pierced the sky ahead. She braced herself for the thunder roll, her skin went cold and she shivered. It was raining hard now, so hard she could barely make out the road, she squinted and leaned forward to peer through a small patch cleared by the windshield wipers. The rain flooded the windows, she could not see at all but she was afraid to stop, afraid to be still, afraid not to be in motion. The light and the sound surrounded her, crashed around her and drowned her in noise, in the staccato drumming of rain on the roof, in a long silver shriek. Was it her? Had she screamed?

She glimpsed something through the water that coursed down the windshield, blinding her, something dark and massive across the roadway . . . Branches? A tree? She pulled hard at the wheel, the car spun, turning and sliding. She felt it slip into the soft mud and stop. The water coursed down the windows so that she could not see out. She was trapped, caught, and the noise of the storm filled her head. Shaking, she put her hands over her ears and longed to cry for help but she couldn't think who to cry out to.

Not mother, not father. No one.

Karin and Faith and the twins were waiting for her at Kit's apartment, waiting for her with streamers and balloons and a banner that said "Welcome Home." She put her head on the steering wheel and sobbed, she emptied herself of tears too long stored and then, exhausted, she sat with her arms wrapped around herself and waited. The rain would seem to let up for a time, but then it came throbbing down again, even more ferocious.

She sensed it before she heard the noise, a rattling. Something was rattling the door handle. She turned her head and saw, through the water, a blur of red, a hand. Swollen, gnarled, pawing at the window. And then a face—misshapen, grotesque, and a mouth, black and yawing open, open and shut.

23

"Oh God," she whispered, "Dear God."

She turned away, hid her face, covered her ears. When she had the courage to turn back, it was gone.

She sat until the rain spent itself, until it grew steady and then stopped altogether. She waited until the sky grew light, until finally it was bright. And then she stepped out into the world and breathed in the freshness of the earth after a summer's hard rain.

She felt tired and drained and quiet. She was alive, and alone in the middle of a never-ending road in the midst of a great empty land. She stood alongside the mud-spattered Mustang which had spun around to face in the direction from which she had come before it sank to its hubcaps in the mud of the great plains. In the other direction a giant sycamore, felled by a lightning bolt, lay across the road.

The air moved only enough to sound a soft rustling through the corn rows, other than that the silence was complete. At first she thought it was nothing, that her eyes were playing tricks. Then she saw that it was moving toward her, moving down the middle of the road. Five minutes more and she could make it out: a tractor. Another five minutes and she could hail the old man driving it, a big thick man in a red rain slicker and a baseball cap. He raised a gnarled old hand in greeting:

"Took me a spell to get back, but then I figured you wouldn't be going noplace." He grinned then, and his big horned face rearranged itself into kind folds.

"You frightened me," she said, and was surprised to hear her voice crack. If he heard she couldn't tell, he was already attaching a chain to the Mustang.

When he had pulled it back on the road he took off his hat, retrieved a big blue handkerchief from its crown, wiped his face and asked her where she was heading.

"Home," she said, her voice strong now, "I'm going home."

2

Karin perched on the window seat in the dining room, hugging her legs to her and resting her chin on her knees. For a time she scanned the wide view of San Francisco Bay offered from the window, then she turned to survey the living room with its high beamed ceiling. The morning light streamed through the French doors to illuminate the fireplace, and the acrid scent of fresh ashes lingered in the air from last night's fire.

"I can't believe how lucky we were to find this place," she said, turning back to the sweeping view of the Bay, dotted now with hundreds of sailboats.

May sat at the dining table, several forms spread out before her, and toyed absently with a fountain pen while she studied her friend. She was thinking of the contradictions that existed between them, of how opposite they really were. Karin was small and soft, curvaceous and warm, with large breasts while May was tall and dark and cool, and not quite flat-chested. Karin's mop of blond hair curled out of control, while hers was straight as a stick and black. Karin was pink and pretty in the Scandinavian way; she was olive-skinned and unusual looking, people guessed she was Mediterranean. Karin was sweet-tempered and easygoing while she could be moody and intense. She sometimes wondered how they could have become such good friends. . . .

"It's what they call an 'old Berkeley house,'" Karin broke in, "meaning brown shingle with lots of wood inside, and tiles and beamed ceilings and such, sort of a civilized rustic. A copy of a Maybeck, or a Julia Morgan. In case you don't know, they were architects who designed houses in these hills in the early part of the century. I've learned quite a lot about West Coast architecture in these past weeks. The people who own this house spent two solid years fixing it up, 'returning it to its 1920s glory,' is the way Kit put it."

At mention of Kit, May looked up. "Has she seen the house?" she asked.

Karin read the note of disapproval in her voice and answered carefully. "No. That's just how it was described to her."

"Who described it?" May probed.

"The people who told her it was for rent. Kit heard about it, and thought we might be interested."

"Then it wasn't luck," May said in a flat voice, making a show of turning her attention back to the papers, "Cousin Kit never leaves anything to luck. She likes to control things, haven't you noticed? I should have known she would have a hand in this."

May could taste the bitterness welling within her, and she was dismayed by it. She had come back because she was convinced she could put it behind her, the old hurt, that it didn't matter so much any more. She knew she could never forgive Kit—the damage had been done, and it was done forever. But she thought she could keep her anger under control, that she could maintain a civil attitude toward the woman who was her guardian. Now, suddenly, all the old anger had flooded back. Part of it was that the others had always been so taken in by Kit—her dad and Sara when they were alive, and Faith and Emilie and Phinney and even the twins. She found Karin's studied neutrality especially annoying.

Karin had turned back to the window, to the wide sweep of the San Francisco skyline. She knew it would not do to come to Kit's defense. May was too soon back, too tense, too quick to anger.

"We've got to decide what to do about renting out the in-law cottage," May said in an effort to restore the earlier, easier mood.

"I know," Karin answered without turning, "Sam wants it but he can't afford the rent. He's hoping to find someone to share it."

May frowned. "Do you think it has enough privacy for two men? I thought maybe we could find a couple—and that we might let them have it in exchange for housework and taking care of the grounds."

Karin turned, her face registering distress.

"I thought we agreed," she began, forcefully for Karin, "I thought it was all decided, that in return for my part of the rent I would do the housework and the cooking. And I was really looking forward to the gardening. I know how . . ."

"I know you do," May interrupted, smiling in an effort to ease the tension that was building. "You can still do all the cooking because you know how badly I cook. But when we made that agreement I was thinking in terms of a nice modern apartment which would require little work. Instead we have a huge old two-story house with grounds to match. You can't handle graduate school and all of this too, nobody could. I certainly can't, and I can see what's going to happen— you'll be working yourself silly, and I'll feel like I have to pitch in and help. I can't have you waiting on me, for crying out loud—we'll both get tired and bitchy."

Karin's chin was set. "I can't be your guest. Besides, I was the one who found this big old house—I got us into it. It's the most beautiful house I've ever lived in. I love everything about it—the fireplace, and the view and the funny old plumbing in the bathrooms and the redwood trees out back. I won't complain, May. . . ."

May looked at her, and smiled as the familiar flood of affection rose inside her. She sighed. "I know you won't complain, K. You never do—and I was wrong about both of us getting bitchy. You never do that, either. Sometimes I think there's something wrong with you, that you just go along with that wonderful calmness . . ." May lifted her shoulders in the slightest of shrugs. "But please hear me out," she said, her tone warm and intimate, "it seems so crazy to me, that I should have plenty of money from Sara's trust, and very soon I am going to be richer than almost anybody either of us knows—richer even than Kit, I'm told—and I haven't done a thing for it. I don't deserve it any more than you do. My dad wouldn't have anything to do with the family money, did I ever tell you that? Sometimes I think that I shouldn't either, except . . ." She stopped herself from veering off the subject. Pulling up short, she said, "But I was talking about you and me and the money. I don't see why it has to change anything between us, why we can't just use it, and yet you refuse to share it with me, or to have anything to do with that part of me, that struggle . . ."

Karin bit her lip; they had been through this before and it had never been resolved. "I did go to Europe with you after graduation . . ."

"I give Kit credit for managing that, at least," May said, too sharply. She had been glad, then, for Kit's manipulations, for thinking far enough ahead to arrange for Karin to work in her company's New York office over spring vacation, so she could earn spending money for the trip.

"It *was* good of her, May. It really was." Then Karin, too, moved away from the subject of Kit, and brought herself back to the one at hand. She continued, carefully, "Money really hasn't anything to do with it, I don't think. At least, not where we are concerned. It's just that I've never had a truly good friend before, a woman friend. And you are that . . . and sometimes I worry that the money, your money, could interfere. And I couldn't afford to have that happen."

May smiled at the small pun, and remembered Kit telling her, at the end of their sophomore year, when Karin refused their offer of a summer at Kit's house in the south of France, about how money could be a problem, and especially between good friends. That summer May had gone to Thera instead. Kit had arranged that, too. She joined a research team from Berkeley that was exploring the only active seabed volcano in the Aegean. Kit was so goddamned good at arranging things, May knew that as well as anyone alive.

"Are you worried that someday I might wonder if it's me you care about, or my money?" May asked.

"That's too simple," Karin answered. "It's not just you and me, it's other people too."

"Like Sam Nakamura?"

"I suppose," Karin said thoughtfully. "He probably thinks I am, well, taking advantage . . . and that there couldn't be any equality, that you naturally have a superior position . . ."

"Why should he assume that?" May bristled.

"Don't be angry," Karin told her, "because of his background. When you're poor as a kid—the way I was, and the way Sam was— and even more when you feel that your race sets you apart, makes you different . . ." She glanced at May to see if the mention of race had registered. May nodded for her to go on. "You come to think that people who have money know something you don't know. Like there's a secret you haven't been let in on. Sam was calling you my 'rich friend' and my 'benefactor' even before he met you."

"Sam has a chip on his shoulder," May put in drily, but when she saw Karin's frown she added, "But he is gorgeous, with that wonderful tight body of his and that satin-smooth face and those black, black eyes that I swear leave burn marks when he turns them on full blast. And he has been helpful, and generous with his time and muscle power. Actually, I'm sorry he dropped off the gymnastics team—I'd love to see him in full muscular glory in white tights . . . Okay? Is that good enough?" Karin grinned, so that May couldn't resist adding, "But you have to admit he has an edge of arrogance."

"Not arrogance so much as something like wounded pride," Karin said, drawing out the words slowly, "but that's because he has this very distorted idea of what it means to be wealthy, and because you seem so sure of yourself. He thinks people with money are automatically secure, never frightened like the rest of us."

May looked at her steadily. "That's ridiculous," she began, her voice rising.

"I know, but I also know that you do appear to be full of confidence. And I *think*—I'm not sure about this, but I *think*—you don't know what it's like to feel *inferior.*"

Karin's face relaxed into an impish smile. "Do you remember in our junior year," she suddenly remembered, "when our History Forum made that trip to Washington and toured the White House? Lord, I'll never forget . . . I mean, I'll never forget the moment when we were all sitting in that elegant little anteroom, and no one knew why we were told to wait there . . . and suddenly Jackie Kennedy appears and in that breathy, cultivated voice of hers asks which of us is Miss Reade, and then asks if you would like her to give us a tour! You would have thought the rest of us had swallowed our tongues, but you just said something perfect, and the two of you went sailing off together chattering like old friends, the rest of us in tow. You were different, May! You are!"

May laughed. "Don't you know how that happened? Didn't I ever tell you? I knew right away why we were getting the royal treatment. Kit gave piles of money to the Kennedys. Think about it, K—that whole production smacked of Kit's little behind-the-scenes maneuverings. She arranged the whole thing with her usual precise manipulation, it's how she controls . . ." May caught herself then, made herself stop before she had moved into that other subject, the one that she could no longer talk about to Karin, not since they had come West and Kit had had a chance to spend time with Karin.

Karin, too, decided it best to sidestep the issue. In a small voice she said, "The point is, you didn't know that Jackie Kennedy was going to appear, but you just took it in stride."

"That," May said firmly, "had nothing to do with growing up with money. But it had everything to do with my father." She stood then, pretending to stretch, and turned to look out at the back garden. She began, as if to herself: "I went with my dad to all of the hearings . . . he was forever being called before one committee or the other. They had all of these names—Internal Security or Un-American Activities—but it was all the same, really. We would get out of the car and reporters would be there, cameras being shoved into our faces, questions being shouted at us. And then we'd walk into one of those big meeting rooms, filled with people and all of them would be staring at us. My heart would be beating so loud that I thought everybody would be able to hear it . . . *There's Porter Reade and his kid,* you could hear the murmur run through the hall. All I had to hold on to was his hand, and every now and then—when he would feel me shaking—he would squeeze it, so I would remember what he told me. 'It's okay to be scared,' he said, 'just as long as you don't let the sons of bitches know.' So I'd stand very straight, my mouth clamped tight so my lips wouldn't tremble, and I'd look the sons of bitches in the eye until they looked away."

She turned then, her eyes bright but dry, and made herself laugh. "After that, Jackie Kennedy was a piece of cake."

"Oh May," Karin said, her voice full of the emotion that May had drained from hers, but the sound of the doorbell severed her sentence.

May waited in the dining room, shuffling through the forms that had to be filled out that day if she was to start classes on Monday, but listening to hear who might be at their door on a Saturday morning. She did not recognize the voice, which was low and resonant and male, but she did recognize Karin's flustered laughter. That meant he was attractive.

She was right. "May, this is . . ." Karin began, leading the way into the dining room, and hesitated because she didn't know his name.

"Hayes Diehl," he said, "Sam Nakamura told me about the cottage you have for rent."

He was tall and thinner than he should be, May thought. His pants rode low on his hips, and she noticed the belt had been tightened a notch. His face was more interesting than good-looking, forehead high, mouth a little wide, his eyes a solid blue, with laugh wrinkles. His hair was a fine, light brown and fell into his eyes; he brushed it back absently, as if the gesture were a habit.

"Hayes is in law school," Karin said.

"Which means I'll be around for a couple of years, so I'd like to find some agreeable digs," he said. "Can I see the cottage?"

He saw the look that passed between the women, and asked, "Or is it still for rent?"

"I think so," Karin said, uncertainly, still looking at May.

"Yes," May said, "Of course you can see it," and she led the way out the back door and across the lawn, moving from one stepping stone to the next to avoid the wet grass.

"No dogs, please God," Hayes Diehl said.

May asked, "Is that a question or a prayer?"

"It's one of the problems with my current apartment," he answered. "The landlady has two Dobermans who maintain a curfew and accept no excuses. One minute past midnight and you don't get in."

Laughter spilled out of Karin, who was pulling up the rear.

May turned to look at him, one eyebrow raised, and asked, "Dobermans who tell time?"

"They even know which way to set their clocks for Daylight Savings," he answered.

When the door to the cottage was pushed open, a musty smell rushed at them. May propped the door with a stone so the air could get in. There was one very large room with a Pullman kitchen at one end, and at the other a huge stone fireplace that rose to the top of the vaulted ceiling. A single bed filled an alcove. "The sofa makes into a queen-sized bed," Karin explained, "and there is a bathroom and a large walk-in closet—and that's about it. It has more charm than space, I'm afraid." It troubled Karin that she and May had not come to a decision about the cottage, or if they would let Sam have it.

Hayes stood silently in the middle of the room, taking his time, looking carefully but not, as May had expected, checking out any of the details.

"You said the Dobermans were 'one' of the problems," she broke in.

"I'm also active in the Stop-the-Draft movement." He grinned. "My landlady calls me 'a rabble rouser.' Actually, I'm not very good at rousing, but I have been involved politically in the peace movement—I guess I'm what the papers would call an antiwar activist, in case that's a problem for you."

"No," May said, and Karin broke in to add, "The hot water heater works fine and the stove is okay, too. I'm afraid the refrigerator is a little small, and noisy."

He said, "I would like to rent it," surprising both of them.

"You haven't asked how much," Karin chided.

"How much?" he asked.

"Two-fifty a month," she told him, and he said, "Does that include the birdbath?"

It was May's turn to laugh. He looked at her, as if he were trying to remember something, and then he said, to make sure they knew he was serious, "I do want to rent it."

May shot a glance at Karin, who looked away, so she said, "Don't you think it's going to be a little cramped for the two of you?"

He looked puzzled. "Two?" he asked, confused.

"I thought you said Sam told you—" Karin began, then started over. "I had understood that Sam was looking for someone to share the cottage."

A look of surprise passed over his face. He thrust his hands into his pockets and for a moment looked away, but recovered quickly. "Sam was talking at his usual fifty miles a minute, and my brain doesn't operate at those rpms—I must have missed a turn." He grinned then, and shrugged. "It looks like I'm going to have to make peace with the Dobermans."

At that moment Sam pulled into the driveway. He was driving the "Winged Victory," his old Dodge truck, well past its prime, which he had painted a bright blue, with Day-Glo pink angel wings sprouting majestically from each door.

"Hayes," he said, jumping out of the car in one long fluid motion, smiling with real delight. "Sorry I'm late . . . you've met my friends."

"I talked my way into the cottage," Hayes told him, "and it is as terrific as you said it was, but a little tight for space, I think. I've got too many elbows, need a room for each." His tone was easy, friendly. It was clear that Sam had not told Hayes about the plan to share the cottage. May glanced at Karin, and wondered if she realized that Hayes was saving face for Sam.

32

Saving face. Her father had taught her how important it was to give people a graceful way out. Why had she remembered that now? She wondered if Hayes was doing it because Sam was Asian. Did that mean that Caucasian-Americans perceive Asian Americans as requiring a different kind of treatment? And isn't that racist?

May was lost in thought, and Hayes had squatted to rub the ears of a friendly black dog which had wandered into the yard. A silence seemed in danger of settling in, so Karin asked, "Are you two old friends?"

Sam spoke before Hayes could: "We went to high school together. Actually, I know Andy better—Andy is Hayes's younger brother. You are what, three years older?" he asked, turning to Hayes, but not waiting for an answer. "I remember you were a senior when I was a freshman. They called Hayes 'Big Diehl,'" he told them, "and Andy was 'Little Diehl.'"

Sam was acting now, he had figured out what must have happened and his high spirits had crashed. "You ladies should know that Hayes here really was a Big Deal—Rhodes scholar, Ivy League, Peace Corps, all round Big Man. Now he's leading the charge against the Establishment."

Hayes shifted uncomfortably. "No, now I'm just hungry and I think I'd better be moving . . ."

"You can't do that," Sam cut in, his voice suddenly urgent. "How about a cup of coffee?" he asked, and when it appeared that Hayes was going to decline, he insisted, "Listen, pal, I'm sorry about the cottage—that it wasn't right, I mean. I should have figured . . . but listen, really, no harm done. Let's all go down to the Cafe Med for an espresso. I'm buying." It was not a casual invitation; May wondered how Hayes would get out of it.

To her surprise, he didn't try. "Sure," he answered. May couldn't resist saying, "We promise to have you home by midnight."

Hayes and Karin and May laughed together; Sam wasn't in on the joke. Karin, contrite, quickly invited them to the house for coffee. "It's silly to go out," she said to Sam, "when we've just brewed a whole pot. And I was just about to make French toast."

Sam started again almost as soon as they were settled around the little table in the dining alcove off the kitchen. "Let's play get-acquainted," he announced with game-show cheerfulness. "You first Hayes, why don't you start by giving us a rundown—really, May and Karin want to know, don't you?"

Hayes was fingering a ginger jar, taking the lid off and then putting it back on again, as if it were a puzzle.

Sam smiled too brightly. "Hayes is reticent, refreshingly reticent."

May saw the annoyance in Hayes's eyes; he was not going to answer, she could tell, and she wondered why. Sam's barbs were purposeful, she knew that, though it took her a while to realize that he was punishing Hayes for not wanting to share the cottage.

"Karin is a getting her master's in art history," May cut in, wanting to take the lead away from Sam, "and I'm in geology."

"Geology?" he repeated, and once again it seemed as if he was trying to remember something, groping for some connection. "Nick Vergetti!" he said, "That's it. You were on the Thera project he ran a couple of summers back—I knew I'd heard your name before. Nick said he'd never seen anyone fall so hard for a volcano in his life."

She laughed, pleased. "Well, that particular volcano is easy to fall for—there is a very credible theory that the lost city of Atlantis is buried there, under a blanket of volcanic ash and pumice—you know Nick?"

"He's a family friend. I was supposed to meet him in Greece that summer, but . . ." he paused, as if he had suddenly run out of steam, and ended lamely by saying, ". . . it didn't work out."

"So," Karin said, smiling, "you guys should already have met."

"Fate," Sam cut in. "Real Kismet Kids, the two of you. The jet set crowd, summers in Greece, winters on the Côte d'Azur. Ah, the good life."

Abruptly, he changed the subject. "How does Andy feel about going to 'Nam?" he asked, but he didn't wait for an answer. Instead he explained to May and Karin, "Andy is my age, you could almost say we grew up together. Andy got me in trouble in more ways than I care to remember . . . to give you some idea, his last big splash— literally—involved a truckload of bubble bath and five naked girls on Ocean Beach. I won't go into the details, but that was Andy's style."

Hayes carefully sectioned a piece of French toast, dipped it deliberately in syrup and answered Sam's question. "Andy seems to feel that Vietnam requires his services."

"Jesus!" Sam blurted. "Didn't anybody tell him to head for graduate school, like the rest of us?"

Karin was frowning. "Not every male at the University is there to avoid the draft," she said.

"However," Hayes put in, smiling at Karin to take the edge off, "that does happen to be a good reason for being here. I don't think we should be in Vietnam at all. I wish my brother agreed with me."

"So do I," Sam said, suddenly sobered. "God, it must have been rough, trying to reason with Andy—I mean, once he sets his mind to something . . ."

"I know, he wrote the book on stubborn," Hayes said, and having reached this agreement both of them seemed to relax.

The conversation moved from one subject to the next, without any particular plan, as it does when people get to know each other. Karin started to break more eggs to make a second batch of toast, and Sam pulled her away, telling her to take it easy for a while and let him take over. The talk drifted aimlessly. At one point Sam asked Hayes, "Didn't you manage to pick up some tropical bug in Africa or something, when you were in the Peace Corps?"

"He seems to know all your secrets," May said to Hayes. He didn't answer, he was looking out the window, seeming to concentrate on the birdbath where several small birds were flicking water over themselves.

Then he said, in a whimsical tone: "It's only a little asthma I got skating against the wind in Flanders."

May had been sipping coffee, and she choked. It took her a while to get her breath. Karin rose to pat her on the back, but she was laughing, both of them were laughing so hard they couldn't stop, and May couldn't catch her breath. Hayes watched, amused and puzzled. Finally, Karin was able to gasp, *"Tristram Shandy!"*—and the two dissolved into another round of uncontrollable laughter. Sam gave May a glass of water and waited.

Finally May, dabbing her eyes, was able to speak, to explain how she and Karin had read *Tristram Shandy* out loud to each other in college, how much fun they had with it. They had memorized several passages—including the one about skating against the wind in Flanders. It had become their personal code—for a while they used "skating against the wind" to describe any ridiculous situation. If they missed the last bus from town, that was "skating against the wind." When Karin, fuzzy from staying up two nights in a row studying, had accepted not one but three dates for a Saturday night and all of them showed up, that was definitely "skating against the wind." And now, with Hayes coming out with their phrase without any warning whatsoever, well . . . She laughed weakly. "You can see how incredible . . ."

Hayes was grinning, but Sam was not. Sam was quiet. He waited for May and Karin to calm down, to finish, to pay attention. When they did he said, "The reason I know so many of Hayes's 'secrets,' as you put it, is because my mother cleans house for the Diehls. She has been their housekeeper for fifteen years now, isn't that right, Hayes?"

"The Diehl housekeeper," May said, shaking her head, when they were alone.

Karin replied, "Poor Sam."

"Why 'poor' Sam?" May asked, irritated.

"Because he is, well . . . ashamed, don't you think?"

"I don't know if it's shame he feels, or envy."

"Probably both," Karin came back, "and that's why I said, Poor Sam. What did you think of Hayes?"

"You tell me first," May answered.

"I think he is *interesting*," she began, deliberately. "We've been disconnected from all of the turmoil, the social movements on campus these past three years, and I'd like to know more about what's going on—and God knows, Berkeley is in the middle of it all. He seems like the sort of person who understands complications, who can figure out things quickly . . . he understands diplomacy, if you know what I mean . . . and yet he's funny, too. Smart and funny and yet . . ."

Karin was silent for a long moment, until May prompted her. "And yet?"

"Well, there was something else about him, as if he were backing away, not wanting to get too involved. With Sam, certainly, but with us, too . . ."

"I'm not sure about that," May said. "After all, he wanted the cottage—until he found out that Sam came with it. I just think he seemed tired . . . Sam said something about him being sick, and I think maybe he hasn't recovered. But I know what you mean . . . he isn't terrifically good looking, but he looks . . . finished."

"Finished?" Karin said, "What do you mean, finished?"

"I don't know, I guess that's the wrong word. Substantial, maybe. Sort of impressive."

"A big deal?" Karen laughed.

"That's it, how original of us." May laughed back.

"I wish Sam hadn't been so abrasive," Karin put in, "He just doesn't seem quite to know how to handle social situations—"

May interrupted, "I think Hayes probably knows that, otherwise he wouldn't have put up with it—"

"Which was lost on Sam . . ." Karin added.

"Which was lost on Sam," May agreed, "but we were talking about Hayes. How could you not like someone who quotes Tristram Shandy? For a minute there I had this feeling that it was some kind of a sign—that he was meant to be connected to us. Do you think we should consider him for our Inner Circle?"

Karin laughed. "What Inner Circle?"

"We could make one, couldn't we?" May came back with mock exasperation.

"Does it bother you that he's a political activist?"

"Bother? You mean because of my father? No. I hated what they did to my father, but I always knew he was right. And I loved him for standing up to them, for 'shouting into the wind' as he called it."

The morning's tension was gone now, so May could say, "You know Sam could become a royal pain, don't you?"

"I do," Karin answered seriously. "Maybe it would be better to let someone else have the cottage. He can be so sweet, you know . . . and I like it that he doesn't come on to either of us, and how easy and helpful he is, like getting up to help with the cooking, things like that. I guess I just felt so grateful to him, and he seems so badly to want to be friends with us . . ."

"I understand that," May said, "I really do. And though I have some doubts, I'm willing to take a chance if you think . . ."

"Please don't leave it to me," Karin interrupted. "In fact, I would rather the decision be yours—either way will be fine with me."

"Why should I make the decision?" May said, feeling herself stumbling into the kind of thicket of meanings, the cloudy mass of innuendo that always exasperated her. "Is it because I'm paying, or is it so I can't say 'I told you so'?"

"No," Karin said, clearly smarting, but not allowing the anger to surface, "neither. It's because I have some real questions about Sam myself, I don't know if I want him in so close. But I also know how kind he can be, when he isn't being defensive or trying to impress you. It's strange, but for a while there when I thought Hayes might share the cottage—well, I would have felt better about that. But Sam alone, I don't know."

May nodded, and touched her lightly on the shoulder to show she was sorry, and Karin smiled to show it was all right.

"I've got to walk over to the campus to turn in my admission forms. Let me think about it," May said.

She walked briskly down the hill, breathing in the sharp medicinal scent of eucalyptus. A scattering of small, prickly leaves rustled in the gutters. Through a break in the houses she glimpsed the San Francisco skyline, shimmering in the autumn light. She remembered a fund-raising party for her father; it might have been held near here. The house had a wonderful big garden with a view of the whole sweep of the Bay. That had been one of the nice times, Dad in the center of things, among admirers, surrounded by people who listened, who hung on to his every word, who told her how proud she must be of her father.

The memory caused her to smile at a boy with long hair who was struggling up the hill on a bicycle.

"Long way home," he said.

"Long way home," she agreed, laughing.

An hour later, her errands run, she made her way back up the hill, past student housing where blankets were hanging out of windows, up the steep winding curve of La Loma, walking slowly now because she could feel the muscles pulling on the backs of her legs.

Halfway up the hill she ran out of breath and sat on a low retaining wall to rest. Behind her, the hills were filled with evergreens and ivy and various bright ground covers planted to grab hold of the earth, to keep it from sliding away. She sat there for a time, not thinking, and then she knew that it had been right to come back. She knew because she was thinking about her father, remembering, and it didn't hurt, the tight feeling was no longer in her chest. She had talked about him easily this morning, had told Karin more than she had told anyone, had said out loud words she had hardly been able to think. It was coming back to her. She had been afraid of it, but it was coming back. *Look the son of a bitch in the eye.* She was not afraid.

She saw Sam working even before she got to the house. He had taken off his shirt in the heat and the muscles of his shoulders stood out, hard and slick and shining with sweat. He had the look of a sculpted bronze figure, in graceful efficient motion. He was pruning an overgrown rhododendron, reaching high, concentrating. She watched his muscles flex in a kind of wonderful rhythm.

"What are you doing?" she called out to him.

He turned, and for an instant his dark eyes registered alarm, so she knew she had taken him by surprise.

"I thought I'd get this pruned before you hired somebody who would come in and butcher it. It's a great old rhoddie, but it's gotten out of hand."

"You certainly look like you know what you're doing," she said.

Without turning around, he answered, "I do. My pop's a gardener and I've put in my time." She heard the edge of anger in his voice, but decided to ignore it.

"Sam," she said, "I have a proposition for you."

He raised his eyebrows suggestively, and she discovered that the eyes that could burn could also shine with fun. "My mother always told me that if I waited long enough, this fairy princess in a frog suit would come along and kiss me . . . Where's your frog suit?"

She laughed, at ease with him for the first time. "Well listen, I mean, gee gosh . . ." She pretended to stumble. He laughed too, balancing on the ladder, his body lithe and alive. This was Karin's Sam: easy, likeable, eager. Suddenly, the decision seemed simple.

"My proposition is—you can have the cottage rent-free if you'll take care of the grounds and be a sort of 'handy man' around the place," she said.

Deliberately, he turned back to his chore and made a few cuts before he said, "It isn't enough."

She watched the muscles move as he continued clipping, and she had a sudden urge to pull the ladder out from under him, to see if that beautiful tight body would be so graceful flying through the air. Anger rose in her throat; she could feel her face grow hot. "What do you think would be 'enough'?" she asked, forcing her voice to go cold. She would hear him out before she told him to go to hell.

"The rains start next month," he said, "and there'll be very little yard work then. As for a handy man, this house is in such good shape it won't require more than an occasional lightbulb to change, or a toilet to unplug. I wouldn't be doing enough to earn my keep."

He had been clipping all the while, but now he stopped and looked at her. "I could help with the housework. Do all the vacuuming, maybe, and the floor scrubbing—the heavy stuff. I know how. If you want, I could do the grocery shopping." All of this had been said in a soft, measured voice with only the slightest rasp on the edges. Then, as if he couldn't help himself, he added, "You could think of me as your Japanese houseboy."

She held his eyes for a long moment. He didn't back off. "Okay," she finally said, calling his bluff, "I'll talk to Karin and we'll decide what would work out best."

Sam returned to his clipping, leaving her to watch the muscles of his back, straining as he pulled at the branches, glistening as if oiled by sweat. She felt as if she could see how hard it was for him, how terribly much he wanted, needed; the struggle within was written there in the tight muscle coil of his back.

3

──── ▭▭▭ ────

They arrived together, May and Karin and Sam, bumping and jostling, laughing and joking. Sam opened his arms to me in an expansive gesture. "Faith," he said dramatically, just as Karin slipped between us to warn, half in earnest, "we told him he could come if he promised to behave."

"You certainly look as if you're dressed to behave," I said, admiring his perfectly pressed slacks, tattersall shirt and tweed jacket. The girls were in jeans and sweatshirts.

"Mr. Ivy League West here," May jibed as she headed for the kitchen, "aims to impress."

"Impress whom?" I laughed, "these are pretty casual affairs."

"I'm never casual about affairs," Sam joked.

Ignoring him, May called back, "Kit. He finally gets to meet the illustrious Mrs. McCord."

Every other Friday evening, May and Karin and Kit would come to my cottage for cracked crab and sourdough bread, salad and wine. During crab season the menu never varied, but the guest list always did. Others were invited to liven the conversation—some of the young photographers who had discovered the work I had done in the twenties and thirties, and had found their way to my door, or people May and Karin had met at the University.

It was an exciting time, those weeks and months that led from the summer of 1967 through the first of the year, but it was a fearful time as well. The ghettos of Newark and Detroit burst into flame during that long, hot summer, even while the young of the land made their way to San Francisco for what was called "a summer of love." The girls in flowing paisley dresses and the boys with flowers in their long hair scattered over Golden Gate Park and the nearby Haight-Ashbury district in a haze of marijuana and incense. The hippies added the only gentle note that fall and winter. A Stop-the-Draft week demonstration in Oakland had erupted in violence, with police spraying marchers with chemical Mace and arresting hundreds. In San Francisco and in Boston and in Washington, D.C., the growing groundswell of opposition to the war in Vietnam could be measured by the hundreds of thousands who turned out for antiwar marches. At the Pentagon, the clash between marchers and police ended in mass arrests. Closer to home, the Black Panthers brandished their weapons in the California state capitol to make their point about "black power."

The talk at my get-togethers was spirited, to say the least. May teasingly referred to them as "Faith's Fortnightly Salon." What she didn't seem to know was that they were my way of bringing her private world into some kind of balance with Kit's, that it was an attempt to bring them together.

In the five months since May's return, she had stubbornly resisted most of Kit's overtures. At first May was polite, making up excuses that sounded plausible. Kit knew they were excuses, but she persevered until May stopped making excuses. When Kit became aware of the struggle she was causing between Karin and May, she saw the girls only at my cottage.

The air seemed to constrict when Kit approached May. Karin did her best to ease the tension and so did I, and it took all of our energy. Still, I was convinced that if we kept at it, if May and Kit were brought together often enough, something would happen to shake May, to bring her to her senses.

What did it mean, *to her senses*? I did not know. I did not know how my view of Kit could be so different from May's. I did not understand how—or why—May had lost faith in a woman who was devoted to her completely, who was prepared to love her without conditions.

Still, I believe that change is possible. I believe that love—that strange act of courage—can be surprisingly tough if well rooted, can lie dormant under the leaves of many seasons. I believed, I fervently hoped, that if I could find where it lay buried and bring it to the light, it could flourish and grow. And so, the fortnightly crab and sour-dough sessions.

I explained this to no one, Kit least of all, but I expect she knew. Little ever missed Kit's notice.

There were times when I thought my plan might actually work, times when even Kit must have felt a flicker of hope. The Friday that Sam Nakamura came was such a time. That evening I had invited two young photographers who were studying at the Art Institute. They had been working on a show the Institute was mounting of my photographs taken in the early years of the war, of the Japanese-Americans who were interned in the so-called relocation camps for the duration under Executive Order No. 9066. It was May's idea to ask Sam, who had been born at the camp at Tule Lake.

When I found myself alone with May in the kitchen she said, "I'm glad you noticed Sam's finery. He's been planning his wardrobe all week. It's all calculated to make the rest of us feel slightly uncomfortable. That's because he doesn't feel very comfortable with tonight's subject."

I nodded. "I would expect Sam to be angry."

"He is," she answered. "Prepare for fireworks." She gave me a light kiss on the cheek and a pat on the shoulder before rejoining the others, and it occurred to me that May was looking forward to the fireworks.

Kit came in a few minutes later, carrying a plastic shopping bag full of Dungeness crab and apologizing for being late. She is as trim at sixty-one as she was at forty-one, I do believe—she looks too young for gray hair. With that husky voice and trim style, she somehow reminds me of Lauren Bacall. There's something glamorous about Kit. Always has been.

Sam introduced himself before the girls had a chance, saying, "I finally get to meet the fabulous Mrs. McCord."

"Fabulous?" Kit laughed. "What a nice thing to be called on a Friday night." Turning to me she added, apologetically, "I had to wait for Frank to crack the crab. I rushed him so he didn't do a grand job. I think I'd better repair to the kitchen and finish up."

"Let me help," Karin said. May frowned into the magazine she had been leafing through. Kit smiled and stage-whispered, "Thanks, but I think I'll enlist Sam. Maybe he'll pay me another compliment."

It was May who started the discussion that night. "Tell us about

Faith's show," she asked a young photographer named Nancy Caravello, who proceeded to launch into the kind of rhapsody that is embarrassing. I intended to interrupt as soon as I decently could but Sam got there first.

"You don't have to describe the pictures, we all know them," he said brusquely, and asked me, "what I want to know is why you took them."

Nancy's face flushed a bright red, and I wanted to reassure her, to take the sting out of his rebuff, but Sam spoke with such urgency that I could only think to answer him.

"It was a terrible time," I began. "Innocent, confused people— civilians, many of them citizens—were being herded into detention camps. Concentration camps, for the first time in this country's history. It was a human tragedy, an American tragedy, and I wanted to record it."

After that awkward opening, the conversation moved easily around the table, everybody eager to take part while the bowls in the center of the table gradually filled with empty crab shells. The photography students entered the conversation, drawing on the research they had done in connection with the show. Their enthusiasm for the subject was greater than their grasp of the facts. The more the two expounded, the more agitated Sam became.

"The war hysteria was part of it," Jeff, an intense young man, ended a monologue. "You have to remember that people actually believed the Japanese were going to invade California."

Sam's patience gave out. "That is not what I have to remember," he said, "and besides, who believed that? Certainly not all those white folks who moved in to take over Japanese properties at five cents on the dollar."

"I'm not saying it was right," Jeff muttered.

Sam came back, "Then what the hell are you saying?"

Nancy, her voice shaking with emotion, rushed in, "What Jeff meant about war hysteria was that you have to put it in the context of the times." Then she added, "And I think it's important to remember that being locked up wasn't the worst thing that could happen. Our people were being killed." Giving Sam a look of quiet triumph, she finished: "My father was killed, by the Japanese, on Guadalcanal."

Sam stared at her steadily for a moment, then said in a tone that was almost conciliatory, "Your name is Caravello. Italian, right? Your father was probably an American citizen. So was my Uncle Hideo. He was with the 442nd Battalion, which was all Japanese in case you didn't know, and he died in Italy at the Gothic Line. Do you think the local Italian community should be held responsible for his death?"

Nancy, flustered, did not know what to answer, so I broke in. "As it happens, many of us disapproved of that executive order and some of us—" I paused to emphasize the next words—*white folks* did what we could to fight it. In fact," I said, "Kit did as much as anybody. She was the one who got me into the camps to do the photos."

Now Sam turned to Kit, his voice betraying a grudging surprise. "How did you do that?"

For a long moment Kit concentrated on removing a large morsel of crab from a leg. She did not like to be the center of attention at these gatherings, and her answer was purposely vague: "I was working with a group who toured the camps regularly."

"Toured?" Sam asked archly, "as in touring the zoo?"

Unlike poor Nancy, Kit would not rise to his bait. "As in touring a prison," she said easily, "to see if the prisoners were being treated humanely."

Sam shrugged but Karin, who had been listening intently, picked up. "What group was it, Kit? And how did you get involved?"

"The Quakers. The Friends were about the only religious group who came out against the camps, and they did their best to help. I was just one of the volunteers. We weren't able to do all that much. Just little things, really. Once I got a special formula for a new baby. But I did get into the camps often enough to make some friends, and when Faith wanted to come in to photograph—to make a historical record, actually—they accepted her."

I went on to explain, "Without Kit, I could never have done the most moving of the photos—the sick child on the cot, the teenage girl looking out through the barbed wire at the young guard, the tiny cubicle shared by a family of seven."

"You didn't answer Karin's question," Sam said to Kit. "How did you happen to get involved?"

Kit hesitated. "Initially it was because I had some friends who were sent to a camp."

"Your gardener?" Sam prodded, "or maybe a housemaid?"

"Cut it out, Sam," May lashed out in an exasperated tone, giving Nancy the courage to add, petulantly, "I thought this was supposed to be a discussion, not an inquisition."

Suddenly Sam smiled, a wide and charming smile, and put up both hands in a gesture of surrender. "Sorry," he said, "I get carried away with the devil's advocacy stuff."

Kit glanced at me. She knew Sam was not playing the devil's advocate, not this time. She also knew he was not going to be satisfied until he got an answer. I smiled in encouragement, she hesitated for a moment and then began in her husky, low voice:

"Mr. Ishigo was no one's servant. He was already an old man when I first met him in 1930 and he was in his nineties when he died at Manzanar." She paused, remembering, and with a small sigh continued, "Mr. Ishigo was a craftsman, a builder of sailing ships in his younger days. In his age he had taken to making models of the ships he had helped to build. He did extraordinary work—beautifully detailed dragon boats, especially. He lived with his daughter and her family out in the Avenues."

Sam pressed on: "How did you happen to come into contact with this old Father—I don't imagine he moved in your social circles."

Kit took a sip of wine and studied him over the top of the glass. "My husband had drowned at Ocean Beach," she said evenly. "He swam there every day and one day . . ." she started to explain, then stopped herself. "So, every year on that day I would take a wreath out to cast on the water." She looked up and smiled, briefly. "And usually the wreath would wash right back in. So I had an idea that if I could put it on a little boat of its own, that boat could sail out to sea. And that is how I happened to meet Mr. Ishigo. I saw a newspaper article about the models he made, and went to see him and he didn't think my request was in the least peculiar. After that, every year Mr. Ishigo and I would go to Ocean Beach together to launch a beautiful little dragon boat filled with flowers. He would check the tide tables, and he knew just how to read a wave. At the right moment he would signal and we would wade into the water together—sometimes we got quite wet—and then we would go back to his house and his daughter would have hot miso soup waiting for us."

For a moment Kit had become oblivious to the group. Her face glowed with the memory, and without realizing it she had crossed her hands over her chest in a gesture that was soft and touching.

Then she caught herself, put her hands in her lap and finished in a tender voice, "We became good friends." She turned to Sam and added, "Mr. Ishigo would take no pay, and after the first time I did not ask. We did that every year until the war, when they put Mr. Ishigo and his family into a camp."

Sam looked at Kit, but had nothing to say. Karin's eyes were brimming with tears, and I didn't trust myself to speak. It was May who broke the silence. With a puzzled look on her face, she asked: "Did my father know about the camps—what you did?"

"Yes," Kit answered carefully, "In fact, you were too young to remember—you must have been about four years old—but I took you to visit Mr. Ishigo's daughter when she came back. I had sent them pictures of you and that day she gave you a little teak sampan that Mr. Ishigo had carved for you not long before he died."

"I have it," May said, "my name is on it in tiny, tiny characters. I thought someone gave it to my father." The look on her face made me think that the revelation was not so much that Kit had been involved with the camps, but that Kit had been involved with her, with the child May, to have taken her to visit the Ishigos.

The next day I found myself going through a box of photographs labeled "May: baby pictures. Age one to four." I was looking for something, I wasn't quite sure what. I can only explain it as a niggling in the back of my mind, a question unanswered—or never asked. I leafed through the prints. May and her grandmother, May and Sara, May and Emilie. The wide, searching look in the baby's little face. Suddenly it occurred to me to separate out all of the pictures of May and Kit together, and there it was, as clear as day. In almost every picture, May was touching Kit. Kit's face radiant, as she gave the baby her bottle, May reaching out for Kit's arms while taking her first steps, holding tight to Kit's skirt as a shy two-year-old, a tired three-year-old tilting her head against Kit's. And then an especially telling picture of Porter, Kit and May a few days after Porter's return. He was strange to the child, still, and she was clinging for dear life to Kit. For the first four years of May's life she had trusted Kit completely, had loved her as a child loves, without question. Something had happened to erode that trust. The question was: what?

I went to the letter file and pulled out the one labeled, *May-letters, 1957–1960*. I leafed through the pages filled with a girl's square hand, until I came on the one I wanted.

Colworth Farm
February 6, 1957

Dear Aunt Faith:

Thank you for all your letters (three since the last time I wrote you! Sorry!) You deserve a nice, long one back and today is the perfect day for me to write because I am home sick with a cold. Emilie has me all tucked in on the cot behind the wood stove in the kitchen. You know that cozy spot. It's my favorite place. Phinney gets up early and stokes up the wood stove so it is warm and cozy when the rest of us get up. It always smells like someone has just cooked a big pot of applesauce.

On Saturday, Phinney is taking the twins to the hardware store with him so Em and I can do some shopping. That should be a scream, Amos and Annie loose in the store. Especially Annie. Phinney says, "I'll just flash my *Phineas Colworth, Prop.* sign at them and they'll know they better behave." He's very proud of the new sign, which was carved by an old man who used to work for Phinney's grandfather.

Em has been helping me with my math. She says she doesn't understand how Daddy could have taught me Chinese and skipped algebra altogether.

I miss him so much. I know you are right when you tell me that Kit misses him too. I suppose that's the only thing she and I have in common. You asked me to write her. If you say I have to, I will. I just wish you and the rest could understand that I don't feel the same way about her as you do. And I never will. Could we just not talk about it any more?

I hope I haven't hurt your feelings. I miss you too, Faith, but I am very glad I came to be with Em and Phinney and the twins, and to go to Colworth School. There is this sign in the main hall that says, "Founded: 1837 by Perseus Colworth." Phinney's right about his rock-ribbed ancestors rattling around all over the place.

I can hear Em and the twins—they went into town for groceries, and they are storming in now, so I'll sign off.

All my love,
May

I called Kit.

"I've asked myself a thousand times what could have made her turn away from me," she told me. "For a long time I thought there must be a reason. Porter didn't know, either. He said she was 'moody'—but Porter was never much for introspection or trying to understand feelings. He was too intent on action. And in the meantime, May just seemed to drift away from me. I could actually feel her withdrawing. It caused an almost physical pain . . . it still does," she admitted, her tone implying that it was foolish of her, after so long a time.

Kit continued to try, because she invited May and Karin and Sam to join us for a gala dinner at Trader Vic's before the opening of my show. Karin had happened to answer the phone, and accepted for all of them on the spot. It was a fatal mistake. Sam and Karin arrived without May, Karin obviously upset and Sam angry.

"May is being a Class A shit," he said, disgusted. "She threw a fit when Karin said we'd come without checking with her and then she really went into a spin when we said we would go without her."

"Sam, I really should have . . ."

"Cut that crap, Karin," he came back, "May is being a bitch and you know it. Somebody needs to tell her that she is way out of line. I elect you, Faith."

"You do?" I said, with as much sarcasm as I could muster.

"Yes I do," he came back, "because you're the only one who can get away with it."

He was right. It was up to me, and suddenly I felt enormously weary. As if I had been told to scale a cliff—I knew it was all but impossible, and I knew I had to do it.

Kit disappeared into her public persona—superficially charming and distantly correct. At the show she retreated into the background. May finally appeared, late and distracted. She was wearing jeans and a black turtleneck, and looked as if she had just come from the lab. Between trying to be polite to mobs of people I didn't know, I watched her. She studiously made a careful circuit of the exhibit, stopping to read the captions on each photograph, careful not to let her eyes wander over the crowd. Karin and Sam saw her, and kept their distance—Sam, I suppose, waiting for me to set May straight. Suddenly, quite without warning, one of my canes slipped and I would have toppled had not someone caught me. A chair was brought, and the crowd that had gathered around me gradually dispersed. May, her face filled with concern, appeared next to me.

"I need to talk to you," I said, in a voice that—to my utter chagrin—sounded desperate.

"You need to get some rest," she cautioned me, "You've overdone. This has been too much for you, Aunt Faith."

"About Kit and Karin, tonight . . ." I started.

Anger flashed across her face like heat lightning. Struggling to control it, she closed her eyes for a long moment. When she opened them again, her eyes were empty of emotion. I shivered at it—the stifling of so much anger, pressing it down inside of her like that.

"May, dear . . ." I tried again, but it was no use. Her face had closed tight to the world and I knew it was no good. I could feel the disappointment well within me. There was no easy resolution, and nothing I could do for the moment, nothing. I had been a silly old fool to suppose I could.

I asked May to drive me home. I wanted so for the words to flow between us, I wanted an outpouring of feelings, I wanted to be able to ask the right questions, to say the right phrases that would unlock all the hurt, all the pain, and let it flow out forever. But the words would not come; I felt mute, struck dumb, frozen. It was as if a heavy, opaque screen had dropped between us and words would not go through. I knew it would take time and emotional strength to pierce that screen and I was too weak. I thought of Sara, who would not have been so weak, and a feeling of despair seeped through me.

May helped me into the house and asked if there was anything she could do for me, but it was a perfunctory question, words to fill the emptiness between us. Then she kissed me on the cheek and left.

I had no idea how angry she was at that moment, no idea that the anger would burst into flame the next day.

The date is clear in my mind: Saturday, February 3, 1968. Ten days before May's twenty-fifth birthday. Had I been thinking straight, I might have read the signals, I might have been prepared, I might have spared us all the anguish.

Or not. I can't be sure. It is possible that it had to happen as it did.

My phone rang at exactly nine that morning and when I heard Karin's voice I knew she had been waiting for a decent hour to call me. "Is May there?" she wanted to know. "I mean, I don't need to talk to her—I just wondered if she spent the night with you."

She had not returned to the house, and Karin was worried.

"I imagine she took a room at a hotel." I tried to sound reassuring. "She was upset last night, you know that, but she seemed quite calm when she left here. I'd be willing to bet she just needed some time to think. I'm sure we'll hear from her soon."

There was an anxious pause. "She was so angry yesterday," Karin said, "I've never seen her like that before. She was mad at me for accepting an invitation from Kit, but I think that was only an excuse. I think she was looking for a reason to be mad."

"At you?" I asked.

"Yes," she answered, pulling out the word slowly, "at all of us . . . all of us who care about her, I mean. It's as if she has to hit out. Kit's the main one, you know that. The target. But she's angry at all of us, and that's what I don't understand."

I was made dizzy by the clarity of her statement. Of course she was right. Of course May was angry with us all. I took a deep breath. "What a wise girl you are."

"No," she said solemnly, "if I were, I would know what was going on with May. And I don't know."

"It's a puzzle we have to put together," I told her, and promised to call as soon as I heard from May.

The day stretched before me, interminable. To pass the time I went through the files again, all the letters May wrote in the years she was in the east. It was not until her second year at Mount Holyoke that she wrote Kit, to ask if Karin might be included in the invitation to spend the summer with us at Kit's place in the south of France.

At four that afternoon Kit appeared at my door, unannounced, her face ashen, all the pain in the world reflected in her eyes.

"May came to see me," she said, breathing erratically, and then she repeated herself, as if the words were stuck in her throat and she had to force them out: "May came, just now," she said, with little gasps in between the words. "And I know . . . know what it was . . ."

"Quiet now," I said, and made her sit down. I held her hand and told her to take a deep breath and to tell me. She did exactly as I said, resting her head on the chair and closing her eyes, and my own eyes played tricks on me: Suddenly she was thirty again, her face smooth and unlined, even then a woman touched by sorrow.

The doorman had explained that Kit had a guest—the son of an old friend had dropped by for a drink, a man in his thirties who was between jobs and who hoped that Kit would help him out. May told the doorman it was all right, that Kit was expecting her.

As soon as Kit saw her she knew that something was terribly wrong. Her skin seemed to be stretched tight across her face, and her eyes were almost translucent in their anger, as if light was reaching them from some great depth. Kit attempted an introduction, but May brushed it aside. The visitor, sensing a crisis, said he had better go, and Kit thanked him for coming, which was a way of saying yes, please leave, using the social formalities to mask confusion.

May stood waiting in the big living room: feet apart stridently, in the middle of the room, the wide view of the Bay in the big plate glass window behind her.

"Your male companions just keep getting younger," May sniped. Kit did not answer.

"I know what you are doing, and I want you to stop," May finally said, the words sharp and hard and knotted.

Kit let the sound float out into the room and settle before asking, in as level a tone as she could manage, "What is it that I am doing?"

"What are you doing?" May mocked, and then told her: "You are trying to win Karin over, you are trying to manipulate her and take control, and I'm not going to let you do it, not this time."

At the periphery of Kit's vision the walls seemed to waver, to shimmer, and she reached for the back of a chair. "This time?" was all she could think to ask.

"This time," May spat back, her voice thick with resentment. "You know what I'm talking about, you know exactly what I am talking about. Don't play dumb. That's one thing you aren't. You are as shrewd as they come, God knows, Cousin Kit."

May began to prowl about the room, stopping to pick up a picture in an old-fashioned, heavy silver frame. "Ah, Porter and Kit Reade. The twins. That's what they called you, didn't they? Inseparable. Like twins? And of course she was no match for you, was she? Not some little Chinese war bride."

Kit was frowning now. "I don't know what . . ." she began, but May cut her off.

"That's not true, Kit. You do know. You know exactly what you did. You got rid of my mother. You made her life so miserable she had to leave. Oh, you covered your tracks, you're good at that, aren't you Kit? You wanted things to be just the way they were before, you and Daddy, inseparable. You wanted him all to yourself, and you would do anything . . ."

Kit stood staring; she could not think what to say, where to begin, she had lost the power to speak.

"No," was the word that formed in her mind, but even that would not come out.

"How do I know?" May asked the question Kit could not, her eyes so black with fury that Kit could not bring herself to look into them. "I know. I've always known. I grew up knowing. I knew for certain a long time ago, a long time. I knew as soon as I was old enough to figure it out. My father told me all about my mother, about how good she was, how full of life and love. He never said one bad thing about her, never, except that it wasn't her fault, that I shouldn't blame her."

She stopped for a long moment, forcing Kit to look into her eyes, and then she said in a rising voice, "She wouldn't have just left us . . . she would not have left us. My mother would not have gone away forever, my mother would not have left me behind . . ."

Then she was crying, shouting and crying, fierce and furious in turn, her face wet with tears that ran in rivulets down the smooth face. She made no attempt to brush them aside, but only stood as if leaning into a storm wind, crying and shouting the same words over and over, in a litany that had at long last broken free: *My mother would not have left me . . .* the words all run together. Kit knew then how deep was the pain, so long stored, and she knew that it had found its way to the surface, had broken through and was spilling out, spewing out in an awful torrent.

"Oh child, poor child," Kit was saying in small, whispering gasps, but May did not hear, would not hear, could not hear.

4

And so the waiting began.
One day, then two.

We sat by our telephones, Karin and I, attached as if by umbilical cord, carrying it with us as we moved about, afraid not to answer on the first ring.

Afraid.

I have lived a long time, and of this I am convinced: Waiting, full of dread, is a part of life not worth living. The numb terror of not knowing, the terrible effort to keep the mind from wandering too close to the edge, to the unthinkable.

Sam called the hospitals. Then he drove Kit through the city streets, checking hotels and motels. Kit could not sit and wait, she had to be in motion, even if that motion were futile. They called at intervals to see if we had heard . . . afraid we would have no news, knowing their voices could only disappoint us.

The hours dragged on interminably. Reading was impossible, television did not distract. You want it to be over, more than anything simply to be over, and when it isn't, the pressure builds until there is a terrible need to scream, to get some kind of relief.

"Damn her!" Sam would swear, smacking a rolled magazine against the table. "One lousy call is all it would take." He said out loud what he would do when he got his hands on her: He would

shake her until her bones rattled, he would shake some goddamned
sense into her.

At the end of the first day, Sam returned to Berkeley, not wanting
Karin to face the night alone.

He found her curled in a corner of the sofa in a faded flannel
nightgown, heavy wool hiking socks on her feet, the phone by her
fingertips. Sam thought she looked as if she were there for the duration, as if her body were molded in that spot and she would never
move until she found out.

Where May was, what had happened.

Sam brought two mugs of tea, handed Karin one and sat down on
the coffee table facing her.

They sipped in silence for a while, until he asked, "Do you think
something could have happened to her?"

"Like what?" she wanted to know, flashing anger.

He looked away.

"Like suicide? Is that what you're thinking?"

He shrugged and shook his head, trying to back off.

"No," she said. "She wouldn't."

"How can you be so sure?"

"Because she told me once . . ." She stopped, then started over, as
if from the beginning, as if she were telling a story to a child: "When
May was eleven or twelve she was living with her father in southern
California, in an old house on the ranch the Reade family owned. He
was going through a really hellish time—you know about how he
was labeled a Communist, and had to appear before all of the investigating committees?"

Sam nodded, and she went on: "Anyway, one day she couldn't find
him. She looked all over. They were alone, and she must have started
to feel pretty panicky. Finally she thought to look in an old shed out
back of the house, and she found him there, cleaning a gun. She'd
never seen her father with a gun before, she didn't even know he had
one, and it scared her. She got hysterical, and I guess it took him a
long time to quiet her down and convince her that he really was just
cleaning an old gun he had found, left over from the ranching days.
He tried to explain how as a boy on the ranch he had grown up with
guns, that cleaning it was just a chore, something mindless to do. I
guess her reaction must have been so violent that he talked to her that
day in a way he never had before. And one of the things he told her

was that suicide went against everything he believed in. That to kill himself would be to deny his whole life, and anything of value he had ever done. He said that things were tough, but that he'd been through tougher times, and McCarthy and his kind couldn't beat him. He told her that he had plenty to live for—and that she was number one on the list, and he planned to be around a long time. It made a tremendous impression on her."

Sam exhaled: "And then the bastard died and left her."

Karin's eyes filled with tears. She closed them, and took a slow sip of her tea, as if in remembrance.

Sam waited for a while before he asked, quietly, "What do you think has happened to her?"

Karin sat up, arched her back, and her breasts swelled loose under the soft flannel gown.

"I think she just got in the car and drove. That's what she usually does, drives. Except I know how upset she is—with me, with all of us—so she is feeling alone, and I know how fast she drives. That's what scares me—that she's out there on the road, all alone." Sam moved to sit next to her on the sofa, and put his arm around her for comfort. She put her head on his shoulder and allowed herself to give in for a moment and to weep, quietly.

At two o'clock the next afternoon I was listening to the radio, an hourly news analysis about the Tet offensive launched by the Viet Cong during the Lunar New Year celebration. General Westmoreland was calling it a victory, the commentator said, but in fact what the Viet Cong had proved was that they could strike at the very heart of South Vietnam, that even the United States Embassy had come under attack with the enemy inside the compound, that there was no light at all at the end of the tunnel.

I was listening to a report about two young California civilians— entomologists with a West Coast engineering firm who had been killed when they tried to flee their house next to the Saigon golf course—when May called.

"Aunt Faith," she said, as if to check to see if it was me, "I'm staying at this bizarre motel in San Luis Obispo," she went on, stumbling over words that came spilling out, "truly strange, you ought to see it. I ought to bring you here, you would never believe this place. The showers in the room are made to look like waterfalls, with real rocks. And everything is pink. Bright pink. Someone told me that the men's urinals operate by electric eyes, so that when you step up to one the water goes on automatically."

I let her ramble on like that, only murmuring an "umm" once in a while so she would know I was listening. I didn't care what she said, so long as she was talking. I allowed myself to enjoy the sweet relief of knowing she was all right, that she had not wandered off the edge of the earth. Any anger I had felt evaporated, the awful pain of waiting was already a memory.

"I've been touring the missions," she said, as if it made perfect sense. "I've always wanted to do that—start in San Diego and head north. I didn't get quite to San Diego, but I got to Santa Barbara. That's a lovely mission. I suppose I lost track of time, but now I'm heading north again."

Knowing I had to be careful, I said, "Do you know how long it will take to drive back?"

She hesitated, and I held back from saying more, determined not to scare her off.

Finally she answered: "I'm not sure. And I want to stop at the mission in Carmel. I don't know . . ."

"Well I do know that mission," I picked up, sensing that it was my turn to chatter on, to hold her fast and pull her in. "I went to a wedding there oh, years ago. I'd love to go back, actually. Father Serra—the priest who founded the missions, you know—is buried there, under the altar. There is something so comforting about the missions, I think because they don't change . . . so you can go back forty, fifty years later and see it and pretend you are young again. There's another mission I like even better, this side of Carmel. San Juan Bautista. They have a wonderful rodeo there in the fall. I'd love to go . . ."

"Yes," May said, her voice calm now. "Let's. I'll drive on home tonight, and we'll plan to make a day of it very soon."

"Good," I answered, and then very quickly said what I had to say. "Can you come here, to see me, first thing in the morning?"

She hesitated. "I have a class," she began. "I've missed one and if I don't show up tomorrow . . ."

I smiled, glad she was worried about missing classes. "Then will you come as soon as you're finished with your class? It is important, May. I wouldn't ask if it weren't."

Again she hesitated. "I don't know if I want to talk about it—about what happened . . ."

"No talk," I told her. "And no questions. But it is time that I fulfilled a promise I made to Sara. She asked that you see some family papers, and she expected you to see them before your twenty-fifth birthday, which is only five days away. I've been remiss, and now I have to ask you please to help me keep my promise."

"All right," she finally said, full of hesitation, and I leaned back in my chair and closed my eyes, thankful that I had been able to convince her, that I had not failed again.

───────────

The letters were arranged in chronological order on the dining room table. I had fussed over them all morning long, fingering the yellowed sheets and sharp folds, pages filled with fading script, carefully protected now in cellophane covers. Touching them had sent me careening back to that other war, of a city filled with boys in khaki and boys in blue. The letters were witness to other times, other troubles.

When May arrived I held on to her hand a bit longer than I should have, and was thoroughly disgusted with myself for feeling so foolishly emotional. "It's just old age," I told her, trying to brush off the tears that had insisted on creeping down my cheeks, "and it's dumb."

May rubbed my back a little, letting her fingers linger on my shoulders, and then she settled down to the task at hand while I withdrew to the sunporch to wait.

Reade Letter File: Box 2, folder 4: Porter Reade, 1942–43 31 July 1942, Liao Ch'ing-Ling to Porter Reade

Nob Hill, San Francisco
USA

My Dear Porter,

I am arrived safe from Honolulu yesterday. Your mother and Miss Sara and Kit all came to boat to met me. I feel how fortunate to be with such kind ladies and in so fine house. We also have Kit's niece, Miss Lucy Reade. She teach biology in Balboa High. It is like Chinese family, everyone live together. Except here is only women.

Kit is very busy work Red Cross and gone much time each day. She says when I have some rest she like me to go too. Now I sit at window and look on that small park across street, like park in Shanghai. But America not how I thought. Kit says Chinatown only a few blocks from here, but I cannot imagine it. Her friend has a clinic for poor people in Chinatown. Kit says they need more doctors now because so many gone to the war.

Our baby grows so fast inside me. Your mother will have a walk with me this afternoon at the park, then we go back for tea with Aunt Sara. They feel so much excited about this baby.

I wish I not miss you so much. Always I remember your face. Your mother tells stories when you were a small boy. She says when you come back, you have no more secrets. I tell her already there no secrets for us, we two like one.

I pray for a boy child, and make you proud. Your mother not agree, says she like girls. I have good health, do not worry. But I cannot be happy and wait for you come back. I so much love you.

> Your dear wife,
> Ch'ing-Ling

2 October, 1942, Porter Reade to Liao Ch'ing-Ling
> Chungking, China

Dear Ch'ing-Ling:

Five of your letters arrived all at once, yesterday. It is always feast or famine around here. (Ask my mother to explain "feast or famine" to you.)

I'll start by answering your questions. 1) I have not been ill, only lethargic. By the time I get my stories filed and off by whatever method possible I seem not to have the energy to sit down and write long letters. I am sorry. I will try to do better. I know how difficult it must be for you there. 2) No, I am not disappointed that you have decided not to work in the clinic in Chinatown. You are, after all, pregnant and I would not want you to do anything to endanger either your own health or that of our child. I am not sure what you mean when you say you find the American Chinese to be "thick." If you mean "rough" or "crude" or "uncivilized," I suppose all I can say is that they are probably like all of the immigrants who came to the American West—risk takers, looking for a better life. California was settled by a bunch of louts, when you think of it. Ask Aunt Sara to tell you about some of her relatives, the ones who helped build the railroad. 3) I am afraid there is little chance of my coming home for the baby's birth. As you know, I'm trying to get permission to get into Shensi province in the northwest of China, to interview the Chinese Communists. So far the Kuomintang won't hear of it, but I keep pressing for permission. What you do around here is wait and wait and wait some more, and then one day when you are expecting nothing the word comes in and you have to be ready to go. Even if I weren't waiting for that, I wouldn't be able to get back. That's not to say I won't celebrate. I have a bottle of twelve-year-old scotch I'm saving, and I expect to lift a few toasts to our child when he or she arrives. We had three births this past month in our company, reason for celebrating. I know you want a boy, but I'll be just as pleased with a girl. Women have made my life happy.

It is important, dear one, to keep your spirits high. The war will be over one day, before too long I hope, and we will be together again, a family. We have much to be thankful for, I know you know that. And you know that I love you and miss you and more than anything that I want you to be happy. I know you are in a strange land, that you are worried about your family in Shanghai. I have tried through every channel open to me to get some word about your family. As soon as I hear anything, I will write. I know that you must feel homesick, but I am glad you are far away from all of the turmoil and sadness of this war. We can only hope that when it is over, there will be a bright, new future for China. And that someday, you and I and our child will return together.

I promise to try to be better about writing and to write longer letters. I wish there were more to write about, other than the progress of the war, which in this theater seems all but non-existent. And you know by now how peculiar the mails are, so don't be hard on me if they don't all arrive on time.

Take good care of yourself,
Your loving husband,
Porter

6 December 1942, Lena Kerr to Porter Reade

San Francisco

Dear Son,

I have lasting faith that you will not, as you suggested in your last letter, expire of ennui. Poor Vinegar Joe! He just can't seem to stir Chiang to action, can he? From newspaper accounts, including your own, I can gather only that nothing much seems to be happening on the China-Burma front. And yet the Chinese Communists are able to harass the Japanese in the north. It seems to me that Chiang Kai-shek is more interested in fighting the Chinese Communists than he is in fighting the Japanese. I suppose if you try to comment on that, it will be blacked out and I do hate to get letters with holes in them, so perhaps you had better tell me what you can in the newspaper articles you write. I feel such a thrill every time I see your byline. You have always made me feel so proud, Porter. I can't remember a time when you ever disappointed me. Though there were a few times when I felt a little bit exasperated. Looking back, those were usually times when you were too absorbed with one thing to pay any attention to another.

I feel a bit that way with you right now. I wish you could manage to write more often to Ch'ing-Ling. She absolutely lights up when she gets a letter from you. And of course, the mails are not consistent so those weeks which bring no letter at all find her quite sad. The pregnancy makes her more emotional, I think. Most of the time Kit can convince Ch'ing-Ling to go for a short outing. Kit and she have become quite good friends, I believe, and we all work to keep up her spirits. But your letters are terribly important, dear. Instead of taking the time to write to all of us, why don't you just include paragraphs for the rest of us in your letters to your wife. That way she could share parts of her letters with us. (Though of course there will be tender parts I would not expect her to share.)

Reading over what I have just written, I realize how demanding I must seem, and how small our concerns are when compared to all that you are facing. I am sorry, son. We are simply a band of women here, more engrossed than perhaps we should be with the impending birth of your and Ch'ing-Ling's child.

I think of you throughout the day, wonder what you are doing at that precise moment, and say a small prayer for all of you. I love you, son.

Mother

24 December, 1942 Porter Reade to Katherine Reade McCord
Ramgahr, India

Dear Kit,

Your letter arrived today, delivered by your friend in the foreign service (you do have good connections). I could almost feel your hot little hand on it. He tells me I have to have an answer ready by 0600 Christmas morning when he is scheduled to fly out, hence this Christmas Eve effort.

I've been trying to think how to answer. In the end, I guess, I will have to be honest. I've never known how not to be honest with you, especially when confronted.

What's going on, you ask. Something is wrong, you say, and you need to know what it is so that you can do whatever you can do. (Why do you always think you can do something, Kit?)

I don't think there is anything you can do, except maybe give me some advice which I may or may not take. Christ.

Here it is. I'm not sure it will translate. I'll have to trust you to read between the lines. (That I do trust you should be obvious, otherwise I would never be writing this.)

I've mentioned, in my letters, the nurses who work here with Dr. Seagrave—some of them walked out of Burma with Stilwell. They are an amazing group, these women. Tough, kind, caring. In spite of the heat and the jungle rot and the terrible boredom of waiting. And of course they are women in a world of men, in a time of war. All the old rules are suspended, they have to be. Marriage and fidelity are ideas that exist in another place, not here, not for most of us, not for me. I have become friendly with a nurse. (*Friendly.* A euphemism.) A big-boned, blond girl called Sunny because she is that, who grew up on a farm in Georgia. She calls herself a Georgia cracker and she probably is one, but she gives me comfort, makes me laugh, she makes this place bearable. She knows I am married, that I am going to be a father, that whatever is between us is temporary. She knows it, but I am not certain that I do.

63

I have never loved anybody before Ch'ing-Ling. There had always been women, but never the time, it seemed, to become deeply involved. I know what you are thinking: Porter became deeply involved with issues, with causes, not with women. I suppose that is so. I know I loved Ch'ing-Ling, and I think I still do, but I won't know for certain how I feel until I return, and we have time together. I know from her letters that she is unhappy with the States, and I think it likely that she will want to return to China. I do not discount that as a possibility. It is just that, right now, all that seems so far away.

If you tell me to give up Sunny, I'll have to tell you that I can not and will not, not now (and perhaps not ever). If you tell me what I can do to make things as easy as possible on Ch'ing-Ling, I will do my best.

Thank you for inviting me to get this off my chest. I know you won't like it, will probably be upset as hell with me, but I needed to confide in somebody, and you always were the right one. I know that after Connor died there were men in your life, and I know that some of them you cared for with something more than a passing passion. I am counting on you to understand the complexities of this situation, the unknowns. I appreciate your going to so much trouble to set it up so that we can write to each other in confidence. Cover for me. You always have, haven't you? When do I get to do something for you? Merry Christmas anyway, Kitten.

Love,
Porter

18 January, 1943, Katherine Reade McCord to Porter Reade
San Francisco

Dear Porter,

The best laid plans do go awry, and mine certainly have. Your letter arrived yesterday and was delivered, according to plan to my house in Pacific Heights. As you know, I've turned it into a hostel for service wives for the duration but I check in regularly to pick up my mail. As fate would have it, Lucy was passing by yesterday and decided to do me a favor and pick up my mail. Since I wasn't at Sara's when she arrived, she simply left your letter and three others on the front hall table.

Yes. Ch'ing-Ling found your letter and the "confidential" on the envelope must have set off all sorts of alarms in her, because she opened and read it.

Dear God I'm sorry, Porter. I would give anything to undo what has been done. Ch'ing-Ling is in her room, where she has spent most of her time for the past two months, and she will not talk to any of us. Aunt Lena and Sara are wandering around the house looking worried. They know about the letter, but they do not know what was in it and I will not tell them unless you ask me to.

I don't know what to tell you to do. You are right, maybe there isn't anything to "do." If you can come back, I think you should. I have this awful urge to tell you to write to her and lie, tell her anything to give her hope. I have this letter going out with an Air Force acquaintance, so you should have it within a week. Please answer at once to tell me if there is anything at all that you can think of for us to do.

I am so awfully sorry, Porter. What a rotten thing to have happen, when you are trying to sort things out. I'm sticking close here, and I'll wrack my brain to do whatever I can.

Love,
Kit

16 February, 1943 Liao Ch'ing-Ling to Porter Reade
San Francisco

Dear Porter,

The baby was born two days ago, a girl not boy, weighs seven pounds one ounce. I stay one month only, until the kind princess who watches over babies give a smile to this child then goes back to heaven. It is an old Chinese folk story about *Songzi Niangniang* and everyone still believes. Till now many babies die before they have one month birthday. If our child grows strong and healthy at one month we have good sign. I go then and leave her stay with old Aunts and Sister Kit.

I cannot take this child because I don't know where I go. Better she

65

stay here, with good people take care of her. If not for them I never can go, my heart would break.

Our marriage was wrong, I know that. You dishonor me. For me, come to this country no good even before. I never can be happy here. I feel that now for many months. Aunts are good, Kit is good, but the voices harsh and English sounds hurt on my ears. I don't want to tell you, away at war, but now I cannot keep silent. It is no good. I leave, and you never can follow. I ask this.

I think sometimes of death. I think of just walk with baby into the ocean. I will not, do not worry for that. Better, I think, is what Hawaiians call "hanai." Giving baby to someone else who is good and wise. I hold baby close for one month, then give to Kit. Kit always asks me to stay, says, "Look at such beautiful daughter, stay with her." I tell her truly I never be happy here, and baby cannot be happy go with me. I tell Kit she is already my sister, now can be happy Mother, have happy child.

I go home to China. Do not follow. Good-bye.

No longer your wife,
Liao Ch'ing-Ling

15 March, 1943 Lena Kerr to Porter Reade

San Francisco

Dear Son,

I have tried, dear, and so have Kit and Sara. We have pleaded with Ch'ing-Ling to wait until you can return, but she would not and we cannot force her to stay. Ch'ing-Ling is determined. She has made up her mind and nothing we say dissuades her. Kit has been frantic, even to considering blocking all paths for your wife's departure. Sara and I finally convinced her not to. Kit blames herself, but I feel certain when the pain of this difficult time has dimmed, we will all be able to think more clearly, and perhaps we will come to understand that Ch'ing-Ling did what she had to do to save herself. She was so very unhappy here, son. Even before your letter to Kit fell into her hands, she was brooding and troubled. We cannot know all that went into her decision.

Your daughter is so beautiful, Porter, such great black eyes that look up at you with such seriousness! And then she smiles, an utterly beautiful little smile. I have never seen such a captivating child, all pink and pretty and with a lovely shock of black hair.

I didn't think Ch'ing-Ling could possibly leave her, but she did. This morning, on a freighter that sailed for Chile. I did not help her make arrangements, but when I saw that she would go, no matter what, I made sure she had enough funds. It was the only thing I could do to try to make things easier for her, and I knew you would want me to help.

I am so very sorry, Porter. You know that darling Mei-jin will be well cared for until her father comes home. We take turns holding her. When I see Kit with her, I am reminded of myself when you and Kit were babies. We love your child, my grandchild, deeply, son. It is as if we have been given a sign that the world is, after all, a good place, a living place, with this small, wonderful girl child. Bless her and bless you. And bless dear Ch'ing-Ling, may she find peace wherever she goes, for all the days of her life.

My love,
Mother

May waited, pacing while the receptionist checked.

"Take elevator E to the penthouse," the girl finally said. "Mrs. McCord's executive assistant will meet you there."

Mrs. Emmons was waiting, smiling in the self-contained way she had always smiled, as if everything had been planned well in advance. "How nice to see you, May." She touched her lightly on the arm, guiding her down the thickly carpeted hall. "She's waiting for you in the little study off her office, where you won't be disturbed. There's a private entrance here." She rapped once on the door, smiled encouragingly, whispered "Go on in," and left.

May put her hand on the doorknob, turned it, and the words began to batter: *It doesn't matter, I don't care.* She closed her eyes as she pushed open the door.

May's teeth began to chatter, her whole body to shiver. She stood, frozen. It was Kit who opened her arms, who moved to close the distance between them, until they clung together, holding hard.

5

"Wake up, wake up, Happy Birthday," Karin called out, laughing as May emerged from under her comforter, blinking. "You've got a big day ahead of you, let's get moving."

May groaned. "You sound like a drill sergeant," she mumbled, then, opening her eyes, added, "you're sprinkled in flour."

Karin laughed. "Look. Breakfast. In bed. Now! Can't you smell it?" She was carrying a breakfast tray on which was a single red rose in a cut-glass vase, an omelette, a brioche, Earl Grey tea in a flowered pot and a funny Valentine with a silver-wrapped chocolate kiss. May propped herself up and read out loud: "Roses are red, violets are blue, sugar is sweet and not good for you but what the hell, have a kiss." She peeled the silver paper from the chocolate and popped it in her mouth, making a show of enjoying it.

They ate breakfast together, May in bed and Karin perched on a chair. The sun was streaming in the window, filtered through a cherry tree in bursting bloom.

"I can't get used to spring in February," Karin said, nibbling on a brioche.

"It isn't spring, it only looks like it and feels like it. There'll be more rain."

"But not today," Karin smiled.

"Not today," May agreed, throwing off the covers. "I have to meet Kit at the Bank of America at ten. I'm off to the shower."

May had to tug open the bathroom door; it gave suddenly and balloons came tumbling out, red, white and pink, and the quivering harmonica strains of "Happy Birthday" sounded.

May looked at Karin. "Sam?"

As he came.bounding up the stairs she turned and hit a balloon at him, hard, and in a few minutes they were all swatting at the balloons, hitting them at each other, both hands flying and balloons bouncing every way.

"Wait, wait," Karin finally called out, breathless, "you haven't seen the best part," and led May into the bathroom, saying, "Look up."

On the ceiling was a mural painted in bright blues and pinks, of May and Karin suspended in clouds, costumed in ethereal Greek gowns and angel wings, staring down from the heavens, each wearing a Mona Lisa smile.

"Oh my God," May gasped, and then, looking at Sam as if she couldn't quite believe it, "That is very funny. But it wasn't there yesterday—was it?" She answered herself, thinking out loud: "I wasn't here yesterday—and it was locked last night, I thought that was strange, but when did you do it?"

"If you look hard," he said, ignoring her question so he would not have to admit the amount of work it had required, or the lengths to which he had gone, "you can see where it says 'Happy Birthday, May' on your lyre."

She threw her arms around him. "Thank you, Sam. That is absolutely the most extraordinary birthday present I've ever had, and I'll cherish it forever."

"Or at least as long as you live here," Sam came back, more pleased than he wanted to show.

"Phinney's got to see this," May said to Karin, "He will go absolutely wild, won't he? I can't wait for them to come out now."

Karin glanced at Sam conspiratorially.

Kit was waiting in a private lounge in the Bank of America's Trust Department. "Happy Birthday, dear," she said as May hugged her, adding, "and Happy Valentine's Day, too." She handed her a box wrapped in silk paper.

"What's this?" May said, as they sat down together, and she started opening the package, "I've been getting surprises all morning. I love it."

Inside was a blue velvet box, not new, the velvet matted from use. "Oh Kit," May said with a sharp intake of breath, staring at the strand of perfectly matched pearls, and grasping her hand.

Kit squeezed back. "This was the first gift my husband ever gave me. I wore them all the time when he was with me, and I was always happy when I wore them. I hope they'll work their magic for you." She attempted a wry smile, bent her head toward May's, and added, "I always meant for you to have them."

"Are we ready, Mrs. McCord?" a tall, balding man interrupted.

"Are we ready, Miss Reade?" Kit repeated, smiling at May.

"I'm not sure," May laughed, but it wasn't true. She did feel sure, and she knew it was because of Kit, that it had always been because of Kit. She wondered, as she settled into a leather armchair, when she would find the words to tell her.

At 12:25 precisely, Kit interrupted the president of the Bank of America to say they had to be on their way, and when he continued to talk on, about the Hunt holdings which May would now control, Kit simply stood and reached to shake hands with him and said goodbye, nicely but firmly. May followed Kit, trying not to laugh.

"What a windbag," Kit exploded when they were alone. "No matter how many assets the two of us represent—and that is more than any other two people in this city, take my word—that man still thinks we 'ladies,' as he kept calling us, should be delighted to listen to his palaver . . ."

At that May burst out, "You're wonderful. I've never seen you in action before. I'm beginning to think that being rich and powerful might even be fun."

Kit grew serious then. "Not really, May. It probably hasn't quite registered yet, how much wealth you control, and the burden of it. When it does you will probably feel scared. It frightens me, sometimes."

"I'm glad you're here to help me," May said solemnly.

"So am I," Kit answered. "Now let's get some lunch."

"You buying?" May asked.

"You're the lady with all the money," Kit came back, and they laughed together, like old friends.

. . .

The maître d' at the Metropolitan Club had been watching for them, saw them leave the elevator, and made a quick motion to one of the waiters.

"Mrs. McCord," he greeted them buoyantly, "and Miss Reade. Happy Valentine's Day to you. A beautiful day, no?"

"A lovely day, yes," Kit answered, pushing May ahead of her. "Lead on, Charles."

Afternoon light streamed into the big room, glancing off the marble pillars and bathing the tables and diners in a hushed pastel glow. May concentrated on following Charles, so she was nearly at the table before she looked up.

She stopped short and stared. "Emilie! Phinney! Annie and Amos! Aunt Faith and Emilie—you knew this all along!"

"Happy Birthday," Annie and Amos called out, too loud in the restrained setting.

"What a wonderful surprise," May said, shaking her head as if she couldn't believe it. "Look at you, just look at all of you. Here. What a wonderful, wonderful birthday present."

She moved around the table, kissing each in turn, flushed with excitement.

"I could hardly stand it this morning," Karin said, "When you said, 'Phinney has to see this' . . ."

"Shhh," May came back, "Not one hint, and be careful—Phinney's awful about wheedling secrets out of you."

Talk swelled and flowered and spilled out over those seated at the large round table, talk about other birthdays and other surprises and all the things a family remembers when it gathers. May sat between Emilie and Amos—happy, animated, excited.

In a lull in the conversation Annie piped up to ask, "Is it correct to call you an 'heiress' now?" And Amos quickly added, in a voice in the process of change, "How rich are you, May?"

"Pretty rich," May answered, wrinkling her nose.

Emilie broke in, speaking just loud enough for those at the table to hear: "This is kind of a family secret, Amos," she said. "If everybody finds out that May has inherited the Hunt estate, then people will bother her."

Amos turned to May, clearly disappointed. "You mean we can't tell anybody you're rich?"

Annie broke in, exasperated, "Everybody knows it's déclassé to flaunt wealth. And it's even worse to ask somebody how rich they are."

"Déclassé," Phinney put in, winking at Amos, "pretty good, Annie. I like that. Déclassé."

Before Annie's feathers could get ruffled, May tapped gently on a glass, sending a small crystal echo over the table.

"I have something to say," she announced. "I know it probably is not in very good taste," she began, smiling at Annie, "but I admit to having come into a nice little slice of the Gross National Product today . . . no no no, no applause," she joked, "and I hope you will all bear with me while I do something we can all agree, at the outset, is . . . well . . . self-indulgent." She cleared her throat. "What I want to do, and what I want all of you to let me do, is to give each of you a present. Please, hear me out before you say anything. I've thought it all out very carefully, and none of the gifts is lavish . . . I'm not going to throw money at any of you, I promise. Okay?"

"You're not?" Phinney said, feigning disappointment. May grinned at him and went on, clearly nervous: "Okay. I'll start with the twins. First of all," she said, "Tickets to the next Rolling Stones concert." Amos sat up very straight and Annie clapped her hand over her mouth. "Also," May went quickly on, "an education fund so you can go wherever you want to go to college."

"Great jumping gold frogs!" Annie squealed, all thoughts of decorum vanished. When the laughter calmed Amos spoke up. "But when are the Stones coming to this country?"

"Who said anything about 'this country'?" May asked, rubbing his arm.

"Next," she went on, "Phinney and Em. I want to give you a tour of Europe—but no backpacks and no hostels. This is going to be a first-class tour all the way. Kit and I will be your travel agents. We'll arrange everything. All you have to do is get Mr. Ambergen to take over the store for you."

"Aunt Faith, you're next," she went on quickly. "You were also the hardest person on my list. However, I have arranged for a special service—a van with a wheelchair lift. The driver will take you anywhere you wish, all you have to do is give them an hour's notice. So you can go anywhere you want, whenever you want. Karin also gets wheels. No, just listen," she said, as Karin started to protest. "Nothing flashy. Just a nice little Volkswagen bug. Yellow. Your color. I thought you needed something safer than your bicycle, especially when you come home late nights from your new waitressing job."

"And last but not least," May went on, "Kit. I would like to give you a vacation to be shared with me at spring break, if you can get away, to the Big Island of Hawaii." When Kit smiled, May went on happily, "You, however, will have to bring a backpack and some hiking boots, because we're going up to the mountains to take a close look at volcano country. No Mauna Kea this trip."

Kit pretended to groan, "But the Mauna Kea packs a terrific picnic lunch."

It was a small, offhand statement, uttered with mock wistfulness, but it had the effect of reminding them that an old hurt was healing. Kit said, quite simply, "Thank you, dear." And the rest joined in, thanking her for the sweet giving of her gifts, until May, tears flooding her eyes, managed to whisper, "Thank you all, thank you all so very much."

Sam took a bottle of beer out of the refrigerator and straddled the chair, facing her at the table, where she had the newspaper spread out before her.

"I hear you're filthy rich," he said before tilting the bottle to take a long swig.

When she didn't answer, he went on, "Does this mean the beer is on the house?"

"Be my guest," May said, still not looking up.

"Should I take that literally?" he asked.

"Would you?" May came back, and without waiting for an answer added, "Playing word games is one of your least appealing traits, Sam."

He looked at her hard. "What would you say are my more appealing traits?"

"I wouldn't," she shot back, glancing up.

"Would you say it is my directness?" he pushed on.

"God no," she answered, "look what happened at Faith's, you blasted those poor, unsuspecting photographers."

"Fools."

"Beg your pardon," May said. She had been ready to laugh with him but hesitated because of the bitterness of his tone.

"I said they were fools, jerks. Her especially. They've read a couple of books and suddenly they are your typical Anglo, pseudo—they don't know anything."

"Anglo," May repeated. "That's the first time I've heard you use that term."

"Is it?" he asked, taking another hard swig of beer.

"It sounds as if it's you against them," she answered.

"Me against them," Sam repeated, then asked, "What about you? Which are you—Asian or Anglo?"

May studied him, trying to find some clue in his face that would tell her what it was he was trying to say, what he wanted to find out.

"I'm both," she finally answered, trying not to sound defensive, "but you know that."

"Your mother was Chinese, your father one-fourth Chinese. Did you know that if you had been an American citizen with one-sixteenth Japanese blood, you would have been sent to one of the concentration camps during the war?"

She shook her head, wanting to hear what he clearly planned to tell her, but determined to be careful too, not to be drawn into one of Sam's verbal traps.

"What happened to your family?" she asked, hoping it was the question he wanted her to ask.

He tilted back on the chair and observed her, making a show of deciding whether or not he would confide. Just as suddenly he brought the chair down again, hitting hard on the floor, and spread his hands before him on the table, as if the answer could be found there.

"My family," he began, "had a flower farm on the Peninsula. They sold cut flowers, you know—carnations, mums. They owned it with my uncles and my grandparents. The country was just coming out of the Depression and things were looking up. When the war broke out, they had more than half of the mortgage paid off. Naturally, the bank foreclosed and they lost it all." He stopped, "God," he said, "listen to me, I even tell the story their way, I've heard it so many times."

"That's okay," May encouraged him, "I haven't heard it at all."

He nodded, intent now. "My grandparents were Issei—that means first generation. They'd lived in this country for forty years, but they had never been able to get citizenship. Their children, my father and his brothers, were second generation—Nisei—and American born, so they were automatically citizens. To complicate matters a little, one of my uncles was 'Kibei,' which meant he was born here but had been sent back to Japan to be educated. The old school tie thing, you know," he added, sarcastically.

"But your father wasn't sent back?"

"No, not Pop. He didn't have the drive. Pop was what they called the 'gentle' son, which translates to 'weak.' When Mr. Franklin Delano Roosevelt told Pop, 'Pack your bags for the concentration camp, Boy,' Pop said, 'Yassir, Boss.' "

She looked at him coldly. "If you blame your father for going along with it, you would have to blame the rest of the Japanese community too."

"No," he said, "it was too personal for that. Too wrong. I had to blame one person, and he was it. He was my father and he let it happen. To me, to my mother. I'll always hold that against him."

She could feel the heat on her neck, climbing to her face. *Why was he telling her this? Was it a trap, was he calling her out, showing her up?*

She stared at him and for a time he stared back. Then he said, "Look, I know he was no more at fault than anyone else. I guess I really blame all of them for accepting it so goddamned easily. Not just accepting it, but for continuing to try to convince everybody they were one-hundred-percent, patriotic, flag-waving Americans. After all the shit they were forced to take." He stood and paced the length of the kitchen three times. The light was almost gone, but neither moved to turn on the electricity. It was talk for the half light, talk that would wither in a searching brightness. Sam stopped, faced her, his voice betraying the pain that lurked behind his anger: "Christ, May—there was an Oklahoma Congressman who wanted to sterilize all the Japanese in the camps. But the truth is, they had already emasculated them. And the truth is also that I don't know what I would have done in my father's place—and maybe that's what goads me, I don't know."

At that moment May wanted to get up, walk out of the room, do anything but continue to listen, but she knew she could not leave. She would have to hear it all, she had no choice.

"Your family was at the Tule Lake camp?" she heard herself ask. "That's up north, isn't it—on the Oregon border?"

"First we were sent to what they called an 'assembly center'—the county fairgrounds. I was born there, in a horse stall. Sound familiar?"

"You mean no room at the inn?"

"Japanese version, without wise men. We could have used some of those."

May thought for a while. "How much do you actually remember?"

"Not much," Sam agreed, "and yet it seems . . ." He started over, "There were all the stories, growing up. You hear them so much they become your memories, you actually think you remember. I have dreams about walking up to the barbed wire fence and looking out at armed guards, but I know I couldn't have done that. Hell, I was four years old when we got out."

"Four years. That's a terribly long time," May said. "I was in San Francisco, and I don't remember anything about those years, either."

"You didn't remember about the boat—the one the old Japanese guy made for you in Manzanar. You didn't remember going there with Kit?"

She shook her head.

Carefully then, in a voice that lay soft on the evening air, he asked, "What about your mother? Do you remember anything at all about her?"

May looked at him. Her throat was too dry, too tight. She could not have answered if she had wanted to, could not have told him how she used to stare at the snapshot of her mother and father on the day they were married. They were standing on a small bridge in a formal garden, he was wearing his uniform, she was in a Western dress of white crepe with a peplum and wore a tiny hat with a veil. She smiled into the camera, and May used to pretend she was smiling at her. Nor could she have told him about the other, the dream . . . her mother sitting under a mimosa tree, reading, her face turned away.

Tears rose, she couldn't stop them. Sam reached across the table, took her hand and inspected the fingers, long and narrow fingers, the nails filed short. He rubbed the ragged nail of her ring finger, broken on a field trip the day before, and told her, in a voice grown husky, that he understood, that he really did.

After a time he cleared his throat and went on, talking because he knew she could not. "Would you like to hear about the 'yes-yes' and the 'no-no' boys?" He made it sound as if he were about to tell a slightly lewd joke.

May nodded gratefully.

"Well, the WRA—that's the War Relocation Authority, the agency in charge of the so-called 'relocation' camps—they put out a form which everybody seventeen and over was expected to sign if they wanted leave clearance. It had an official name, but in the camps it was called the loyalty questionnaire. It turned the camps upside down. Two questions on the form caused all the trouble. One asked if you were willing to serve in the armed forces of the U.S. in combat duty. And the other asked if you would forswear any form of allegiance to the Japanese emperor. Nice, huh? A real Catch-22. The people in the camps—the draft-age men especially, but the Issei too, because they had no citizenship—got it coming and going. If you said Yes, I forswear allegiance to the emperor, it would sound like you had pledged loyalty to the emperor in the first place, which in almost every case was not true. And if you said no, it would sound like you weren't loyal to the U.S. government. If the Issei said 'yes,' they would be stateless, with no country, no place at all to go."

May asked, "What happened to the draft-age men who said 'no'?"

"You mean said 'no-no'—to both questions—that they would not serve in the U.S. Army and that they would not forswear allegiance to the Japanese emperor. Remember that. There were plenty of them, including my kibei uncle—the one who had been sent back to Japan to school. He considered himself a loyal American, but he said to hell with a government that would put his family in a concentration camp and then expect him to go off ready to kill Germans and Italians to keep America 'free.' He was thrown in the stockade as a troublemaker, and after the war 'repatriated' to Japan. Actually, he did pretty well—came to see us a few years ago, got himself a room at the Mark Hopkins and hired a limo to get around. But my other uncle, my father's second-youngest brother, Uncle Hideo, he was the one-hundred-percent All-American boy; he answered 'yes-yes' to both questions, and went to Europe with the 442nd Regimental Combat Team and died in a burst of glory."

"He died in Italy, you said the other night."

"Actually not. I bent the truth a little—otherwise the little witch wouldn't have got the point. He really died in France. In a famous battle in the French Vosges the 442nd rescued the "Lost Battalion"— about 300 Texans who had been surrounded for a week. It took the 442nd half an hour to wipe out a Nazi stronghold that other Allied forces had been up against for five weeks. In the process, however, the Japanese unit took sixty percent casualties—the Germans killed more Japs than the Japs saved Texans. There's a little irony there, wouldn't you say? My Uncle Hideo was one of the dead Japs. The

U.S. government gave my grandmother a silver star with an oak leaf cluster to remember him by. Some glory, huh?"

Sam got up, put his empty bottle in the trash can under the sink, and stood looking at his reflection in the darkened window. His intensity made him both darkly handsome and powerful. Suddenly he said, "Do you know that during the war, the government passed out leaflets telling people how to tell a Chinese from a Japanese?"

She looked at his reflection, but could not see his eyes.

He went on: "There was this girl in the camps—she was only about twelve when she went in, and she was all alone. Her mother was Irish and her father had been Japanese, but he had died before the war and her mother remarried a Caucasian and had two more kids. When the relocation notice came, Emerald had to go alone. A twelve-year-old kid. My mother took her in with us—I guess she helped out with me a lot. She still sends me a birthday gift every year."

"How good of your mother," May said.

"Yeah, well, my mother's heart is almost as soft as her head. And she has this habit of taking in other people's kids."

"Where is she now, Emerald I mean?" May asked.

"Married. A Japanese guy, I think he has a grocery store in Mountain View, someplace like that." He shook his head. "She could have passed, but she wouldn't. Dumb."

"Was it?" May said cautiously.

"You have to ask?" he came back.

"Yes, I have to ask."

"Don't be so damned coy, May," Sam said. "You know you pass, and why the hell shouldn't you? What law says you have to proclaim your parentage? Who asks Hayes Diehl what percent of his blood is German and what percent is Swedish or Scottish or whatever else mix is in there, as long as you can't see it on the surface? The only possible clues are your eyes and the black hair. I mean, I know some Jews who have darker skin than yours."

"I'm part Chinese. I've never tried to hide it," May interrupted.

"You never talk about it either."

"Why should I?" she demanded.

"That's the point," he came back, "you have a choice, not to tell. If I had that choice, I'd take it in a minute. This country may be a goddamned melting pot, but the folks with the black skin and the big lips and the slanty eyes seem to need to bubble in the pot a whole hell of a lot longer than the fair-skinned folks. If you think racial hatred is going away in this grand land of the free, just think about what happened in Watts and in Detroit and all the other big city ghettos . . . and it's not over. Burn, Baby, Burn, that's the current slogan—they've begun to understand that holding hands with white college kids and singing 'We Shall Overcome' isn't going to do it for them."

She stood abruptly, scattering papers over the table and the floor. Words churned inside her, heaved and rolled and tumbled, contradicting each other and herself.

"I don't know," was all she could manage to say. She wanted to believe he was wrong, but she didn't know.

6

If May's fascination with volcanoes had begun on the Greek isle of Thera, it reached the level of obsession on the island of Hawaii, where she and Kit tramped through the desolate lava fields of the active volcano called Kilauea, hiking down into the caldera and as close as they could come to the steaming firepit called Halemaumau, where the Hawaiian fire goddess called Pele is said to live. That spring May decided that volcanoes would become her major field of study.

In the months to come, May would learn to read the signs of an impending volcanic eruption: the swelling of the mountain along a rift zone, the seismic swarms—hundreds of earthquake tremors—that mark the movement of the magma, the churning molten rock deep within the earth that from time to time works its way up through the mountain mass, to explode in primitive violence.

Had May been charting the social rumblings deep within the country throughout the spring of 1968, she would have been alarmed at the stresses that were gathering, the pressures building. In March President Johnson, unable to end the war in Vietnam, announced that he would not seek office again. In April, Martin Luther King, Jr., fell in another war, victim of an assassin's bullet. One great, terrible wail reverberated throughout the land, and then the frustration and anger spilled over and there was rioting in the cities. That same month,

Columbia University students rampaged. Police became familiar on American college campuses.

In the air that spring, masked by the heavy sweet perfume of wisteria, was the scent of dread: of patience lost, of chances missed, of things gone wrong. And we, not knowing what else to do, repeated our daily routines, lulled by the sameness, yet with the disquieting feeling that there was something we were forgetting, something important we had meant to do, but we could not quite think of what it was.

I do not mean to suggest that we were at all times preoccupied with a sense of foreboding. For some of us—for Kit and May on an idyllic Pacific isle—this was a time of understanding and thanksgiving. Kit wrote from Hawaii:

READE letter file, box 3, folder 6:
Katherine Reade McCord to FMG, April 2, 1968

The Mauna Kea Beach Resort,
Kohala Coast, Hawaii

Dear Faith:

We are spending our last few days of May's spring break at the Mauna Kea. She had planned it all along, thinking I would need a rest after all the hiking we did on the mountain. In fact, I am so exhilarated by this time with May that I think I could have hiked forever, but it is nice to bask on this lovely curve of beach, and look forward to a perfect mai tai on the flagstone terrace at sunset and a bed with proper sheets at night. Right now May is snorkeling with one of the young men who has been on her trail since we arrived yesterday—a stockbroker from Connecticut, I believe. She has only to walk along the beach in bikini and flowing pareau and you can fairly feel the air crackle with the young men's sexual tension. She is so elegant to watch—those long, slender, limbs of hers and that tanned cocoa skin. (And yet, only a few days ago she looked almost plain in her khaki shorts and big dusty boots as we were trudging through the empty lava fields on the mountain.) It is quite strange and wonderful to be the companion to such a chameleon creature.

I had all but forgotten what it was like, being young and beautiful on a tropical island. May feels the difference here. She said the most peculiar thing the other day. We were eating at a local restaurant that was filled with young Island people, and she said, "I fit in here, don't you think?" I didn't know quite what she meant so I asked her, and I was astonished to learn she meant her racial background. When I had time to think about it, I realized how stupid I had been. Of course it must trouble her, otherwise she would not have denied that part of her which is Chinese for so long. From what little she is willing to say on the subject, I gather Sam has pushed her to think about it. Perhaps that is good.

My memories of these Islands are rather bittersweet. Porter and I were here as children—Aunt Lena and Sara brought us to Honolulu and we actually stayed, I remember, in a thatched house right on Waikiki Beach. That makes me feel ancient, somehow, when you see all the big hotels crowding out the dear, marvelous old Royal Hawaiian, where I spent my honeymoon with Connor. (Remember the party in our stateroom on the Lurline just before we sailed?) For a long time after his death I could not bear to return, but I did come once again before the war, with Aunt Lena and Porter. We came to meet May's mother, who was in medical school in Honolulu. Porter was desperately trying to court her, and her family was not cooperating. Aunt Lena and I had to pose as friends of one of her professors, in order to get an invitation to tea. I remember that day vividly. Ch'ing-Ling was, I thought, the most exquisite human I had ever seen with those wonderful high cheek bones and the kind of natural grace you have to be born with. Remember how wonderfully she moved? Small wonder her daughter is so lovely. And yet, what a mixed legacy she left her child—and it seems to me the racial part is the least of it.

On that same trip I danced with a young Naval officer until all hours and then we walked barefoot on the beach to watch the sunrise. May and I stopped over in Honolulu for a day to go to the Arizona Memorial at Pearl Harbor. My dashing young officer went down with that ship and I have always meant to make a pilgrimage. When I mentioned it to May she insisted we go together; we found his name engraved on the wall and ran our fingers over it, and had to share my handkerchief to blot our tears.

The scene was made even more poignant by the presence of two young men in uniform, on leave for a few days before shipping out to Vietnam. One was black and one was white with flushed pink patches on his cheeks. They were wearing highly polished boots which seemed too large, too clumsy, and all I could think was that they were playing soldier. They are so very young, Faith. And worst of all, they have no memory of the names that are etched in marble at the military cemetery at Punchbowl, names that still catch in my throat: Tarawa and Guadalcanal and Truk and New Guinea, all those battles where so many boys, just their age, died.

It has been twenty five years now, but it seems only yesterday. When we listen to the evening news I can only wonder if the names we are hearing now—Khesanh and Quangtri and Dakto—will evoke the same chilling effect on May's generation.

And now that LBJ has removed himself from the fray, I think we can assume Bobby Kennedy will step forward. In confidence, I can tell you that his people tracked me down here yesterday to see if I would, as they put it, 'come on board.' I said yes. I think Bobby may be the man we need at this critical juncture in our history.

May has unlocked all manner of memories for me. I can't tell you how good it is to be with her, to be *accepted* by her. I know you always believed it to be possible, but I have to confess I was skeptical. For so many, many years she resented me because she was convinced I had sent her mother away. I was sure those feelings, so long harbored, would be corrosive. I expected, at best, a kind of civilized rapprochement.

On the mountain one night, when we were tucked into our sleeping bags after a long trudge and were just about to float off to sleep, May asked: "Do you know about whipping boys, Kit? They were companions to little princes or noblemen's sons, and when the royal brat did something wrong, the whipping boy took his punishment for him. I think that's what you've been—a whipping boy." That was all she said, but perhaps it is enough to explain how she could become, with such seeming ease, so genuinely fond of me. To me, that is the miracle.

The girl at the front desk greeted me in that lovely straightforward way the Hawaiians have by saying, "You look so happy." The manager, whom I have known for some years, also remarked on my glowing good health and I found myself telling him, "My niece and I have just had the most wonderful outing on the mountain."

May has suggested she be introduced as my "niece," which of course delights me. More important, she trusts me enough now to begin to ask questions. Yesterday she wanted to know what happened to the nurse her father had fallen in love with during the war. I explained that Porter had gone to Georgia to see her, and that when he came back all he would say was that it had all been a matter of "time and place." May shook her head and frowned, but later she said she could understand. I hope that she can. She is so mature in so many ways, she seems more thirty-five than twenty-five.

I admit to being concerned that her memory of her father might be diminished by the letters. I don't think it is time, yet, for me to offer any opinions—to try to explain how her father, who was so wonderful in so many ways, could have been so naive about women and love. Porter had so many disappointments in his life, but May was his great joy. She must know that, must have it to hold on to. But as you say, she must also give up any schoolgirl idea that he was a saint, and infallible. She has not yet asked me about her mother, though we both know that painful subject is there, in the wings, waiting.

I expect May will return to Hawaii this summer to do her required field work. She is mesmerized by this Big Island, as it is called, and the volcanoes which created it, especially the two which are still active: Mauna Loa and Kilauea. The scientists at the USGS (United States Geological Survey) have agreed to allow her to work out of their observatory which is perched on the rim of the great caldera of Kilauea. The truth is, she is fascinated by volcanoes. It is wonderful to see her so rapt, so totally immersed in the subject.

May must leave tomorrow, but I am staying on for a few days, perhaps even a week. It has been such a long time since I have been able to relax this completely, and I am going to hold on to it for awhile. Think of me lying under a palm tree, the scent of frangipani in the air.

I hope your gift from May is proving as enjoyable as is mine.

My Love,
Kit

My gift from May had changed my life more than any of us could have dreamed. My "new mobility"—as we called the van and driver May had provided—combined with the gathering storm of events to bring my old and rather comfortable reclusive life to an end.

There are times, I honestly believe, when the powers that be conspire in ways that are wonderful to behold. Surely that is the only explanation for my having had the great good luck to acquire as my driver one Israel Dobbs, a large, middle-aged and wonderfully good-natured black man who was part preacher, part performer and, when it came to moving me and my chair about, a veritable magician. Israel viewed his position with extreme professionalism. No doctor could have been more attentive to a patient, no lawyer more concerned that a client be accorded her full civil rights. Israel's mission in life was to take me wherever I could safely go, without creating so much as a stir. He would never simply ask anyone to let us through; rather he would boom out in his deep basso profundo: "All give way for Faith and Israel," followed by, "We thank you so very much and hope you have a simply glorious day." He was courteous and he was humorous; he caused people to be happy to have us in their midst. So it was Israel who made it possible for me to go out in the world again. Without him, I would not have been at the epicenter.

You could feel the forces gathering, hear the rumble of the troop trains as they made their way across the country to the Oakland Army Depot where protesters tried to stop them. On the evening news I watched the crowds swell in numbers, saw them march with flags flying, passing out pamphlets, burning and looting, and straining against the old order throughout the summer and into the fall of 1968. And nowhere were the seismographs more sensitive than at Sproul Plaza at the entrance to the University of California at Berkeley.

I had lived through two world wars; I knew it had to stop and I had to do my part, I could not retire to the small world of my cottage, my garden. There are no small worlds, and no excuses given my new mobility. At first I volunteered one day a week for a group called "The Peace Coalition," which was attempting to act as a clearinghouse for the various peace groups in the community. Before long I found myself running the Berkeley office in a battered old apartment above a shoestore on Bancroft Avenue. From this vantage, I could look down on Sproul Plaza, which had become the epicenter of political activity.

Karin and Sam dropped into the office to see me almost every day. May's visits were less frequent because most of her waking hours were spent in the Life Sciences Building on the far side of the campus, where she had immersed herself in such arcane subjects as stratigraphy and tectonics, sedimentary petrology and the structural analysis of deformed rocks. Sam and Karin could sometimes be coaxed into an hour or two of typing or collating the lists of schedules of rallies, demonstrations and teach-ins. Since so many of the leaders of the antiwar groups fed us information, we became a central clearing-house of sorts. When the press made its way to our door, our status was confirmed.

By late morning a crowd would begin to gather in Sproul Plaza. The rallies started about midday with the amplified sounds of voices raised in passionate challenge, backed by strumming guitars and sometimes the pure high quiver of a folksong. And the students came; they emptied out of classrooms and filled the plaza, bringing with them a sense of purpose, a belief that they were, here and now, going to change the way the world worked. Wars were madness, they said; the military machine had to be dismantled, they said; the Third World must be addressed.

Not everyone was convinced that the student movement would succeed. Sam was not. "As far as the Great American public is concerned," he liked to say, "the college kids who are demonstrating are just a bunch of ungrateful brats who ought to be kicked out of school."

Hayes Diehl wasn't convinced that the movement could succeed, either. I met Hayes when he came into the Peace Coalition office. Sam introduced us, making a point to tell Hayes about my connection to May and Karin. Hayes explained that he would represent the Boalt Hall law students in the Peace Coalition. Later, Sam told me that Hayes had left the Gene McCarthy camp to become a West Coast campus coordinator for Bobby Kennedy's campaign.

Whenever Hayes came by he would stop to say a few words to me, either sitting or kneeling beside my chair so that we were face to face and he wasn't towering over me. I liked him for that. Israel liked him, too. Everyone else in the room might be talking revolution, but Israel and Hayes would be in a corner talking basketball. Israel told me later, "That white boy knows whereof he speaks when he's discussing the NCAA, but he's definitely soft on the big boys, the pros, oh yes, quite definitely soft."

Karin walked in one day, bent to kiss me, but before I could say 'Hello,' she spotted Hayes and blurted "Do you remember me?" The question raised a chorus of catcalls from several of the young men in the room at the time, and one of them suggested that if Hayes could forget Karin he must deviate from the sexual norm. Karin blushed, and then laughed as Hayes went into a teasing "Was it in Paris?" routine. A while later I noticed the two of them talking quietly in a corner.

Karin waited until the office emptied to tell me about their first meeting with Hayes. "It was strange," she began, "I think May and I took it for granted we would be seeing him again—I know we wanted to. But there was something awkward about it, with Sam I mean. We didn't make any attempt to get in touch with Hayes, and I suppose he must have felt the same way, because he didn't make any moves, either." She nibbled on a fingernail. "Somehow that doesn't seem right, does it? Holding back because of some third person? Just now I asked him out for coffee, but he had to go to class. That's what he said, anyway. What he didn't say was, 'Can I have a rain check?' I think he figures that Sam has staked us out as his territory, and that he should stay away. And it just makes me . . . sad. And a little bit mad, too."

"That you can't get to know Hayes, or that Sam should have 'staked you out,' as you say?" I probed.

Karin's face registered a small, thoughtful frown, and then she said deliberately, "Both. And the truth is, if Sam had been around today, I'm not sure I could have been so friendly with Hayes. And that makes me mad at myself. Suddenly, today—meeting Hayes again and having that same feeling that here is somebody worth it—if you know what I mean—well, it just seems very wrong to me. Giving in to Sam like that."

"What makes you think Sam wants you to give in?" I asked. "After all," I went on, "Sam was the one who brought him round in the first place. Sam was willing to 'share'—the cottage, and presumably his friendship with you and May."

"Possibly," she said slowly. "We thought it was because he needed the money, but maybe . . ."

I broke in, "When I see the two of them together, the feeling I get is that Sam resents Hayes, but he wants to impress him at the same time."

"Or wants his approval?" Karin asked.

"Maybe," I answered. "Hayes does seem to mean something to Sam."

Karin sighed. "Sam is so . . . volatile . . . I think he would do anything for us. When May was gone and I was so worried, he sat up with me all night. The three of us get along well enough, but sometimes I think it is because May and I are careful not to rock the boat."

"It's your boat, you know," I told her. "Maybe you should try a little careful rocking." She squeezed my hand and bent to nuzzle me in that easy way she had. I hugged her back, caressing the thick blond hair that fell loose to her shoulders, and thought once more what a warm, dear girl she was.

———————

Other campuses erupted that spring, and there was rioting in cities across the country. At Berkeley, a momentum was gathering until at times it seemed the very earth vibrated with all of the amplified speakers set up on campus. There were political rallies now, in advance of the summer conventions, and Hayes Diehl was keeping what Sam called a "high profile" for the Kennedy campaign.

What was called a "Vietnam Commencement" ceremony was held in Sproul Plaza that May, though Governor Reagan had warned that to hold it would be "so indecent as to border on the obscene." Sam and I watched from across the way and I moaned, "I would give anything to get down there and photograph that."

I had, in fact, brought my Leicas into the office, hoping that there might be a vantage point from which I could do some long shots. I knew it was hopeless, but the urge was there and wouldn't seem to go away. I wanted to get into the crowd, close up, to show the young, intense face of this antiwar movement. Israel outdid himself scouting possible locations, but in the end agreed with me, there was no way for me to photograph in the crowd.

It surprised me when Sam said, "Can I take the photographs for you?" When I didn't answer right away, he added, "I know a little about cameras, maybe you could tell me what you want and I could try to get it."

I thought for awhile. Sam didn't understand that I needed to be behind the camera myself, moving with the action, interpreting it in my own way. And yet he was eager to help, to do something for me. "I could preset the cameras for you, we could try it at least," I told him.

The next day was foggy and gray. "I'm setting a basic exposure—500 at 8," I explained to Sam, showing him how to focus, using the rangefinder to bring the split image together. I put a 35mm lens on one camera for wider shots and a 90mm on the other for closeups on faces. "Get as near as you can without drawing attention to your-self," I told him. "You want to be invisible, but you also want to be involved," I added, loading the cameras with black and white film. "Watch for gestures, for intensity. And remember to compose each frame so that the design adds to the tension."

From my office window, I could see him work his way into the crowd, pushing forward, moving up close. Sam did not hesitate and the students made way for him, dressed as he was in jeans and an old surplus jacket decorated with peace buttons. That first day he shot three rolls of Tri-X film. When it was developed and printed onto contact sheets, I looked them over carefully and found five strong photographs—pictures which were sharp, well composed and with strong content. I looked at Sam in amazement. For a first time out, he had done remarkably well.

After that, Sam went out every day and, as soon as his film was developed, we would study the contact sheets together. I have never known a student so eager for criticism. "This is very good," I would say, and he would come back with, "Why?" And then he would insist I tell him what he did wrong and what he should have done.

Near the end of November, when what was to have been a peaceful sit-in at the Student Union erupted into violence and police dragged off student leaders, Sam was up front, close enough to photograph one student's face contorted with pain as his arms were pinned be-hind him. That night the photo went out over the AP wire, with Sam Nakamura's credit line.

We celebrated Sam's success with pizza, beer and Louisiana hot links—Israel's contribution to the party. My desk became the table, the young people sat on the floor, their backs against the wall. Sam was looking through one of my cameras as if to photograph May. She held a rib between two fingers, studying it as if in preparation to bite into it, and looking directly into the camera said: "Faith thinks you're a natural."

Sam came out from behind the viewfinder.

"I don't know what there is about it," he said, "I just know I like doing it. There's something so immediate—the picture is there but just for a second, and you have to see it and get it. It's all so fast, you don't really have time to think, you just have to react and it's both exacting and, well . . . terrifically exciting."

He stopped, surprised at himself.

"So what now?" Karin asked.

"I'm thinking about a change of careers . . ." Sam answered, looking at me, "and my teacher here has offered to help."

"I offered to give you a few contacts," I corrected him, "and to loan
you my equipment until you can get your own. Other than that,
you're on your own."

"Are you thinking about leaving school?" Karin broke in.

"Are you crazy?" Sam answered. "And lose my deferment? I might
be willing to shoot some film in Vietnam, but that's all. What I need
is for Faith to get me in with her friends at Time-Life, and then I'll
have it made."

I laughed and reached to pull Sam's ear. "You've only just begun,
boy-o," I told him, "and you've still got a whole lot to learn."

"You said I was good enough to be a pro," he came back, an edge
of accusation in his voice.

Israel was sitting across the desk from me, quietly passing food,
pouring beer and listening, but now he broke in, a cautionary tone
in his preacher's voice: "Sam good son," he said, "remember what the
Proverbs tell us: Pride goeth before destruction, and an haughty spirit
before a fall. I should only add, my fine friend, that few people in
this world are blessed with the advantage of a fine teacher. It is
always right to acknowledge a debt and to give credit to your master."

Sam, for the first time since I had known him, was humbled. "You
are right, Israel," he said, adding with real sincerity, "and I am grateful, Faith." He grinned mischievously then, and added only half-
teasingly, "I'm especially grateful that you're such a damned good
photographer—anyone of lesser talent couldn't have brought me
along so fast."

"Well, hallelujah!" May put in, to which Israel boomed out a loud
"Amen," and we all laughed, even Sam, in spite of himself.

When Robert Kennedy made his last sweep through northern California before the June primary, Kit arranged for us to meet him at a
small private reception at the Press Club.

Sam made the most of the opportunity, moving in so closely with
the cameras that the senator finally stopped him by playfully grabbing the lapels of his jacket to examine the collection of buttons. "I
like this one," he said, fingering a button that said, "Make love not
war." Looking at Karin he added, "I do my part." Kit, standing next

to the senator, gave his sleeve a maternal pat and warned: "You do have a lovely big family, Bobby."

On election night we gathered at my house to watch the returns. By eleven o'clock the networks had named Kennedy the big winner of the California primary.

"On to Chicago," Kit announced, beaming. She and May had helped bankroll the Kennedy campaign.

"It's nice being on the winning side," May teased, poking at Karin and me because we had voted for Gene McCarthy.

"Some of us are *loyal,*" Karin jibed back. "Some of us don't change horses in midstream. Some of us don't desert sinking ships."

"Some of us see the writing on the wall," May answered.

"Right," Karin came back, the good loser, "and it says, 'Go home now. Don't wait for victory speech.'"

"It *is* late," May said, switching off the television. "Time to get across the Bay."

My clock radio buzzed on the next morning, crackling in an annoying way as if it were between stations, a voice trying to make itself heard over the static. I lay there and listened, alarmed by the tone of the voice. Something had happened, something terrible. I sat up and for an instant did not know if I wanted to tune the station in or turn it off.

It could not be, I told myself. This could not happen, not again. And then the voice on the radio told me it had: *Senator Robert Kennedy was shot in the kitchen of the Ambassador Hotel last night, and lies near death in a Los Angeles hospital.*

I stayed in my garden that day and considered the poppies and talked to no one because I could think of nothing to say.

7

It could be said that Robert Kennedy's death launched Sam's professional career. The photographs he took at the private reception Kit arranged were suddenly in demand. Calls came in from *Newsweek*, from *Time* and *Life* and *Paris Match*, and from publications as far afield as Turkey. Sam was, in turn, flattered, confused and annoyed. Flattered by all the attention, confused by the question of payment and rights, and annoyed that I did not want to act as his agent in dealing with the magazines.

Among my own favorite Sam Nakamura photos was one he made early on, of Hayes and Joan Baez standing together on the steps of Sproul Hall. The singer's hair is blowing across her face but she doesn't appear to notice, so intent is she on what she is saying to Hayes. I made a print of the photo, pinned it on the office bulletin board and waited for Hayes, but he did not come. Others stopped to look at it, a few added cheeky captions. May read them and asked me what he thought of them but I had to say I didn't know; Hayes had not been around and nobody seemed to know what had happened to him.

"His folks have a place at Stinson Beach," Sam said when I asked him. "I know he spent the summer out there—but he should be back by now. This is his last year at Boalt."

When finally Hayes did surface it was in a setting that was, as Kit described it, not only wonderfully theatrical but altogether out of the context of the times—a black tie benefit at the Opera House in San Francisco.

That evening May arrived at Kit's wearing the long white Givenchy she had bought for the occasion, a clinging white matte crepe with one shoulder bared. Over her shoulders she had thrown her grimy, rumpled raincoat, and her hair was blowing and wispy.

"I washed it just before leaving," May explained, "to get it dry I opened the car windows and let it blow in the wind. Are you absolutely sure you want to be seen with me?"

Kit laughed and told her she was halfway there, but that the coat would have to go and her hair needed to be tamed. "Give me ten minutes," Kit commanded, "and absolute cooperation."

When they left May was wrapped in white ermine, her dark hair was caught up on one side by an astonishing art deco ormolu clip in the design of a cobra, encrusted with lapis lazuli. On the street, two young women stopped and stared.

Once settled in the back of Kit's car, May confessed, "I feel like Cinderella with a cobra over her ear."

"You look absolutely smashing," Kit answered, "and I wondered when you were going to ask about the lapis cobra."

"Now," May told her, "tell me now."

"I bought that clip in London in the winter of 1939," Kit began. "Your father was in hospital there, recovering from a serious war wound—you know about that, about the Spanish war and the Lincoln Brigade and what happened. I went over to be with him and fetch him home, but it was several weeks before he could be moved, so I had a lot of time on my hands. I didn't want to wander too far from the hospital, so I took to haunting the little shops nearby. They all called themselves purveyors of antiques, but it was really pretty much junk. There was this one shop—the man had an absolute passion for art deco and Victorian jewelry. Some of the pieces were outrageous—Lalique stomachers, and Forquet bracelets of opals and lavender enamel. They were out of style already, and of course in 1939 there wasn't much reason to dress up."

She paused, and May pressed her hand so she would go on. "Anyway, I kept dropping into this little man's shop. It was usually empty, and he was friendly and liked to chat me up, as the Brits say—he knew stories about all the heirloom pieces.

"Only a day or so before we were to sail for home, he brought out

the lapis cobra to show me. I remember thinking it was both outrageous and beautiful. He told me that it had been made for Sarah
Bernhardt, but I doubt that. I can't imagine the divine Sarah wearing
ormolu. Still, I felt I had to buy something—I'd spent so much time
in the shop. And I was quite mesmerized by it even though I couldn't
imagine myself ever wearing it, but I didn't want to leave without
it—and that's how I got the lapis cobra."

"It's stunning," May said.

Kit sighed. "On you, yes it is, dear heart—on you it has all the flair
I knew it could have. You weren't even born, but if I believed in fate
I would say it was put in that shop in London in 1939 just so you
could wear it tonight."

May was standing at the top of the grand staircase, waiting for Kit,
embarrassed by the eyes that scanned her. From that vantage, she
picked Hayes out of the crowd. He was with an older woman whose
hair was dyed a dark red. The woman was talking and he was listening attentively, so that he did not look up until they were almost to
the top of the stairs. For a moment he did not recognize her, and then
he did.

Kit had returned and the red-haired woman called out in a deep
whiskey voice:

"Katherine McCord! Aren't you nice to come tonight!"

After introductions had been made, Kit explained that Marylee
Diehl, Hayes's mother, was the chairman of the benefit. There was
no time to say more, because Hayes's mother was marshalling them
toward the bar. The two older women walked ahead, leaving Hayes
and May to fall in step behind.

"If the folks back in Sproul Plaza could see you now," May began,
teasingly.

"You mean in my Fred Astaire uptown suit?"

"Did you forget the top hat?"

"You aren't quite dressed to man the barricades, either," he said,
pulling back slightly to look at her, "but has anybody told you there's
a snake in your hair?"

"There is a story to this snake," she said, touching it.

"There always is," he came back in a voice full of innuendo. "Are
you going to tell it to me?"

Kit, having decided against champagne, was waiting in front of the
entrance to their box.

"Of course," May answered quickly, "how about tomorrow? Dinner."

"Dinner?" he said, hesitating. "Is it that good a story?"

"You will always wonder . . ." she began, but he laughed and said, "Seven sharp. I'll pick you up."

Watching him push through the crowd after his mother, Kit said, "Give the girl an ermine and a snake and she turns into a vamp."

"What's a vamp?" May wanted to know, and that caused Kit to laugh with such delight that an elderly man turned and looked at them quizzically.

"My niece doesn't know what a vamp is, Mr. Burney."

"That's all right," the old man told them, "she's pretty enough to get away with whatever she's up to."

As the orchestra began warming up, Kit answered May's questions about the Diehl family:

"She was Marylee Hayes—at one time the Hayes family owned a good part of the San Joaquin Valley. I don't know the whole story, but it seems to me there was an ugly divorce and a big custody battle and Marylee's mother was cut off without a cent. It's one of those sad stories about money and how one generation tries to control the next by manipulating them with trust funds. I don't see Marylee much. I know she is considered something of a joke by the social powers-that-be in this town. She's a talker, for one thing, and she drinks too much, for another. They think she involves herself with too many 'social' issues. She won't raise money for the opera or the symphony, but if there is a famine in Africa or a flood in Italy or an earthquake in Peru, you can bet that Marylee will be chairman of the committee."

"What about her husband?" May asked.

"I think he's a banker. I've never met him. But now it's your turn. Tell me about young Mr. Diehl."

"He's a political activist," May said, "and I know he was working for Robert Kennedy."

"Oh my," Kit said, pained, and May nodded and answered, "Yes."

The house lights went down then, the curtain went up, and May and Kit settled into the first act of *Eugene Onegin*.

When she opened the car door, the smell of food—hamburgers and french fries—rushed out at her.

"Dinner?" she asked, lifting a box and looking at it quizzically.

"Dinner," Hayes answered, grinning. "You've heard of needing to eat and run? Well, we're going to eat on the run. Can't be late."

"Late for what?"

"Late for what?" he repeated, pretending amazement. "For the basketball game. You didn't think I'd let you miss it? Surely you had more faith than that . . . I said to myself when I saw you the other night—standing at the top of the staircase in your long white gown, snake wrapped around your ear, I said, 'Anybody that glamorous would have to be passionate about basketball.' "

"Is that what you said to yourself?"

"Exactly. And knowing that, I knew I would have to make a herculean effort—I'm good at those—and spare no expense, even if it meant bribing several high officials, to secure for us two tickets to tonight's game. Cal against UCLA. The hottest college team in the nation."

"Cal?" she said, and he grimaced.

"A game not to be missed," he went on. "You are about to have the time of your life. Better dig in before the fries get cold—nothing worse than cold fries."

"Nothing," she agreed, unwrapping a hamburger for him.

They threaded their way up the bleachers, balancing as they pushed through the crowd. When they finally found seats, high up in the gymnasium, he said, "You look different. No furs. No jools."

"I make it a practice not to wear jools to basketball games," she shot back, and then, seriously: "Why didn't you just say you were busy tonight?"

He half turned in order to look her full in the face.

"Exactly how much do you know about basketball?" he asked skeptically.

"Exactly plenty," she answered. "Full-court press, fast break, slam dunk . . ." She took a mouth full of popcorn so she wouldn't have to say more. At that moment the teams came onto the court and the sounds of the crowd, mixed with the hard, fast action, bounced and ricocheted off the walls and caught them up in the fast drama of the game.

Hayes sat forward, elbows propped on his knees, his attention riveted. May watched him as much as she watched the game, fascinated by his total immersion in the action. She had been disappointed when he picked her up, sorry that they would not spend the evening talking, but now she was not sorry. Suddenly the crowd was on its feet as a Cal player shot from the backcourt and the ball swished clean through the hoop.

As the place erupted in pandemonium, Hayes turned and pulled her to him and May wrapped her arm around his waist and hugged him back, laughing with the excitement and pleasure of the moment.

They stood like that for a time, arms around each other like comrades, and he looked down at her and told her he thought she might be all right, after all.

"You must have played basketball in school?" she asked.

"I'm not sure that's what the coach thought I was doing," he answered. "It was more like I went out for basketball at school. I sort of made a profession of doing that—going out for sports."

"Didn't you ever get to play?"

He grinned. "When the team was twenty points ahead, sometimes they would let me in. And I got to play the last game of my senior year—well, actually only the first quarter. But I was always voted the most determined player on the team."

"Still is," a low voice boomed at them from behind. May turned to see an amazingly tall black man fold himself on the bleacher behind them. He put both his big hands on Hayes's shoulders and started massaging.

Hayes introduced him as Eli Barnes, his "basketball guru."

"I keep telling this white boy it's not just that his feet are too big," Eli said, "it's that they don't always go in the same direction."

"You can't be serious," May came back, "he's just been explaining how he was all-state in high school, and I love the part about how close he came to being a candidate for All-American in college—though of course that was Ivy League and we all know they don't count when you're talking basketball."

Eli whooped and slipped his arm around Hayes's neck, holding him in a mock hammerlock. "Is that right, boy?" he teased. "Is that what you told this nice lady? Confess or I'll break your lying neck."

Hayes coughed for effect and said he confessed, adding, "Remind me to steer clear of ladies with snakes in their hair."

"Is that you?" Eli asked.

"Afraid so," she answered.

"Who would have thought it?" he came back, and they all laughed.

The two men talked about the game for a time, and it seemed to May as if they were speaking another language. Then Eli turned to her and said, "Don't you want to see our boy here play basketball? Listen here, if it isn't raining in the morning, why don't you come on out to Oakland and watch us. We play there every Saturday morning and I just know . . ."

"She's too busy for such kid stuff, Eli," Hayes cut in. "May's working for a doctorate, she's serious, man . . . beyond all this bouncing ball stuff, and she certainly doesn't want to go hanging around some ghetto playground . . . she has better things to do."

"No I don't," May said as innocently as she could.

"Terrific," Eli told her, clapping Hayes on the back as he rose to go. "Lincoln Recreation Center, corner of Eleventh and Harrison, around eleven. Our friend here will give you one of his All-American exhibitions, and after that we'll take you out for lunch. How about that?"

"Fine," May said, smiling up at him.

"You hear that Hayes? The lady says fine."

"Tell me about him," May said when Eli had left.

"Where do I start?" he answered. "I guess in Mississippi. I had gone south to help with voter registration one summer vacation, and so had he. Eli was already something of a celebrity—he had made All-American in his junior year in college. Even little kids in backwater towns knew who he was. The thing is, he comes from a middle-class family in some small Minnesota city—his Dad is a CPA and his Mom is a nurse. Eli was a good student and a great athlete, so he hadn't really had all that much experience with racism. He wasn't any more ready for Mississippi than I was.

"We slept on the ground together, read each other's books, got eaten by chiggers, knocked on doors, got spit on together. All the fabulous fun things you did down south. Then at the end of the summer, I left but he stayed on, working for SNCC." He laughed. "I remember his coach came all the way down to this little four-corner town way back in the country, the kind of place the bus goes through every other day—to try to talk sense into Eli, all about the importance of being an 'educated man' and how he could help his 'people' by being a 'role model.' I remember the guy said to Eli, 'Kid, do you know what you're giving up?' and Eli said, 'Yeah, and it has nothing to do with being a kid.' When the coach finally figured out that Eli wasn't buying it, he spit on the ground and called him an ungrateful Negro son of a bitch. I happened to be there at the time, and of course I had to open my mouth and say how obvious it was that the coach was an educated man himself because he said Negro instead of 'nigger' like the other rednecks, and the guy hauled off and slugged me. I landed on my ass with a look on my face that sent Eli into convulsions, he laughed so hard. Anyway, we kept in touch. He always meant to get his degree, so this year I convinced him to come and finish at Berkeley. That was a few months back, but he hasn't quite gotten around to enrolling yet."

"Why not?"

Hayes looked uneasy. "He's listening to Stokely, I think. And the Black Panthers."

"Black power?" she said, and he nodded. "Who will be playing tomorrow?"

He laughed. "Mostly guys who were good high school players a few years back, but not good enough to get college scholarships—or a few got them and flunked out. Some are unemployed, they just hang out, so the Saturday morning games are a big thing for them. You might even see a little action on the side . . . some of the local bookies turn out."

"Are you the only white?"

"Afraid so. Eli is the big star. They tolerate me because of him."

"That doesn't sound like much fun, for you I mean."

"It's okay," he said, and because she didn't know what he meant she asked if it would be better if she didn't show up.

"No," he said slowly, "it's okay to come. But it's up to you, if you don't feel easy . . ."

"I feel easy," she answered.

He pulled into the drive behind the Winged Victory. "Sam's here," she offered, "would you like to come in?"

"Big game tomorrow," he told her, "coach says I have to turn in early."

She got out, then leaned down to speak through the window: "You've got all sorts of excuses for being home before midnight. First the Dobermans, now your basketball curfew . . . I'm beginning to wonder if you turn into a werewolf or something at midnight."

"Some one of these nights you'll have to find out," he told her in a Dracula voice.

It had rained during the night, but when May got up the next morning the sun was shining, and the air seemed almost iridescent. She pulled on jeans and a loose Italian knit sweater, then she asked herself why she had taken Eli's dare. (By then she was certain it had been that: a dare, not so much testing her as teasing Hayes.)

She was ready to leave and Karin was still in bed so she left her a note: "Borrowed your car. Keys to Jaguar on my dresser."

On the way out she ran into Sam.

"Where you heading?" he asked.

"To the lab," she lied.

He watched as she climbed into the Volkswagen. "What's wrong with the Jag?" he asked.

"I'm leaving it for K," she answered evasively, irritated that she did not want to explain where she was going or why she didn't want to drive the Jaguar.

When she pulled up at the playground a few minutes after eleven, a small crowd was gathered—a cluster of boys and middle-aged men. A knot of girls, about high school age, May guessed, were noisily calling out to the players.

Eli saw her and waved as he called out to Hayes, who turned to wave as he loped down the court.

"He you boyfriend?" one of the girls asked.

Before May could answer another chortled, "Who you think? He the only white man here."

"Maybe she come to see Eli," the other snapped back.

"I've come to watch both of them play," May answered.

"Eli, he play basketball," the first girl offered, "the rest, they just flop around the court, chasing after him." The other girl said in agreement, "No shit."

Hayes, May could see, was better than he made out to be, was probably as good, she thought, as most of the men on the court. What was obvious was that none of them could hold a candle to Eli. While the others pounded down the court, breathing hard, Eli seemed to dance with the ball, dribbling and smiling, moving with a grace that suggested he was making no effort at all.

"Hayes—here!" Eli called from the free throw line. Hayes fed him the ball and watched as Eli turned, executed a perfect four-step which delivered him under the basket where he jumped, pirouetted in the air and dropped the ball perfectly through the basket.

"The Skywalker," somebody shouted in awe. They crowded around Eli then, jostling him and joking, patting and touching, so you knew they were grateful to him for being there, for reminding them of their own glory days, too short and too long ago.

Hayes grabbed a towel, mopped his face and joined her. "The last female who came out to watch me play on a cold Saturday morning was in high school. Her name was Bunny Felderman, but that was before she had her nose fixed."

"Minor confession time?" May said, lowering her voice. "The ladies here," she said, nodding at the high school girls, "say you play okay for a white boy, but they also say that Eli's the whole show. I have to admit," she added, "I think I've never seen anyone move so . . . elegantly."

Hayes looked at her for a long moment. "You're right," he finally said. Then: "I need a shower. If you'll give me a lift back to my place, I'll let Eli take my car to drop some guys off. He'll meet us there."

Hayes lived in a duplex on Benvenue on the south side of campus, a wide street with old trees and lawns and shingled houses built fifty or more years before, except for an occasional newer building made to blend in with the old. His was one of these, brown-shingled with its own deck and set back in the privacy of sycamore trees.

While Hayes showered, May studied the living room. It was furnished in what Karin would call "student semi-classic"—bookshelves put together by stacking cement blocks and two-by-fours, a desk fashioned of a door balanced on two-drawer filing cabinets, several canvas chairs, a sofa that was vaguely Danish and a wicker chest that doubled as a coffee table. A calendar hung on the wall over the desk; it was, May noticed, filled with notations.

The room itself was neat enough; his desk, which on first glance had appeared to be cluttered, was actually organized. May stood back, trying to decide why the room seemed so impersonal. Finally she knew: there were no pictures on the wall, no mementoes, little that was private.

She heard the short, shuddering noise of the water being turned off. She glanced at the books in his shelf. Most were law books, but one corner had a small cache of volumes: *Pride and Prejudice, Huckleberry Finn, Let Us Now Praise Famous Men* and *Tristram Shandy*. She opened this last; on the frontispiece was written: To Hayes from Mother, Christmas 1952. Quickly, so he wouldn't find her looking at it, she put the book back. In her haste, she almost toppled a coffee mug. It was of plain white glass, the cheap kind you can buy at the dime store, and on it—printed in ragged letters in red fingernail polish was: For Hayes. Selma, 1965. Love, Doolie.

"Who is Doolie?" she asked, without turning around.

"The most beautiful female in Alabama," he answered, coming into the room in a wash of warm, moist air from the shower.

"How old?" she asked.

"Ten then, fourteen now."

His hair was damp, his shirt, fresh from the laundry, was sharply creased and, she noticed as he moved to stand behind her, he smelled of soap.

"Sounds like love," May offered lightly.

He was, for once, serious: "She was the sweetest child you can imagine. Her hair braided and tied with pink ribbons. White patent leather shoes and pink socks to match the ribbons."

She turned to face him. He put his hands over hers on the cup; at his touch, May felt her breath catch.

"You must be hungry," he said quietly.

"Not very," she answered.

The words did not matter, she was not listening to the words but to the warm throbbing of her body, the rush of heat that began between her legs and moved, shimmering, into her stomach. Their faces were close, their voices hushed.

"What did you think of my form this morning?" he asked.

"I liked your form," she told him.

She ran her fingers over the tips of his starched collar; he pulled her to him, his hands moved up her back while he whispered into her ear, "Do you know anything at all about basketball?"

"Nothing," she confessed in the moment before his lips pressed on hers, lightly at first, then hard; before she felt the heat race through her body. They held together, swayed. His hands caressed her back, moved up her sides to her breasts.

She pulled him to her. His mouth was on her neck; she put her head back and opened her eyes and saw the white cup with the bright red printing and tears stung her eyes. She reached for his mouth again, breathless.

The doorbell rang, sharp and shrill.

He held her close for an instant, then with his hands strong under her arms held her away to look at her. She wanted to cry but she tried to smile, and he bent to kiss her forehead.

"One second, Eli," he called out, and lowering his voice said, "I'm sorry."

May shook her head in protest and wrapped her arms hard around his neck. "Don't be sorry," she whispered. "I don't want you to be sorry."

8

The noise scratched at the corners of her sleep; May heard it, tried to ignore it, could not. She lifted her head enough to see from the glowing hands of her bedside clock that it was not yet six. The noise billowed, low and humming and then swelling. It was a day-time sound but it was not yet day, not yet light. She rolled out of bed and stumbled to the door, shivering in T-shirt and underpants. As she moved down the hall, her bare feet guided by the carpet, she could see a light in the living room. The sound grew louder, reached a crescendo.

"Sam," she shouted over the din, "turn that damned thing off." When he did not hear, she grabbed the cord to the vacuum cleaner and yanked, pulling the plug.

"What is this all about?" she managed to ask, dangling the end of the cord in the air like a dead snake.

"I'm cleaning house," he said.

"I can see that," she snapped, "but why now? Why at this ungodly hour on Sunday morning when people are trying to sleep?" She slumped against the door frame, too tired, almost, to be angry.

When he said nothing, she went on: "Let me see if I can make you understand. I was up until three working on a paper. That's right, Saturday night and you were out carousing or doing God only knows what, and I was working on a paper. I had planned to sleep until nine, Sam. Six hours of sleep, then up again to finish my paper. It seemed a reasonable plan, at least until you decided to sabotage it." She tried to stifle a yawn and couldn't.

"You're cold," he said, "better put on a robe."

"I don't want to put on a robe," she answered, "I want to go back to bed."

"Put on a robe. I've already made the coffee."

She groaned. "I don't want coffee, Sam. I want to sleep."

"I need to talk to you," he persisted.

She held the cup to her lips and let the steam rise to fog her vision. He sat across from her at the table, and watched as she took a first, tentative sip.

"What's this about you and Hayes Diehl?"

"Is that why you got me up? To ask about Hayes?" She glared at him for a long moment. "If that's it, I can set your mind at ease real fast. We went to a basketball game once, to lunch once and to see a Woody Allen movie once. That was three weeks ago, and I have not heard from him since. Now that I've made my full report, may I please have permission to go back to bed?"

He grabbed her hand. "Hold on, hold on," he said, "I didn't mean to set you off, and I didn't mean to make you mad. I was the one who introduced you to Hayes, remember? I have some problems with his family—his mother drinks like a fish, and his old man is dour as hell. They're quite a pair. And Andy is a hell raiser like you've never seen. Hayes is the only normal one in that family."

"Then why the cross-examination?" she demanded.

"What cross-examination? I only asked what was going on between you, that's all."

May ran her hands through her hair. "To answer your question then, nothing is going on between us."

"Okay," Sam said, as if to accept an apology. "What I need to talk about is my schedule. I'm having problems—classes require a certain minimum, and I'm cutting that very close. My work hours at the chem lab are set, and I can't get around them. The thing is, I can't garden after dark so that means the housework has to be done at night or very early in the morning, and that is messing up my shooting schedule."

"What shooting schedule?"

"My own," he answered. "If I'm going to make it as a photographer, I need to shoot as much as possible. That means using the early morning light, and it also means being free to photograph whenever the occasion arises—the demonstrations for instance, and all the things that are going on in San Francisco now in the Haight, the hippie kids."

"Make it?" she repeated.

"Become a professional photographer, make a living at it."

"That's what you want? You're sure?"

"I've been at it for six months. I'm good, I know that. But to answer your question: Yes, I'm as sure as I've ever been of anything."

The dense gray of the dawn had become a soft pewter, and it caught the determination in his face. May reached across the table to touch his hand.

"So what can I do . . . short of getting up at five in the morning?"

"I don't know," he answered, "help me figure out how to juggle everything. And I have to get my own photo equipment, cameras and lenses. I can't keep using Faith's, and besides, hers is out of date. I can't drop out of school, and I can't get another job because I don't have time to do the ones I've got."

"Maybe if we get someone else to do the house and garden?"

"Then how do I pay for the cottage?"

She hesitated. "You don't, Sam. Listen, we've all lived here together for more than a year now, and you've done twice as much work as you needed to, you really have. As far as I'm concerned—and I know Karin agrees with this—you've got a nice fat credit built up, and I think you should cash it in now. The cottage is yours. Maybe you could find someone to garden for us, and we'll hire someone to clean the house."

"I don't know."

"Why not?" she asked. "When you start making big bucks as a photographer, you can pay rent."

He hesitated. "Are you sure?"

"Yes I'm sure, especially if it means you don't get me up at the crack of dawn again."

He managed to combine a groan with a grin, and they sat in silence for a time, the coffee aggravating the dull ache of sleeplessness May felt in her stomach.

Sam broke the silence. "Now all I have to do is figure out how to get my equipment."

She looked out of the window; it was light, soon the sun would flood in, the kitchen would be bright and full of air. Now it seemed marble cold.

"I could make you a loan," she offered carefully.

He said nothing.

"I'm sorry," she added quickly, "I didn't mean to offend . . ."

"You didn't," he cut her off, and then he repeated purposefully: "You didn't."

"Does that mean . . ." she began.

"It means I'll think about it," he answered.

"One more thing," he said as she got up to go back to bed, "I've got myself into something of a corner, and I'm hoping you and Karin will help me out."

What more? she thought, but she said, "What's that?"

He stood, shoved his hands in his pockets and began to pace. "My parents have been after me to bring you and Karin down to the house for what my Mother calls a tea party. I know how busy you both are, and I didn't think you'd be all that wild about spending an afternoon at my folks'. I've been putting them off for months, and they keep after me. Somehow, a couple of weeks back, I guess I agreed to a date . . . and then I forgot about it. Mother called to remind me yesterday. She's been baking for a week, and it seems to have become something of a big deal for them . . . for Mother and Pop."

"When?" May asked.

He raised his eyebrows and shrugged: "Today."

"Oh Sam," she said, leaning her head against the wall and closing her eyes. "I am so tired and I've got this paper to do, and if we go it means I'll be up all night again . . ."

But she knew, even as she said it, that they would go. She climbed the stairs slowly, pulling herself up by the bannister, the bitter taste of coffee and disappointment in her mouth.

She went back to bed but she could not sleep. She was chilled, the sheets were cold, all the warmth had left them. She closed her eyes but there was no drowsiness left in her, only an empty weariness. Hayes moved into her thoughts, she ran the memory through her mind one more time, as she might a loop of film, searching for some new meaning in his words, going over them again as if they held some secret code, some message she had not been able to decipher.

Throughout the movie she had been conscious of him, distracted by his closeness, by the touch of his sweater against her arm, by the sound of his laughter. She had to make herself pay attention, she was impatient for the film to be over, she wanted to be alone with him.

They walked across campus, pausing in front of the campanile, stopping to sit on a bench under the plane trees. It was early still, and unusually warm. Knots of students passed on the paths by the library, the sounds of their voices drifting in short, cheerful bursts.

She had expected him to ask her back to his apartment. She had wanted it, her whole body ached for him, but sitting on the bench in the evening warmth she knew it was not going to happen. She felt a stab of disappointment.

"Sam said you'd been in the Peace Corps . . ." she began, not to let a silence fall between them.

"Sam said," he repeated, making it sound like a question.

"I suppose we should talk about that—about Sam, I mean."

"Why?" he asked.

"I don't know why," she answered, and she didn't. She did not want to talk about Sam, she wanted to talk about him. About them. "Why did you join the Peace Corps?"

"Good question. In fact, it turned out to be the Big Q." He sat forward, and spread his hands as if to study them: "I joined the Peace Corps because I believed that John Kennedy had pressed some golden button, and I was excited that it had happened in my generation, and I guess I was convinced that I had something to give." He stopped, turned to grin. "I didn't stay convinced very long. I had been in Africa about two months when I finally figured out what I was doing there . . . what most of us were doing there. It was a grand adventure, going into this impoverished Third World and exuding all this wonderful good will, showing them how righteous we were in the USA . . . Except, most of us didn't know how to do the things they needed us to do. There weren't many carpenters or plumbers or engineers among us. About the only thing we were qualified to do was to teach and spread good will. And in the end, for a lot of us—myself included—it was a relatively safe way to test ourselves, a helluva lot better than the old-fashioned way, war being a chancier business all around.

"The Africans were amazingly patient with us . . . with me, particularly, because I managed to get sick enough to require being shipped out for treatment. Africans who get the same vicious amoebic critter swimming around in their bloodstreams aren't nearly as lucky. But then, they weren't members of the shining generation." The self-

109

mockery in his voice made her want to touch him but she did not.

"I'm talking too much," he said.

She answered, "I'm listening. What happened after Africa?"

"Are you sure you want to hear this?" he asked, and when she said yes, he waited a while, as if trying to decide. "Okay, I'll give you the abbreviated version. I went south after that. It seemed straightforward enough—voter registration. I could measure my effectiveness through the numbers of people I signed up to vote. In the end, those results were mixed, too."

"When the black civil rights workers decided to go it alone?" she asked, and he nodded.

"That brings us up to date—Berkeley and the antiwar movement."

"And Robert Kennedy."

He said nothing for a time. A silence settled on them. The light from the standard reached them obliquely. It seemed to May that they existed in a shadow world that was separate, closed off. He sat forward. She wanted to put her hand, palm down, to feel the small of his back through the rough wool of his sweater, but she stifled the urge.

It was Hayes who broke the silence: "I spent a day in the library reading about your father," he began.

"Why?" she asked, puzzled.

"Because I knew his name—old lefties and new radicals still speak of him in hushed tones—but I never really knew much about him, what he'd done. And I thought knowing something about him might tell me something about you."

She waited.

"He seemed to know, your father I mean—what he was doing, what his place in the world was. I have been trying to make some sense of it all—where I've been, what it's all about. My batting average isn't terrific. I've been blundering around, trying to figure out some reasonable way with nothing much working."

He shifted to face her, allowing his hand to rest on the back of the bench almost, but not quite, touching her shoulder. He tried to shift the subject, tried to get her to talk about her father, her own past, but she could answer only superficially. She did not want to talk about herself, she wanted to talk about them.

As if reading her mind he said, quietly, "I'm a little bit afraid of you, May Reade."

She looked at him, incredulous. "Why?"

"Why?" he repeated, laughing a little, trying to shrug it off. "Because you are formidable. Because you're Porter Reade's kid. Because . . ." He stood, ready to go, to end the talk, end the evening. She remained seated on the bench, staring up at him.

"Why?" she repeated, standing abruptly so that she almost bumped into him. Without thinking, she lifted her face and kissed him, pressing her lips lightly against his at first, until he put his arms around her and pulled her in, holding her to him for a long, hard moment.

"That's why," he said, as if short of breath.

Lying in bed, playing the memory one more time, it occurred to her that they had never gotten around to talking about Sam.

May insisted they take the Jaguar and that Sam drive so she could sleep on the way to his parents' house. She could tell by the way he caressed the wood paneling he was pleased. She put the seat back as far as she could, and dozed off to the Beatles singing "Nowhere Man."

Sam's parents had been listening for the car because his mother came out to meet them, smiling and laughing. His father stood on the small porch of the bungalow, as if not quite certain where he should be, but smiling too. May took the rosebush they had brought as a gift. He said "Thank you, thank you," and fondled the leaves with a gnarled old hand.

"It's a 'Sutter's Gold,' Pop," Sam told him, "yellows, shaded oranges."

"I see," the old man said, then smiling shyly he looked at May and added, "and here we have *R. chinensis.*" Mrs. Nakamura burst into laughter and explained: "That's the Latin for the old-fashioned China Rose, my dear—the source for all the very best roses—and you must take it as a compliment." Her enthusiasm washed over them all. She seated them in her immaculate little parlor, where a table had been laid with a dozen dishes of sweets and an elaborate tea service which, May guessed, was used only on special occasions.

"What a beautiful tea set," Karin said.

"It was in my husband's family for very long time, his father's grandfather, and before that even . . ." Sam's mother explained, pouring from the old pot with its panoply of willow trees and birds. "When the war came, and we had to leave everything, you know, had to sell in two days, that was all, we could only take what we could carry, no more, and we had to leave Father's tea set." She laughed then, as if embarrassed at introducing such a serious note.

Karin noticed the frown that flickered across Sam's face, but May did not so it was she who asked, "How did you get it back?"

Mrs. Nakamura finished the story she had started to tell: "After the war, the lady I work for, Mrs. Diehl, she did it. She went to our farm, and found out where those people sold our things, and she kept looking and looking and finally she found it, in an antique place up in San Francisco. I wanted to pay her for it, but she said no, it had to be an anniversary present. It was the best present, wasn't it Minoru?" We all glanced at her husband, who only nodded, then she went on, "We never knew how much she had to pay, so I can't tell you how much it's worth."

Sam sat nibbling on almond cookies, one arm looped over his father's chair so that his hand just touched the old man's shoulder. The men listened to the women talk; May had settled in a rocking chair and the gentle motion, combined with the hot tea and Mrs. Nakamura's easy laughter, made her feel glad she had come. It was the same for Karin, May could tell from the soft set of her mouth, the ease with which she moved to hold her teacup under the spout of the beautiful old pot. What they had envisioned as an onerous chore was turning out to be a lovely afternoon. May looked at Sam, his arm placed protectively on the back of his father's chair, and was struck by the exquisite lines of his profile, by the blue-black gleam of his clean, clean hair. He was wonderful looking, she thought, especially here, in his home with his mother fussing over us all and laughing with pleasure and his father rocking and smiling.

Had the visit ended at that moment, with the sweet taste of almond cookies and green tea lingering, they might have made their way north again, over the Bay Bridge in the late afternoon haze, feeling warm and good together.

Sam's mother sounded the first disturbing note when she told him, "Andy is home. He will be leaving in a few days for Vietnam. I thought you would want to see him before he leaves, so I've asked him to come by this afternoon." When Sam said nothing, his mother turned to them and went on, as if she did not notice. "Andy is the son of the lady I work for. He and Sam practically grew up together . . . when they were little boys they were great friends," she said to May and Karin, "they did everything together—fish, swim . . ."

"In the Diehls' pool," Sam cut in.

"Yes," his mother agreed, sensing his displeasure.

"It's getting late," Sam told her, rising, "and May has a paper to write so we have to get going."

"Yes, I understand," she said, her eyes lowered to absorb the rebuke, and May thought perhaps she did understand.

But it was too late; at that moment a car pulled up, skidding to a stop in the graveled driveway. "Mama Miyo," a voice called out, and Sam's mother could not help herself, her face filled with light.

"It's Andy, Father. And look—Hayes, Hayes too. Son," she said, turning to Sam, her eyes pleading.

"A party," Andy Diehl said, sweeping Sam's mother into the crook of his arm, "You are having a tea party, Miyo mother, and you didn't invite me." She could not help herself, she laughed.

"Yes I did," she corrected him, knowing he was teasing, but unable to help herself, "I told your momma that Sam and the young ladies were coming, and you should all have tea . . ."

"Sam, dammit," Andy said, releasing the mother to grab the son around the neck. "Introduce us to your young ladies." His eyes had been scanning them, and now he gave May and Karin his full attention.

Introductions were stumbled through. Hayes met May's glance and grinned, but said nothing. No one seemed quite to know what to do. She and Karin waited for a signal from Sam, but he made no move to leave. It seemed to May that everyone in the room was ill at ease, with the exception of Andy Diehl, and she knew instinctively that Andy Diehl was never uncomfortable in a crowd.

Andy was the original fair-haired boy, she thought, all charm and glib talk. He was not so tall as his brother, but he was more powerfully built and better looking in an uncomplicated, blond way.

It was Hayes who spoke up. "We can't stay, Miyo—Andy has a lot of people to say goodbye to, we've got to be off."

"There's time for a cup of tea," Andy came back, settling next to the tea table, carefully choosing a candied lychee and eating it, delib-

113

erately. "Miyo's tea parties are world class," he said. "You even hear about them in Saigon. Come back, sit down," he laughed. As if playing out some sleepwalking game of musical chairs, the rest of them found places to sit, with Andy in the center.

He directed the talk as he might have directed an orchestra, pointing the baton first at one to perform, then another, but his eyes kept returning to Karin. They flickered over her, exploring her breasts under the peasant blouse she was wearing.

"I'm going back to the wars tomorrow, Sam. To Vietnam," he said, almost singing the syllables. "Why don't you come along, keep me company, have some fun."

"Some fun," Sam came back. "You think you're playing war again. I always knew you were crazy Andy, but I didn't think you were stupid."

Sam's mother frowned, then looked confused and relieved when Andy smiled his big, charming bad boy smile. "You are right, brother Sam," he said, "absolutely and totally right, just like brother Hayes here, but it's the only show in town, isn't it?"

Andy looked at Karin again and suddenly May felt afraid, she didn't know why. She wanted to step in front of Karin, to shield her, but it was Hayes who moved between them, saying "Time to go pal," to his brother.

Goodbyes were ragged, disjointed. Sam's parents stayed on the porch, in the shelter of their tiny home.

"Whose Jag?" Andy asked in what they all knew was the opening salvo.

May returned his fire firmly. "Sam is driving his two young ladies home to Berkeley."

"No, no . . . listen," Andy came back, "we all have to eat, even Sam, right Sam? And when will we ever have the chance to be together again, think of that. I'm going off to war, Sam!" He was laughing at himself. Karin was the first to smile.

"Look," Andy went on, "I know you're all part of Hayes's gang— and you want to end the war and bring all us boys home. But some of us are being shipped out anyway, surely you won't hold that against us? And how about a little patriotic, Stagedoor Canteen action?"

Hayes sighed and shook his head as if he'd played out this scene before.

"Come on Sam," Andy pretended to plead, "I'm not asking you to sing Yankee Doodle Dandy, just to have a little last supper with me. At Rosie's. Hayes, Sam, tell the ladies about Rosie's. The best to eat, the very best. Terrific enchiladas. Terrific quesadillas, absolutely fantastic margaritas." The words were rolling off his tongue, smart and smooth and mesmerizing. "Look, we'll meet you in town. Hayes, you go with Sam and May, in that By God riotous green Jaguar. I'll take Karin . . . we're off—let's go, troops. To the ramparts!"

His hand was on Karin's elbow and he was guiding her toward a two-seater Triumph.

She looked back at them, smiling. "Come on, May . . . Sam . . ." she said. "Just for . . ."

"Wait!" May called after her. "I can't go anywhere except home, I've got a paper to finish." She turned toward Hayes and managed to keep her voice firm when she said, "So it's time to say so long and good luck." It wasn't clear who she was talking to.

Karin stopped, and for the first time in a very long time May did not know what she was thinking.

Andy moved into the hesitation. He took possession by putting his arm on Karin's shoulder. "Meet us at Rosie's," he called back.

She watched them climb into the sports car. A small explosion of dust marked their departure.

Sam climbed into the driver's seat of the Jaguar as if he belonged there. They gave Hayes a ride to his parents' home, down a country road lined with great blooming bushes of oleander, red and white and pink. Sam drove fast and said nothing at all.

May was tired and confused and exasperated. For a time they rode in silence. Then Sam blurted angrily, "You never know what the hell that brother of yours is going to do."

Sam pulled up in front of a large, rambling house hidden behind a phalanx of oak trees. As Hayes climbed out of the car, she asked, "Will he get her home all right?"

"I'll catch up to them," he answered, patting the back of her seat.

May felt better then. She would have liked to talk to Sam, to ask him about his parents and about the Diehl family, but she could tell by the set of his mouth that he did not want to talk. Instead, he threaded his way through the familiar streets of the town where he had grown up with the Diehl boys, driving too fast but handling the car expertly, using its speed and its power, until he swung onto the ramp that led to the Bayshore Freeway.

Sam negotiated the loop in a single, long swift motion and merged into traffic at top speed, moving between two cars with no space to spare.

It was five o'clock, and the Sunday drivers were moving sluggishly back into the city. Sam began to wind his way through the lanes, moving two, three at a time, slipping into spaces, then pulling out again in one long, fluid motion. He was dancing up the freeway, feeling the throb and pulse of the engine, responding with sure, swift moves. He did not brake, not once; speed was imperative, speed and the rush of the wind through his open window. He played the car, played the traffic, letting the Jaguar full out.

She wanted to ask him to stop, to slow down, to pull off the freeway and let her drive. She did not ask because she was afraid to break his concentration, afraid that one spoken word could send them careening out of control into the back of a truck, over the edge of the freeway to burst into flames. Instead she concentrated, made the decisions with him, and it was not until they turned off at the University Avenue exit that she became aware of the cuts her fingernails had left in the palms of her hand.

May was still typing when Karin slipped in at two in the morning. She went directly to bed without saying anything, and was still sleeping when May left at nine the next morning.

At dinnertime May found her standing at the stove, methodically breaking apart a block of frozen peas and dropping the pieces into a pot of boiling water. She was wearing jeans and a faded flannel shirt left behind by some boyfriend.

"What happened last night?" May asked.

Karin shrugged without turning around.

"Did you have a great time seeing Andy off to the wars?" May persisted, an edge of sarcasm in her voice. Karin did not answer.

May waited for awhile, caught between anger and concern. "How did you get home?" she finally asked.

"Hayes drove me," Karin answered in a small voice, feeding another small block of peas to the water.

"What about Andy?" May prompted. She had by now glimpsed the dark circles under Karin's eyes, and concern overtook the anger.

"He got drunk," Karin told her, dropping the last of the peas into the water and lifting the cold tips of her fingers to her eyelids in a gesture that was, May thought, at once both brave and terribly sad.

The kind of silence that cannot be broken began to grow between them; Karin could not talk.

The lethargy set in on Tuesday. Karin had work to do but she could not bring herself to begin. She went to a lecture on Hieronymus Bosch and the fifteenth-century Dutch painters but she might as well not have, for all that she heard. On Wednesday she could scarcely get out of bed, and when she did she stood looking at the pile of clothes on the floor, trying to decide what to put on.

May found her there. "I can't believe this." She tried to hide her alarm by joking, "Miss Neat has finally succumbed to filing her clothes on the floor like the rest of us." When Karin did not answer, May said, gently, "K, it's obvious you are both distressed and depressed. I think it has to do with whatever happened last Sunday night, with Hayes's brother. Can we talk about it?"

"I can't," Karin said in a small, miserable voice.

That week May did what work she could do at home to be close to Karin. Sam had made himself scarce. He mowed the lawn and mended a fence on Wednesday, but made no move to come into the house. On Thursday he came to the door to tell her he would be in San Francisco for a few days. "Photographing hippies," he said, "around the Haight-Ashbury." May was relieved.

"My mother made me a dress out of material like this," Karin said, fingering the yellow and orange flowered voile in her lap.

May had been lying on her stomach on the living room floor, reading, but now she turned on her side and looked at Karin, sitting primly on the sofa. "Are you going to make that dress today after all?" she asked carefully.

Karin went on, as if she had not heard, "Mother used to starch it very stiff, and iron it just right so that I could wear it to Sunday school. It had a ribbon for a belt, a green ribbon that matched the leaves on the flowers." She ran her fingers over the material as she talked, and May saw that her nails were bitten below the quick and had been bleeding.

"There was some material left over," Karin went on, "and she made a little collar for herself, to go on one of the brown dresses she always wore. Housedresses, they called them. Cotton and starched, too. But he wouldn't let her wear it, he said it was too frivolous for a grown woman, so she had to take the collar off."

May looked searchingly at Karin. Finally she said, "That's the most you've ever told me about your mother and father."

Karin looked at her, and her eyes were filled with hurt.

May sat up, feeling a need to be upright.

Tears began to slip down Karin's face. She used a knotted tissue to wipe her nose. May rose on her knees to reach for a box from the end table and handed her a fresh tissue.

Karin sighed and shifted; her eyes were red now, but the stunned look of the preceding days had given way to a kind of panic. She choked out the next words: "My father said I was a whore, and sometimes I think he is right."

May moved closer and wrapped her arms around Karin's legs, as if to hold her up. Then May took a deep breath and asked, "Why would he say that, K?"

Karin shook her head violently; she was sobbing now, soft wet sobs that shook her body and caused her voice to come out in short swallowed gulps.

"Tell me, K, please."

"Oh God," Karin started, gathering momentum, "oh God," and it came tumbling out then, in no order at all: "I was just a little girl, but I developed early—breasts, pubic hair, hips. And men started looking at me—the way Andy did at Sam's, their eyes running all over me, at the store and at church. We'd come home and be in the parlor, the three of us, and my father would be reading the Bible, and the message was always the same. I was tempting those men with my wantonness, I was causing them to lust after me. From the time I was twelve, I had to sit in our parlor and listen to my Father ask forgiveness for my sins. I didn't know what they were—I was never allowed to go out, not even to school parties. They were very strict with me. They knew where I was every minute of the day, my mother knew I couldn't be doing anything wrong . . . but he was convinced that I would if I could. The prayers got longer and more violent, and more unforgiving until one day I left. I ran away. I went to the only person who had been kind to me, a teacher in our high school. A sweet, ineffectual little man . . . he had lived with his mother all his life, in a little house on Barton Street. She died the year before this happened. He may have been gay, I don't know—I don't remember him ever being close to anyone except his mother. Anyway, I asked if I could stay with him and as soon as I said it, I could see he was scared to death. I felt so sorry for him, and I knew I had made a big mistake. I mean, he was a good man but he just wasn't able to help me."

She paused and blew her nose. "So I went back home, and of course this time Father had actually caught me . . . I mean, I had run away and he was certain I had been with a man. He said I had become an offense in the sight of God, that I flaunted myself. And then he demanded to know who I had been with."

She stopped to take a deep breath. "I wouldn't tell him, of course. But it wasn't hard to figure out. I didn't have any friends, the only person who paid any attention to me was this teacher. So my father confronted the poor guy, who admitted I'd come to his house and asked to stay with him. That was all my father needed. He went straight to the school board and said my teacher was a sexual deviate, a seducer of young girls, and demanded the man be fired. And they did, they fired him. It was a terrific scandal . . . and my father caused it.

"I went to our principal and tried to talk to him but he wouldn't listen, he wouldn't even look at me. Nobody would listen to me, nobody wanted to hear what had really happened. Of course everybody in town was talking about it, just not to me. For me, a wall of silence went up and stayed until I left home."

Karin sat, lost in thought.

"Your mother," May finally said, "what did she do?"

Karin sighed. "I used to blame her, at the time I blamed her more than him, really. Because I hated him, but I loved her."

"She should have left him rather than let him humiliate you like that," May said fiercely. "That's what a mother is supposed to do, protect you."

"She did the best she could, May, I know that now. My father was a fanatic, a man of God, remember. They were all afraid of him, I think. So much that they allowed him to destroy a teacher's reputation, his career. That was the real sin."

"Christ!"

"Yeah, well, He wasn't around when I needed Him either." Karin tried to laugh, but her voice cracked. "Anyway, it was my mother who got me out. Somehow, she found out about all kinds of scholarships, and she and I filled out the applications and sent them off without his ever knowing about it, so when I got the chance to go to Mount Holyoke he couldn't stop me."

"Did he want to stop you?"

"Oh yes," Karin shuddered, "oh yes, he did. But it's all over, and I survived better than they did, out on that poor old farm all alone with their Bibles."

May stood, stretched and then she sat down next to Karin and said, "But what has this to do with now, and with Andy Diehl?"

Karin bit her lip. "There are times when I do something that brings it all crashing down on me again . . . when it seems as if he must have been right . . ."

"Your father?" May asked. "Right about what?"

Karin only grimaced. "Andy took me to this place called Rosie's, but we didn't stay there very long . . . after that he made the rounds of two or three other places, bars. I had something to eat but he didn't, he was just drinking and laughing and joking with people. At first I thought he knew them, but it turned out he didn't. He just seemed to speed up, as if he had to do everything very fast, and the bars kept getting more and more raucous. He was drinking a lot, but he seemed to be holding it and I guess I thought he could handle it, I don't know . . . then he looked at me and said he wanted me. Just like that. He said I had a neon sign bobbing on my breasts that flashed on and off, and it said, 'Climb on, honey, and come if you can.' He was saying all of this very loud, everyone could hear. People were looking at us, May, and they were laughing, and I felt like . . . I felt like what they all thought I was: a quick lay. A whore. He pulled me out, smiling and laughing at them as if they were an audience, and . . . they applauded. They applauded!"

She was sobbing now in deep, hard gulps and May could only sit beside her and rub her arm, and make soothing sounds to try to comfort her. Twice Karin tried to continue speaking, but couldn't. "Shh," May said, "give yourself some time, K, take it easy now."

Finally she was calm enough, and insisted on continuing. "In the parking lot he was pulling me toward a dark area, some trees, a picnic table I think . . . he was laughing and singing, and he had his arms around my waist, pulling . . . I started to cry, I think I must have been hysterical because this is a little hazy . . . But then a car was driving straight at us, its lights on and Andy stopped and stared at it. Hayes got out. I think I screamed because I didn't know what was going to happen, but then he was helping me into his car, and saying I was safe and that he was very sorry about what had happened, and I could tell by his voice that he meant it. He wasn't laughing at me . . ." She took a deep breath, as if she were about finished. "He said he'd take me home but he had to talk to Andy for a minute." She blinked, then she said, "I don't know what he said to him, I couldn't hear. I just know that in about five minutes he came back to the car and drove me home."

"Did he ask you what had happened?"

"He asked me if Andy had hurt me. I told him no, not really. He said again that he was really sorry it had taken him so long to find us—I guess he went to every bar he could think of. And he asked if there was anything he could do. That's about all."

"K," May said carefully, "you know it's not true—what your father said."

"You mean about my being a whore? Yes, I know it isn't true. But knowing doesn't keep you from feeling, sometimes."

"Those drunken Neanderthals in the bar—you can't possibly . . ."

Karin spoke sharply. "What I can't possibly do is erase a painful, horrible memory. That's what I can't do. Of course I know it was my father's problem, of course I know the kind of people who sit around bars getting blind drunk aren't likely to have any sensibilities. But when it happens to you . . . when people look at you like you're a piece of meat. Yes! And they do sometimes, May, you know they do. Don't you remember at school, when some of the girls in the dorm got mad at us—and somebody pinned up that nasty cartoon with you as a 'Chinese Dragon Lady,' and me as 'The Slut'?"

"I remember," May said, wincing.

"Sure you remember," Karin said firmly, "you went tearing into the dean's office, demanding to know who had access to your personal file, because you didn't think anybody but me knew about your Chinese background."

"I remember," May said, as if she didn't need to be reminded. Then she added, "It's strange, isn't it, how intensely you can feel about something that happened when you were so young? I guess Sam's right . . . about my not wanting to acknowledge that part of me that is Chinese."

"Your mother didn't acknowledge you, so you won't acknowledge her . . . or that part of you that is her."

"Psych 100, Introduction to . . ." May said, wryly.

"Are you ready for confession number two?" Karin asked, trying to manage a smile. "When I've slept with men I've cared about . . . guys I wanted to be with . . . it was never . . . I have never . . . I can't feel anything."

May stared at her, aghast. "You mean you've never had an orgasm?"

Karin shook her head.

"But it shouldn't be that way," May told her. "Sex is something you share . . . I thought you of all people . . . We've talked about it a million times and you always made me think . . ."

"I faked it," Karin confessed, grinning.

"Oh Lord," May answered, leaning her forehead against her friend's.

"Oh Freud," Karin joked, and the two started laughing then. They laughed until they had to gasp for breath, laughed until the tears flowed and they daubed each other's faces with tissues. When finally they stopped Karin managed to say, "I feel as if a hundred-pound block of ice has been lifted from my chest."

9

_S_ he saw him before he saw her. He was wearing a white shirt which blazed bright in the sunlight and dazzled her eyes; she was already smiling when he looked up. He was, he said, heading for one of his weekly meetings in the barracks left over from the Second World War, which now housed an assortment of offices peripheral to the main purpose of the university. She was, she said, on her way to Earth Sciences for a seminar on Finite Strains. Their schedules had meshed, their paths colliding like atoms, setting off a chain reaction. She felt it first in her stomach, a rise and a catch and then a soft, glowing spread.

"So," he said, shrugging—but not anxious to be off, she could tell.

"So," she answered, allowing a very small smile, but not making it easy for him, either. It was up to him. He was the one who had held her at arm's length.

On her way to Earth Sciences the next week, she found him waiting for her.

"What would you say," he began slowly, "about skipping out for an hour or two?"

She looked at him as if she were trying to solve an equation.

"Why not?" she said at the same moment he said, ". . . unless," and they laughed. He took firm hold of her arm to turn her around, and guided her to one of the trucks that drive onto campus at midday to sell sandwiches. They peered into the polished aluminum racks, chose a chicken salad and a ham and cheese, two cans of Pepsi, oranges and packaged brownies. Walking quickly across campus they encountered a man dressed in T-shirt and baggy dungarees who raised his hand for Hayes to stop.

"Later," Hayes called to him, not breaking stride.

"You mean this," she said, taking longer strides to keep pace.

He guided her through an opening in a hedge beaten down by years of students intent on a short cut, and into a parking lot where his car waited.

They drove up the hill behind the University, past the botanical gardens, and on to the Lawrence Hall of Science. She said nothing all this while, only sat next to him in the front seat with the brown paper bag that held their lunch in her lap—the Pepsi cans cold through her jeans. She glanced at him; he did not look at her but he knew she was looking at him and he grinned. She turned away, smiling.

They sat on a grassy hill overlooking the whole of the Bay, spread out before them in the warm haze of the day. He stretched out full length, his head propped on his arm, and looked at her. Self-consciously, she took a bite of her sandwich and pretended to look at the view.

"There are so many things I want to talk to you about," he said.
She waited.

"I want to tell you about my brother, my crazy brother who does things that are inexcusable, who can be the world's worst screw-up . . ."

"But?" she said.

He smiled. "Yes . . . there is a 'but.' Andy does have some redeeming qualities, as hard as that may seem to believe, given his performance that Sunday."

"I'm afraid I don't know him well enough to be forgiving," she said quietly. "I don't like what he did to Karin. I certainly don't like the way he treats women."

Hayes sat up, squinted out at the Golden Gate. "No, you're right. That's one of the things I wanted to talk to you about. If I had known that you and Karin and Sam were going to be there, we would not have come by Miyo's."

"I thought Sam's mother had told yours."

"She didn't. I'm sure you've figured out there is a problem, maybe Sam has told you . . ."

She twisted a thread that was coming loose from around a button-hole on her blouse. "Actually, no . . . but it's hard not to see how he resents—not you, but your family, his own family's position . . ."

"I'm not sure I blame him. There have been times when Sam's mother has put my family—Andy especially—ahead of her own. She carries devotion to an extreme—and of course, she can't see it. Neither can my mother, for that matter. She just goes along, pretending we're all the best of friends, perfect equals . . . Mother and Miyo have this great fantasy they've dreamed up, that we're one big happy family."

"And you aren't?"

"Not their MGM version. Actually, in a looney tunes sort of way our family is happy. And so is Sam's, separately. But not together. As Sam told you the day we met, his mother is my family's housekeeper. That's the reality of it."

He turned on his back, one hand firm around a can of Pepsi and the other flung to shade his eyes. She studied him: He had not shaved that morning, and a soft bristle covered his jaw. A strong jaw, strong face, she thought. A good face. Not sharply handsome like Sam, but good.

They tempted a squirrel with bits of brownies. It sat up straight and considered them, its bushy red tail twitching. "Watch the tail," Hayes said, "you can tell what it's thinking by the movement of its tail."

The talk drifted easily, like a raft on a slow-moving river, touching on this and that and moving on when some new subject floated into sight. Her foot cramped and she had to get up and hop around, then he rubbed it for her until the feeling came back. He lay back then and closed his eyes. "God," he said, "the sun. I keep forgetting it's there."

"It always is," she answered, absently. "Don't you know it is sinful to forget the sun?"

He sat up suddenly and with a passion that caught her by surprise said, "Do you know how old-fashioned that word sounds? Nobody talks about *sin* or *sinning* today. It's not with it, not cool . . . you rip off or you trash or you violate, you're a reactionary pig or an imperialist dog or a mass murderer—but nobody sins, and nobody is ever called a sinner."

She knew it was just starting, that everything inside of him was in motion, spinning wildly around, and that he could no longer contain it, no longer hold it in.

"Jesus!" he hissed, low in his throat, and then, shrugging as if at the irony of it. "Sin and Jesus, I'm beginning to sound biblical. I didn't bring you here for this."

"I think you did," she said, controlled, knowing she had to be careful.

He sat up, his body no longer relaxed, and he had forgotten the feel of the sun on his face in the mad colliding rush that was going on inside of him.

"Maybe I did," he repeated, looking at her so steadily that she felt, for a moment, she would not have the courage to stand up to it.

"So here it is," he began, clearing his throat and then stumbling over the words (so she knew, after all, that he had not planned it this way): "I'm sick of all the rhetoric, all the words, all the anger. It's become so rote, so studied, like a play we keep putting on, over and over again, and the people who make the difference . . . who make the decisions . . . some of them came to see it on opening night, thought it was a nifty little entertainment, and laughed all the way home. We didn't get it, though, so we keep going on, pretending it makes a difference. One award-winning performance after another and it's all so damned self-deluding . . ."

The gates were open now, he couldn't stop. She used a paper napkin to blot up a puddle of Pepsi he had spilled on the blanket and hadn't noticed. His voice was hoarse so the words came out grating: "It's all a charade, a game we play to make ourselves feel as if we have some control . . . pretending we can make changes. My mother— you've met my mother. We laugh at her, affectionately of course, because she's a good woman with a good heart. A good woman with her ridiculous good works, sending all those boxes full of old clothes—Brooks Brothers suits and sequined Saks dresses—down to Ecuador for the flood victims. But it's sheer hypocrisy for me to laugh at her when what I'm doing is worse. It's empty, posturing. More and more I hear myself talking and some other me whispers, 'Hayes, that's pure bull and you know it. . . .' I know we should not be in Vietnam and I know black people are systematically put down in this country and I know that prison abuses exist and that all of those things are wrong—are *sins*—but I've come to believe . . . I guess that's the right word, believe, an act of faith of a kind, that nothing I do on any committee or say from any podium is going to expiate any of our multiple sins."

He turned away from her, dropped his head and ran his hands

126

through his hair. She looked at him, at the big hands with their long, slender fingers, at the thick tumble of light hair which curled slightly behind his ears. She wanted to touch him, but knew she should not. He wasn't done.

"What is it you're trying to decide if you should tell me?" she asked, and his head snapped up, his eyes registered surprise.

"You know?"

"I don't know why you're hesitating. Unless it's a confidence."

"No, not that," he answered, frowning.

"Then I think you should tell me."

"Why?"

"Because it is part of all this . . . the sin, the reason for everything that is, or isn't. For you, and for you and me. Part of what I need to know."

"Need to know," he repeated, squinting into the distance. "That's a phrase the intelligence services use, and the government, in some classified programs. You should know only what you need to know to do your job. Which means everyone hides everything they can from everybody else. It isn't what I want with you."

It took all her courage to ask it: "What do you want with me?"

He looked up at the sky now; a white cloud had moved over the sun, as if to shield them from the glare. "Too much," he said.

"Then you will have to tell me."

He sat for a while, looking at his hands without seeing them, and she knew he was trying to find the words to begin: "There was this guy," he finally said, "I roomed with him for a while in Africa, when I first got there, before I got sick. His name was Ernie and he was from some little ranch town in Arizona, one way back off the main road was the way he described it. He was a real cowboy—I mean, he could ride and he'd been brought up on a ranch, and he didn't talk much, it was like he'd never had much practice.

"Anyway, after we were there about a week he started having nightmares. Nightmare, I should say. It was always the same. Sometimes he would just sit bolt upright in bed, other times he would scream out, but every time he would be sweating and shaking. This would happen about two, three in the morning.

"He started trying to stay up, not go to sleep, I think he must have had a million ways to keep himself from dozing off. He got haggard looking, his eyes had terrible dark circles and he walked around like a zombie. It was wearing both of us out, and finally I guess it just wore him down enough so that he told me. What had happened, the reason for the nightmare."

He frowned, and his voice became tight. "When Ernie was ten years old he had this friend, a boy his own age whose father was a ranch hand when he wasn't riding the rodeo circuit. The father was a bronc buster, it seems, and a bar brawler. He drank too much and messed around with other men's wives and just generally raised hell, except where his kid—Ernie's friend—was concerned. He loved his boy, everybody knew that . . . The mother had died, and this guy had raised the boy, and the two of them just loved each other . . ."

May stole a quick glance at him, she wanted to see if he knew his voice had changed into the short, terse phrases of the Arizona back country. Hayes, his jaw set, moved into the troubled story: "One day the boys were at a local rodeo. Small town stuff, just a little ring and some rickety bleachers out in the middle of a dusty field. And everybody who was there knew everybody else, local folks. Ernie and this boy were sitting almost at the top of the bleachers. And just as the boy's father was in the chute, waiting for his next ride, this man comes running in . . . He was a big guy, a cowboy, dressed in jeans and wearing one of those western shirts with big sweat stains around the armpits, Ernie remembered that. But mostly he remembered the man's face, which was tortured. Twisted into something beyond anger. Beyond madness, Ernie said, and deliberate. Like he knew exactly what he was going to do and nobody could stop him. He was wearing a gun, one with a long barrel.

"Everybody in the stands just stared, frozen, as he went tearing up the bleachers, two at a time, fast—and purposeful, with that demon look in his eyes. People made a path, and he was coming right for Ernie and his friend. Before anybody knew what was happening, this man had grabbed Ernie's friend and hauled him to the top row of the bleachers. He just stood there, he had the boy by the hair and he was holding him up . . . up off his feet and he had a gun to the kid's head. And he stood there like that until everything got quiet, and everybody was looking at him."

Hayes saw the shock in her face and said, "I'm sorry May, I shouldn't . . ." She gripped his hand and shook her head so that he would know he had to continue. In a curiously flat voice he went on: "Ernie wanted to shut his eyes, turn away, do anything but watch . . . but he couldn't. He couldn't move. All he remembers is the

128

father's scream rising out of the ring, and his friend's eyes in the moment before the gun went off."

"Oh dear God," May said, letting her head fall against his.

"Yeah," Hayes said, his hand cupped around her jaw, "a sin, yes. Several sins. The slaughter of the innocent, and then, now, the slow, slow torture of Ernie . . . the nightmare in his head, playing the scene, like a tape, over and over again."

"Poor Ernie," she said, leaning into him as he caressed her face.

"Yeah, poor Ernie," he repeated, "who joined the Peace Corps and went to Africa to help the black man, the Third World, the under-privileged. Except he really went to Africa because he believed that it was where he could get to the source of it all."

"The dream? The nightmare? How? I don't understand."

"He thought," Hayes said, watching her closely, "that it all began in Africa—the bloodletting. He thought he would find the wellspring of anger, primeval human anger, and violence. He figured it had started there, in the beginning there had been the jungle, and blood and anger seeping up like blood out of a wound. So he came to Africa to confront it, to look it in the face. He felt it was the only way he could get rid of the nightmare."

May could not think what to say; her leg had gone to sleep again and sent sharp jabbing pains at her, but she couldn't move. Hayes saw and took her hand and lifted her, made her stand, slipping his arm around her waist to give her support. Gingerly, she put her foot down and a shower of electrical pains shimmered into her leg.

"But how?" she asked. "How could he come to that . . ."

"I don't know," Hayes answered, "the reason I am telling you this is . . ." He grinned, though his eyes were not smiling. "I don't know why I'm telling you this. Funny. I've tried to tell a few other people about it, and I've never been able to. Get the words out, I mean. I'd want to but I couldn't." She could see his mind working, could see he was trying to understand something else. "But the real reason I told you, the true reason . . . *true:* there's another word to go with 'sin' . . . is that my running around day after day, making speeches and going to meetings and being the total political activist makes about as much sense as Ernie's going to Africa to find the root of evil."

They sat close together on the blanket then, holding tight to each other's hands, looking out over the haze that hovered over land and water. They could see the afternoon fog piling up behind the Golden Gate, waiting to work its way into the Bay.

"You know all the wrongs," she finally said, "but you don't know the rights."

"Something like that," he answered. "We know what we don't want . . . and we go, sheeplike, to our rallies and we write our diatribes against the power elite and the establishment and the pigs in the police department and in Washington, but we're just another kind of sheep . . . all of us, in our radical uniforms with our pat radical speeches."

"How do you find another way?"

"God," he said, rubbing her hand fiercely, "I don't know. I don't even know if it is possible to create a compassionate society."

"You know what I would really like?" he went on, with more passion than she thought could be left in him, "I would like for us to be one of those missionary couples who go off together into the jungle, ecstatic with the love of God and absolutely and totally certain that what we were doing was right. Never a doubt in our minds, ever." And then, because he had just thought of it, "I envy Eli because he is black and he can work from the inside. Part of an historical movement that includes him. A belonger. Eli is going to make a difference because in the end, he is going to do something to make life better for the black people in this country. And it will be worth it, his life I mean."

"And your life?" she asked.

"I sometimes think my life is going to be an unending series of meetings in which people I usually don't know and don't love drone on forever, saying what's wrong—wallowing in the wrong—while I sit there sick of it, sick of myself most of all."

She knew she must not talk, must not say anything at all, certainly not the obvious. She knew she must not ask, "Why are you telling me this?" What she also knew, and knew absolutely, was that she wanted to be with him. Like this, able to talk from the heart, from the mind, no detours. Straight, close, like they were now. Sitting side by side, listening, all the doors wide open between them. No barriers.

10

A January sun sent cool tremors of morning light through the
dust-spattered windows on the third floor of the Earth
Sciences building where May shared an office with two other graduate students. As the wind shifted, an errant branch of a giant pon-
derosa dipped and waved and scratched at the pane. Had she looked
out of the window at that precise moment, she might have seen Karin
enter the campus at North Gate. Absorbed in reading, May neither
heard nor saw.

"Tell me what you know about Krakatoa," Jeremy Wemers said.

May looked up, vaguely surprised. She had not noticed him enter
the room. "I'm not reading about Krakatoa," she answered, trying to
deflect what she suspected was coming.

Every attractive female graduate student knew Jeremy's approach.
He always opened with a question which had something to do with
her major field of study. Though as volcanoes go, May thought,
Krakatoa was just a trifle too obvious, even for Jeremy. If she bothered to answer the question, he would interrupt as soon as he could
by saying either, "That's interesting!" or "That's terrific!" and then
shift quickly to the question at hand, usually an invitation to some
university function at which he was expected to appear with a date.
An associate professor, he had burrowed into the academic life as a

mole might. His myopia was real; he wore glasses that sat heavy on his small nose so that he had continually to push them up.

"What *are* you reading?" he asked, determined.

May sat straight in her chair, and for the measure of a breath considered not answering at all. "A report on a joint U.S.-Brazilian study of continental drift," she began reluctantly, "—the idea was that if the continents of Africa and South America were once joined, then the rock formations should match up. And they did—formations of two highly distinctive geological ages were found in Ghana and on the coast of Brazil, exactly where they should have been."

"Fascinating!" Jeremy said.

"Yes?" she replied cautiously.

"Yes. Terrific," he answered, quickly adding, "I've been invited to a cocktail party and I thought you might like to go." A look of doubt must have crossed her face, because he hurried on, "It's at Philip Ward's . . . you know, our pop professor."

"I thought he was an astronomer . . ." she said as Karin appeared at the door.

"How can you not know about Dr. Ward?" Karin asked, "He's terribly famous . . ."

Jeremy interrupted, "As I said, our very own media star—bestselling author and pop political scientist. Loves to rake ugly Americans over the coals and gets paid properly for it. Don't you read the gossip cols? Marlon Brando just bought his latest for a movie."

"I read his books," Karin came back defensively, "I like what he has to say."

"Why did I think he was an astronomer?" May asked.

"Because he is," Jeremy answered her. "Unfortunately, when he chooses to publish it is fiction and outside his field and for the popular press. He hasn't made much of a mark in astronomy."

Karin disagreed. "He's one of the best teachers on campus—his lectures are always packed. It's almost impossible to get into them, I know because I tried."

"Exactly—he's popular," Jeremy said, sniffing as he pushed back his glasses.

"Jeremy was just inviting me to a cocktail party at Ward's house," May told Karin.

"Really?" Karin turned to Jeremy. "I'm impressed. How do you know him?"

Jeremy plunged both hands in his pockets and rocked back on his heels, a stance he assumed in the lecture hall when he was on shaky ground and trying to hide it. "We've been serving together on a faculty committee," he admitted. "Actually, he's invited all of us, and a guest."

Karin blurted, "You don't suppose you could wrangle me an invitation too, do you Jeremy?"

He stood back as if to inspect her. Her hair was loose and curled to her shoulders; she was wearing sandals, a long peasant skirt in muted Indian designs. When she slipped off the Peruvian knit cape she had been wearing, you could see the rise of her nipples through her cotton blouse.

"Very tempting," he told her, "showing up with a gorgeous hippie and a Eurasian geologist. But . . ."

"I'm not Eurasian," May cut in.

"No?" he murmured, surprised at the sharpness of her tone.

"I suppose Amerasian would be the label, if you feel you have to slap a label on me. But I don't approve of identifying people racially, so if you feel you must include a qualifier, I'd prefer being called an American."

He wasn't certain if she meant for him to laugh—Jeremy Wemers had trouble with subtleties—so he coughed instead, but managed still to ask: "Do you think you'd like to go?"

"She'll go," Karin answered, grabbing May by the arm and pulling her out of the office, calling back to Jeremy, "I'll see she's ready," and whispering to May, "and I'm depending on you to get me an invitation."

"I have to go out with Jeremy the Creep so that you can meet Philip Ward?"

"You've got it," Karin laughed as they took the stairs arm in arm, running down in fast matched double steps, moving quickly into the January sunlight and across campus, toward a low rumbling emanating from Sproul Plaza. The Third World Liberation Front was about to begin another rally demanding a student strike to force the issue of an independent Third World College for minority students.

"Funny," Karin said as they walked across the sunsplashed campus, "you object to being identified by race, and the Third World Liberation Front insists on it."

"I don't agree with them," May told her.

133

"I suspect Jeremy doesn't either," Karin answered. "That's what is so confusing about all this. You find yourself agreeing with people you absolutely, fundamentally disagree with."

They hurried along the path behind South Hall, the steady throb of bongo drums urging them on. "I wanted to tell him," May said, "that I probably have a better claim to be called an 'American' than he does—measuring by his standards. My grandmother's grandmother was a Randolph of Virginia. And when you think of it, almost all of the blacks in this country have been here longer than most whites. I don't understand why they should want to be known as Afro-Americans. This is their country, they helped settle it, their ancestors did all that hard work and now they want to turn back, to become something they never were—Africans. 'American' doesn't mean 'white.' "

"Doesn't it?" Karin asked. "Isn't that the popular conception? Both my parents were born in Norway, but nobody calls me a Norwegian-American. If you are white, you can drop the label as soon as you speak the language without accent. But if you are dark-skinned you can't."

At Wheeler Hall they stopped. The doors were cordoned off by strips of yellow plastic and the acrid smell of charcoal lingered in the air. Two nights before the auditorium had been gutted by fire; it was arson, almost certainly set by one of the radical groups, though none had claimed responsibility.

"I hate this," May said fiercely. "This awful rage that erupts into violence almost against oneself—students setting fire to a campus building, blacks burning down their own neighborhoods. Can't they see how self-destructive it is?"

Karin linked her arm in May's and said, "When I asked Eli that question—about black people burning the ghettos—he said there are just times when the frustration gets unbearable, and there's nothing left to do but strike out. And he thinks the rage is better than acquiescence, that burning down your own house is some better kind of a statement than dying in it without anyone ever knowing you were there."

"Is that what Eli said?"

"Something like that, yes, and while I can't agree with him I believe in him, somehow. And in Hayes . . . sometimes I think the two of them could find some answers . . . does that make any sense?"

"I don't know if it makes sense, but I know what you mean. When

134

they are together it's as if each gives the other something he couldn't have alone. I'm pretty sure Hayes knows it, and I think Eli does, too, but he's fighting it."

"I think Eli is fighting Eli most of the time," Karin said. "Have you seen Hayes lately?"

May continued walking, head down, not looking at Karin. She muttered, "As a matter of fact, yes."

"Stop right here," Karin said, loud enough to make a few students passing by look up. She lowered her voice to add, "Let's declare this neutral territory so we can talk."

"What do you mean, 'neutral territory'?"

"I mean out of the house, away from Sam. I get the feeling that Hayes is a forbidden subject, so I thought that if I could find some neutral territory you might . . ."

May sat on a wide stone ledge and began to laugh. Karin sat next to her, smiling and waiting.

"Okay," May finally said, taking a deep breath that was meant to signal a move into a serious frame. "Okay," she repeated, "you're partially right, I suppose. I have been seeing Hayes and I haven't been talking about it, but not because of Sam. At least, I think not because of Sam, or not totally because of Sam." She smiled again, this time to acknowledge the confusion.

She told Karin about the chance meeting with Hayes, and about the day on the hill by Lawrence Hall. "After that," she went on, "we started running into each other every few days . . . but of course it isn't chance, we plan it—casually, always, nothing at night or away from campus. We always meet in full daylight, in public. Where it's safe."

"Safe from what?"

"Sex. Love. Commitment."

"Oh."

"Yes, 'oh,'" May said, turning to look at her friend. "Is that what you wanted to know?"

"Yes. No. No, not nearly. I want to know how you feel about him, and what is going on!"

"Only that?" May cried out, "That's all you want? Come on, let's walk."

They dodged bicycles and two large dogs that came bounding through the fountain, splashing water and leaping against each other. May began, "Mostly we talk about ourselves—our families, what it

135

was like growing up. My father, his brother. My mother, his father. You, Eli. Everything. We just . . . talk. We walk into town sometimes, and go to coffee shops and sit there for hours. Sometimes we hold hands, sometimes he loops his arm through mine or puts his hand on the small of my back to guide me someplace, and when he does, this little electrical storm goes shimmering through me. I can't remember ever feeling this way before. Just all . . . well, all what? I don't know."

"It sounds like love."

May's face flushed. "I know," she said weakly, "I know, but we can't let it happen, not now." She struggled with the words to explain. "It's hard really . . . because each of us has a dilemma, something to resolve. And we both know—and we can't let each other get in the way because that could stop us in our tracks. Oh God, K, I don't know if this makes any sense at all but there it is. I've never felt this way about anyone, and I'm terrified I never will again. Every time I'm with him my whole body practically shrieks with wanting, but I can't. Not yet."

"Your mother," Karin said.

May nodded, looked away, lifting her eyes to the hills. "My mother," she repeated. "I keep thinking it is going to fade, and one day I'll wake up and she'll be gone, out of my mind, out of my thoughts, no more questions, no more pain . . . she will just have faded away and I'll be free of it, free of her. But it isn't going to happen, not like that."

Karin waited.

May put her hand on Karin's arm as if to steady herself. "I've got to find her," she said, "there is no other way."

They walked up Euclid Street, each deep in thought, May setting the pace. When they reached the steep part of the hill, Karin stopped, winded. "I need to sit," she said, collapsing on the steps to someone's house.

Looking up at May she said, wistfully, "You never see Hayes at night?"

May laughed. "Remember that party I went to a couple of weeks ago? You were so surprised that I would go? I went because it was given by a good friend of Hayes's, and I was pretty sure he would show up. He did."

"And?"

"And we spent most of the evening together. The room was

packed, full of smoke and noise and it was hard to talk. I was sitting on the edge of the piano bench and the phone was behind me. To make a call, Hayes had to lean into me and balance himself by putting his hand on my shoulder. It was just so . . . strange . . ."

"Strange?"

May sighed and laughed. "That I wanted it so much, the touch . . . I could have stayed there forever, with my face pressing into his chest."

"That's not strange, May. That's wonderful."

May smiled. "It was, it really was. I felt so connected to him, so important. When he put the receiver down he let his hand rest on my arm for a few seconds and I felt perfectly content. Then his friend Arnie, who was giving the party, called out to Hayes to come into the kitchen and he pulled me along. He could have taken me anywhere and I would have gone."

"But he didn't," Karin said, wryly.

"No, he didn't."

"It sounds like some kind of water torture to me—being together yet not allowing yourselves to *be* together."

"Very often I think to hell with it," May answered with sudden bitterness, and then, more softly: "Passion casts such a strange light. Sometimes, when I have to stifle it, it makes me feel almost . . . incandescent."

"If I see you glowing in the dark, I'll know why," Karin offered, dryly. "Why don't you just go after him, for what you can have together now?"

"Because I'm afraid he'll say we shouldn't see each other at all, and I'm not ready to take that risk."

To hide her surprise, Karin shifted the subject: "When you and Hayes talk, does the subject of Sam ever come up?"

"Hayes thinks that Sam has reason to be mad at his particular world."

"Well I don't agree," Karin snapped back. "He still holds it against me for going off with Andy Diehl that night. It's as if I did it to spite him—all actions revolve around Sam. It is perfectly obvious that his parents care about him, care deeply. His life hasn't been any bed of thorns."

May decided not to answer. Sam had become a sore point. Karin went on, "Have you thought that Sam might be one of the complications, as far as you and Hayes are concerned?" When May didn't answer, Karin continued: "Has it occurred to you that Hayes is everything Sam wants to be and never will? Sam is mad at the world, and blames it on his being Japanese and coming from a poor family, and he can't see that neither has anything to do with it."

"No, you're wrong there," May flung back at her, "race has everything to do with it, and poverty doesn't help."

Karin stared at her, and for a moment a flare of anger threatened to overcome them. Then Karin started laughing: "Do you realize we've switched positions? Great political theorists, we two."

May caught her breath and came back with: "What do you expect of a geophysicist and an art historian?"

———————

Philip Ward lived high in the Berkeley hills, in a house surrounded by a high wall painted the color of siena. From the street you could see nothing of the house. Inside was another world entirely with a beautifully tiled courtyard, dominated by a pepper tree, a fish pond bright with carp, the house itself, all plate glass with French doors that opened onto a profusion of flowers. Camelias in full, pink bloom were reflected in the gothic windows.

"Not too shabby," Jeremy said as they entered.

When a maid, in black uniform and white apron, took their coats, Jeremy murmured again, "Not shabby at all. Maybe it pays to write potboilers." They made their way into the living room, which struck May as more like the main hall of a British hunting lodge with its rough, heavily beamed roof, and huge stone fireplace. The floor was covered with deep red Oriental carpets and it was furnished in over-sized linen-covered sofas and English antiques.

"Karin says they aren't potboilers," May told him, raising her voice just enough to cause Jeremy to look around to see if she had been heard. As they stood in line to meet their host, May had a chance to study Philip Ward. He had to be nearing sixty, she knew, but only his hair—which was thick but silver—gave it away. His face was surprisingly youthful, and his build, while slim, was athletic. She took note that he was wearing a tweed jacket which would have been tailored in England, and the kind of tan acquired on a tennis court. What surprised her was his manner: she had expected flamboyance but he was, rather, restrained. He smiled and listened attentively to what each guest had to say, tilting his head in a way that made it seem he closed out the rest of the room and concentrated on the person whose hand he took, and held perhaps a moment longer than one usually would.

"Reade?" Philip Ward repeated when they were introduced and he was tilting his head toward her. "I don't suppose you happen to be related to Kit Reade McCord, do you?" She was surprised. She had expected him to name her father, most people of Ward's generation did. When she told him her connection his voice became vibrant with interest. "I knew Kit years ago—I manage to keep track of her through the business pages. I notice she is still good at keeping her name out of the society columns."

May smiled. "She hires someone to do that for her, I believe."

"I met your father once as well," Ward went on. "It was a great honor. I admired him." He said this in such a straightforward, disarming way that May answered, "Thank you."

The wife of the chairman of the department swept down on them in a storm of words, arms out to claim Philip Ward. May moved to leave, but Ward caught her by the elbow and told her, with what seemed a certain urgency, "I will need to speak to you again before you leave."

Jeremy made for the bar, where he stood, entranced by the choices. He murmured: "Chivas Regal or Johnny Walker Red, Heitz's Cabernet or Stoney Hill Chardonnay. Christ. Coming with me?" May took a glass of chardonnay and drifted away from Jeremy as soon as she could, approaching a group of women standing by the window.

"We're discussing our host," one of the women said, pulling her into the group. "I'm Marge Fromberg." She introduced the others, all faculty wives, and said, "I hope you don't disapprove of a little academic gossip."

"I've only just met our host," May answered, "so I won't be able to contribute . . . I'm afraid he struck me as charming—does that disqualify me?"

The women laughed. "Join the club," Marge answered. "Philip *is* a charming scamp—except on the tennis courts. He plays with my husband twice a week and I understand he does not take the charm onto the court. Of course, that's probably sour grapes on Hank's part, because Philip usually beats him."

"Who cares about charm?" another of the faculty wives put in, lowering her voice to add, "I wish my Joe looked that good."

"Philip is big on health," someone offered.

"Would that Ariel had been too," another said, and the mood darkened.

"Ariel was Philip's wife," Marge explained to May. "She died of lung cancer a year ago. We figure this is Philip's 'coming out' bash. His reentry after a year of mourning. Not formal mourning—he simply has done no entertaining. And he's a wizard at it, believe me. He loves to mix people, interesting groups of people—Philip and Ariel gave wonderful parties."

"Oh yes," Eleanor added, a touch of acerbic in her tone, "they worked hard at leading interesting lives."

"Are there children?" May asked.

"A boy and a girl," Marge answered. "Thea is thirteen, a lovely child. She should be here," she said, scanning the crowd, "and Daniel is sixteen."

"Has anybody seen Daniel?" someone else asked. "Or has he been allowed back in the house?"

"Daniel is away at school," Marge answered evenly. "Philip says he is doing very well—it's been a rough year for all of them." She smiled at May and said, "I think I'd better mix a little, so Philip will ask me back. He frowns on ladies who congregate."

May stayed only long enough to hear one of the women say, "I do believe Marge was trying to tell us not to speak ill of the dead."

May moved about the room making polite conversation for almost an hour before going to look for Jeremy. She found him in deep discussion with a pale young man he introduced as, "one of the chancellor's fair-haired boys." May had no idea what that meant, and decided she wasn't interested enough to ask. Jeremy put his hand on her arm possessively and returned to the conversation. May wanted to wriggle out of his grasp. She did not like cocktail parties, did not like having to make conversation, did not like talking to someone and having him scan the room over her shoulder. But now she did just that: scanned the room so she didn't have to get involved in the conversation, all the while trying to figure a way to convince Jeremy that it was time to leave. Philip Ward caught her eye and motioned her to join him.

"I'd forgotten how annoying these kinds of parties can be," he told her, "all silly talk, and usually not with the people you want to talk silly to." She smiled. "Before we're interrupted again," he went on, "I wanted to ask if you and your friend—Dr. Wemers is it?—might like to come again. I'm hoping to do more entertaining this spring—smaller dinner parties, where we might have a chance to talk."

She did not answer for a long minute. "I would like to come," she finally said, "but without Jeremy if you don't mind."

"I don't mind in the least," he said, eyes sparkling.

It gave her the courage to ask, "Could I bring a friend? Karin Rolofsen is her name. She's read your books and she wants to meet you."

"Good," he answered, touching her arm in confirmation, "I like her already. And now I get the feeling you are ready to go? Shall I tell Wemers that you're waiting for him in the foyer?"

"Yes, please," she said, grateful to him for helping her escape.

That spring of 1969 the campus and the center of town shook under a revolutionary barrage: birdshot and bottles, rocks flying, fire bombings, tear gas and shattered glass. It was a war zone, a long, steady scream of resistance, of change. Almost daily through January and February demonstrations boiled over, waves of students surged down Telegraph Avenue. Trash cans were heaved through plate glass windows, and the police moved in swinging billy clubs.

They found their marks: somebody's child, yesterday's polite kids who had been raised to be seen and not heard, to speak when spoken to, above all to be polite. They had been children with shining faces and neatly cropped hair who had in the short years of their coming of age assumed a righteous indignation. They grew their hair long and wore rag-taggle clothes their parents did not approve of, sprinkled their vocabularies with four-letter words and announced they didn't trust anyone over thirty. If they happened to be black they were saying "Freedom Now" and "Burn, Baby, Burn." If they were white, and of draft age, they were chanting, "Hell No, I Won't Go" and burning draft cards.

They fought for a "People's Park" and they spoke in the name of the People, though in fact this was a presumption. Many, perhaps most, of the people of the land believed these student rebels to be spoiled, disrespectful children of privilege.

All the old slogans came into play, and I could not help thinking of May's father, who had been bloodied in labor disputes on the San Francisco waterfront fighting for another generation's rights. Quite purposefully during those months I chose to work on Porter Reade's papers from the 1920s, the period when he was a student at Berkeley. "It is exciting to me to see how intensely Sally feels about these issues," he wrote his mother about a woman who had once been his tutor, "and how she translates that intensity into action. It makes me feel that people who are totally convinced, who know what is right and stick with it until they can make others see, are the ones who will change the world." Attached to the letter was a yellowed copy of the words to "The Internationale." He had underlined the two lines that read:

> The earth shall rise on new foundations,
> We have been naught, we shall be all.

I could close my eyes and see him still, a tall and gangly young man full of fire, of righteous indignation. There were times at the Peace Coalition office when I was certain I heard him in the next room, holding forth on some political issue. "Your father would have been in the thick of this," I told May.

"That's what the Revolutionary Student Army people keep telling me," she answered, her voice bitter. "They want me to march at the head of their line, in what they call 'my father's place.' Isn't that wonderful? The man's dead, and they still want to use him."

Police and demonstrators engaged in running battles. A new style came into vogue: bandanas, bright red and electric blue worn cowboy style so they could be pulled over the nose and mouth whenever police—some in low-flying helicopters—flung out cannisters of CS gas.

One sunlit morning the National Guard rolled into town, hundreds of men in battle gear standing in army trucks, bayonets drawn. The heavy silence was broken by the slow-rolling, ominous rumble of those trucks and the responding low recitative of the disaffected—the students and the street people and the blacks joined by a strange amalgam of townspeople, all those against the war, against racial discrimination, against poverty, against what some—but by no means all—of them called "The Establishment" and the "Pigs" and the "warmongers." In truth, against mistakes made by all the generations that had come before them, mistakes they wanted to correct now, all at once, and for all time.

One afternoon I stood at the window of the Peace Coalition's second-floor office, looking down at the gathering storm. May stood next to me; Karin was late.

"She'll have trouble getting across the street," May said.

"Perhaps she's already on this side," I answered, hoping it was so.

A strange, animal sound lifted from the crowd. It seemed to signal a movement down Telegraph Avenue. A distance away we could see a line of police in riot gear blocking the whole of the street. Directly below us, a rangy young man in a buckskin coat held a cigarette lighter high, touched it to a rolled-up paper and used the torch to set fire to a trash can; a whoop rose with the flames; a bottle bounced soundlessly off a plate glass window, and then we heard glass shattering and a fusillade of bottles and rocks was flying, and war cries pierced the air.

May gripped my arm. "Look, just under the bookstore sign," she pointed. A blond girl wearing a knit Peruvian cape was trying to push her way through the human maelstrom, which had washed over the sidewalks. What the girl could not see, but we could, was the current of movement that snaked down the center of the street. She was knocked down, and for a moment we couldn't see her at all. Then we saw that she had been caught up in the rush of it, was being pushed ahead, swept away. She was being carried into the line of police who stood, clubs raised in anticipation.

At that moment Karin appeared, out of breath, in the doorway behind us. When we turned back to the window, we could no longer find the girl in the Peruvian cape.

Philip Ward did not equivocate. He supported the student antiwar movement. While several of the men gathered at his table did not agree with him, most had assured their wives they would not become embroiled in a heated argument. Philip Ward's table was viewed by some as the last civilized place in Berkeley.

Karin bought a dress for the occasion at one of the shops that made new dresses in old styles: an ankle-length blue tie-dyed silk of cornflower blue, trimmed with velvet and bits of old brocade which she wore with boots. With her hair loose and curling over her shoulders she looked like a Renaissance princess. May put on what had become her 'dressup' uniform, effected so she did not have to think about clothes: a heavy cream-colored silk blouse edged in braid and a leather miniskirt from a Paris boutique which made them for her in a variety of colors. Tonight she wore the aubergine, with matching shoes.

A young girl opened the door. She had long, Alice-in-Wonderland hair caught up with a blue ribbon and was wearing a long dress, but it was her face that completed the fairytale effect: she looked like the little princess in the tower.

"You must be Thea," May said.

"Let them in, love," Philip Ward called, and then he appeared behind his daughter and her smile became radiant.

"May," he said, giving her a small kiss on the cheek as if they were old friends, "and Karin Rolofsen," he added, taking her hand.

There was an awkward moment then, when no one said anything. May thought it strange, that the charming Philip Ward should be at a loss for words.

"Thank you for letting me come tonight," Karin managed, a flush spreading on her neck.

"Thank you for wanting to come," Philip answered, regaining his composure.

May's name card was at Philip Ward's right at dinner, Karin was at the opposite end of the table, between a political correspondent on his way to Vietnam and the curator of the Asian art collection at the de Young Museum. By the time the lobster bisque was cleared, the correspondent was making pronouncements about the war to his end of the table, with the exception of Karin and the curator, who were having their own quiet conversation.

Philip scanned the table and, satisfied with the way the talk was going, said to May: "I thought Karin might enjoy talking to Byron— she is an art major, isn't she?"

"You certainly do your research," May laughed.

"Old habit," he grinned, slightly embarrassed. "That really is all I know about her."

"What else would you like to know?"

"Oh, everything," he answered lightly, touching her arm as if to convince her of his sincerity, even as he turned to answer another guest's question.

When they moved to the living room for coffee, Philip skillfully negotiated the seating so that Karin was at his side.

May slipped into a chair next to Marge Fromberg. "What's new on the academic gossip circuit?" she asked in a teasing tone.

Marge laughed and lowered her voice. "Well, for a while there at dinner the money was on you—but I'm afraid it's shifted to your friend."

"Is it a burning question in the department?"

"Maybe not burning," she answered, "more like smoldering. I have to admit the man has good taste . . . if only she wasn't so confoundedly . . ." Marge raised her eyebrows archly.

"Young?" May filled in.

"Yes," she made a show of sighing. "Both of you. Young and beautiful and bright. An unbeatable combination."

"Move immediately," the voice boomed out over the speaker of a patrol car cruising downtown Berkeley, "You are in violation of the governor's declaration of emergency."

"Our movie star governor thinks Berkeley is a war zone," Sam said as he slouched in the van, tired and angry at having been shoved and pushed by both demonstrators and police. "Thanks for giving me a lift—a couple of minutes more and I think they would have loaded photographers onto the bus for Santa Rita. Jesus! Mass arrests, this is insane."

Real insanity was reported every night on the evening news, up close and in color: TV taught us about Apbia mountain—"Hamburger Hill"—where North Vietnamese defenders rolled hand grenades down on the advancing American paratroopers as they crawled to take the summit of the 3,000-foot peak. "Sure we want the hill," a twenty-year old Specialist 4 from Oakland said on camera, "we want it because we can't get the hell out of here until we get it."

May ran into Marge on the sidewalk outside the Co-op Pharmacy. They stood together for a few moments, watching the National Guard trucks pass in some sort of review, on their way, someone said, to the encampment. An older woman came to stand next to Marge and in a heavy East European accent repeated, over and over again, "Is turrible, turrible, here to see."

"This *is* terrible," Marge said, "like a bad dream. I'm supposed to go to a piano club tea but under the circumstances that seems surreal.

Or this does, I'm not sure which. Do you have time for a quick cup of coffee?"

"I've been wanting to call you," May told her when they were seated at the counter. "I need to ask you about something—I'm hoping you won't mind."

"Let me guess," Marge smiled. "It has to do with our mutual friends—who, I hear from the grapevine, are seeing quite a lot of each other."

May nodded. "They are—Karin is in what another of our friends says is a state of acute dazzlement. She can't believe he could be interested in her. But really, what I wanted to talk to you about is Philip's wife, Ariel—what she was like."

"Why would you ask me?"

"Because when I met you at the cocktail party that day, several of the other women had some rather biting comments to make about her. One of them said that in the end, you were the only friend she had left. So I thought you could tell me something about her."

"Are you asking for your friend, for Karin? Because if you are, I'm afraid I'll have to give you the proper line."

"I'm only asking for me."

Marge considered for a long moment, "The proper line would have been: Ariel was handsome and bright and talented. She and Philip had what appeared to be a good marriage—I say 'appeared' only because I am convinced that no one can tell, from the outside, which marriage is 'good' and which is not. I sometimes felt that their life together was planned, almost blueprinted, and I think that Philip was the architect."

"Did you like her?"

"No, I suppose not," she answered deliberately. "But I didn't dislike her, either. There was no . . . peace . . . in her. I think she would have been terrified to find herself with an empty afternoon."

Marge moved to allow a girl with a large backpack to squeeze by before going on: "I get the feeling that Philip is ready to get on with his life. I hope he finds someone who can make him happy. My turn now to ask you some questions. Do you think that someone might be your friend Karin? And do you approve of him?"

Marge had been honest, and now May felt she had to be, though it made her uncomfortable. "I'm not sure if I approve of him for Karin," she began. "He is charming, no doubt, but his life seems somehow contrived—the carefully choreographed parties, the English tailors, the 'cultured life.' But what I think really doesn't make any difference, because I do believe that Karin and he might get together. She is quite enchanted with him—I know that sounds like an old-fashioned word, but in this case it is exactly right. I assume he is just as taken with her because of the amount of attention he pays and the time they are spending together. I was curious to see if Karin was anything at all like Ariel. From what you say, she isn't. Any objections I might have as far as Philip is concerned are really a matter of style, anyway. I assume the substance is there."

"Yes," Marge said, "under all that mannered charm and cultivated gentility and raging ambition breathes a reasonable, decent man. And a troubled father."

"That was my next question," May said.

"Karin must be a very good friend," Marge commented, and went on: "Thea is just fine. Rather quiet, self-contained and very self-sufficient. Ariel left her to her own devices quite a lot—when Thea was nine, she was taking the bus by herself to ballet lessons in San Francisco. She and Philip are close, I believe. Certainly closer than Daniel and he."

"Daniel is a problem?"

"Sixteen-year-old boys often are," Marge said. "I've got three boys, and I know. But Daniel is having a worse time than most."

"How?"

"He ran away the first time when he was thirteen. Philip had to fly to Philadelphia to collect him. After that it was a series of schools, and a series of trips to various places to haul him home. Once he got as far as Alaska, and had signed onto a fishing boat. I think Philip was rather proud of him for managing that, though of course he'd never admit it. But mainly, the two are at loggerheads, they never spoke the same language and Ariel either couldn't or wouldn't translate for them. Whenever Daniel would take off, Ariel would manage to have to make a long trip in the opposite direction. I remember she was involved with some gourmet food fair in New Orleans when Daniel had his Alaskan adventure. Ariel's funeral was the most poignant reminder of how a child and parent can manage to miss connections. Daniel was terribly distressed . . . he sobbed uncontrollably and Philip couldn't seem to go to him, I had the feeling he was embarrassed. Thea was the one who comforted her brother. Anyway,

Daniel's going to a private school near Bishop which is strong on survival skills, outdoors things, and he seems to be doing well, cross your fingers."

"I get the feeling you like the kid."

She laughed. "I do—I suppose I've had some practice in seeing the good, sweet boy underneath the surly exterior. Boys are very good at surly exteriors." Suddenly intense, she asked, "Why is it that we don't expect plumbers' sons to follow in their father's footsteps, but we expect professors' sons to? If Daniel finishes high school, he will have accomplished something. I'm not sure Philip will look at it that way. So if Philip does marry again, I hope he marries someone who can be Daniel's ally."

———————

Karin was not to go to the cottage for the Friday night that found Eli and Israel and Hayes discussing Black Power. That weekend she drove to Bishop with Philip, to meet Daniel and become his ally.

11

A girl who called herself Sunshine and who cleaned my cottage on Wednesdays told me she had been an Indian rain dancer in another incarnation, and I was tempted to believe her. She moved with meticulous grace and infinite patience, whether polishing my old and worn silver or reaching high to waft cobwebs out of the corners.

Sunshine believed that certain psychic forces had converged to create, that fall of 1969, a plethora of spiders, many of which had invaded my cottage. Some were microscopic in size, but quite capable of creating gossamer constructions in all the farthest niches. It became something of a game for us, moving about the house to discover all the webs spun since Sunshine's last sweep. It was not unlike looking into a tide pool: The longer you look, the more you see.

"Webs, webs, everywhere," Sunshine would chant as she made her way through the cottage, wielding a broom wrapped in an old T-shirt which she used to scan the ceilings and sweep away the webs, *"the spiders weave in double time, web within web, no reason, no rhyme."*

Occasionally she would come upon a web that was especially beautiful and call me to come see. Once we spent the better part of an hour watching a spider on the other side of the window weave its web using two of its long front legs as knitting needles, over and under and over again. The smallest of breezes would shiver through it, setting web and weaver trembling.

"Perhaps we should not think of them as nuisances," Sunshine said, "perhaps we should consider them works of art."

"Perhaps," I answered her, "you would like to come in here some day and find me caught in all their webs?"

In fact, that last year of the decade we were caught in webs that spun round from all directions. On a bridge at Chappaquiddick, a cruel quirk of fate compromised the political future of the last of the Kennedy brothers, the family that had come to symbolize the promise of a new historic hope. Two Black Panther leaders were killed in a police raid in Chicago. In Los Angeles, the crazed followers of a madman named Charles Manson performed ritualistic murders. The world was awash in blood; the peace talks in Paris came to nothing, the killing continued in Vietnam. A forest of umbrellas sprouted in San Francisco, raised by 150,000 protesters against a drenching November rain on the day set aside to mark a moratorium of the war in Vietnam. And then the story of American atrocities in My Lai began to unfold, showing all who would look how corrupting war was, how the horror and the violence it unleashed threw its awful web around the innocent, those women and children murdered by American boys. But those boys were our sons, some only eighteen years old, and it became necessary to ask who the victims really were.

I did not go to the Vietnam Moratorium. The heavens opened that day and the rain came down in sheets that looked like cellophane. "You will rust," Israel said, and I told him I certainly hoped he was referring to my wheelchair. So we stayed, the two of us, in the office, which had emptied for the occasion.

Israel settled in to read the dictionary; he had embarked on a vocabulary building program. For twenty minutes each day he memorized words, and was now up to the E's. I was making some headway with a budget report when Eli came in, followed by a young man whose blackness was emphasized by his costume: tight black pants and a black turtleneck T-shirt under a black leather jacket. He sprawled in the chair next to the door, feet splayed out before him.

"Hayes said to meet him here. I couldn't remember if he said at two or three," Eli told me with his usual slow grin, "Must have been three because it's past two and he isn't here. You know Hayes, he's an on-time dude."

Just then a long-legged girl named Esther came running up the stairs, her hair streaming wet in her eyes and her army poncho dripping water. She did not see the legs stretched out, could not check her momentum and went sprawling. There was an ugly scraping sound and the thud of books hitting the floor.

Israel jumped to help her, and Eli began gathering the scattered books and papers. The man who had tripped her did not move, did not even draw his legs in but sat motionless, exactly as he had been.

It was too much for Israel. "Pick up your feet boy," he shouted.

"Come on Elmore, Hayes is late," Eli said, stepping between them. "Let's go."

Elmore was smaller than either Eli or Israel, but the determined set of his body hinted of power. He stepped around Eli and leaned into Israel's face, his chin thrust forward. His words were slow and deliberate: "Listen to old Uncle Tom here . . . Uncle Tom, who you calling 'boy,' you black Tom nigger faggot?"

Israel roared in anger, his eyes wide, the whites marked by yellow. He had lost control, I was sure of it. For an instant I believed he wanted to kill Elmore, and in the time it took for the thought to flash through my brain, I was sure he would do it.

Eli held Israel off as he wrenched Elmore down the stairs in front of him. Hayes was just coming up. "Later, man," Eli told him as he brushed past, not even pausing.

All of this happened in a matter of minutes, maybe two—no more. "Faith?" Hayes asked, but I was too worried about Israel to explain what had happened. He was sitting in the corner, his hands covering his face. I cleaned the nasty scrapes on Esther's knees and talked to Hayes to give Israel time to regain his composure.

When finally the three of us were alone, I asked Hayes about Elmore.

"I don't know him," he said, "probably he's one of the Panthers working on prison reform. I've been doing some legal work for them."

Hayes looked at Israel, still sitting with his head in his hands. "Some of those guys have mean mouths," he told him. "I get the feeling they spend a lot of time figuring out which buttons to push."

Israel looked up then. "He surely did get my goat," he said wearily—I had never heard Israel sound weary—"He certainly did that." He walked to the window and stood with his back to us, looking out on the rain-drenched campus, staring back at a weeping world. And then he said to Hayes, without turning around, "I don't know why you let them use you like that, those two. They aren't the answer, don't you know. They don't speak for us."

Hayes surprised me then. He walked across the room, put his hand on Israel's shoulder and simply stood there, without saying a word. After a while Israel sighed, "Oh, well yes," as if something had been settled.

All that night I lay awake and tried to sort out what had happened. It was a puzzle, a perfect conundrum. Israel and the man called Elmore, Eli and Hayes. Each of them a different, terribly complicated piece of the puzzle. Along about morning I became convinced that Israel and Eli and Hayes had something to say to each other, and I wanted to hear what it was.

"Are you sure?" Kit said when I told her I was planning to invite them to a Friday evening. "Don't you think it might be a little risky?"

"It will be the three of them and Karin, May, you and me, that's all," I told her. "I don't want Sam, or anyone else who might throw things off. But yes, you're right, I do think it's a risk but I believe it's one that needs taking."

———

May and Kit stood side by side at the kitchen sink, May washing the greens for the salad and Kit peeling an avocado. "Karin and Philip are going to Bishop this weekend to meet his son. I think she's a little nervous."

"This sounds serious," Kit said.

"I'm beginning to think so," May answered. "Philip's daughter, Thea, has already announced that she wants them to marry. Karin's thinking hard about it, I know."

"There's quite an age difference, isn't there?" Kit asked.

May laughed. "Somehow, coming from you that surprises me. Wasn't there *quite an age difference* between you and your wonderful Connor?" Then she remembered: "Philip said something about knowing you—I've been meaning to ask and I keep forgetting . . . when was that?"

Kit concentrated on slipping the knife under the hard skin of the avocado. "Let's see," she said, "just after the war, I think—a long time ago. Before he went back East to teach."

"He would have been . . . what? In his mid-thirties then? He's about your age, actually," May said, but was interrupted by Israel's call for help from the front door. May grabbed a towel to dry her hands and went to open it for him.

When she left I said to Kit, "I take it you and Philip didn't stay in touch."

She had busied herself removing the crabs from their butcher paper wrappings. "No," she said, "you know how those things go . . ." and she let her voice trail off.

Israel appeared, filling the door frame: "I saw Hayes circling the block, looking for a parking place. They'll be along in a minute. Now what can I do, Lady Faith? Shouldn't I move in here and get that crab all fixed up nice? Or would you want me to whip up some of Israel's Special Crab Dipping Sauce? Move over Lady K, make way for some fancy fingerworks here as I prepare to dazzle you with an impromptu concerto for six Dungeness crabs . . ."

From the kitchen I could see May standing in the door, as Eli and Hayes approached; their smiles, I assumed, reflected her own. "Damned if it isn't the basketball kid," Eli said, slipping his arm easily around her for a hello hug. Then it was Hayes and May, facing each other. He put both hands on her shoulders, that's all. But until that moment I did not know how much there was between them.

I cleared my throat.

"We are about to be called to order," Israel announced, coming back into the room with some freshly cut sourdough.

"Something like that, I suppose," I began, surprised to find myself feeling a bit nervous. "All of us around this table are friends, I think. I hope. But we all know that those friendships have been complicated by race—by color. The incident the other day in the office—between Israel and that man named Elmore—brought it all rather sharply into focus, how much dissension there is, how quickly it can flair into violence." I glanced at Israel, but he was calmly spreading butter on a slice of bread. "I thought if we could explore a bit, learn something of what each of us thinks about what is happening or what should be happening, we might . . . I suppose . . . be a little wiser about each other. For instance, I don't really know what 'black power' means—every explanation I hear is so fraught with fear, and I don't know what the goal is. I was hoping you could tell us, Eli, what it means to you. I am hoping you can make us understand."

Eli shifted and put his elbows on the table. He opened his large hands once, showing the pale inner parts of his palm, spreading his fingers as if he might find the answers there. Then he began, his voice at first hesitant, but after a while gathering resolve:

"Black power . . . it starts off sounding violent, or at least I think that's how the white world interprets it . . . as if blacks are going to rise up and put the torch to the white world. But that's not what it means, at least not to me. You don't get power without respect, and you don't get respect without respecting yourself. So to begin with it means accepting what you are and liking it: starting with your black skin, your family, your culture. That means not believing what you've been told all your life—which is that if you're black, you are inferior. I know that sounds pretty simplistic, and I also know the slogans would sound pretty pathetic to most white people, if they were linked to nonviolence. It's the threat—the fear—that makes whites listen. Martin Luther King, Jr., could have marched forever, preaching nonviolence, and some white people would have followed him and sung 'We Shall Overcome' and cried real tears forever, but it wasn't going to make any difference. In the end, blacks are going to have to do it themselves—nobody's going to give them a share of the power because it's the right thing to do. And violence, or the threat of it, is the only thing that seems to move the people who have the power. The white man that put a bullet in Martin may have done more for the civil rights movement than the marching ever did."

"Is integration out, then?" Kit asked.

"I think integration is only acceptable when it is between equals. It's time we quit begging to be allowed to live next door to people who don't want us, and create black neighborhoods we can be proud of. We've tried meekness and it hasn't worked. Now it's time to stand up and demand what should have been ours all along."

"You say integration is only acceptable when it is between equals," May put in. "That sounds good, but I don't believe it ever has worked that way. 'Equal' means too many different things to too many different people. What I do understand is the idea of blacks demanding what should have been theirs all along, by law."

Israel had taken a pair of reading glasses out of his pocket and made something of a show of unfolding a piece of paper. "I brought this tonight," he spoke up, looking out at us over the glasses. "I read it back in 1944, when I was in the army, and for a long time I carried it around with me, and I'd recite it whenever I could. It was written by Mr. Gunnar Myrdal, a famous Swedish economist, in a book called *An American Dilemma,* which I found in the library in a little nothing town in Georgia."

His face took on a pulpit demeanor, he cleared his throat and in his preacher's voice he read: "America can never more regard its Negroes as a patient, submissive minority. They will continually become less well 'accommodated.' They will organize for defense and offense. They will become more and more vociferous . . . They will have a powerful tool in the caste struggle against white America: the glorious American ideals of democracy, liberty, and equality to which America is pledged not only by its political Constitution but also by the sincere devotion of its citizens. The Negroes are a minority, and they are poor and suppressed, but they have the advantage that they can fight wholeheartedly. The whites have all the power, but they are split in their moral personality. Their better selves are with the insurgents. The Negroes do not need any other allies."

He took off his glasses, folded the paper and returned it to his shirt pocket. "I submit to you Eli," Israel finished, summing up what he had come to say, "that your Black Power movement will alienate the better selves of those white people who would help us. That young buck you brought up to the office the other day—he wasn't being proud of being black, he was being arrogant, he was doing everything he accuses the white man of doing."

Eli shifted defensively. "I don't necessarily agree with all the brothers' actions," he began, "but I do agree it's time to take some action that shows we mean business. And I know that nonviolence is never going to work, not in any lifetime."

"Where does that leave you, Eli?" I asked.

He didn't answer for a while; then he looked up and surprised us all by grinning sheepishly. "Damned if I know," he said, breaking the tension, instantly transformed to the black kid who grew up in the white suburbs of Minnesota and felt most at ease with his white friends. "My problem is I've got these pale-faced pals I can't seem to shake off."

He gave Hayes a playful poke. Hayes caught Eli's fist and held it for an instant in a gesture that signaled his own seriousness: "I guess I have to say I'm with Israel and Gunnar," he began. "The laws are on the books, now what we have to do is make people obey them. There are white people who know what is right—some of them might not like it, but they'll go with the law if it comes down to it.

I hear myself saying this, and I can almost hear you thinking, 'another jive-ass white boy telling me to wait another generation or two . . .' I don't really have any answer, Eli."

Israel spoke up, all thought of vocabulary abandoned in his passion: "Eli's the one's jiving. Talk about black people respecting themselves. Talk about that boy Elmore you brought up to the office the other day. He don't respect nothing. You think I'm ever going to respect that? No way, not ever. Eli, you going to be in big trouble if you don't stay away from that black trash."

A flash of anger flaired in Eli's eyes: "Don't talk to me about 'black trash'—that's not something I need to hear from a black man."

"Isn't it strange," I stepped in quickly, "how epithets have a way of triggering anger." (*Black Tom nigger faggot* Israel had been called.) "They seem to short-circuit any rational feelings, all that verbal violence rolled into a couple of words and flung at a person."

Israel, brushing away my interruption, answered Eli: "Maybe not, but there are some things you and your militaristic Black Panther friends could learn from the black men of my age, those of us who've actually been off to war. And maybe from the black kids who are coming back now from Vietnam. That's not playacting, that's not strutting around with guns spouting out slogans. We've already proved ourselves . . . as men and as black men. We've gone out and fought for this country by God, and some of us never did come home . . . and some black boys aren't going to come home from this war either. And what I want to know is, how the devil you and your Black Panthers friends think you can teach those boys and their folks pride?"

"You're right there, Israel," Eli said, backing off. "Nobody's trying to put you down."

"Yes they are!" Israel raised his voice. "Your friend Elmore, didn't you hear what he called me? What do you mean, nobody's trying to put me down? That prison bait, that lowlife nogood. . . ."

Hayes broke in: "Eli, do you remember that time we were with a local CORE guy named Slim out in the backroads of Mississippi, I think it was near a little town called Pawtonville, or something like that? We met this grizzled white man wobbling down the road with the help of a cane. Slim told us he'd been wounded in the war. We were downwind of the guy, and he smelled like he hadn't had a bath since the Battle of the Bulge. Anyway, we could see a black guy coming down the road in an old wagon pulled by a mule, and when he gets up with the other guy he stops. Neither one of them said anything, but the white guy climbs up into the wagon and off they go. Slim said they'd been doing that twice a week for twenty years. Just outside of town the black guy would stop and let off the white man, so he wouldn't be seen riding in a mule cart with a Negro. I asked Slim why the black guy bothered, and Slim said he asked him once."

Hayes paused, remembering.

"And?" May prompted.

"And the black guy said he felt sorry for him."

Israel, calmed, said: "That's right, that's exactly right."

"Maybe so," Eli added, draping his arm loosely over Israel's shoulder, a gesture of reconciliation. Suddenly he looked at his watch and said, "Christ! It's after eleven—I'm supposed to be meeting somebody in the Fillmore right now." Turning to Hayes he added, "Think you could hitch a ride home with Magnificent May here?"

"Magnificent May," Hayes said, turning to her, "what are the chances?"

"Call me pretty names and I'll take you anywhere," she answered, laughing. When she bent to kiss me goodnight, I felt her cheek burning warm against mine.

May eased the Jaguar slowly onto Broadway, glad for the tangle of traffic in front of the striptease and topless joints. A barker with a top hat and an English accent called out to Hayes: "Come on in, mate, there's things in here—great galloping balloons you'll bloody well never see again in this lifetime."

"Great galloping balloons," Hayes repeated as they picked up speed, and he rolled up the windows. They slipped easily onto the freeway that curved along the edge of the Bay. May was glad to be alone with him, glad to be in the car sealed off from the rest of the world. The air seemed to expand; she held the Jaguar back, wanting to make the ride last.

She took a deep breath. "I've missed you," she said, exhaling.

"You've missed me?" he repeated. "Funny. I haven't missed you all that much. I never think of you."

"Never?" she came back, ready to play.

"Not in the morning when I'm drinking my Ovaltine and eating my crunchy granola. And you never pop into my mind when I'm circling the campus looking for a parking place and I see a tall, willowy, dark-haired female person walking by."

"Not even then?" she sounded the refrain.

"Not even when I was in the Lowie Museum the other day, looking at some terrific masks from New Guinea. I didn't wish you were around to see them with me."

"Nope?"

"Nope. Never think about you at all. Not in the shower. Not even in bed at night."

"Wait a minute," she laughed, "or I'm likely to run us off the bridge."

They entered the tunnel, the lights flickered through the car and she felt, suddenly, lightheaded and happy. Then they were in the dark again and the lights of the Oakland waterfront blazed bright against the night sky. She slid the car easily into the lanes marked for Berkeley and felt a strange elation. She considered kicking hard on the gas and going on, driving up highway 80 to Sacramento and on to Lake Tahoe, driving on and on through the Nevada desert to Salt Lake.

"Whoa—University Avenue coming up," Hayes warned as she picked up speed.

"You've passed the bar," she said as they moved up the wide street. "What next?"

"I'm not sure," he answered. "I have an offer to go to Washington, play penny ante with the power brokers . . . Don't laugh, I might just do that. I'm also thinking of getting out of the country for awhile, see if that helps."

She pulled up in front of his place on Benvenue.

"Are you going back to Hawaii next summer?"

"June and July," she told him. "I have to be back here for a project in August."

"You like it there?"

"I love it. The Big Island, especially. I can't quite explain what there is about it—there is just this clarity. It's such lovely big empty land, so gentle, floating out there in the middle of the ocean. And the volcanoes are so accessible . . . they all but invite you to study them."

"Sounds civilized."

"It is. Why don't you come out while I'm there?"

He looked at her. "You and me and the sea and the sand?"

She nodded.

"Christ," he said, leaning to touch his lips lightly to hers as he opened the door.

She put her hand on his arm to stop him. "Wait. Hayes. Please." She was searching for the words, and they were coming in short bursts. "I can't pretend anymore . . . I think it's time . . . we need to talk . . . about us . . ."

He put his head back and closed his eyes. The silence settled on them, May felt herself sinking under the weight of it. She pulled herself up, grasped the steering wheel firmly and waited.

"I'm sorry," he said, his eyes still closed.

"You keep saying that," she told him, a sting in her voice.

"What I'm sorry about," he said slowly, the words were hard in coming, "is that we had to meet now . . . in the middle of all this . . . what I'm sorry about is that our timing has been so lousy."

The taste of bile rose in her throat. "What are you trying to say . . . right girl, wrong time . . . something like that?"

He didn't answer, but grasped the door handle as if he were about to leave. She could not let him go, not yet. She knew she shouldn't do it, shouldn't say it, shouldn't cling but she could not help herself. Panic rising, she pleaded. "Does that mean forever?"

He touched her face. "God, I hope not," was his answer.

When everyone had left the cottage that night and I lay in bed, phrases flew about the room, bombarding me, but the one that stuck in my mind was: *You know how those things go,* which Kit had said when I asked about Philip Ward. There was something, I knew, some small detail tucked away in a dusty little unused room of my memory: And then I got it. Of course.

I climbed back out of bed, pulled on my robe and cursed my old bones for taking so long to move. It took a while to find the right file and longer to find the right letter.

June 4, 1944, Lena Kerr to Porter Reade in Burma.

I scanned the fragile onionskin page covered with Lena's feathery script . . . news of a cousin in Los Angeles . . . an almost tangible feeling that the war in the Pacific is winding down, will soon be over . . . And then: *"Kit has not yet been able to resolve her dilemma over Philip Ward. I can only wonder what has made her so cautious, so suspicious of passion."*

12

"Don't expect too much," Philip said, "from Daniel, I mean. He's not very articulate, and his social graces are just short of nonexistent."

"Just short of?" she smiled.

"He might say 'hullo.' Then again, he might not."

The two-lane blacktop shot straight down the empty valley floor, the highest peaks of the Sierra Nevadas looming on one side, the White Mountains on the other. There was no color, only shades of black and white and a dark, dark green. It was a strangely menacing landscape, desolate and beautiful in the January cold. Karin shivered.

"More heat?" he asked, reaching for the control.

"No, no. It just looks so cold out there. And I guess I'm a little nervous. About Daniel. I want him to like me."

He reached for her hand. "The kid may not be swift, but he's sure as hell not stupid. The way I figure it, he'll take one look at you and figure there must be more to the old man than he thought. My ratings should go up considerably."

She pressed his hand to her cheek and said, "I'm very serious. Daniel has to accept me if this is going to work."

"This?"

"Us."

"Don't do that, Karin. Don't make us contingent on Daniel. That's too much for me to handle—Daniel's produced more than his share of disappointments already. And it's too much to lay on the kid."

She looked out the window, focused on a tall stand of alders in the half-distance. The sun glinted off a frosting of snow that lay on the open land, creating a surreal brilliance that made the mountains stand out sharp against the hard blue of the sky.

"Dear God this is violent country," she said, breathing out.

"I've always thought of Owens Valley as the True West," he answered, glad to move away from the subject of his son. "It has the scope and the geographic terror . . . Can you imagine the Sierras here being heaved up out of the earth? Think of the magnitude of the earthquakes, the volcanoes. Mind boggling."

"I was just thinking about volcanoes, and May. She's been here several times on field trips . . . and always said this was magnificent country. It really is. But it's . . . well, what you said. Terrifying too. At least to me."

"To me, too. Given the choice, I'll take Manhattan. But Daniel likes the out of doors, the rugged life, and this is the first school he hasn't run from, which is something." He glanced at the odometer. "The school should be coming up just . . . about . . . now."

He swung open the gate while she drove the car through, over a cattle guard. They could see the school in the distance: a cluster of low buildings grouped around a stand of barren trees. "Looks like a prison camp left over from World War II, doesn't it? Now that I think of it, one of the Japanese internment camps was near here—Manzanar."

"It seems very Spartan," she answered, "But that's the idea, isn't it?"

Daniel was waiting for them in the cafeteria. He was sitting on a table, wrapping the red cellophane strip from a packet of crackers around his little finger. He looked up when they walked in; his glance flickered but could not meet his father's, so he looked at Karin instead.

"I'm Karin," she said, before Philip could introduce her.

"Dan," the boy mumbled.

"I'm glad it's 'Dan.' I thought maybe you wanted to be called 'Daniel.' The problem with Karin is that you can't have a nickname, and I've always envied people who have them."

162

"Is that right?" Philip said, amused.

Karin was looking at Daniel when she said, "Sure is."

A slow, half smile played around his lips. He stood, put out his hand and said, "Hello, sir."

Philip took his hand and held it. "Sir? I thought this was a survivalist school, not a military camp."

The boy looked at the floor. "Mr. Egon—he's one of the teachers here—says the two go together. He says discipline and survival and manners are all part of the same scheme."

"We could use Mr. Egon in Berkeley these days," Philip laughed.

Daniel, serious, answered, "True. You need somebody to bash a few heads together up there—between the dopeheads and the antiwar jerkoffs."

Philip flinched. Karin quickly put in, "Where is everybody? It seems awfully empty around here."

"In the mountains," Daniel answered, "every Saturday the whole camp goes for a day trek into the mountains, rain or shine—anything short of a white-out."

"Did you want to go?" Karin asked.

He shrugged.

"Thanks for staying behind this time," she went on. "I really did want to meet you."

They had lunch at the only place in town that served food, the Wagon Wheel Cafe, where the Saturday special was Mady's Real Beef Stew.

"What is 'Real Beef Stew' and who is 'Mady'?" Karin asked Dan.

He answered, "You've got to take things literally out here. Real beef stew means real beef, not horsemeat, which Mady is suspected of using now and then, it's so tough. And Mady is about a hundred years old and still dresses the way she used to dress when she was dealing blackjack in Reno back before electricity, I think. Mr. Egon says she looks like she's been soaked in brine, that's like being pickled—you'll know her if you see her. And she has a few young . . ." his hesitation was heavy with innuendo, ". . . protégés hanging around. To catch guys passing through between L.A. and Reno."

"I was getting worried, Dan," his father said, "but now I see you are getting an education, after all."

Karin noticed the "Dan."

On the drive back to Bishop Philip was elated. "I'd almost forgotten what a terrific laugh the kid has. It's been so long since I've heard it. You were wonderful, K. God. I can't believe the difference. Part of it is the school, but I think you were able to make him feel easy . . ."

"It's too bad we couldn't have met Mr. Egon. He seems to be a major influence."

"When Daniel was showing you the grounds, I had a talk with Dave Powell, the guy who runs the school. Egon is an ex-Marine, very gung ho Corps but, according to Powell, reliable. He assured me that Egon isn't training killers behind his back."

"Is that what you thought?"

"Daniel's remark about 'bashing heads in Berkeley' bothered me, yes. And surprised me, too, since I remember a time when his room reeked of pot. I suppose I'm relieved to find him antidrug, because he's an obsessive kind of kid and I can see him getting caught up in the whole drug culture. His half-baked ideas on the war don't please me, but frankly I didn't want to bring up a subject that could have been divisive. Not today."

"I know. And it's Dan."

He looked at her quizzically, so she repeated, "He wants to be called 'Dan.' He told me."

"So is that how it's going to be?" He laughed. "You are an amazement, Karin Rolofsen. You and Dan teamed up against me? Making me change old habits?"

"Afraid so. If you want me, you've got to take Dan and Thea too."

The car hit a patch of black ice and swerved; Philip swung it around, turning with the spin. Karin tensed, concentrated. The road was empty, the mountains revolved around them as the car made a full revolution. Philip eased it back into the northbound lane. They drove in silence, catching their breath, trying to take in all that had happened in a few seconds.

"Did I understand you correctly?" he finally asked.

Karin laughed. "Yes!" she cried out. "Yes I will marry you. Yes we will survive."

He slowed the car to a stop, opened his arms and she came to him, mouth open to breathe in the clean, safe smell of him.

A shrill, whining blast from an air horn pierced the silence; a big rig came barreling down the highway toward them. As the driver passed he gave them a 'thumbs up' sign.

. . .

"As you know by now," Philip said as they entered the outskirts of the town of Bishop, "in some ways I am incorrigibly old-fashioned."

She reached for his hand, brought it to her lips and kissed it.

"Now that we are officially *betrothed*—isn't that a nice old-fashioned word?—now that we have agreed to plight our troth," he said with mock seriousness, "we have to make a few personal decisions."

She laughed, a pure clear trilling sound that caused him to look at her with delight.

"God, I love the way you laugh," he said.

"And I love you for being incorrigibly old-fashioned, in some ways."

"We have to spend the night in Bishop," he went on. "I reserved separate rooms." He touched her hair and spoke softly, as if reading a line of poetry: "There is time aplenty now . . ."

Karin felt a surge of gratitude. Philip's touch was light, certain. Never fumbling, never groping. Philip knew how to caress, how to respond to her own shy advances. When she put her arms around him, Philip did not assume she wanted to be physically overwhelmed. He understood affection. When she began to worry that she was not giving him all that he wanted, he sensed what she was thinking and made her understand that he was happy, in fact quite content, to go slowly. Not just for her, but for himself. It was important, he said, that both of them feel ready. She had cried, that a man could be so sweetly understanding. That she did not have to worry about satisfying him.

"Do you suppose we could get adjoining rooms?" she asked.

She positioned herself rather primly on a small settee and watched as he opened the burgundy leather case, took from it two silver flasks, a small bottle which held maraschino cherries and two glasses of heavy lead crystal. "Old-fashioneds," he told her, chuckling. "Appropriate, don't you think?"

"Nice in this cold climate."

"The perfect nightcap," he said. "I guarantee you will sleep well."

"Oh, I intend to," she smiled at him as she used her fingers to dip into her drink for the cherry and bit into it. She took a sip and held it in her mouth, allowing the warmth to slip down her throat a small amount at a time.

"Please, come sit next to me," she invited.

"That would be my great pleasure," he answered.

They moved in slow motion; he sat, drank from his glass, put it down, moved his hand to caress her neck. She put her hand over his, guided it to her chestbone, held it there for a long moment. Took a sip, touched lips, laughed at the taste of cherry on the tongue. Her hand still on his, guiding under her gown, tenderly. A sharp intake of breath as he lowered his head to kiss the soft place where her breasts met and rose, his hand exploring the great pink rise of her breast.

He pulled her face to his and kissed her forehead. "Sweet," he said, "you taste sweet."

She took another sip and let the warm liquor trickle down her throat. "I like your hands on me," she said, her fingers on the tie to his silk robe. He kissed her on the lips, three times, lightly. She pressed her mouth into his, hard.

"You have to finish your nightcap," he whispered into her ear, "that's part of the ritual." They toasted each other, Karin could feel her face flush warm. They drained the glasses; he set his down very carefully, then took hers from her, carefully.

He stood, pulled her to him, held her close. She could feel his erection through the silk, and pressed herself into him. He put his hands firmly about her waist and said, "Come with me."

They sat on the side of the bed. He held her face between his hands, looking at her, kissing her eyes, the tip of her nose, her exposed throat. She felt herself grow warm and wet; she wanted to put her hands on him, pull him into her. With her tongue she flicked into his ears. Slowly, slowly, he lifted her into the bed, gently pulled the cover over them, turned off the light, slipped out of his robe. She could feel the coarse hair on his chest, she took him in her hand and felt a shiver run through him.

She turned and raised herself so that her breasts fell loose against his chest. She could feel his heartbeat; "My sweet, sweet girl," he whispered into her ear, while his hand explored the contours of her stomach. "You are so beautiful," he sighed as he entered her.

She arched her back, made a small thrusting motion. He began the rhythmic movement, kissing her, talking to her. "Here, is this good? Tell me."

She fell into his rhythm, and it was as if they were dancing, as if their lovemaking had been choreographed. The tempo picked up, faster and faster until it reached a crescendo, he moaned and she moaned with him in one long sustaining sound . . . then they lay quietly in each other's arms, breathing in the sweet smell of sex.

When he could speak, his voice was soft and lyric: "That was better than wonderful. Better than marvelous. God." He caressed her breast. ". . . yes?"

"Yes," she lied, kissing him sweetly on the lips.

———————

"Put on your archivist's hat, Faith," May said, "I need to dip into your seemingly limitless knowledge of the old family history." She raised her eyebrows as if what she was about to say might shock me. "I want you to look into your crystal ball to the period around the end of the war. The big Two, I mean. Zero in on Katherine Reade McCord, rich and beautiful and in her early forties. And see if you come up with any cross reference to . . ." She paused, made sure she had my full attention, ". . . Philip Ward."

"Aha," I said.

"Aha?" she repeated. "What does 'aha' mean?"

"It means I wondered when you'd get around to following up. The first time you asked was weeks ago, and then you asked Kit."

"She was evasive."

"Yes she was. What does that suggest to you?"

May looked at me and shook her head, "You fox, you," she said, "you picked up on it and found out, didn't you?"

"I plead nolo contendere," I said. "Anyway, you are going to have to press Kit for an answer. I may be an archivist but I'm no snitch."

"Just tell me this much," she said, "all you have to do is nod your head if I get it right."

"No telling, no nodding, no nothing. Talk to Kit."

"Listen, Auntie, please . . ."

"Don't give me the 'Auntie' treatment, May, you aren't going to get a thing out of me on this subject."

"Just tell me this, will Kit go to the wedding?"

I threw up my hands and said, "You are impossible, girl. No she won't go to the wedding, she has to be in New York that weekend. But she's going to offer to give them a big lovely reception at Wildwood after the wedding trip. Now that's all I'm going to tell you, period."

167

. . .

I phoned Kit to warn that May was on her way, loaded for bear. Kit was waiting, two very dry martinis in place on the bar.

"This is a dry martini subject?" May asked, sipping hers.

"I'm afraid it's still my drug of choice," Kit said. "But you want to know about Philip Ward and me."

"Faith called ahead," May pouted.

"Faith is our guardian angel, didn't you know? But there isn't all that much to tell. I met Philip Ward here in San Francisco near the end of the war. He was . . . in transit, in a way . . . trying to figure out if he wanted to go back to Columbia to teach or if he would try for Berkeley. He finally decided he'd do better at Columbia."

"You've skipped something, I think."

Kit smiled. "Yes. There was a short, rather intense episode. I . . . was rather attracted to him at the time. During that period in my life I was rather attracted to a number of young men. I emphasize *young.*"

"Philip isn't that much younger than you. What? Six or seven years?"

"It wasn't just age, and Philip wasn't the only man I had an affair with. There, I've said it: affair. It's always been such a compromising word. I have to keep reminding myself that your generation doesn't react to it so hysterically as mine did."

"So you were a 'loose lady'?" May teased.

"Don't make fun. It wasn't funny," Kit told her, then took the edge off by raising her martini glass. "Want another?"

May waved her off. "You said 'age' wasn't the only thing—between you and Philip. What else?"

Kit sighed and moved to the window. The sun was casting long shadows on the city below. "Philip was very ambitious. He had a plan, and I realized that I didn't fit into the plan. He needed someone more . . . malleable. Remember, by the time I met Philip I had been on my own for almost twenty years, and I liked it. Besides, I had a lot of obligations. But the point is, my fling with Philip was just that: a fling. History. It never really had a chance of being anything more, not for either of us. It seems fairly obvious that Philip has not mentioned anything about this to Karin, and frankly I would prefer she didn't know. I like Karin so very much, and I think it might cause her to feel differently about me."

May nodded, then asked: "Was I one of your obligations? It must have been that time before Dad came back, when you were taking care of me—"

"I never thought of you as an obligation," Kit cut in, "and you mustn't think that. Remember, your grandmother was still living then, and Sara. And Faith and Emilie. If anything, you were in danger of being suffocated with love and attention. There were plenty of 'mothers' for you, my dear."

"Except my own."

Kit started to pour another drink, but stopped.

She looked at her watch. "It's five-thirty. When did you say you had to meet Sam and Karin?"

"Six. Sam's cooking dinner for us, which means spaghetti. I suppose I'd better be going, but I still need to talk to you."

"That's just what I was thinking. Can you get away this weekend? I'm going down to the ranch—to do some riding, just to get away and into the mountains."

"I'd love to see the ranch again," May said.

"Why is it that Karin is always early and you are always late?" Sam asked May. "My spaghetti sauce is probably ruined."

"Your spaghetti sauce is indestructible," May answered, moving a pile of books and papers from the end of Sam's table so she could set it.

Karin was breaking vermicelli into a pot of boiling water, her face turned away from the rising steam. Sam leaned against the far wall, watching them through a camera.

"This is nice," he said, "the two of you, steam rising all around, nice." The doorbell broke his concentration.

Standing in the doorway was a couple in their twenties, May guessed, maybe younger—it was hard to tell under the long hair and hats they wore. The girl had on a long skirt and a tunic that disguised her thinness. The boy had long, thin blonde hair and for some reason made May think of a chimneysweep.

"We need a place to crash, man," he said to Sam. Sam looked at him for a few moments, then asked: "Do I know you?"

"Yeah," he answered, "Don't you remember? You took some pictures of us the other day. You said if we ever needed a place we could come on over. You gave us your address."

The girl thrust a piece of paper at Sam, as if to offer proof.

"Oh yeah, sure, I remember now. You were in the loft with Star and Wanderer. What're your names again?"

"James," he said. "This is Michelle."

"James, Michelle, come on in. We're having spaghetti. Are you hungry?"

Each carried two shopping bags filled with their possessions, including, May noted, a high school letter sweater. "Spaghetti with meat?" James asked. "We don't eat meat. But a bath would be good."

"Be my guest," Sam said, showing the way. Michelle followed James into the bathroom, and they closed the door behind them.

May looked at Karin, both looked at Sam. He grinned, shrugged and all three had to stifle their laughter. They heard the water turn on. "You know what they say," May couldn't resist: "Cleanliness is next . . ." Karin burst out laughing, May and Sam joined her.

When they caught their breath, May asked, "What made you give them your address?"

"I thought they would be good subjects . . . *The Saturday Evening Post* is supposed to be doing a big story on the hippies, especially the drug scene. So I thought if I did some really strong pictures I might land the assignment."

"So are you going to take pictures of James and Michelle?" Karin wanted to know.

"Maybe. If it works out."

"Stoned?"

Sam frowned. "If they are, and if they don't mind."

"How can they know what they mind if they're stoned?"

"I'll ask them when they aren't stoned."

"Where's Philip?" May asked, to change the subject.

Karin took a while to answer. "He had an Academic Senate meeting . . . something about the Ethnic Studies program."

"At least he's one of the good guys," Sam put in.

"Just exactly who are the 'good guys'?" Karin challenged.

"Hell, don't ask me. I thought I was one of them until a bunch of long hairs rousted me at the last demonstration—because I was shooting for *Time* magazine. One asshole put spit on his thumb and rubbed it into my lens. Now I tell them I'm with the underground press."

"You never were 'one of them,' " Karin said.

"What do you mean?" Sam asked, on guard.

"I mean, you never got involved with the issues—you were never committed to building a People's Park, were you? Or to the Free Speech Movement? Or even to ending the Vietnam War."

"I think I was about as involved with People's Park and the Free Speech Movement as you were, Karin. But you're wrong about the war. I think it's stupid and anyone who would get sucked into fighting is either incredibly stupid or incredibly naive . . . or just maybe unlucky. But I'll tell you this, and you can think what you like, I hope it doesn't end before I can get over and photograph it."

"So what you believe in is photography," Karin pursued.

"That and sex, drugs and rock and roll," he came back, trying to regain his balance.

May decided to help him. "Don't even try to figure Sam, K, he moves too fast, you know that."

"Sometimes I don't like the way he moves at all," Karin said, rising from the table so fast a stainless bowl clattered to the floor, spilling spaghetti. Nobody moved to pick it up. In the silence, they could hear the splashing from the bathroom.

Sam ignored it. "I don't know what's going on with you, Karin," he finally said, his jaw set. "You've been bitching at me all night, for no good reason that I can see. Is it the wrong time of month or something? Or is this what marriage is going to do to you?"

Karin stared at him and, to everyone's amazement, burst into tears.

May knew Karin's bedtime ritual: She would pull on a flannel nightgown, wash her face and then rub it with a clean, lemon-smelling creme. She would do a few situps, brush her hair and plump her pillows and prepare to read for an hour or so, however long it took to make her sleepy. May listened, and when she knew Karin was in bed knocked on her door.

"Time to talk, luv," she said with what she hoped passed for a cockney accent.

Karin grinned. "Sam was right. I was being bitchy. I don't know why."

"Don't you?"

"Well . . . yes . . . at least I have an idea . . ."

"Tell me."

May settled in at the foot of the bed, while Karin sat up straight, clasped her hands together and began to talk.

"It's so odd, May. I went over to the house this morning and let myself in. It's the housekeeper's day off and no one was there. It was the first time I'd been in the house alone, and it was just very . . ." the words came out slowly . . ." lovely. Peaceful. I felt so content, so calm. For a long time I just stood there and looked and loved the way it made me feel. Safe. I guess that was part of it, peaceful and safe and substantial, sort of. The way Philip makes me feel.

"Everything was in perfect order, except that Thea had left a pink sweater hanging on the back of the chair next to the phone. I can't tell you why, but it seemed almost heartbreakingly sweet to me—that crumpled little sweater. Then I went upstairs, into the master bedroom. Philip had asked me to pick up a package for him—but the package turned out to be a present for me. One of those big brown and white I. Magnin boxes was in the middle of the bed, and he'd left a note." She paused, sighed, attempted a smile.

"I guess I expected some sort of designer dress, something like that. But it was a pair of grey wool slacks, a matching cashmere sweater and a paisley Liberty silk scarf."

May widened her eyes. "Did they fit?"

"Perfectly." She pursed her lips. "Philip knows my measurements. He's very thorough."

"I'll bet," May said, and they both laughed a little.

"I tried them on, and pulled my hair back with the scarf and took a good look at myself in the mirror. Then I read the note Philip had left, and decided I had better think about it. So I folded the new clothes and put them back in the box, then I pulled my old jeans back on, and that orange Indian tunic with the little mirrors and embroidery, and my mocassins, and left."

"The note," May prompted.

"The note," Karin repeated, grimacing. "I think it was meant to be a joke, in fact I'm sure of it. But the kind of joke that makes a point. I don't remember all of it, but there were two lists: 'Ward Don'ts' and 'Ward Do's.'

"Some of them were very sweet: Do Kiss Hello when reentering room, that kind of thing. And 'Don't fail to wake me if you wake in the night' . . . But there were some others."

"Like?"

"Like, don't wear red shoes, and do read the *New Republic* and *The Statesman* and don't bite your fingernails."

"Don't bite your fingernails? Just like that?"

"No, not just like that. He knows it's a real problem but he believes that once we're married I'll feel secure and then it will just be a bad habit that needs to be broken. I don't think it's going to be that easy."

"So that's what is bothering you?"

"Partly that. Mostly, it's knowing that Philip has this plan, this way of living, and that if our marriage is going to work I will have to fit into it. And I want to, May. I love everything about his life—I adore Thea and Dan, and I know I can be good for them. I want so much to be part of it, I'm just not sure I can . . . I looked so different in those slacks, with my hair pulled back. I almost convinced myself that I could do it, could pull it off. And then, right in front of the mirror, I started biting my fingernails! Right there!"

May started laughing, she couldn't help it. "I'm sorry," she said, "I know this is anything but funny but I can just see you doing that . . . you always did, you know. Bite your fingernails when you were anxious. Why is that so terrible? It seems to me it's a whole lot healthier than smoking or drinking or shooting heroin. I mean, who are you hurting except your cuticles?"

Karin sat for a moment staring, then with both hands she slowly pulled the pillow from behind her and took a full hard swipe at May. May lunged, grabbed the other pillow and the two of them hit and laughed and laughed and hit until they were exhausted, and fell gasping across the bed.

"Follow me," Kit said as she flicked her horse into a trot. May breathed in the warm, dry air and was glad to be back on the southern California ranch where her father and Kit had been born, and where they had grown up. She nudged the chestnut mare and followed Kit up a path which headed into the mountains. They rode for the better part of an hour, single file along a narrow path cut through a wide, grassy meadow, then up into the hills, into the welcome shade of an old eucalyptus grove. Kit stopped, turned and when she saw the beads of sweat dripping down May's face said, "Am I setting too fast a pace?"

"No!" May laughed. "You're just a much better rider than I am— Phinney touts himself as the world's best trainer of riders, but Phinney could take some lessons from you."

Kit pulled her horse around, to come alongside May. "Your dad and I spent a good part of our childhood roaming these hills—I get carried away every time I come back. Let's rest a while."

As Kit rummaged in her pack for the Thermos, May studied her:
She was wearing a pair of worn jodhpurs that had gone out of style
long ago, riding boots that were well oiled but cracked with age, and
a plain white shirt. For an instant that morning, as Kit had set about
saddling her horse, May glimpsed the girl she had been: small, boyishly built, intense. As the early morning light played through the
stand of oaks that shaded the ranchyard, May suddenly understood
what life must have been like long ago when all of this land for as
far as you could see, all the way to the ocean, had belonged to Kit's
mother, before Kit had been forced to sell off large tracts to save any
of it.

"Wait a minute," Kit had called, running back into the barn. She
came out carrying a shapeless felt hat which she slapped against her
hip to get the dust out: "This was your dad's riding hat. You'll need
it."

Now May dismounted, pulled off the old hat, and with the back
of her wrist felt the sweat that had accumulated around her forehead,
where the band had been.

"I've never seen this part of the ranch," May said, sipping the cold
water. "When Dad and I were here we never went riding . . ."

"I know," Kit said, "he was worried about his heart—that something might happen when the two of you were out alone."

May looked up to the softly curving hills that rose to the west, long
green winter grass dotted with tiny flowers. "I didn't realize he knew
that early—about his heart, I mean."

"He didn't want you to know. He thought you already had enough
to handle. I remember Porter telling me once that he would give
anything if he could give you the kind of childhood we had here, on
the ranch."

"And I remember you came down when I was here, and wanted
to take me riding and I wouldn't go."

Kit looked at her, smiled gently. "You had every reason in the
world to be angry, May. Your mother left you and your father was
fighting for his life. I remember feeling so . . . damned . . . impotent. . . ."

May reached for the Thermos and touched Kit's hand. To change
the subject, Kit asked, "What did you decide about Philip and
Karin?"

May lay her head back on the saddle and wet her lips with the
water. "Well, I decided I wouldn't be breaking any faith with Karin

by not telling her about you and Philip. And I guess I've decided that the marriage might be good for K. I had some doubts, and I think Karin does too, we had a long talk about them the other night. She knows the kind of life he lives, and the part she will be playing. She's convinced me that she really does want it. She only worries that she isn't up to being the wife of the dazzling Philip Ward. I have a lot more confidence in her than she has in herself . . . and Philip does too. I think he can make her happy."

"I'm glad," Kit said, tightening the cinch on her saddle. "Let's ride for a while longer—there's a place over the hill there where your dad and I always stopped for a picnic."

The climb took the better part of an hour, but now Kit set a slower pace and May could look about, could breathe in all of the wide country—the fresh tangle of grasses and animal sweat, the steady blue of the sky at midday, the dry rasping calls of insects rising from the warm earth, interrupted by a sudden sharp bird song from above. She lifted her face for the sun to warm, and opened her eyes to see Kit waiting on the crest of the hill ahead.

"Behold the wide Pacific," she said, arm outraised.

May stared: They were on a knoll overlooking the ocean which stretched, empty and blue and perfectly calm, to the far horizon. For a moment she thought she could no longer breathe. "Dear God," she finally whispered.

"It's as close as you'll get to Him on this Earth," Kit answered, laughing as she dismounted. "I've been aching to bring you here. . . ."

May stood, hands limp at her sides, unable to speak. Kit led the horses off, tethered them and busied herself with lunch. "Hard-boiled eggs, tomatoes, cold fried chicken legs, a Thermos of fresh lemonade made from Meyer lemons, and Trinidad's tortillas. Josepha makes them almost as good as her mother did. This was our favorite trail lunch, your dad's and mine."

They ate in silence, May's eyes continually scanning the wide horizons of land and water. Kit leaned back to rest against a large rock, enjoying the warmth of it through her blouse. She began in a soft voice that seemed to May to have a small echo, as if coming from a long distance:

"I think I knew from the moment I saw your mother that a marriage would be disastrous for both of them. I understood perfectly well how he could love her—she was exquisitely beautiful . . . not pretty, but beautiful . . . that extraordinary bone structure, that's where you got those wonderful high cheek bones . . . But more than that, too. Her face was very animated, you could look into her eyes and see how bright she was.

"She was also very Chinese and extremely traditional. Honor was more important than love. Porter knew this, but I don't think he ever grasped how firmly Ch'ing-Ling was committed to it. Then too, like most Chinese she felt herself superior to Westerners. She was a member of the ruling class so democracy did not make much sense to her. The point is, she was repelled by so many things in this country, though she tried hard to hide these feelings because she didn't want to offend us. And then she became quite homesick for China. All of this happened before she found out about Porter and the nurse. For Ch'ing-Ling there was no margin for error.

"I think there was never any way that she could have been happy here. Your father agreed, you know. He understood the Chinese well enough, and he knew she would not change her mind. Even so, he wanted to go after her, to talk to her—for your sake more than anything. He knew you would want some answers and he thought you deserved them. But by then he wasn't allowed to travel abroad." She sat quietly for a time, thinking. Then finally she looked up at a hawk gliding overhead, riding parallel on the wind, close enough that it seemed possible almost to reach up and touch it. "We did manage to get some information. We were able to keep track of her until the Communists took over. And then something strange happened. Most of her relatives went to Taiwan with Chiang Kai-shek, but your mother stayed behind. For a while she was in Shanghai, then she moved out to a village far out in the countryside, in one of the most primitive provinces. . . ."

May's eyes had been following the hawk, but now her body tensed. She put her head on her knees and began to shiver uncontrollably in the noonday heat.

Kit, alarmed, put her arms out and May moved instinctively into them. Kit stroked her and whispered calming words . . . "It's all right, darling, it's all right . . ." Finally the shaking stopped, and Kit kissed her forehead and asked, delicately, "What was it dear? What happened?"

May sat up, wiped her forehead with the dampened handkerchief Kit gave her. When she could speak her voice quivered: "It's so strange," she managed, "but until this moment, until you told me where she was, I had never really thought of her as being . . . alive. She was my mother, and I knew she existed, once, but I guess I didn't really *know* it. Until now. That she is somewhere out there—" she looked out to the sea, flat and vast—"right now, breathing and talking and being . . . and she has been there all along, my mother." She put her head down again, and sobbed, and Kit let her, knowing it was good for May to cry, knowing it was the first step. And while she waited for May to spend herself, she looked up at the wheeling hawk and thought about her own mother, who had known everything about the birds of prey, and who had spent so much of her life in a losing battle to keep this ranch clear of man's encroachments on their wild habitat.

"Daddy was right," May finally said, "I do want some answers and she's the only one who can give them. I have to see her, Kit."

Kit sighed, nodded. "I thought you might, so I made some preliminary inquiries through my contacts in Hong Kong. It isn't going to be easy, not right now. You can't get a visa to go into China. The borders are closed to foreigners, particularly Westerners, while Mao tries again to shake up the bureaucracy and has another go at creating his perfect classless society. This time the intellectuals are under fire, and all things Western are strictly forbidden. I know the name of the village where she was living four years ago. She had been there for seventeen years, so there is a good chance that she still is. It's a very primitive village called Kau Peng in a western province. She's the only doctor in the village, but she operates a small clinic where she has trained a number of paramedics. It's an area where most doctors have no desire to go, so she has been left pretty much alone. I was told that she never remarried, that she lives a very simple life and that the peasants of the area revere her. I'm afraid that's all I've been able to find out. Except that until the current troubles abate, getting into China will be not only very difficult, but very dangerous."

May listened as she concentrated on peeling an egg. "Do you think I could pass?"

Kit looked at her sharply. "Pass? You mean go in as a Chinese?"

May nodded.

Kit exhaled, "No, don't even think about that, you could end up in prison or worse. There has to be another way and we'll find it, but please don't do anything foolish . . ." Something distracted her, a sound. A mechanical grinding noise.

"Damn!" Kit swore as a white Mercedes appeared, its hood seeming to ride the waves of grass on this soft plateau. Kit's face registered her astonishment: "A road, somebody's put a road through here."

The car stopped, and the mechanical rattle of its engine ceased. May stood, but Kit remained seated against her rock, too dismayed to move.

A blond woman wearing a lavender linen dress and matching oversized sunglasses got out and picked her way toward them, stepping carefully through the rough grass in high-heeled sandals.

"What are you doing here?" the woman demanded.

When Kit didn't answer May said, "We're having a picnic."

The woman looked at the horses with disapproval. "This is private property," she told them, hand on hip, "and we have a lot of trouble up here with fire, so I'd suggest you be on your way out—and next time take the no trespassing signs seriously."

May waited for Kit to tell her, but Kit seemed unable to speak. "We have permission to ride here," May said. "The owner is an old friend."

"Is that right?" the woman came back, looking both of them over suspiciously, not impressed with Kit's worn riding clothes or May's jeans and T shirt.

"Yes that's right," May answered, allowing some steel into her voice. "I'm sure the owner would appreciate your concern for fire hazard. If you'll give me your name, I'll be sure to tell her."

The woman's tone changed. "Damned right I'm concerned. Damned hippies come out here, set up their teepees and smoke their damned fool dopeheads off. Going to burn us all out one of these days. I'm Evie Shurz—my husband's granddad owned all this land to the north here." She waved her hand vaguely. "We're selling off lots. I'm Evie's Realty, down in town. I didn't catch your names."

Still Kit said nothing.

"This is my aunt, Mrs. McCord," May spoke up, "and I'm May Reade."

There was a long, thick pause. Evie Shurz looked at them through her lavender glasses, as if there was something she had meant to remember. Then, tossing her blond head as if to shake off some troublesome buzzing insect, she raised her hand in a gesture of dismissal. "Like I said," she threw back at them, "there's fire hazard up here."

The hollow clacking of the Mercedes engine echoed over the hills, and when the silence returned and wrapped around them, May said: "She had no idea who you are."

Kit only sighed and said: "It will never be the same again—not when you can get here by car."

May looked at her. "I don't know whether to laugh or cry. But I'll tell you what I do know. Someday I'm going to bring my children up here and I'm going to tell them about the day you and I came, and about the blond bombshell real estate agent who wanted to know what we thought we were doing up here, and how you wouldn't tell her you owned a big chunk of the damned place. And then, just before we leave, I'm going to get a big tear in my eye and sigh and say to them, 'But it'll never be the same again . . .' "

Kit's face softened into a smile. "I didn't know you were planning to have children," she said. And May answered, "Of course I am, and as soon as we can get them on horses we are going to bring them here. With hard-boiled eggs and homemade tortillas. I've just decided. You and me and little Porter and little Kit. I've already named my children, so you see how serious I am! All you have to do is promise never to sell the ranch or this piece of land."

"I promise," Kit said, wiping at the tears she could not keep from welling. "But first things first. Now it's time to begin plotting the China Project."

13

The forecasters lied. They told us that the worst was over, they
lulled us into a false complacency, we were not prepared for the
storm that was to break over us in those first days of May, 1970.

On May 1 we learned that combat troops of the U.S. First Air
Cavalry and B-52 bombers had invaded Cambodia in an attack ordered by President Richard Nixon "to wipe out the headquarters for
the entire Communist operation in South Vietnam."

The newspapers reported 6,500 U.S. troops searching for the secret
headquarters they were never to find. It was, I suppose, macabre, but
I began to clip news reports of the war and paste them into the *Reader's
Digest Great World Atlas.* I clipped a wire photo of a group of young
Cambodian women tied together in an open field, suspected Viet
Cong collaborators the caption said. Their faces were filled with
terror, their bodies bowed. I had pinned this photo to my wall, but
found that I could not bear to come upon it so often, so I pasted it
in the atlas, over a conic projection of Southeast Asia, covering the
southern half of Cambodia. A country visited long ago in that time
of my life now relegated to dreams, a country that lies on my memory
like the softest gauze, stirred on a summer's night. Once I could close
my eyes and conjure up the young girls dressed in their flowing
gowns, tittering as they made their way down the streets of Phnom

Penh. Now all I could see was the faces of the girls in the clipping: tormented, terrorized.

———

On May 2 Karin and Philip were married in the walled garden of Philip's house. Only family and the closest of friends attended. Dan and Thea were there, and May and Marge and Hank Fromberg— Hank's rumpled corduroy suit in rather nice counterpoint to Philip's sartorial splendor. Karin was radiant in an old-fashioned dress of ecru lace with a high collar; Philip was spilling over with high spirits. The ceremony had been timed for the sun, when the bank of deep red rhododendrons against which the couple stood to repeat their vows was in full light. Philip's plans were, as always, both precise and elegant. Although the forecast had been for possible showers, the sun shone brightly and on schedule, dazzling Karin's blond hair. There was just the right amount of ritual, nicely balanced by intimacy. Thea held Karin's hand throughout the simple ceremony performed by a retired justice of the state supreme court, an old friend of Philip's. A string quartet played "Jesu, Joy of Man's Desiring," Sam took photographs, and I cried as quietly as I could, glad for this small, happy reprieve in that tormented time.

The vows were said, the couple embraced and then, in an instant of silence, a mockingbird warbled out one clear lyrical phrase. We looked up to where it perched in the birch, the new green leaves draped gracefully over the garden, and Marge whispered: "That is too beautiful not to be prophetic." Thea threw herself into Philip's arms and Karin turned to Dan and asked, "Would I embarrass you terribly if I hugged you?" The boy wrapped his arms around her awkwardly, and for a small, tender moment buried his head in her hair.

May put her arms around Karin and they rocked back and forth for a while before she kissed her on both cheeks, then May hugged Philip hard and said something to him that caused him to lower his head and answer her solemnly.

I watched May. She busied herself passing champagne; her smile was, I thought, just a little too quick, her attention a bit splintered.

"Come talk to me," I said as soon as I had a chance. She sat and took my hand and held on to it tightly, as if to quiet some turmoil within. Tilting my head close to hers, I asked if she could tell me what was troubling her.

Her eyes grew too bright, and she smiled to stave off the tears. "It's just," she began, and had to stop to take a deep breath before starting over in a calmer voice. "I'm going to miss K of course," she said, "we've been so busy these past weeks, with plans for the wedding and all—I suppose it's just hit me that she won't be coming back to the house." Her voice began to quiver.

I patted her hand and said, "But that's not all, is it?"

Now tears filled her eyes and she turned away to struggle with them. I tightened my grip on her hand. We were too small a group, it would not do for the others to see May cry. "Are you thinking about Hayes?" I began, to help her.

She nodded. "Karin and Philip . . . everything just seems so clear, what they want . . . and in a way so easy . . . but for me, for Hayes . . ." She sighed and took a deep breath. "For us everything is so complicated, absolutely nothing is clear and I'm not sure it ever will be. I think it's going to be impossible to sort it all out, too much depends on things we seem to have no control over . . . it's just such an ungodly mess . . ." Suddenly she looked at me frantically. "Please . . . don't think . . . I'm terribly happy for Karin, I would not have wanted anything to be different . . ."

Sam's approach caused her to break off her sentence. I patted her hand so she would know I understood. "I'm bringing the two of you some wedding cake," Sam said, grinning. "Aren't you supposed to take it home and sleep on it or something, so you are the next one up to bat?"

I laughed. "You two can sleep on it if you wish, but I've been out of the ballgame a long time so I plan to eat mine right now."

By four-thirty the newlyweds were on their way to Carmel, leaving the rest of us to sip champagne and face the empty evening.

"Want to keep me company?" I asked May.

Sam answered for her. "Don't worry, Faith," he said, "I'll take care of her."

The house was as May and Karin had left it that morning, an empty shoe box on the dining room floor, mounds of tissue paper scattered in their rush to get off to the wedding. Sam picked up the shoe box and stood holding it; after a time he put it down again and said he was going to the cottage to change.

May sank into the sofa where Karin always sat. A spool of green thread and a bone china thimble had been left on the table. She put the thimble on her finger and studied the tiny violets painted on it. She squinted against the last of the day's sunlight, but she could not find the energy to get up to close the shades. A strange lethargy had overtaken her. She had sipped two glasses of champagne, but had eaten nothing so her stomach felt hollow and echoing. Still, the effort it would take to go to the refrigerator was more than she could manage.

Sam returned, sat next to her, rolled the film out of his cameras, marked it for the lab. "I'm going to drop this in the city, want to ride along?" he asked.

"I don't feel like the city," she said petulantly, "I feel like being alone somewhere in the middle of nothing. On the flank of Mauna Loa, preferably. Or in a desert. Anywhere away from here."

Sam looked at her abstractedly, he was figuring logistics. "Okay," he said, all action, "let's throw our sleeping bags in the truck, we can drive through the city to drop off the film to be developed and keep right on going over the Golden Gate and out to Point Reyes. There's nothing out there—I mean nothing. Just windswept beach and sand and ocean. I've got camping gear in the back, ready to go. What do you say?"

She looked at him, bit her lip, shrugged. She did not think she could move. "I'm hungry."

"We'll eat on the way. At Giovanni's. I'll pay, you can deduct it from what I owe you." He grinned to show he was teasing.

"Okay, sure," she finally said, making the effort to unfold herself and stand. Her leg had gone to sleep and she grimaced. "Why not?"

The rain started about two in the morning. May was wakened by a sudden shock of cold water on her neck, washing into her down bag. Sam had placed his sleeping bag on slightly higher ground, and was still dry. He ran to the truck, came back with a blanket and a tent. While Sam put up the tent, May stripped and wrapped herself in the blanket. The rain was falling steadily now; she was thoroughly chilled and her teeth were chattering. They crawled inside the tent and huddled together on top of his sleeping bag.

"Can we build a fire?" she asked.

"Not in the dark," Sam said, "not in this rain."

He put his arms around her and felt her shivering. "Poor kid," he said, soothing her, rubbing her arms and back to try to warm and comfort her. "We'll still be seeing a lot of Karin . . . she couldn't do without you, you know that." She could feel his breath warm on her neck. "And I'm here too," he said, trying not to sound so serious. "As a matter of fact, I have wanted to be here for you for quite a long time . . ." He moved his hand tentatively under the blanket, touching the soft place under her breast.

She sobbed, and took his hand in hers, removing it. "You will always be my friend, Sam," she said, burying her face in his neck, "you and Karin and me . . . we will always be great, great friends . . ."

And though he did not move and scarcely breathed, she could feel him withdraw from her, she could feel the cold, angry blanket of his disappointment settle over them and she knew, she understood in a flash of awful clarity, that Sam had wanted to be more than her friend for a very long time.

"Great, great friends . . ." Sam repeated, using sarcasm to mask the anger, but he could not stop himself from adding, "It's Hayes. Right?" It was not a question. He knew.

I clipped the story, pasted in it the *Great World Atlas:* On May 2, the day of the wedding, on a hockey field on the campus of Yale University police fired tear gas into a gathering of Black Panther supporters and an explosion ripped through an arena as tensions gathered. On May 3, Eli spoke at a Berkeley rally held for Black Panthers in Provo Park.

The uneasy peace that had settled over Berkeley was shattered in those early days of May. Four hundred campuses across the country suspended classes, students gathered, their numbers bolstered by Americans infuriated by the invasion of Cambodia. The day before his wedding, Philip Ward had helped draft the Academic Senate's statement, which called the invasion "unwise, immoral and dangerous . . . and deeply exacerbating to the distrust of students and faculty of the U.S. government." Once again there was the sound of glass breaking, as students rampaged along Telegraph Avenue, heaving trash cans through store windows. The air was filled with the acrid smell of burning, as Army trucks and ROTC buildings were set afire. A state of emergency was declared.

I clipped and pasted and wondered if I was losing my mind. Over a map of the subcontinent of India I pasted this special report from Cambodia: "The monsoon rains have come early and washed out our airstrip, so that hundreds of armored vehicles that spearheaded the morning thrust started to bog down as the thick clay turned to red mud. Rain fell all of Sunday, for four hours straight. American soldiers are putting the torch to homes because they might be useful to the Communists; they are killing livestock for the same reason. A young tank commander said: 'I had orders to burn everything.' "

When my neighbor of fifty years, Mrs. DeLucci, came to tell me that her grandson Charlie was missing in action—little Charlie with the great, soft brown eyes and endearing smile—I held her hand and cried with her, but could find no words of comfort.

On May 4, members of the Ohio National Guard fired into a group of demonstrators on the quiet little campus at Kent State and four young people lay dead. Four young students, some of them carrying their books, just about Charlie DeLucci's age.

I began to think crazy thoughts; I began to wonder if Charlie DeLucci might have met one of the Kent State girls, and married her, and old Mrs. DeLucci would move in with her daughter Cara so the young couple could have the house and raise a family . . . if not for this war, if not for this terrible war. It was too much. I could not go to the Peace Coalition office in Berkeley, I could not bear to watch any more. My eyes filled with fluid and the view was streaked and dark. I felt old and tired.

Kit, returning from her New York trip, found me sitting on the sunporch of my cottage, unable even to find solace in my garden.

"You've got to come to Wildwood with me," she said. "It's going to take a massive effort to get everything ready for the wedding reception next Saturday, and I can't do it alone." I said I couldn't. She put both her hands on my shoulders, looked me square in the eyes and said, "You can and you will, if I have to carry you."

The next day Israel loaded me into the van, along with thirty large boxes filled with family silver and crystal and monogrammed linens and we were off for the country and the magnificent estate Connor McCord had built for himself in the first decade of the century, and called "Wildwood."

The great house and surrounding acres of gardens are now operated as a public trust established by Kit, and thousands of people tour the place every year. Kit retained the right to use Wildwood for special occasions but she has exercised this right only two or three times for charity functions.

"Perhaps I just need a few days in the country, away from it all," I told Kit in a worn-down voice.

"Not a chance," Kit answered. "We've got work to do and you, my dear, are going to be in the thick of it. I told Karin and Philip to invite as many people as they wished. We've got almost three hundred people coming four days from today, and I'm determined to make it a grand occasion." She must have felt she did not have my attention, because she cried out, "Faith, listen to me—in all this sorrow we have a chance to carve out a little island of pleasure. There's nothing crass about it, we need this time—it's the only way we can stay sane . . . and human."

It was Kit's way of shaking some sense into me, and it worked. We had to mark the marriage of Karin and Philip, to make it a grand occasion—for Charlie DeLucci and the girls at Kent State, for all of the young people who would never have the chance.

Kit knew something about grand occasions, and Wildwood with its acres of formal gardens and reflecting pools and great smooth flagstone terraces was the perfect setting for one. No sooner had we arrived on Tuesday than the caterers began to troop in, checking out the kitchen, planning where to set up tables for the twilight supper. The decorators and florists came next, discussing flower arrangements and where the little flower stalls that would dispense champagne would be scattered around the grounds. Then came the musicians—a representative of the chamber orchestra which was to play in the small pavilion near the pool and the manager of a group called "Sweet Relish" which had what May said was a "Mamas and Papas" sound. When Kit opened the doors to the grand ballroom, the young man fell into a fit of hacking when he saw the polished parquet floors, the crystal chandeliers and the stage.

Kit assigned bedrooms for those of us who would be staying over. Her own was at the far end of the second floor hall, a suite of rooms she had shared with her husband—the only rooms in the house which remain reserved for her personal use. Karin and Philip were to share the room at the opposite end of the hall, and the rest of us—May and Israel and Thea and Philip's sister Germaine from Philadelphia—would occupy the rooms between.

Dan had called Karin to ask if she would mind if he didn't come, because he had an important math exam on the Monday following, and he wasn't doing all that well in math. She told him she would miss him terrifically, but that she understood and maybe when his finals were over they could all take a trip somewhere together. He answered that when he came home he would like to take her and

Thea on the Nimitz trail in Tilden. It was a pretty easy hike, he said, and he thought she'd like it. She said she knew she would, and that it was a date. Later, when Philip asked her about the conversation with Dan, she repeated all but the Nimitz trail part.

On Tuesday, May 5, Sam had an hour and fifteen minutes to pack his gear and catch a plane to Ohio, to try to photograph the parents of the slain students at Kent State for a German magazine. May was to drive him to the airport, and they were almost out the door when the phone rang. Sam grabbed it and May heard him say, "Listen Eli, I can't talk now but I'll explain everything when I get back. No . . . it wasn't like that, no . . . listen . . ." he said, but Eli wasn't listening so he hung up.

"What was that all about?" May asked as she threaded the Jaguar through the narrow hill streets.

"Nothing," Sam said, preoccupied with checking his camera case. "It's too complicated to go into. If Hayes calls, just tell him there's no problem."

She kept her eyes on the road and said nothing. It was the first time Hayes's name had been mentioned between them since the night of Karin's wedding. They had maintained a correct silence; it was as if they had an unspoken agreement not to mention what had happened, what had been revealed in the cold rain at Point Reyes.

But now Sam was involved in some way with Eli and Hayes. She frowned, but said nothing. She knew not to push; Sam was always nervous when he was leaving on assignment. Once he quit checking his equipment he would lean forward, drum his fingers on the dash- board, and she knew his mind would be a thousand miles away, in Ohio. Also, according to the unwritten rules of their fragile peace, she had to be careful around the subject of Hayes.

"Will you be back for the reception on Saturday?" she asked as she dropped him in front of Western Airlines.

"Can't say," he called back, already on the run, "I'll try. You'll see me when you see me."

She saw him on Friday night. When she came home at eleven he was lying, fully clothed, across her bed and was sound asleep. He reeked of pot; she saw the remnants of a joint in the little bone china dish by her bed. He must have wanted to talk to her tonight, she thought. Probably he wanted to tell her about the assignment, he

188

often did that when he returned from a job that was charged with emotion. Always before she had been excited, listening to him. But not tonight. She backed out of the room quietly, not to wake him, and went to sleep in Karin's room.

If the wedding had been Philip's, the reception was Karin's, not by plan but by time and circumstance. Wildwood was the perfect setting for a dress-up party. A few years before, the dress would have been very proper, quite prescribed. "Dress-up" in 1970 was a free-for-all: any time period, or any mix, fantasy was fine and so was fun, and a large number of the five hundred who came took full advantage and made it something of a costume party.

Guests poured in from all parts of the country: Philip's publishing friends in New York came, and the movie people he knew in Los Angeles, along with many of the Mount Holyoke girls who had graduated with Karin and May, and a large contingent from Berkeley.

Karin set the tone. Her long flowered dress had been designed by a young woman with a romantic theatrical flair. It was pink and green and vaguely Edwardian. May's was simpler. Of yellow silk, it was ankle length and skimmed her body. Her hair was pulled back with a spray of white orchids.

May had flower leis flown over from Hawaii, and floated them around our necks so we could breathe in the fragrance of frangipani and ginger and tube roses. The setting was sublime, we could lose ourselves in the loveliness of the day and the place and the music and the people.

"A little island in time," Kit reminded me, "grab and hold on tight. Isn't that right, Israel?"

Israel stationed himself beside me on the pretext that I might have difficulty maneuvering my wheelchair over the flagstones. He looked splendid in a beige silk suit he had borrowed from a cousin, set off by a midnight blue silk shirt, but I could tell that he was not entirely comfortable in this setting. That changed when Eli and Hayes arrived, escorted by May who came beaming, arm and arm between them, saying, "Just look who I found lurking about."

"Hey brother," Eli called to Israel. "I admire your style, I certainly do, and I especially admire that pretty lady you came with." He kissed me on the cheek and Hayes stood holding one of my hands while May clung close enough to him so that I could hear her when she told him to remember to find her again when the music started.

. . .

Sam's wedding gift to Philip and Karin was to be an album of photographs from the wedding and the reception. He shot from four o'clock, when the first guests began to arrive, until all light was gone and the Japanese lanterns were lighted, transforming the gardens. He was making his way back to the house with his camera equipment when he came upon *Time*'s bureau chief and his Swiss wife. Sam asked if they would like a private tour of the house. May happened onto them in her bedroom, where she had gone to get an aspirin for one of the Mount Holyoke classmates.

"Miss Reade," the woman, whose name was Eugenie, said in thick accents, "I am so happy to meet you. I am reading about you just yesterday—I wonder do you know about that *Paris Match* story, the one called 'America's Rich Girls'?

May frowned and said she didn't know.

"Oh yes," Eugenie went on, her hands with their bright red fingernails shaping the air, "it is all about women beneath"—she said 'be-knees'—"thirty, who are very wealthy, and they say you are one of them, and that little is known about you—you are mystery. The photograph of you was, I think, when you are little girl, with your father in some courtroom, I believe."

May sat down on the bed. Sam put his hand on her shoulder, rubbed it. "Not all that many Americans read *Paris Match*," he said, "I don't think you have to worry."

May tried to smile. "As long as *Time* magazine doesn't decide to do a little feature on rich girls."

"What rich girls?" the *Time* man said gallantly.

May found Eli walking back from the tennis courts. "You can get high just breathing in down there," he told her. "That little chubby blond woman from Iowa, the one with the innocent eyes? She must have about ten pounds of what she swears is Acapulco Gold. Did you know one of your old classmates is a dealer?"

May laughed. "It's her looks. That flower-sprigged innocence covers a charming, larcenous little heart. Carrie likes money and men and wild parties, in that order. Dope falls into the first category—I hope she isn't selling it today."

Eli shook his head and slipped his arm around her. "While we're on the subject of old college pals, I've been wanting to ask . . ." he began.

Sam waved to them from across the pool; May noticed he was still with the *Time* couple. Seeing Sam reminded her, and she interrupted, "I've been wanting to ask you something, too. What was it Sam did that he had to explain to you? I heard part of the telephone call."

Eli tightened. "No big deal," he said.

"Maybe it isn't, but I know it involves Hayes, too, and I'd like to know."

Grudgingly, he told her, "I thought Sam had used our names—mine and Hayes's—to get into a meeting of the Panthers that was supposed to be closed. He got one of the Brothers to pose with some guns . . . not a very smart thing to do, given the current climate of public opinion. Anyway," he looked away, "Sam worked it all out, it's okay."

She knew by the way he said it that it wasn't. "My turn now," he went on, "while we are on the subject of Hayes."

She took his arm, moving him across the terrace to the ballroom. He bent his head to hers so he couldn't be heard. "Hayes and you—what I don't understand is why, if it works, you don't let it."

"If it works," she said, "I'm not sure it does."

"I'm sure it could," he came back.

She tried to explain. "Hayes is full of doubts . . ."

"About himself, yes, but not about you," he answered.

"But he has to come to terms, sort things out . . . and I have some things that need to be resolved before I can be any good for anyone . . ." She stopped, looked at Eli and something about the way he looked back at her moved her to speak with a searing, blunt honesty. "My mother deserted me when I was one month old, and it crippled me. I've been trying to come to terms with it—her walking out on me—all of my life. I don't know why it gnaws at me . . . I hate it . . . but I know I have to settle it before I can get on with my own life."

"Hayes knows about this?"

"Yes," she said, smiling wistfully, "he knows that I have to find her, to tell her . . . so I can get free of it. . . ."

They walked for a time in silence. "I'm sure it could work for the two of you," Eli said softly, "and I think it should. You could make him happy, pretty May, and he deserves to be happy, my friend Hayes does. I have a powerful wish to see the two of you together, where you belong."

She slipped her arm around his waist and leaned her head lightly on his shoulder, to show him how he had touched her.

"Miss Reade," called a small man with a moustache that brushed big on his face so that his mouth looked like a small, pink, wet thing. "I'm Ira Rossman—Philip's agent in L.A. I'd like to speak to you—privately, if I could." He shot Eli a glance of dismissal. Eli looked at May, she tugged him closer.

"Well Ira Rossman," she said, "I'd like you to meet Eli Barnes . . . friend, lover, Boy Scout, Black Panther, to name a few of his accomplishments. Eli and I have no secrets—except for Panther meetings which I am not allowed to attend. Bunch of racist snobs, the Panthers."

The small man snorted and sneezed at once to cover his confusion. Eli's laughter saved him. May gave in and smiled.

"I see," Rossman said, laughing to show he could take a joke. "What I wanted to talk to you about . . . I read this article in *Paris Match* about you . . ."

May cut in. "About me?" she said. "What did it say? What could it possibly say? What was the article called? Tell me."

Her quick switch confused him. His hands tried to shape the air into an answer. "Well, I didn't actually read it myself, I heard about it—the gist of it—and it seemed to me there might be something there . . . I mean, I know a lot of people in the Business and . . ."

"What business is that, Mr. Rossman?" May came back, mock innocent now. Eli watched, fascinated. He had never seen May so taunting.

"The movie business, May," the little man said, his pink gums flashing between swaths of moustache. "I think we might be able to put together a package . . ."

"A package of what exactly?" May came back. "You say you haven't read this story, but you think there's 'something' in it. Perhaps they talked about my work—is that what interests you?"

Ira Rossman tried grinning and shrugging, a gesture meant to be boyishly charming. "I think we could . . . it would be possible, certainly . . . to work that in."

"Work what in?" May demanded.

"Man," Eli laughed in a big, loose-jointed way and lapsed into street language: "You got to do your homework before you come lookin' after the doctor here. The doctor, she don't suffer fools graciously, you've got to know that. She likely push your belly in boy, send you flyin' out on one of those vol-canoes she done study all the time. That's so, man, that's perfectly so, you don't watch your step this lady here about to blow, like Stromboli, like Krakatoa. No shit. You got to watch out there."

Ira Rossman lost control. He began to trip over words. "Investments . . ." he said, "Many people find films an interesting investment, not just dollar return but the people you meet. A whole lot of very interesting people . . . Brando," he said, his voice rising, "John Huston," he went on, "fabulous people."

"John Huston you say?" Eli repeated. "No shit."

"Miss Reade?"

"I could never bear fabulous people," May told him, "ask Philip."

May and Eli walked toward the music. The sky was a deep, dark blue, the night was almost upon them. The colored lanterns lit their way, swaying in a soft and welcome breeze, come to cool the day's long warmth.

"God this is a good party," Eli said, shedding the accent he had affected for Ira Rossman. "I said to myself when I came in here today that I would leave the rest of the world outside, the whole bloody mess, festering out there. Today I called myself a time-out, just to be with my friends and have a nice time for now, that's all."

"Don't stop being my friend, Eli," May said, "or Hayes's. Please."

She could see his teeth shining against the dark of his face, and his eyes studying her. "Hayes is the best man I ever knew," Eli said, "black or white. If the two of you don't find each other sometime, some place, I will never forgive you. Never. Because I love you both, you two honkies. God help me, I do."

He gave her a fierce look and said, "Come on woman, let's dance." The "Sweet Relish" version of "I Heard it Through the Grapevine" drifted out to them, soft and throbbing. She swayed down the path, moving with the beat, soft and easy and rhythmic. Eli lifted his hand to Hayes who put down his glass, as if their movements were synchronized. He walked to meet them. "I'm going to ask the bride to dance," Eli said to Hayes. "You take hold of the bridesmaid here."

"Always the bridesmaid." May sighed as she moved into Hayes's arms. "Never the bride."

"Bridesmaids have more fun," he told her, pulling her around in rhythm, singing the words of the song into her ear.

"Are you sure about bridesmaids?" she teased, moving her hips in an easy sliding motion.

The sound pulled them in, throbbing and rising.

"Absolutely," he answered over the thick twang of the electric guitars, as if it made all the sense in the world. He smiled at her and she at him, as they moved to the music and the flickering lights, caught up in the steady, hard rhythm of it.

"Move aside white boy," Eli nudged him, "make room for the Bride and Count Dracula."

"Yes, move aside," Karin laughed. She was shimmering with happiness. As Eli threw her out from him, her hair came loose and tumbled around her shoulders. She shook it out. "Yeah!" Eli called to Philip who was watching from the terrace doors, "Your lady is hot tonight!"

Philip smiled and saluted. He watched a few moments, enjoying the way they moved—Eli and Karin—the grace of the dance, the easy soft sway of their hips to the music. He could not master it himself. He had tried once, with Karin, and failed. He knew he had failed because she had never asked him to try again.

"Ah for a little Benny Goodman," Kit said.

"I'd settle for Kay Kaiser."

"Or Tommy Dorsey."

"Glenn Miller would be perfect."

" 'Tuxedo Junction.' "

" 'Pennsylvania 6-5000'."

They laughed. "Come walk with me a bit," Kit said. "If we pretend to be deep in conversation, perhaps no one will interrupt."

"I don't have to pretend, Kit," Philip said, I've been trying to get a moment alone with you for some time—to thank you."

"You don't have to do that Philip," Kit said. "The truth is, I gave the party for Karin."

"I know that," he answered, "I didn't mean thank you for that, though it is a damned good party, even without Benny Goodman."

Kit smiled. "I am extraordinarily fond of Karin," she began.

"I know," Philip answered. "What I wanted to thank you for was giving me the benefit of the doubt."

She looked at him quizzically.

"It's been a long time since that summer after the war," he said. "What was it—six weeks? Long enough. You were right to send me packing, Kit. No, hear me out, please . . ." She had tried to stop him,

194

and seeing that she couldn't began to lead him away from the terrace, away from the crowd. "You were too smart for me, Kit. Too sophisticated, and I mean that in the best sense. God, when I think of how callow I must have seemed . . ."

"You weren't callow, Philip. But as you say, it was a long time ago . . ."

He leaned back against a low brick wall and looked at her. "Nothing is ever over, Kit. I will never forget that time—it has a cherished place in my memory. And to be honest with you, until Karin came along I didn't think I'd ever feel so intensely about a woman as I felt about you. And this time, I think, I am finally mature enough."

"Karin looks radiant," Kit said. "Marriage suits her, I think. She seems so happy with you and Dan and Thea, and that makes me very happy."

He leaned against the wall, turned toward the darkened drive and lit a cigarette.

"Have you been happy, Kit? I told myself I'd never ask you that, but now I find I must. Did you make the right decision?"

She sighed. "I've made so many decisions, Philip. Some of them were right." She looked up to the top of the little summer house and smiled. "The first time I came to Wildwood I had made a decision, and it was right. I know that. The man who became my husband had run away from me. He came here to hide, and I followed him and seduced him. Right here. In this house. But you weren't talking about my marriage, I know that. All I can tell you is that what happened between us was a lovely interlude for me, but I think for Karin's sake it would be best not to mention it again. Can we do that?"

The end of his cigarette glowed red in the dark. "Of course," he finally said. "I simply wanted to say 'thank you.' For then, and for now as well. And I wanted to tell you something else—that Karin is very like you."

"That's a great compliment," Kit said.

"It is truly meant."

"I know."

As the band swung into "A Natural Woman," May said, "No more, I can't breathe . . . air, air, air . . ."

Hayes followed her off the dance floor, his hand on the bare of her back. Alone on the terrace he pulled her around to face him. "Let me take your pulse," he said, pressing his hand firmly under her breast.

"Most doctors use the wrist," she answered, leaning into him.

"Dumb doctors," he said, and then he dropped the bantering tone to tell her, "It isn't working, May. Not for me. I want to be with you too much, I want . . . need . . ."

She pulled him to the edge of the terrace. "See that little summer house over there," she said, trying to keep her voice calm, "there's a family story. It's about Kit, she seduced her husband there."

"Seduced, you say?" he answered, trying without success to go back to the bantering tone.

"We can talk there—and even touch without everyone looking at us."

She tugged at the old screen door until it opened, and the pungent smell of marijuana rushed out at them. She entered quickly, pulling him into the darkness, turning to wrap into his arms, to find his mouth and press hers into it, hard and hungry. A surge of passion washed over them. Small, pointed cries of pleasure escaped from her; she heard them and pressed closer, and every small nerve fiber in her body translated for her: Love, she loved him, she wanted him, she could not be without him.

Their bodies had taken over, reason was overwhelmed . . .

"Jesus, May, I love you," Hayes said, in a voice that was low and husky and unguarded.

The voice came from the far corner. "You've got him where you want him now, May. I heard it all, I'm your witness." A cigarette glowed in the darkness. They could not see who it was, but they knew. Sam, it was Sam's voice. He had been there all along, smoking, watching, stoned.

"Maybe I should have waited to speak up, let him screw you, maybe you'd get lucky and get pregnant . . . then you'd have the Big Diehl where you want him. An old trick, old, old. I mean, he's an honorable man . . . marriage, family, all that shit." His voice broke loose: "God, May, I thought you were better than that . . ." Then again, under control, "Actually, the two of you make me sick . . . May, you throw yourself at him like all the love-crazed puling Anglo females. And Hayes—Andy's Big Bro—the Great Activist who does nothing but good for mankind, can't bring himself to make a simple little commitment to a lady who is breathing hard to drop her pants for him."

He stood, made his way to the door, sounded a grunt of derision and threw back at them, "Carry on, my fine fucking friends."

14

It was as if they had been catapulted into separate orbits, as if the gods in their anger had banished them, hurtling them into the heavens to circle the Earth, passing but never to touch like errant beings punished by the Fates.

It was not fair. May knew that. One moment she was spilling over with anger, the next she felt only despair. For the disappointment she knew Sam felt, for the hurt she had inflicted.

Hayes knew, too. They had sat side by side, drained of passion, on the flowered chintz love seat in the old summer house, trying to make sense of it.

"He wants you too," Hayes had said, "and if I were to be truthful, I'd have to say I've known from the beginning . . . from the first day . . . and it's one more complication."

"No," she had all but shouted at him. "No, I refuse to let Sam come between us. In fact," she said, realizing it for the first time, "in a strange sort of way, I think he always meant for us to be together . . . I think he wanted it . . . But even if he didn't, even if he had not brought us together and I had never met you, it wouldn't change how things are between Sam and me. We are friends, important friends. But no more, never any more. And he knows that, I promise you he knows."

Hayes sighed. "What now?" he asked.

For once, it was May who said, "I guess we'd better call another time-out."

She did not see Sam for several days. When finally she came home and found the Winged Victory in the doorway, she could feel her pulse speed and throb. She knocked on the door of the cottage. He did not answer at once, and for a long moment she thought that maybe he would not, would leave her standing there, knocking until the knuckles on her hands became red and bloody and sore. When he opened the door, his face was cold and closed.

"I think we need to talk," she said.

"There's nothing to say," he told her.

She wanted to get away, and Mauna Ulu cooperated. A new mountain on the eastern flank of Kilauea, it had been building for the better part of the year, pushing up, shooting fountains of lava as high as 1,800 feet into the tropical Hawaiian sky. This new volcano had pumped viscous hot lava into Alae crater until it was full to spilling over. Sinuous red lava streams slid down the mountains, snaking all the way to the pali, all the way to the cold ocean where it sizzled and surged and solidified and, finally, added hundreds of acres to the mountain. Kimo told her when she called to ask: "She's getting ready to blow. Come on over and watch the fireworks."

"What does Auntie Abigail say?" May had asked, and Kimo answered, "She say no foolin', Pele messing around for sure."

Sam took her to the airport. "I don't think I'll be here when you get back," he offered, his mouth tight.

"I know," she said, "but if it comes through I think you should take it."

"It doesn't matter what you think," he snapped back.

"All right," she allowed. She had not been able to talk to him, to work anything out. She had tried but it hadn't been any good. She felt as if a thick, muffling wall had been sprayed between them, the way workmen sprayed insulation into buildings. He could not hear her, she could not get through to him.

"Besides," he added, his voice cutting, "it'll be nice to be in a part of the world where everybody looks like me." She glanced at him. His face was handsome in its anger.

"Nobody else looks like you," she said softly.

He shot her a hard look that glanced off her face. "I understand there's a surgical procedure that changes the Mongolian eyelid from a single to a double. I thought you might like to know about it."

"Don't," she said, determined not to let her anger take over, not now when she was leaving.

"Don't," he mocked.

The silence that had been disturbed rose like dust, then settled and thickened and swelled until her throat felt dry and sore. He stood, hands thrust into the pockets of his fatigues, while she checked her luggage.

"Through to Hilo?" the attendant said. "Lucky you."

"Lucky me," she repeated to Sam, grimacing. "You don't have to walk with me to the gate . . ."

He walked half a step ahead of her down the long corridor and she did not try to catch up. She hated the hard, tangled knot that had come between them. She wanted to put her hand on his arm, to stop him and make him talk to her but she knew she couldn't. Time was out.

She fell back into the practicalities, the only language they could speak now: "When did they say you might be leaving?"

"Three weeks, maybe four. Whenever my credentials come through."

"Vietnam," she said. "You're going after all."

"If I'm not here when you get back I'll leave the keys with Karin and have her take care of things at the house."

The loudspeaker switched on: "We are now boarding our first-class passengers," the voice said.

"First class. That's you." Sam could not keep the acid from his voice. "I've been meaning to tell you—I thought I'd be able to pay you back before I left, but it doesn't look like I can. I should be able to send it to you from Saigon."

She started to tell him to forget about the loan, but she didn't because she knew he would read it wrong, they had been through that labyrinth before. *The money isn't important* she would say and he would answer *Nothing is important to you.* She was afraid, even, to say she was sorry. The knot that had been lodged in her chest seemed to move into her throat. She swallowed and, before he could back away, put her cheek against his and then walked, quickly, into the aircraft.

. . .

She did not know why she always felt better in Hawaii. The mountains had something to do with it, softly rising from the ocean floor. Mauna Loa was the biggest mountain in the world, more massive even than Everest, though most of that mass was hidden in the ocean depths. She loved the idea of treading these mountaintops, which rose so easily out of the sea. She thought of them as great beasts, gentle to the touch. There had been times, on the mountain, when that touch had given her a kind of peace she had known in no other place. She thought that the mountain had something to tell her and she listened for its whispers. Once, in the middle of Kilauea's great caldera, she had been certain that she felt the beat of its surging lava heart.

Others found the lava fields desolate. She thought them almost painfully beautiful and never failed to be moved by the ferns that pushed up through the burnt crust surface. New green and tender and perfect. Life at its most insistent.

Her mother and father had been happy in these islands, those few brief weeks after Pearl Harbor. She had been conceived on Oahu. "In a little grass shack on the leeward coast," her father had told her once. He had been joking, she was certain, but whenever she pictured them together it was on a quiet little beach of their own, near a little thatched palm hut. There were times when she could almost feel their happiness, her father's laughter, her mother's arms.

She looked forward to driving the two-lane blacktop from Hilo to the observatory on top of Kilauea. The road would be empty at this time of day. She could open the car windows and wait for the small popping of the ears which would signal that she was rising, steadily. These islands were, she sometimes thought, her high: moments after stepping onto the tarmac at Hilo or Lihue or Kahului, when the trade winds would catch and billow her slacks and blouse, the drifting scent of jasmine or plumeria would brush over her and she would feel a euphoric rush.

"Dr. Reade," a voice called, and when she didn't seem to hear repeated, louder, "Dr. Reade."

She turned, her face registering pleasure when she saw him: "Clarence—what are you doing here?"

The boy grinned, put a lei of plumeria and tube roses around her neck and gave her a shy kiss on the cheek. "Aloha, Dr. Reade," he said, "Pop told me you were coming—I've got my wagon waiting."

His brown muscled shoulders bulged under a torn T-shirt as he reached to take her bag.

"How did you know what plane?" she asked.

"I figured it pretty good, huh?" he laughed. The wilted flowers of the lei told her he had been waiting a good part of the day, but she said nothing. Clarence had been tagging after her since she had first come to the observatory four years before, when he was thirteen.

"What's happening on the mountain?" she asked.

"Everybody up there's wired, waiting for Mauna Ulu to go. Charlie at the ranger station is taking bets. Most of them put down in the next twenty-four hours, but that baby mountain, she can fool you."

"What does Abigail think?"

"Auntie's not saying."

"Smart lady."

Clarence Kaleikini should have graduated from high school that year, but wouldn't because he spent so much time on the mountain. He knew more about the Big Island volcanoes, May sometimes thought, than she did. It got in the way of his schoolwork. Clarence had once told her, "How can anybody think about English when the earthquakes are coming in clusters and you know the lava is making its way up, getting ready to go?" He had been born in Kalapana and so had his father, Kimo, who was one of the assistants at the observatory. Neither had any notion of leaving the island, or the volcanoes.

"No school today?" May asked as she pulled herself into the old jeep.

Clarence grinned sheepishly and changed the subject. "All the action is still in the east rift. Alae crater's full and flowing over, dropping down to the pali to make some new real estate. Mauna Ulu is growing up. You got to see her in her glory, Pop says maybe some dome fountains in one of the vents this time. I'm supposed to deliver you to Auntie's. She got your bed all made up, using her *kamakani kaili aloha* quilt."

"What does it mean?"

"It's the name of the quilt: Something like 'A gentle breeze that sends love from one to another.' Means you pretty important person."

May smiled. "Do you know when I first came to the mountain I practically had to beg for a bed to sleep in? Now you guys have it all arranged."

"Now you belong to this place, Dr. Reade."

"What is this 'doctor' stuff, Clarence? I'd like it a whole lot better if you called me 'May.' "

They could see a rain squall ahead, moving toward them. Clarence pulled over so they could raise the top and she jumped out to help. "Move it, May," he shouted as they tugged at the canvas, and they both laughed.

She spotted a tiny vanda orchid growing wild in the ditch, picked it and tucked it in her hair, behind her ear, before she climbed back into the jeep. The air was warm, the sky was blue all around, except for the squall about to overtake them. It wouldn't last long and then there would be rainbows all around. But as the rain enveloped them she felt a quick, sharp chill and goosebumps appeared on her arms. For weeks she had been preoccupied with Hayes. Now he slipped into some safe, back compartment of mind and heart, where she could put him on hold.

At the observatory she picked her way around the stacks of files and boxes that cluttered any spare space, and headed for the clattering machines. Kimo waved her in. "She's rumbling and she's grumbling," he said.

"Maybe tonight?" she asked.

He laughed. "It's like a woman having a baby. She's all swelled up, you know it's going to happen, all the signals are there. You can tell when she goes into labor, but nobody can predict when the baby's gonna come."

"Any other action along the rift or on the summit? Kilauea quiet?"

"All quiet on the western front," he said. "See for yourself."

She walked out to the rim of the caldera, the top of the mountain, which had long ago collapsed in upon itself to form this vast crater, two miles across and four hundred feet deep. She had hiked across the crater any number of times, had come close enough to the firepit called Halemaumau to breathe the steam which issued from it. Nothing was happening today, not here. Then the ground lurched beneath her.

"Felt that one," she said to Kimo.

"Labor pains," he laughed. "The earthquakes are picking up, coming in clusters now . . . that one should tell us something. You got a helicopter standing by?"

"Sure have. Corey's waiting for the call. Want to go with me?"

"You trust that wild, bearded hippie?" he joked, then answered her question: "I can't go, but you know who will."

"Tell Clarence to pick me up when it goes."

Abigail Penwell was seventy-eight years old, tall and stately with the carriage of a dowager princess. She was, in fact, descended from Hawaiian royalty. Her full name was Abigail Victoria Kaumakaokalani I'i Penwell. Her great-grandfather had been a New England sailing man. She liked to say that as far as she knew there were no missionaries—she said the word as if she were holding it at arm's distance—in her family.

"Sit, girl," Auntie Abigail said. "Eat." Half a pink papaya, May's favorite, was waiting on the table. May sat and spooned out the fruit while the older woman watched.

"So," May said when she had finished. "When, Auntie?"

"Why you ask me? You think I know something about this crazy place?"

"I know you know something about this crazy place," May told her. "My personal scientific opinion is that you have some sort of a direct line to the fire goddess Pele, and she tells you what's going on."

"You talk like that, girl, and they're going to lock you up. Some scientist. Who believes that Pele stuff?"

"Sometimes I am very tempted," May told her.

"Is that what they gave you that Ph.D. for?"

"Okay," May said, "Tell me now. Mauna Ulu's getting ready . . ."

"For sure."

". . . when do you think it's going to happen?"

"How would an old lady like me know?" she asked, her face all mock surprise. "I'd sleep near the top of wakeful tonight though."

They sat on the lanai of Abigail's little cottage until dark, listening. At nine May got up to call Corey and Clarence. "Auntie says to sleep light," she told them.

It was the sound of jet engines revving. May looked at the clock: two in the morning. The sky was bright. She pulled on her jeans and a shirt, made a quick stop at the bathroom, grabbed her boots and by the time she ran out of the cottage Clarence was waiting in the jeep.

Corey lifted off, skimming sideways to gain speed. She could see the excitement in their faces in the red glow of the fountain.

203

"There she blows!" Corey yipped. "Look at that Mother!"

"Oh yes," May whispered.

It was more than she had imagined, this birthing of a mountain. It was, she thought, creation. Blood-red bursting in a great fountain high into the night sky, trailing sparks and roaring bright. Neonatal fireworks; throbbing lava flows burning down the charred side of the mountain, dropping off the pali in licking tongues of fire. The copter lurched as a wave of heat hit it. She glanced at Clarence and looked away, knowing he would not want her to see the glistening wet on his brown face. She bit her lip to keep from crying out, then Corey did it for her: "Holy Mother of God," he shouted over the roar, "Armageddon!"

She was up for twenty-four hours, marking and measuring and making the kinds of observations you can make only in the hours during and after a major eruption. She slept for four hours, falling asleep in a cot in the observatory, not bothering to take off her clothes which reeked of the smell of burning wood, then she was up for another twenty. Clarence would not have slept at all, had she not insisted. She could feel the heat through the thick soles of her boots; Clarence wore rubber thongs, and seemed impervious to the heat. When she took off her boots, the bottoms of her feet were blistered. Clarence's were clear. "I'm oven-proof," he explained.

After thirty-two hours of fireworks, Mauna Ulu settled down to the business of pumping molten lava down to the crater, and the staff of the observatory swung into their posteruptive phase routines. On the Wednesday following, Kimo came looking for May at Kealakomo, an ancient village site which lay directly in the path of the advancing lava flow.

"You gotta call Peter Rensaeller," he told her. "He's in Honolulu and he says he wants to talk to you pretty fast." May had met Peter Rensaeller twice. Dr. Fuller, the head of her doctoral committee, had introduced them at a Washington symposium. Peter was, Fuller had explained with a wry little laugh, a "political geologist of international renown." His name seemed always to turn up on new commissions.

"I heard you had moved to Washington," she said. "What brings you to the boonies?"

He laughed. "Probably the same thing that brought you out: volcanoes."

"Then why are you sitting on Oahu? The action is over here."

"Not those volcanoes, May. I've come to talk to the fellows at the University of Hawaii about a major study. That's what this call is about. It's strange, you know, how things sometimes seem to fall into place through what seems like a series of accidents. I happened to be talking to Fuller a couple of weeks ago, and he mentioned that you hadn't decided on a postdoctoral project. The very next night your name came up again in a different context—my wife was reading *Paris Match* . . ."

She groaned. "Actually," he said, "the position I'm about to try to talk you into taking is a volcanologist's dream, but like most dreams it has a nightmarish aspect. In this case it is the salary, which is an embarrassment. I won't say it is nonexistent, but almost. However, I thought perhaps you might be willing to consider . . . and if you decided, well, that you could afford to sign on . . . well, it would be an absolutely wonderful solution for us—a first-rate volcanologist to act as a kind of second in command on a U.N.-sponsored study. And I tell you, May—I believe, I expect it to be one of the most exciting scientific explorations to take place in this century. . . ."

Her future was settled in just five days. She would be a staff geologist supervising the field work on an international study of the volcanoes that rim the Pacific Ocean—called the Circumpacific Ring of Fire—aimed at accurately predicting eruptions. Heading the study would be Dr. Jorge Obregon-Mendonez of Guatemala, professor emeritus at Harvard, winner of the Penrose Prize for his work on tectonic plate theory and, so far as May was concerned, the finest possible choice for such a major study.

Most of the countries involved would be cooperating. Even the USSR had agreed to allow controlled access to the Kamchatka Peninsula, long off limits because of the number of military installations in that cold place so near the Aleutians. The U.S. and Canada, Mexico and Guatemala and most of the rest of the South American countries on the Pacific Coast would cooperate, New Zealand and the Philippines were in, along with Taiwan and Japan, New Guinea and Indonesia. Each country would provide men and equipment, with the U.S. Geological Survey doing the lion's share of the work, especially in some of the underdeveloped countries. Because of its central location in the Pacific, Hawaii would be headquarters for the project and a staff was already being assembled. Officially, May would be a staff geologist, but she would not need to concern herself with administrative procedures, Peter had assured her. She was to work directly with Dr. Obregon-Mendonez, who had accepted the position on the condition that he have an assistant to act as his eyes and ears. "Jorge," Rensaeller explained, "is too old to go into the field himself. Unfortunately, the budget for the project includes no provision for such an assistant—which explains the tight money situation. I can come up with . . ."

"You are right," she interrupted, "it does sound like a dream. But you said you were offering me the job. Wouldn't Dr. Obregon have to meet me first?"

"I did get a bit ahead of myself, you're right," he answered. "We had to advertise the position in some of the scientific journals, but no one who is qualified will work for what we could offer. I persuaded Fuller to send me some of your records, and took the liberty of giving Jorge a rundown on your qualifications. I talked to the good doctor today—he says you seem 'impressive' and that he would like to meet you. I have no . . ."

"Where and when?"

"Tomorrow at three in Honolulu. At the Ilikai. Can you be here?"

"If I have to swim."

She cradled Abigail's old telephone to her chest. It was right, she could feel it. Right time, right place, right work. Obregon-Mendonez. God. Moving on, moving out. She could almost feel the center shifting. She sat down in a rocking chair in the little parlor, lay her head back and looked up. A small stained glass decoration hanging in the window moved with the breeze and scattered patterns on the ceiling. She watched the flickering shadows move and bend, shimmering out and coming back again. Suddenly she felt as if she had made a deep dive in one of the lagoons and was rising now to the surface, coming up through the clear water turned aquamarine by shafts of sunlight. She felt the exhilaration she always felt when she was just about to break through to the surface, knowing she would feel the sun on her face again and fill her lungs with sweet air. "Thank God," she gasped, wrapping her arms close around her, "and *Paris Match.*" Then she began to laugh.

Five days later, when Clarence took her to the airport for her return flight to California, she told him, "In about six months I'm going to be needing some help in the field. I'm offering you the job right now, but you don't have to give me your decision until I come back—that should be in about a month. You can tell me then. No, wait," she said, seeing that his enthusiasm was about to spill over, "there are some conditions. First, you have to get your high school diploma and then you have to agree to take some special geology courses at the U while you're working with me. Otherwise, no go. Think about it, okay?"

He stood on the tarmac, his hands on his hips, until she got into the small plane at K'eahole. The pilot banked and turned, and as they came around she saw him standing there still, his face turned to the sky, and she wondered if he felt as if he were swimming upward, toward the light.

15

Karin insisted on meeting the plane, even though May had said she shouldn't, especially since it got in at such an ungodly early hour. May scanned the group at the gate and for an instant didn't recognize the blonde in the tailored slacks and matching silk shirt.

"Karin, my God, look at you," she said as they hugged. "Did Philip have to burn your Levi jacket to get it off you?"

"I still have it," Karin said, "to remind me who I really am."

"Actually," May told her, standing back to appraise her, "sleek suits you. Maybe your hippie phase is over, maybe this is the real you."

"I've so much to tell you I'm about to burst," Karin said as they made their way to the baggage claim, "but first I want to hear all about the new job."

"Is that why you got up at the crack of dawn to meet me?"

Karin's face clouded. "No," she admitted, hesitating, "I just didn't want you to go into the house alone. There's a small problem—no," she said, seeing the shadow of concern on May's face, "nothing life-threatening—Sam asked me to take care of it before you got home but I didn't. You'll see. But first tell me about—" She paused and concentrated to get it right: "—the Circumpacific Ring of Fire. I've never heard you so excited about anything."

May told her about her meeting with Dr. Obregon-Mendonez,

how the little man in the oversized black suit had held on to her hand, looked at her with eyes that sparkled with humor and asked, " 'Do you think you could tolerate a forgetful old man and his neurotic dog?' Turns out he has this old cocker spaniel he calls Esme who can't let him out of her sight. She actually starts to shake when she can't see him, refuses to eat, exhibits all the symptoms of acute paranoia— he convinced me! His daughter gave him the dog to keep him company and, he told me, 'The poor, dumb animal took it literally.' So the two are inseparable."

"How will it all work out practically—what will you be doing?"

"Headquarters will be in Hawaii—Obregon . . ."

"And Esme," Karin interrupted.

". . . and Esme," May added, "will be in Honolulu most of the time, but there will be close ties to HVO—the Hawaiian Volcano Observatory on the Big Island. I'll keep a small apartment in Honolulu, but I've already arranged for a house on the Big Island, a place roomy enough for visitors. Right now I'm not sure how much time I'll be able to spend in either place. I said I'd be back in three weeks."

"Three weeks," Karin interrupted, dismayed. "How can you possibly manage? You have to finish that research project you've been working on at Cal, and Kit said she needs at least a week of your time to get all sorts of business details worked out—and we have to put the house in order."

"I'm glad you said 'we'—because I'm going to need lots of help. They're already working out my visas for a first sweep of the South American countries involved, so I can meet the staff in each and get some notion of who they are and check out their qualifications. Obregon is worried that some brothers-in-law or nephews might show up on the roster—I'm supposed to nip nepotism in the bud, he says. Even after the program is in place, I'll be making regular trips to the field—and of course, whenever a volcano erupts I'll have to be on the first plane out."

"Sounds exciting."

"It is. I still can't believe my good luck. The timing was perfect—to be able to work with Dr. Obregon on a project that almost certainly will have a profound impact, far far into the future."

"Saving lives, you mean?"

"That is primary—and important, when you think of it over many years' time. HVO was started by a New England geologist who was horrified by the death toll of Saint Pierre on Martinique. He was there right after it blew in 1902 when the whole town was wiped out—twenty-eight thousand people. So prediction is the main thing, but it will also mean gathering all kinds of new information on how volcanoes work, deep down. By feeding it to computers we may be able to learn something about interactions. It's like moving into a whole new realm!"

"And you're going to be at the epicenter."

May laughed: "Exactly. Hanging on tight to Dr. Obregon's very large coattails."

"And Esme's."

"And Esme's, true."

They were on the freeway before May brought up the subject both had been avoiding. "What about Sam?"

Karin nibbled on a fingernail. "I only saw him for a few minutes before he left. He brought over the wedding pictures, which are wonderful—though I think he went a little overboard with pictures of you and Hayes looking pleased with each other. There must be half a dozen of those." She paused, shot May a glance. "But aside from the pictures, he gave me a lot of instructions on where to send the stuff he left in the cottage, in case you should be leaving the house before he comes back."

"When will that be?"

"He has no idea, but he was pretty sure he would be gone at least three months."

"How was he?" May asked.

"How was he?" Karin repeated, as if it were an exam question she couldn't quite grasp. "I don't know. Angry, I think, but that's nothing new. Mainly he was just very single-minded about going to Vietnam to do photos. He is certain it is his big break. Ambition seems to have crowded out most of Sam's other qualities—especially the ones I liked best."

"Maybe it wasn't ambition," May said carefully as Karin wound her way onto the Bay Bridge. She felt pit-of-the-stomach tired after the night flight, and the fog shrouding San Francisco Bay did not lighten her mood. "Maybe it had something to do with me."

Karin shot her a questioning glance.

May felt too tired to explain, but she knew she had to try. "I disappointed him. Turns out he wanted to be more than friends. It was bad enough, I guess, that I didn't feel that way about him. But

Hayes made it worse . . . you know how he feels about Hayes's family, all the resentments. God, it's all so complicated . . . Sam has been such a good friend, he made me understand things about myself that I hadn't understood before . . ."

"The Asian mystique," Karin said, more caustically than she had intended.

"Yes," May came back sharply, "if you want to call it that."

"I'm sorry, May, I really am, but I think Sam used it to take advantage. Also, did you notice that Sam's romantic interest in you seemed to develop at about the same time he learned that you and Hayes were getting together?"

Puzzled, May asked, "What are you saying?"

"I suppose I'm suggesting that just possibly, Sam is more interested in hurting the Diehl family than he is about getting romantic with you."

May frowned in disapproval. "Sam has been a good friend to both of us, K. I don't quite understand why you're so down on him, but let's not talk about it now. Tell me about Philip and the kids—how is marriage?"

University Avenue was filled now with morning commuters, and it was not until they turned onto Shattuck that Karin could manage an easy tone. "Marriage is great. It's such a luxury, no papers to write, no tables to wait on . . . I feel spoiled—I have this dream where a very large woman calls me into an office with only an enormous desk, and she tells me that it is all a mistake and I have to report for work at eight the next morning. Philip said he'd have a time clock installed in the front hall if it would make me feel better. Unfortunately, he said it in front of Dan, who refuses to recognize his father's humor."

"Bad scene?"

"Very bad. It's the only cloud on my horizon. Thea is wonderful and so is Dan, but he and Philip are not good together. I sometimes wonder how we are going to get through the summer. Right now Dan is doing a 'we shouldn't be in Vietnam if we aren't there to win' number. With anybody else Philip would be the very soul of patience and reason, but Dan gets to him. I try to mediate, and that seems to make Philip angry with me. I think it's just another way for Dan to hit out at his father, but part of it is this ex-marine instructor of his at school. Dan thinks the guy has all the right answers, and to make matters worse, he's even talking about joining the marines as soon as he is eighteen."

"What does Philip say?"

"Can't you guess?"

"Something like 'over my dead body'?"

"Something like." Karin sighed. "It's still almost two years away. Pray the war is over by then."

"Sometimes I wonder if this war will ever be over," May sighed. "It was just really getting under way when we came to Berkeley, remember? Five years ago—it's been raging all this time."

The fog swirled around them as they climbed into the hills. Karin shivered. "Sometimes it seems as if I can actually hear it—a kind of dull thunder that's always in the back of the mind."

Karin pulled up to the house, turned off the engine but made no move to get out of the car. "Before we go in," she said, "I need to prepare you for something." She began to bite a fingernail. May caught her hand and held it.

"Just tell me," she said.

"Sam's story is that he let some kids stay in the cottage while he was away, and that somehow they found the keys to the house and went inside. He said he didn't know if they threw a party or what, but when he came back, he said, the house was a mess and some damage had been done to the upstairs bathroom."

"Is anything missing?"

"Nothing," Karin answered. "Your topaz set was lying right out in the open, and a Cartier watch. Nothing was broken either, or even damaged. Sam said he cleaned up, except for the bathroom. He wanted me to have it painted before you got back. He said he figured we'd have to paint over all his pictures anyway before we left."

"Are you ready for this?" Karin said, and opened the door to the bathroom.

May stared: Scrawled on the ceiling, over the angel pictures of the two of them, spray-painted in large, ugly black letters was the word "Bitch." Slowly, May scanned the walls, defaced now with epithets: Whore. Cunt. Fuck. Obscenities repeated, round and round on the walls until they became a litany, choking out all the innocent pink and blue beauty of the birthday paintings.

May clapped her hand over her mouth to stifle a cry. Karin pulled her away, led her to the bedroom.

"I don't understand," May whispered.

"Neither do I," Karin said, holding her tightly by the shoulders.

"Why would someone who didn't even know us do that?"

"That's a very good question."

May wiped her eyes and looked at her. "You think Sam did it."

"I think that's a logical conclusion. I also think it's a little sick. What I've been trying to figure out is if he really wanted me to have it painted over before you got here, or if he knew I'd show it to you first."

May lay back on her bed, her arm flung over her eyes. "He wanted me to see it," she said.

It took four calls for Eli to find May at Kit's office.

"Eli," she said, happy to hear his voice, "I've been trying to reach you . . ."

"Listen hard, lady," he interrupted, his voice tight, "I can only talk a minute. Hayes has just taken some bad news, very bad. His brother Andy caught it—in Vietnam."

"Andy? Dead?"

"Stepped on a land mine, blown apart." His voice was urgent, he hadn't time to go easy. "Hayes called me about an hour ago and he's all broken up. Andy was a screw-up, but Hayes loved him right-eously. Listen to me May, now, I haven't got much time and I've got to make this very plain. Hayes's calling me means he wants some-body with him, but I can't go. Don't ask me why, just believe it. The only two people in the world he would tolerate right now are me and you. That means it's got to be you. Now. Right now."

"Eli," she broke in, "how can you be so sure?"

"I am sure," he whispered hard into the phone, in a way that made her think he would be shouting at her if he could, "Don't you think I want to be there? Damn it May, I'm not giving you any choice. He's at his folks' beach house over at Stinson. You got a pencil? I'll give you directions."

She left her car just outside the gate, as Eli had directed, and walked down the beach to the house at the end of the spit, the one with a Monterey pine bent by the wind so that it arched protectively over the roof. Fog blew in gusts so that the house seemed to appear and disappear. The rough dune grass pulled at her skirt and she sank into the sand up to her ankles as she made her way up the dune. She reached the top and could see into the house, through the wide windows that looked out to sea. There was no sign of Hayes.

She made her way around to the road. His car was there. What looked like an old temple bell had been hung near the front door. She pushed it cautiously. One low, hoarse note sounded. She pushed it harder. The sound echoed out, low and clear, until it was absorbed by the fog. She tried the door. It was open.

"Hayes," she called out from the entry. "Hayes, are you here?"

It was cold inside the house. The bright flowered covers on the furniture only made it seem colder.

"Hayes?"

"Here," she heard.

"Where?"

"Here."

He was standing in the doorway to a bedroom—she could see the rumpled bed behind him—wearing a down jacket, unshaven and weary.

"Eli told me." It was not what she had meant to say.

He only looked at her.

"It's cold in here. Could we build a fire?"

He looked at the fireplace as if it were a problem too large to solve, but she was already on her knees crumpling newspapers.

Smoke swirled into the room, stinging their eyes. "The damper," he said, moving in beside her to open it.

She coughed. "I'm sorry," she said, "Hayes, I'm so terribly sorry."

He nodded.

They walked on the beach. She held on to his arm, and told him about Eli's call, and asked if he could talk to her about Andy and he said no, no he couldn't, but that he wanted her to talk.

"What shall I talk about?" she asked. "What is it you want to hear?"

"Stories," he told her, "the sound of your voice . . . tell me some of your family secrets."

It was as if she had it all down on tape somewhere deep inside and she had been waiting for someone to hit the play button. She could even listen to herself—to her own voice, low and mesmerizing:

"You know about my father," she began, as they settled in front of the fireplace with half a bottle of Teacher's Scotch between them, "But let me tell you about my grandfather. You may not believe it, it is such a fantastical story. He was born in China—his mother was Chinese, his father British. His name was Wing Soong and he worked

215

as a gardener on the Malibu Ranch, which Kit's parents owned. My grandmother lived there too—she and Kit's mother were sisters. So, my father was the illegitimate son of a Chinese gardener and a spinster lady. Kit and he were born within weeks of each other, so they were reared as twins, and he was brought up as one of the Reade children. It suited the sisters perfectly, you see. Because Kit's mother wasn't very interested in being a mother and Lena, my grandmother, was. She raised all of the Reade children."

She paused, poured several fingers of the amber liquid into each of their glasses and settled back into the cushions she had placed in front of the fireplace.

"But it's my grandfather I wanted to tell you about, because he was extraordinary—and Kit feels it is still too dangerous for anyone to know, so I really am telling you a family secret."

He had been looking away and she wasn't sure he was listening so she touched his arm. He turned, and she continued. "My grandfather, Wing Soong, was a political activist—a follower of Sun Yat-sen. Grandfather had been organizing in southern California, actually training young Chinese for military roles, and when the revolution began—my father was a boy, about ten I think—my grandfather returned to China with a contingent of soldiers trained in southern California.

"You probably know your modern Chinese history better than I do—anyway, Grandfather was part of that group that eventually followed Mao Tse-tung and became the Chinese Communists. The story goes that my grandfather would have liked to find some middle ground, but there was none—Chiang Kai-shek represented everything he abhorred. So Grandfather made the Long March, and eventually he became quite a high functionary. He was close to Chou En-lai.

"After he left California, my grandmother saw him several times— always in secret. Once in Hawaii, again in Macao and, the last time, in Shanghai in 1929, just before Chiang started exterminating Communists. I've read my grandparents' letters—they are in the family archive." She stopped, took a small, precise sip of scotch and smiled. "If there is such a thing as a 'great' love, they had it. My father was with them in Shanghai—he was about twenty-five and already had a reputation as a radical. Wing Soong had spent a lot of time with Dad and Kit when they were young and both of them adored him. Dad was in his thirties before he learned that Wing Soong was his father. They hadn't told him because they wanted to protect him—Grandmother had witnessed the Communist witch hunts after World War One, and she was afraid for Dad. It's ironic, I suppose—the committee that investigated Daddy never did find out that his father was a top-ranking Chinese Communist, but they hounded him to death anyway. Am I talking too much?"

"No," Hayes said, "but you are making this up, aren't you?"

"I swear I'm not," she said, "truly."

He reached for her hand, she held tight to his and went on: "My father was in the China-Burma theater during the war, as a correspondent, working with General Stilwell's staff. With Stilwell's help, he managed finally to get into the far north of China—"

"Shensi Province," Hayes said.

"Right, Shensi near Yenan, where the Communists were encamped, to interview Mao and Chou, but mostly to see his father, to tell him . . ."

"That he knew?" Hayes asked.

"Yes, and that he was terrifically pleased and honored. The way Daddy described it to me, a group of war correspondents was finally allowed to go to Shensi, General Stilwell arranged it with the help of a couple of young U.S. foreign service officers who thought we should at least be willing to talk to the Chinese Communists. There were about ten of them, in all, in the group, and they had to fly over the Hump—the Himalayas. By the time he got there he was half frozen and almost deaf from the noise, so he kind of stumbled onto the tarmac. That was when he saw this very tall, very straight figure standing off to one side. The wind made his eyes water, he could hardly see but he said he knew. He just knew. So he used the figure as a guidepost, and headed straight for it, and when he got there it was Wing Soong. 'Just the same except in an old man's body,' Daddy said, with white hair instead of the black he remembered.

"My Dad said, 'Father.' "

"Wing Soong said, 'Son.' "

"They stood together on the tarmac for a long, long time, with their arms around each other, and suddenly my father was no longer cold, and he could hear perfectly and see clearly."

Hayes was looking at her.

"I'm sorry," she said, "I didn't mean to cry." She smeared the tears that were running down her face with the back of her hand. He took her wet hand, held it between both of his, then put his arm around her and pulled her to him. "I know you loved him," she whispered, her face pressed into his sweater so that she could feel his heart beating.

After a while Hayes said, "Go on . . . Wing Soong. What happened to him?"

"He died at a ripe old age—nearly ninety, I think, at the beginning of the Cultural Revolution. It was in the papers. *The New York Times* even ran a photo of him, with Chou and Mao in the 1930s. He was well over six feet tall, and he towered over them—though Chou was tall, too. The *Times* obituary mentioned nothing of Grandfather's California years, it only said that he was father of Tsiao Jie, a top party functionary. She is out of favor and is supposed to have been banished to the countryside near the Manchurian border."

"Did you know about him?"

"Her. She's my aunt. Grandfather's pet name for her was 'China Rose.' Her mother's name was Tsiao Min, she was a peasant girl who was on the Long March, and they were living in a cave when the baby was born, that would have been about 1935. Something went wrong—the baby was crippled, and the mother died not long after. Wing Soong raised the little girl, and then she took care of him in his old age. I don't know why she took her mother's name because she and her father were devoted to each other."

"Strange," Hayes said in a weary voice. "Neither of his children, or his grandchild, took his name."

May thought about it. "I suppose he thought it would be safer for her—sadly, it didn't seem to help her in the current troubles. Daddy met Rose when she was eleven, right after the war. She would be about thirty-five now. He said she was quite small and very plain, except for the eyes—which he described to me as 'great and dark and filled with sweetness.' He said she made it possible for him to leave, that he would have been heartsick going away from his father had not Rose been there to help them both. He always hoped to go back and spend time with her. And maybe he thought I would go, too. He did insist that my birth certificate carry the name Wing Mei-jin. He really wanted to believe that one day China and this country would come to some kind of a rapprochement."

Night had closed in, surrounding them; the only light in the room was from the fireplace, and it was burning low. Hayes rose, slowly, made his way to the kitchen and returned with a kerosene lamp. The bottle of scotch was empty.

"Should I get another?" he asked.

"This one didn't seem to help," she told him, so he threw another log on the fire and sat staring into the flames.

"Tell me about your mother," he said.

"My mother," she repeated, and sighed. "What I feel is that I have to find her, look at her face to face, confront her. I suppose you're thinking: 'Ah, she wants her mother to put her arms around her so she will not feel cold, so she can hear clearly and see clearly and feel wonderful.' I know it isn't going to be like that. That's not what I want. Sometimes I think I want to tell her off, to let all the anger I've felt all these years out, get rid of the bitterness. Like lancing a boil, I suppose. Wing Soong stayed with his son when he was young, and helped him and loved him, and when he left it was for a great cause. My grandmother understood that, and so did my father, who after all followed in his father's footsteps. But my mother simply left, walked away from a newborn baby, and all I can tell you is that I have to ask her why. To her face. And she has to look at me, I'm going to make her do that."

When she didn't speak for a time, Hayes prompted her with a single word: "How?"

She sighed. "Kit has been doing some digging for me. I think she must have a direct line into the CIA or else she has a connection with the Hong Kong tongs. She found out about China Rose being sent to the far north when no information was coming out of China. I do know that it was through Rose that Kit learned the name of the village where my mother was working as a doctor. Kit thinks that Grandfather may have seen my mother before he died, and she knows for sure that Rose visited her and, at least before these current troubles, kept touch with her. It's still hard for me to think about my mother as a living person. In a way, I've always thought of her as if she were dead."

The word reverberated through the room: It seemed to echo, to move up into the high ceilings and fly back at them . . . dead dead dead dead.

She chose her words carefully: "Can't you please talk to me now, can't you find some words to say about him?"

He shifted, took an envelope out of the pocket of his shirt, and handed it to her. "This came on Monday."

She looked at the return address: Cpl. A. L. Diehl. She opened the letter, held it close to the lamp and began to read in the flickering light. Andy wrote in a square, boyish scrawl:

Hey, Bro,

Prepare yourself for a miracle. A letter from the Brat. It may take awhile for me to finish it—in between mortar rounds and fire fights and all the shit that goes on out here—but I've got a lot to say, so let's get started.

I'm not going to bore you with the gory details of life in the trenches, putting up with a bunch of jerks from Kokomo, Indiana and places like that. Actually, the guy from Kokomo isn't a jerk, but he's about the only one who isn't. Where do they get these crackers? Forget I asked, I'll only get a lecture from you on how the U.S. Army scoops up all the poor dumb kids who couldn't figure out how to go to college or get braces on their teeth or fake heroin addiction to stay out of this shit-kicked war, and sends them over here to catch all the fucking fire the Cong are throwing in this direction.

Time out. Chow. At least that's what they said it was, but I won't tell you what it looked like to me. God, I keep thinking of Miyo's teriyaki. I can almost smell it.

I've been thinking a lot about all of that—I mean all of us, back home. What it was like. Mom and Pop and you and me at home. About all the shit all of you put up with, with me. My being such a screw-up, I mean. I'm not going soft in the center, or make any big apologies, all I really want to say is thanks. "That's okay Andy boy," you are supposed to say now, "you were worth it." Then you laugh a har-har laugh. Got it? Just kidding.

Kidding aside, I think a lot about things we've done together. At the beach summers, taking along a shovel so we could dig all those goddamned deep holes just for the hell of digging a hole you could stand up in. Have you noticed how people always need explanations? You're the only one I never had to explain to. You're also the only one who kept helping me climb out of the holes I dug myself into. Even that last night, even when you were mad as hell at me, you helped me out. I can't figure why. I think I wouldn't have done it, but what I wanted to tell you is that if I get out of this hell hole you won't have to do it again.

Don't think I've found God or anything. This place is more likely to make you believe in hell. Lots of fire, lots of stink and sweat and stupidity. Mainly stupidity for being here where we don't belong. But I have found someone who has turned this massive mistake of mine into a massive miracle.

Her name is Le Tien An. She is Vietnamese, and she is beautiful. And very, very intelligent. She was educated at the Sorbonne, she speaks five languages, her family is wealthy and what Mother would call "historically important." They do not think me a worthy choice for her, and they are right. But—this is the miracle—she does. I still can't believe it. I tried to tell her what a fuck-up I am, but she didn't understand. Or she understood but refused to believe it. And the strangest thing is, I don't feel like a fuck-up around her. She makes me feel like a whole person. A man. This must sound pretty weird. I mean, I'd proved that a long time ago, right? Wrong.

I know it now, and that is why I need to write this letter to you. To act like a man. Pop would call it being responsible, which has never been my long suit.

An is going to have my baby. I wanted to marry her before I left Saigon, but there were too many obstacles, some of them thrown up by her family. I've got everything arranged now, all I have to do is get back to Saigon, but just in case . . .

What I am saying is, if for some reason—if you were here now, you could hear some of the reasons whistling in—I don't get back, I want you to know about An and the baby. Somebody's got to know, to help them if they need it, and you are the only somebody I can count on. This fucking war has got to end one day, and when it does I want An and the baby in the States with me. Or without me, however it turns out.

So that's it, Bro. I hope I won't need your help, I hope we'll all be back at the beach together one day, digging holes with my kid. But if I do, I know I can count on you. And thanks for the memories.

Love.

Andy

She folded the letter carefully and slipped it back into the envelope. Hayes took it from her, his eyes down, and suddenly—she didn't know why—she caught his face in her hands and made him look at her. The hurt she saw there was so palpable she heard herself make a sad whimpering sound. He pulled her to him and they lay back on the pillows, exhausted.

When she woke the first time, she found he had spread a blanket over her and saw that he was sitting in a chair close by. It was full light the next time she woke, and he was gone. She lay there for a moment, listening. Water was running in the kitchen; she could smell coffee. Her mouth was sour from the scotch, her clothes smelled of wood fire and she had to go to the bathroom.

The sun was out. She could see patches of blue through the bathroom window. Too much had happened; she pushed it away from the surface of her mind. She wanted to clean it all out, to feel fresh again. That was when she noticed the water on the floor. Hayes had showered and a razor was out, so he had shaved as well. She looked around for a towel but there was none. She stripped off her clothes, turned on the shower and stepped in. She put her head under the water and let it course over her. She lathered herself with soap and rinsed it off, then lathered herself again. When she stepped out Hayes was standing in the doorway with a cup of coffee. He held it while she took her first sip, hot and warming, then he came back with a large towel which he wrapped around her. Tiny droplets of water fell from her hair onto his shirt. He began to dry her hair.

"I hate what happened," she said.

"I know," he answered, and pulled her to him as if he were holding on to all that was left.

They made love slowly. He touched her gently, and took comfort from the soft thrust of her hips, the smooth curve of her breasts. She lifted herself and moved onto him, pulling him into her so he could forget, thrusting in singing rhythms so he could touch the place that would give him succor . . . *succor, succor* . . . the word came singing into her mind as if from nowhere as she held him in her arms, and she breathed into his mouth as if to send the old ballad singing into his mind and heart:

> *"Curst be the heart that thought the thought,*
> *And curst the hand that fired the shot,*
> *When in my arms burd Helen dropt,*
> *And died to succor me!"*

He began to breath deeply. It was as if he had not been able to get enough air and now he could. She felt a great, wide swelling within her and then the softest silence, pure and empty of pain. He lay in her arms then and he cried. She listened to the sounds of the ocean breaking on the shore in counterpoint to the small, tender sobs wrenching out of him, and did not think at all.

They slept, and woke to make love again, and pulled the blankets up around them and she pretended the bed was their island, lost in time.

Late in the afternoon they walked down the beach to where her car was parked, and before she left he held her close. "Wing Mei-jin," he whispered, burying his face in her hair, but he did not say good-bye.

She drove straight to my cottage. "I need to curl up on the sun-porch and pull myself together," she told me with the smallest of quivers in her voice. "I feel," she said, "like a volcano when the microearthquakes begin to swarm, lots of seismic activity here," her hand cupped under her heart.

I gave her a cup of hot tea and convinced her to eat some scrambled eggs and biscuits spread with apple butter. She ate meticulously, as she had as a little girl on this old porch, then she allowed me to pull a comforter over her and within minutes she was sleeping soundly.

When you are old, routine is important. I turned on the evening news, careful to keep the sound low so it would not disturb May. I was fidgeting with the controls when I heard the disconnected words *. . . we interrupt for a news bulletin . . . three are known dead, and a superior court judge is being held hostage in a breakout attempt in progress at the Hall of Justice. . . . We switch to our reporter on the scene . . .*"

Lights flashed behind him as the man with the microphone spoke in hushed tones: "What we know at this point is that three black men armed with automatic weapons made their way into Judge Harrison Modar's courtroom at three this afternoon in an effort to free two Black Panthers scheduled for a hearing. One of the assailants was shot by a guard before a rain of fire left two guards and one of the Panthers dead. Two assailants and the surviving defendant took Judge Modar as hostage and attempted to escape in a black van. Police have the van surrounded at the north end of the parking lot, and are negotiating now for the release of Judge Modar."

I watched as one would a horror movie; I wanted to turn it off, but I could not. Instead I turned the sound down so low I had to strain to hear, not to waken May. At midnight, a reporter excitedly broke into a commentary to say there had been some gunfire, a flurry of activity, something had happened . . . Ten minutes later, a solemn-faced police captain made his way to a bank of microphones to read a hastily prepared statement: "At 1133 hours this evening, when it was determined that the three gunmen who were holding Judge Harrison P. Modar as hostage would not negotiate, a unit of the SFPD special services attempted to enter the van. In the ensuing firefight, Judge Modar was executed by the suspects, all three of the suspects were subsequently shot and killed."

Twenty minutes later the names of the gunmen were released. Eli was not one of them. Until I felt the surge of relief I did not know I had thought he might be.

At four o'clock in the morning the telephone rang. I reached for it, but May had already answered. I recognized Hayes's voice. Five minutes later May came into my bedroom, her clothes thrown on in haste, her hair not yet combed. "I've got to go, Auntie," she said, bending to kiss me.

"Wait," I tried to say, "there's something you don't know," but she was already gone.

16

The Golden Gate was shrouded in fog, all that was visible was the
yellow glow of the lights on the bridge. On the radio station she
was tuned to, Dylan was singing "Tambourine Man." She could
not handle Dylan's grating voice, not now, not this morning. She
pushed the button for the news station and came in mid-sentence:
". . . bloodbath in a San Francisco courtroom yesterday during a Black
Panther trial, Judge Harrison Modar was executed, his kidnappers
slain."

Her throat went dry.

Oh God. Eli's call, close to panic, begging her to go to Hayes because
he couldn't. Then Hayes's call, asking her to meet him at Ft. Point,
no questions. It could not be coincidence, there had to be a connection. She turned on the windshield wipers, hoping it would help her
see through the mist. She only vaguely remembered the turnoff to Ft.
Point. The Presidio, that must be it.

Hayes's car was parked near the breakwater. Her headlights caught
him, standing alongside the car, the collar of his windbreaker turned
up against the breaking spray as the waves washed high on the rocks.
She leaned to unlock the passenger door and he slid in beside her.

Neither spoke. She thought: Yesterday belonged to Andy, today is
Eli's. She wondered if their day would ever come.

He ran his hand through his damp hair and began, choosing his words carefully. "I'm going to ask you to do me a favor, but first I need a promise." She said nothing, so he continued, "I need a loan, and I need it today. I can't get to my own money for about five days. I'll give it back to you then. But here's the catch—I need ten thousand dollars in cash, and most important, I need you not to ask any questions."

"Eli," May said. "This has something to do with Eli."

He shook his head and took both her hands. "May, please. No questions, not one. I wouldn't be asking you for this kind of a favor if there were any other way. There isn't, but you have to do it my way."

"It's about Eli and the killings. Eli must need the money, he must be on the run. You wouldn't do this for anyone else."

"Stop, please . . . don't say anything more," he pleaded. "Forget what I've asked—go back to Faith's, please . . . just forget it."

"And you think that you can protect me, keep me from being involved, if all I know is that you asked for a loan."

He was shaking his head. "Listen to me," she said, her voice fierce, "just drop the charade. I want to help, I want to be in it with you. It's too late for me to turn back, even if I wanted to—which I don't. But I have to know what happened. Tell me."

In a voice drained of emotion, he told her what had happened in the courtroom and then he said, "The police are looking for Eli, they think he helped get the guns."

"Did he?"

"One was registered to him. It was part of the Panthers' cache of weapons. But Eli would never have provided it for that kind of purpose."

"He knew something was going on," May said. "I could tell by his voice, he sounded . . . desperate."

Hayes said, "I talked to him for a few minutes yesterday morning . . . I wanted him to know about Andy. He said he couldn't talk just then, he said he'd get back to me as soon as he could. Any other time I would have known by his voice that some very bad shit was coming down, maybe I could have . . . I don't know, Eli was always struggling . . ."

"How do you mean? What was he struggling against?"

"The Panthers have factions, just like any other political group. There are guys that want to shoot it out, the 'black cowboys,' Eli calls them. He's not one of them; if he knew about the shooting in advance, he would have tried to stop it. I know that, May."

"That was my next question. I can get the money as soon as the bank opens, and I'll give it to Eli gladly . . . as long as I know he tried to stop the killing. How do you know?"

"I know Eli."

She thought for a moment.

"Then why not try to get him to turn himself in? We'll get him the best defense in town. Faith is an old friend of Colin Riordan—he'd take the case if she asked him. His father represented my dad—the Riordans don't lose . . ."

"Eli is convinced he'll die if they take him in . . . he thinks the police . . . prison guards, someone on the inside will kill him. You know some Panther leaders have been gunned down in Chicago and Los Angeles. I won't ask him to turn himself in because I'm not sure he'd be safe—and I couldn't handle that . . . Eli's death, I mean."

She took his hand and lifted it to her lips. "We'll help him get out of the country, and we'll do it together."

"Jesus, May, I keep wondering where it will all end," he said, his voice breaking. "I didn't want to involve you," his hand caressed her hair, "but I'm not sure I can handle it without you, either."

She left the Jaguar in the Safeway parking lot in the Marina and they drove in Hayes's car to the phone booth near a Chevron station on Lombard Street. They were supposed to be there by seven; at ten minutes past, the phone rang.

"Can you get the money?" a voice asked.

"We can have it by eleven this morning, maybe eleven-thirty."

"In cash?"

"Yes. But we have to see him."

"No way."

"Then no money. Tell him. He'll agree."

"You and the lady he mentioned?"

"That's right."

"You wait. I'll call back in five, ten minutes."

They sipped hot coffee from paper cups and waited.

"You insist on going in with me?" Hayes asked for the third time. "Couldn't you just take my word?"

"Of course I could take your word, and I would. But I want to see Eli . . . I just want to see him, to make sure he's okay, and because it could be a long time . . ."

Hayes shifted his coffee from his right hand to his left, so he could caress her arm. His hand was warm from the coffee, his touch sent an electrical shower spraying through her stomach. "I care about him—for himself, and for what he is to you. It never occurred to me that I could be part of you without being connected to Eli."

"He's the only brother I have left."

"I know," she said as she watched a young woman in striped Ben Davis overalls approach the telephone booth.

May was out of the car before Hayes knew what was happening. "Oh, excuse me," she said to the woman, as if she were out of breath, "I wonder if I could ask if you would mind awfully using another phone . . . we're waiting for an important call from the East . . . our phone is out of order and my mother is ill, the hospital said . . ."

The woman's expression turned from annoyance to sympathy. "Sure," she said. "Sorry . . . hope it works out."

Hayes's look made her laugh. "See how well I adjust to the circumstance?" she asked.

"Your mother . . ." he said.

"Mothers always work," she answered. "People understand about mothers." She grinned, so he would know she was aware of the irony. At that moment the phone rang.

"Here's the drill," he told her as he turned on the ignition and the car roared to life, "we get the cash, put it in brown paper bags and pile some groceries on top. At eleven-fifteen we are supposed to be at a phone booth out by San Francisco State. Someone will be watching us, to make sure we aren't bringing the police. If they find out anybody is following us, the dude on the phone said we'd be in an unlucky situation."

"Unlucky?" she repeated.

"He meant dead," Hayes said, his voice tight. "I don't want you to go, May. I think we'd better call this whole thing off."

"Look," she told him, playing for time, "It's not even seven-thirty yet, we've got more than two hours before we can get anybody at the bank. I need to take a shower and clean up—I haven't even combed my hair—and maybe we can even get a little rest."

She sat on the bed in the motel room combing out her wet hair. "Who could possibly be on to us?" she asked. "It isn't all that generally known that you and Eli are close, is it?"

"He pretty much kept me separate from his Panther friends," Hayes admitted. "I'm on a lot of lists, I'm just not sure if I've been connected to Eli. It's hard to say how good the FBI really is. Sometimes I think they're inept. The Berkeley police would know about me and Eli, but I don't think the feds take them all that seriously."

"Did anyone except Eli know you were at the beach house?"

"No, my folks knew I took off by myself but I didn't tell them where I was going. They expect me back late this afternoon, to help plan a memorial service. The guy who is going to take over my apartment in Berkeley is there now, doing some painting. He knows about Andy, he'd tell them."

She looked at him. "When is the service?"

He pinched the bridge of his nose. "I don't know, next week some time I guess . . . it depends on what the folks want."

She waited awhile before saying, "I didn't know you were giving up your place."

He had been lying on the bed with his hands behind his head; now he sat up, his feet on the floor. "We both know our timing is off, May. A period of separation is inevitable. You had to take the position with Dr. Obregon . . . I agree it was the right thing to do, and you knew it too—you didn't even have to stop and think about it. And I know, I've known for a long time now, that I have to get away. At first I thought I'd go to Washington, see how things worked close up, see if there is any way in the world I can work from the inside." He laughed, a harsh laugh. "Blasphemy, I know. But I'm tired of trying to scale the city walls with toothpicks for grappling irons." He frowned. "Now, with all this—Andy, Eli—I think I have to get out of the country. I'm not sure where, just away."

"Europe?"

"Probably."

"Why not Asia?"

He looked at her, thinking. "I want to go to the other side of the earth right now," he said, "as far away from the Stars and Stripes and Vietnam as I can get."

Timidly, she asked, "Do you know for how long?"

"Do you?" he came back.

She shook her head and asked, "Will we be able to see each other?"

He answered: "I sure as hell hope so . . . you're the only sane thing in my life."

"So isn't it a little bit crazy . . ." she started to ask, but stopped herself.

She was going with him to see Eli, she gave him no choice. "They are expecting two of us," she argued. "If I don't show up they'll suspect something is wrong."

"I don't like it," he insisted. Before they left the motel, she wrapped her arms around him and kissed him with great tenderness, her lips soft on his, and she could feel him relent.

Hayes put in a carton of guacamole dip, some taco chips and topped the bags of cash with loaves of bread and cartons of eggs.

"Why guacamole?" she asked.

"Eli's favorite," he answered.

"Why eggs?" she wanted to know.

"When was the last time you grocery shopped?" he asked, and without waiting for an answer explained that bread and eggs always go on top so they don't get smashed.

They parked close enough to the pay phone to hear it ring. "I still can't believe it took you only twenty-five minutes to go into the bank and walk out with a shopping bag filled with cash."

May laughed. "The poor assistant manager—I'll have to call and apologize to him. He started to tell me that I would need to give them so many days advance notice for that kind of a withdrawal, and I just didn't have time to be polite."

"So how did you do it—how did you get the cash?"

"Kit showed me how."

"You talked to her this morning?" he said, alarmed.

"No, another time I wanted to get some cash fast—I forget now what it was for, but some assistant was balking and telling me I would have to come back, and Kit made one phone call. To the CEO. He had the money delivered to me, as I remember."

"Money talks."

"Most of the time I try to keep the volume turned down, but obviously I'm capable of blasting it out if I have to."

The ring sounded once, then again before they realized it was the phone.

Hayes jumped out of the car, grabbed the receiver so fast he almost dropped it and shouted "I'm here." Then he said, "yes," and "yes" again before hanging up. He made a few quick notes and returned to the car.

"We have to do a little aimless driving on the Great Highway, so they can be sure we aren't being followed. Then we go to a house in Daly City."

They drove in silence, May holding the bags of groceries on her lap. She could smell the corn chips, her stomach rumbled with hunger.

Hayes heard and said, "We'll eat when this is over."

It was a tidy little stucco house with a square of meticulously trimmed lawn in front, and a birdbath; only the birdbath distinguished it from all the other houses on the block. May followed Hayes up the red concrete walk and they stood—each holding one of the bags—on a doormat that said, "Welcome to our Happy Home."

Hayes rang the bell. They could hear chimes echoing within. No one came. May whispered, "Wrong house? This one seems preposterous." He pushed the bell again. A young woman with a plain, freckled, uncomplicated face opened the door. A child, about two, was clinging to her skirts. "C'mon in," she drawled in what might have been an Okie accent, and stood back so they could push by her, into the tiny house.

May glanced into the living room. A playpen took up most of the space. Beyond it, a young man with a thin blond beard watched television, the sound turned off. He did not look up at them.

"That way, down the hall," the woman gestured, and we walked ahead, aiming for the door she pointed to.

It opened and Eli filled the frame. *He is too big for this* went through her mind, *He is just too big.*

His presence seemed to fill the tiny house. Tears rushed to her eyes. Eli pulled them into the room and closed the door. He stood, shaking his head as if he couldn't stop. "What a sorry mess," he said. "Andy . . . now this." His voice cracked. Hayes grabbed him, hugged him hard and Eli reached to pull May into their embrace.

The shades had been drawn, casting the room in an eerie, filtered orange light. The bed was covered with a pale blue satin spread, and a homemade pillow, heart-shaped and elaborately ruffled, was perched against the headboard. May's eyes scanned the room. It was, she guessed, the master bedroom. There was a framed wedding photograph on the dresser: bride and groom in front of a church altar, parents on either side, all of them smiling. May couldn't tell if the

231

bride in the picture was the plain-faced girl who had opened the door for them; she couldn't remember what she looked like.

The room was too cramped to move about. They arranged themselves in a small circle, May sat on the bed, Hayes and Eli in straight-backed chairs, their knees touching.

"I couldn't stop it," Eli told them, "I tried, but I couldn't, and we all lost."

In a voice so low she had to strain to hear, Hayes said, "Why not an anonymous tip, a warning?"

Eli put his head in his hands. "Yeah—why not?" he answered, in an anguished voice.

May reached to put her hand on his shoulder. "Where will you go?" she asked.

Hayes broke in, "He can't tell you."

"I can't, babe," Eli said, "but I thank you for saving my black ass—even if I'm not sure it's worth saving."

"It's worth saving," Hayes told him.

May had to ask, "Will you be all right?"

"If they know what a basketball is where I'm going," Eli tried to joke, and stood to show it was time for them to leave. "Before you go," he said, "I want to say I think the two of you should be together, should hold on to what you've got. Can you do that?"

May looked at Hayes. "It's what I want," she said, as if taking a vow.

"It's what I want," Hayes repeated, solemnly.

Two nights later she was packing books at two in the morning when she heard the knock on the door. One long, then three short raps.

"I drove by about midnight and Karin's car was still here. I decided to try again . . . to see if by chance a light was on . . ."

His eyes were rimmed in red, he looked haggard and worn. "I know," she said, wrapping her arms around him, laying her cheek against his chest, "I wish I could be with you all of the time."

"The FBI questioned me today. I took a risk coming here, it would be bad if they connected the three of us and started investigating you . . . and found out about the cash withdrawal. God, I shouldn't have come May, but I had to see you again before you left . . . I couldn't sleep . . ."

"Come sleep with me," she said quietly, and she led him up the stairs.

They made love tenderly, touching each other with great care; slowly, to remember. He was breathing as a swimmer would breathe, evenly and deeply. She felt as if they were underwater, their bodies suspended in the wet warmth, gliding and turning easily, inter-twined. And then they burst to the surface in a great gasp, laughing at the enormity of it, their immersion in each other.

He slept, and she watched him, and then she watched both of them lying in a tangle of sheets, she watched from some point above, knowing that she would need this image in the months to come, this memory.

May sat in the back of the Stanford Memorial Church, giving herself over to the Bach prelude and fugue. The organ music swelled and waned, resonating into the high beamed ceilings of the great dark chapel, entering her bones. She had not told Hayes she would be there.

The family and friends of Andrew Diehl were in the front pews of the church; the rest were filled with students who had come to protest the war in Vietnam. It was clear they saw the memorial service as a platform from which to deliver a message against the war.

Marylee Diehl turned to look back at the students packed in the pews. Her face had been ravaged by sorrow; now, looking at the crowded chapel, the sorrow was complicated by confusion. Hayes sat next to her, put his arm around her. He was explaining, May thought.

Three students crowded in beside her, pushing her into the corner of the pew. "Jesus, this should be something," one of them, a young blond woman in overalls, said, as if she were looking forward to a theatrical performance. Several students in the pew ahead turned and smiled.

May's face burned with anger. She leaned across two students to tell her, "No, this is not going to be 'something'—this is going to be a memorial service for a man who died too soon. If you didn't know him, or if you didn't come here to offer some comfort to the family that mourns him, then you should either be quiet or leave."

The blond girl looked at her defiantly. May stared back, all of her pent-up anger focusing on this blond, blue-eyed girl. A fierce silence hung over the pew. Then May felt it, the sudden shift as the students next to her moved to give her more room—and as they moved, the music seemed to swell, as if J. S. Bach was scoring a victory.

Hayes came to the podium. He stood, looking out at the sea of faces, tall and elegant in his sorrow, and May had to bite her lip to keep from crying out. He waited until the noise died and the students decided to listen to him.

Into the profound silence that fell over the chapel, Hayes said simply, "My brother died in a war I did not believe in. But I believed in my brother.

"Most of you who have come here today, to this memorial service, did not know my brother, Andrew Diehl. Andy. Many of you think he was wrong to have volunteered for this war, some of you think he was the enemy and you have asked if you can come up here today and state your views. Our answer—my parents' and mine—is that you can, if you are willing first to allow us our memorial."

A loud rumbling made its way, in waves, through the audience. Several students, juggling books, rose and made their way out. Others squirmed uncomfortably. May looked at the blond girl and the others in her row, but they would not look back.

Hayes leaned into the microphone. As he began to speak the noise died down. "My brother Andy was a patriot," he began, and a small hissing sounded through the chapel. "That shouldn't be an ugly word, certainly not in Andy's case. His heroes were Washington and Jefferson and Adams. He read everything they wrote, and as much as he could find written about them. When we were kids and my mother insisted we choose a psalm to say as our prayers at night, Andy talked her into letting him substitute the Bill of Rights. He said it out loud, as he would a psalm. If I close my eyes, I can hear him repeating the words still. He believed them. And he believed that this country was somehow blessed because of the extraordinary men who set its course.

"Those of you who did know Andy know he tested the rules, and often enough he broke them. He wanted people to think he volunteered for Vietnam as a lark. He didn't. Andy was intensely loyal, to the people he loved on an individual basis, but also to his country. Even when he knew there was a good chance that his country was wrong. He went to Vietnam because he felt he could not exempt himself. He felt it was wrong to let poor black and poor white kids go off to face the horror alone. His conscience wouldn't allow it."

234

He squinted out into the audience, lowered his head and then raised it again, almost defiantly. "So my brother Andy went, while we stayed behind to fight the war on the homefront. But he died, and we didn't.

"Andy won't be coming back from Vietnam, but others will be. Some are back already, without their arms or legs, with memories we can't even begin to imagine. What I want to say today, right now, is that these men—and the memory of those who did not make it— must be treated with respect. They are not the enemy, they never were."

He stood for a minute, as if there was something else he wanted to say. The silence filled the great chapel, there was not so much as a cough, a shifting. He looked out over the heads of all those crowded into the pews, and for a moment May thought he was looking at her.

She realized, then, that he was looking at the group as a whole, waiting for someone to come forward, to speak out against what he had said. An uneasy silence lengthened, expanded. No one was coming; Hayes had won. Quickly then, he moved to his mother's side, and the service continued.

"Walk with me," he told May, and she fell in step beside him, moving along the leafy green pathways of Stanford in the late afternoon light.

"I don't like this place, I never did," he told her angrily.

She looked up at him, surprised.

He shook his head. "I guess I don't like any place about now. I'm leaving as soon as I can, May. I'm going to be on the run too."

She put her hand on his arm so that he would stop. "I'm leaving tomorrow," she said. "It's better if I go first, I think."

"It would help," he answered, pulling her to him and walking on, his arm tight around her waist.

17

———▱▭▭▭▱———

FMG: Notes, Reade family file, box 16

The Malibu

New Year's Day, 1971

It is six o'clock in the morning. Yesterday's warmth is trapped in the house but here on the verandah the air is summer morning cool. It will be a while yet before the sun lifts from behind the mountains; it is wondrously still now, the only sound is the birds flickering inside the trees, ruffling the leaves.

I am the only one awake in this big old house. The young people were up until three, welcoming in the New Year. I know the hour because I could hear their stifled laughter as they bumped against one another in the hallway on their way to bed. Their swimsuits are scattered like flags on the porch rail; I suppose they went for a moonlight swim. At dinner Kit was telling about some New Year's high jinks she remembered which ended with a swim in a cove where bootleggers used to put in.

With some effort, I have managed to wheel myself onto the verandah, pen and pad in hand. I had to be very quiet not to waken Israel, who is sleeping in the little study off the library. Israel does not approve of my solo flights. My head is full of thoughts I must not lose; I need to commit them to paper now, this morning, before they slip from me. I can no longer trust myself to remember.

This holiday was—for me, for all of us, I do believe—the myth come true. This Christmas on the old Reade family ranch was in the grand tradition, better than any I could ever have imagined. There it is. If that sounds maudlin, or more to the point, perhaps, if I seem to be regressing, so be it.

So much has transpired these past days, so many details that are part of the story. I must organize my thoughts so that I leave nothing out.

First, the background. Kit and May decided some months ago that we would all gather at the Malibu ranch this Christmas. Back in the 1950s, Kit restored the old family home which sits back into the mountains, in the middle of the four hundred acres that remain of the family property. She and Porter grew up in this house with its wide verandahs and dusty grounds filled with great trees, and I think Kit felt it would make a good retreat from the troubles that were plaguing Porter at the time.

Kit flew into action early in December. She had the house cleaned inside and out, all the upstairs guest rooms opened and aired and made ready. The caretakers—Josepha had grown up on the ranch with Kit and Porter, she and her husband Julio have lived here for thirty years—went out into the hills to gather the wild berries and fragrant boughs that had been part of the Christmas decorations in the old days.

Kit had wanted me to fly down with her but I convinced her to let me come in the van with Israel. I wanted to approach the Reade home slowly. It has figured so largely in the family history, and thus in my life these past decades. To be honest, I never thought I would get to see the old place, and there were times when I was not sure if I wanted to. I was afraid the reality might be disappointing.

I need not have worried. As we drove up the dusty road, the old house appeared at the end of a long avenue of trees, exactly as I had imagined it. A huge wreath of bright red dried peppers hung on the front door and inside, in the cool depths of the hall, the scent of pine mixed with the sharpness of eucalyptus from the great boughs decorating all the doorways. Josepha held the door open for us, all smiles. Israel pushed my chair over the threshold and we were in that other time. For a moment I forgot to breathe.

The next day Israel ferried between Los Angeles International and the ranch, bringing Kit and Karin and Thea in the first trip, then Emilie, Phinney and the twins. May has been in South America these past weeks and since she didn't know when she would be arriving, she rented a car and drove herself, getting in early on the morning of the 23rd.

Arrivals are so wonderful: laughter and hugs and excitement, together again with so much to say, everyone tripping over their own words, their own wonder. Emilie and I holding hands, tightly, watching all the others, knowing we would talk later, when we would have time alone. And then the plans: Kit herding everyone into the front parlor where a great tree was already in place, waiting to be decorated.

"Let me tell you a little bit about the few arrangements I have made," Kit said, "and then we can all do what Phinney tells us to do."

Cheers, catcalls from the twins, May and Karin. Thea, who had only just met my son-in-law, looked astonished. Phinney took her hand, held it high in the air. "Pay them no mind, sweet maiden," he said, with a Shakespearean flourish. "Thea is to be the angel in our Christmas pageant."

It was the first any of us had seen of May since September. She had covered the southeastern section of the Pacific rim; post cards arrived from Colombia and Peru and Chile. Now we gathered round her, rapt, to listen to her adventures. She was wearing white shorts and a T-shirt and—seated as she was in a white wicker chair with a bright yellow cover—I was amazed at how dark she had become. "The sun is closer in the mountains, not so much atmosphere to filter it. I really do pass for a native now," she laughed.

She told about hiring a small plane to circle the 20,000-foot Mt. Chimbarazo in the Colombian Andes, and—her hands lifted in a kind of supplication—described her first glimpse of El Misti in Peru, with a plume of white vapor trailing out of its perfect cone.

"Where are you going next?" Karin wanted to know.

"To the Philippines," May told her, "with a stopover in New Caledonia and the New Hebrides, then back to Hawaii. I'll wait till summer to swing north to the Aleutians. I want to hike into the Valley of Ten Thousand Smokes." The look on Amos's face made her add, "Want to come along, college man?"

"Don't tempt him," Emilie answered for him, "he's already talked us into flying lessons—I don't think I can manage that and have him dodge volcanoes too!" We all laughed, Emilie too, though I knew she did not find Amos's adventuresome spirit much of a laughing matter.

"What about northern California—doesn't the Ring of Fire come close to home?" Kit asked.

"It does," May answered, looping her leg easily over the chair arm, "in the Cascade range—you find the Vesuvian type of cones where the magma is viscous and the gases are trapped inside, so when one blows it really blows.

"But those were active in the late Tertiary time and became extinct in the Pleistocene ice age. Not much action there, I'm afraid. Right now, more is going on in South America and the Philippines—which have volcanoes in the solfataric stage."

"Speak English," Annie told her.

May nodded. "Right. It's the stage when gas is being emitted, and that's usually a signal that something is going on. You know," she winked at Annie, "all that rumbling and grumbling down deep in the bowels of it."

"Sounds like a bad Cole Porter tune," Annie offered, attempting sarcasm.

"It does sound as if it could be dangerous," I echoed Emilie's concern.

"For me? No, the chance of my being there when one blows without warning is infinitesimal. It's the people who live in the villages on the flanks of those mountains who run the risk. A lahar can be horrifying—that's an avalanche of liquid mud, a mix of hot volcanic debris that comes boiling down the mountainside at high speed—you can't outrun it, it buries everything in its path."

"Sounds simply wonderful," Annie deadpanned.

"Yes," May laughed at her, "terrifying, but in an awful way, almost wonderful."

Philip caught a flight from Minneapolis where he had delivered a paper, and arrived late in the afternoon on Christmas

Eve. Dinner that night was formal; dozens of candles lit the huge old dining room. There was enough of a chill to justify a fire in the fireplace, and it crackled and glittered, reflected in the mirror that hung over the sideboard. We gathered in the front parlor for sherry. Annie, who was finally coaxed into giving up her tattered jeans for a dress, announced that she felt as if she had walked into an Agatha Christie film and couldn't wait to see if the butler did it. I could feel Emilie flinch, but Philip set things right by riposting: "I would say Henry James. One of the BBC productions—maybe *The Golden Bowl.* You would make a splendid Maggie Verver, Annie."

"Oh no—Charlotte. Annie would have to be Charlotte," Kit chimed in, joining in the game.

"I agree," Phinney answered, raising his sherry glass as if for a toast, waiting for the rest of us to raise ours and only then pausing dramatically, "except . . . if I remember correctly . . . Charlotte was the one who did it."

Phinney's joke caught Karin unawares. Half choking, half laughing, she leaned against Philip, who patted her briskly on the back and then hugged her to him. For once, Annie had no comeback, I suspected because she hadn't a notion what they were talking about.

"It would serve her right," Emilie whispered to me a few minutes later, "if someone put a copy of *The Golden Bowl* in Annie's stocking."

The talk moved to other subjects, humming low. I listened to Kit tell Thea about some of the antique decorations on the tree . . . a plump old Father Christmas that her father had brought from Germany when he was a boy. And then the humming stopped, and a hard silence brought us to attention: May had appeared in the doorway, dressed in a yellow silk chong san, her dark hair loose about her shoulders.

Philip was the first to regain his composure. "May," he said, "you look absolutely stunning."

But it was Annie who blurted what we were all thinking: "You look absolutely Chinese!"

"That's the idea, Annie," May said, obviously pleased. "I thought this would be a good time to make my announcement. Henceforth, I am Wing Mei-jin." She paused and, sensing our confusion, added, ". . . known to her friends as just plain Mei. . . ."

At dinner she explained, eloquently, her decision to live, as she put it, "the Chinese part of her heritage."

"I've had the idea of it for a long time," she said, "but until recently, it seemed so theatrical, so forced . . . I had, after all, a wonderfully WASPish upbringing. Look at all of you," she laughed, charmingly, "—my family, for sure, and not a . . ."

"Slant eyes?" Amos offered, grinning wickedly.

May almost shouted: "Yes! Not a slant eyes in the group." When the laughter died down she went on, "Then, when I started traveling in countries which were not English-speaking I discovered that, somewhat regularly, I was thought to be Asian. And it was this easy acceptance that convinced me that it wouldn't necessarily be playacting to develop that identity, the one I know so little about. For the first time, it seemed as if I could step out as the me that is Wing Mei-jin . . . I hope this doesn't sound either too schizophrenic or hysterical. I would just like to learn to feel as comfortable with Wing Mei-jin as I do with May Reade, both of whom, by the way, are . . . is," everyone laughed at her confusion, ". . . extremely happy to be sitting here right now, in the embrace of the Reade family history, with all of you."

"A toast," Kit said, raising her glass, "to Wing Soong, grandfather of our Wing Mei-jin . . . he would have been so pleased, and so proud, of you tonight. As I am, as we all are."

"Here, here," Phinney and Philip echoed, and I would have joined them, had I been able to speak.

I have felt Wing Soong's presence in this house. There have been times, these last days, when the past has seemed to embrace the present.

After dinner Phinney led us in Christmas carols and Annie gave a wonderfully robust reading of "A Child's Christmas in Wales," Amos's choice. On Christmas morning Israel, looking especially hilarious in a makeshift red Santa suit, passed out gifts.

When it was all done and everyone had scattered, I stayed behind to collect the ribbons and fold some of the prettiest pieces of wrapping paper to use again, an old habit. Kit found me there, and I knew from the look on her face that she had something on her mind. For a while we rolled ribbon and folded paper in silence. Then she said, "May asked me once if I thought she could pass."

"Pass?"

"She meant, could she look Chinese enough to pass in China. I think she is planning to go in—secretly."

"To find her mother?"

Kit nodded. "And it troubles me terribly. I think she could probably manage to get a visa, eventually anyway. But she thinks it could put her aunt—Wing Soong's daughter Rose, in China—at risk. It is also true that if Rose is in disfavor, it would almost certainly mean that the visa would not be issued for her American niece. At least that's what my China contacts in Hong Kong tell me, and I can't discount their advice. I wish I knew what I could do."

"All you can do is tell May everything you know, give her your best counsel. She has to do this, Kit. You can't do it for her. That's the hardest lesson any mother has to learn."

It took her a moment to realize what I had said. Then her eyes filled. As she leaned over to hug me, the Christmas papers crinkled between us. "Thank you," she whispered in my ear.

Daniel Ward arrived late in the morning, having driven over from his school where he had chosen to spend the holidays. Karin told May that she had to plead with him to get him to come at all. By the time he arrived, Thea was thick with Annie and Amos. She tried very hard to bring Dan into the group, and I must say my grandchildren were cooperative, all of them urging Dan to join them for a hike into the hills. When he wouldn't, Thea stayed behind but those of us who witnessed the scene could tell she was torn. "Go ahead," Dan told her, "these are boring hills, but you can't expect Eastern dudes to know any better—you can still catch up to them." Emilie overheard, and so did Philip.

"Those 'Eastern dudes' could teach you more than a few things, boy," Philip snapped, "starting with manners."

After that Dan had nothing to say. It was easy enough to get lost in the crowd that day. About a dozen or so of Kit's relatives and a few old family friends drove out from Los Angeles for Christmas dinner. The day was warm and bright, there was rack of lamb as well as turkey, and French as well as California wines. It was an elegant meal, elegantly served on long tables set up on a wide expanse of lawn shaded by the great oak and pepper trees.

Israel went into Santa Monica to pick up Aunt Cadie, who is well into her nineties, and sharp as a tack. I have wanted to meet her forever. She was close to Kit's mother, and had such wonderful stories to tell about the ranch in the old days that I was quite absorbed for the best part of the afternoon. Thus, I missed the small scene that ended with Dan abruptly leaving, driving too fast down the lane, leaving a dust cloud and a very angry father in his wake.

Emilie described it to me later. "Philip was furious with the boy, I don't know why. I could tell that Karin was trying to work things out between them. I feel badly for her—I suppose because I know a little bit how Philip feels. Sometimes, when Annie is being obnoxious we get into it, and Phinney tries to be the peacemaker. Sometimes I am furious with him, it feels as if he is betraying me. It takes us a long time to work it out, but Phinney has helped me see that Annie has a right to be Annie. I hope Karin can do that for Philip and Dan."

These days between Christmas and New Year's have been sunny and warm. Emilie and I sat in the yard under the old pepper tree, our arms bare, and peeled apples for the pies as the others moved about us, small groups going this way and that.

One morning Kit and May, Phinney and the twins saddled up and went off for a long ride into the mountains. When they returned in the afternoon even Phinney, for once, was at a loss for words. Later that day Amos sought me out to tell me, in that quiet way of his so touched with awe, "Aunt Kit took us to the top of this ridge, to a place that looked out over all of. the Pacific—it was just . . . vast. And peaceful, and that was all there was: us, and the grasses blowing in the wind, and the ocean. I think I've never felt so . . ."—he frowned, groping for the right word, then shrugged and grinned—"large . . . and small, at the same time."

While this has been a joyous time, it has also been a time of revelations. Of glimpses, impressions, fast takes. Karin and Philip are too polite to each other. I know they quarreled when

Dan left, and they have not made up, though they do a good job of hiding it. It is times like these—watching a couple contend with the tensions between them, at the same time hiding it from the rest of us—that make me glad I didn't marry again. But I am wrong, of course. Dan needs Karin, and so does Thea. Pity the poor child who connects with neither parent, and praise God Emilie and I were good for each other. Yet I know, and it saddens me, that Emilie is not close to her daughter. I know Annie needs her dad.

Glimpses, impressions, fast takes, caught over these past few days from my perch on the verandah: May and Karin, carrying the long tables back into the house, one on either side. May stumbles, tumbles, swears. Karin moves to help her up, May takes the offered hand but gives her a hard tug and Karin goes sprawling too. The two lie flat on their backs on the grassy lawn, laughing.

Impressions: Philip and Phinney in the library, examining the volumes. Philip leaning against the big desk, slowing turning the pages of an old book; Phinney on a ladder, reading the titles out loud from the top shelves. Revelation! They are the same, these two, of an age, Eastern educations, a certain attachment to the New England tradition, to the classics. They have the same stance, move with the same certain stiffness of the joints. The difference is in execution: Philip is what Phinney might have become, or the other way around. Philip followed the marked path, doing what was expected of him: the ancient discipline, the distinguished career. Phinney rejected that course in favor of a hardware store and a community, of hearth and home and an active life as husband, father, friend. Roaming the woods, reading, discovering; Philip may have read *The Golden Bowl,* Phinney can quote long passages from it. Phinney's ambitions parted company with Philip's—when? The war had something to do with it, that is what Em thinks. Philip is trying to understand, I'm certain of it. He is watching Phinney; he pretends to read the book, but really he is watching Phinney.

Fast takes: Amos sitting on the barnyard fence, working to untie a knot. Thea standing nearby, her coltish young body swaying tentatively, ready to jump back, move away, skittish. She watches him. He does not discourage her.

In a few hours now this holiday will be over. I can hear

Josepha in the kitchen, rattling pans. Israel will be up soon to make the first trip to the airport. I wish I could hold them all here, together, but that of course is the impossible dream. Enough that I have had this time with them, this perfect Christmas.

18

She read the directions on the package: *Plant September-February, one inch deep and space eight inches apart in a sunny or part shade location. Blooms in spring, produces many double flowers up to five inches across.* Perfect, she thought, for the space along the edge of the back patio. She loved renunculus, their gaudy color, the layered petals that looked so much like crepe paper, but most of all she loved the long, elegant stem that seemed too fragile to hold the perfect big blossom.

She probed in the newly turned earth with her fingers and set the first bulb. She fell into the rhythm of planting, humming and probing and setting the bulbs, shifting slightly as she moved along the patio edge, aware of the sun on her back and the soft, warm sound of the breeze as it rattled the dry leaves of the sycamore tree. She would have to go in early to shower and clean her hands. They had tickets for the symphony tonight, she should probably start putting things away now, but she couldn't. The garden had become her favorite place. Philip teased her about it, but he was pleased, she knew, that she had become so absorbed in what he called "the flower art." She wondered if he understood that it was an escape of sorts, a place where she needn't think, where she could wear jeans and get dirt on her hands and sometimes her face, where she could feel more like the Karin she used to be.

"Karin," he called to her.

She sat back on her heels and turned to the door. "Time got away from me," she called back. "I've only a few more renunculus to plant."

"You're fine on time," he said, "I'm home early." He took off his jacket and hung it with precision on the back of a lawn chair, then he stretched out on the chaise, his hands behind his head.

"Hard day?" she asked.

"Not so much hard as disquieting," he answered. "Have you ever met Dr. Offenbach? He's an emeritus professor in the department, I suppose he must be in his mid-eighties."

She shook her head and continued her probing in the earth, setting the bulbs as she listened.

"No, I suppose you wouldn't have met him . . . since we haven't been to the kind of department functions he would still be invited to. He asked me today why we have been 'keeping ourselves aloof.' "

"And that bothers you?"

"No," he said, squinting and pinching the place between his eyes. "What bothers me is that here is this fine old man who has always been the soul of civility. Suit, immaculate white shirt, bow tie trademark. He was a fine scientist in his day. He's collected any number of awards over the years and he deserved them all. He has always been the sort of man you just naturally respect. Except that lately he's been turning up on campus wearing an aloha shirt with blazing purple orchids on it, and a head full of what he calls new ideas. He says he has had this surge of new energy, that he's just brimming over with projects—but it's all crackpot stuff. And he wants to talk about it—for hours, to anybody who will listen. And that's not even the worst of it—his wife died last year, and he's started to ask some of the secretaries to go out to lunch with him. His standard line seems to be, 'You have such beautiful, soulful eyes.' "

"He's fighting it," Karin said, taking comfort in the soft, damp earth on her fingertips.

"Fighting what?" Philip asked.

"Old age. Impotence. Time."

Philip sighed. "I guess. His mind is going, maybe he knows it . . . that would be frightening as hell. How do you know . . ." He stopped, pinched his eyes again, sighed. "I'm not sure how to handle this. It's so damned sad."

"Gently," Karen told him, rising and stretching. "You handle it very gently. As you said yourself, he's earned it."

Philip frowned.

"Another headache?" Karin asked, carefully.

He didn't answer, but lay his head back and closed his eyes.

"Let me get you some iced tea, then you can rest before the symphony."

"I forgot! The symphony . . ." he started to get up.

"Please Philip, don't get up. Maybe we should skip it this time," she added, hopefully. "I know the Brauns would love to take our tickets."

He shook his head, "No. The Reshauers are counting on us. Besides, they're playing two of the old war-horses tonight. Beethoven's Ninth, Schubert's Unfinished, you know me—I'm a sucker for those, no taste at all."

She tried to laugh. "That's you, no taste at all." Then, working to keep her voice even, added, "Dan is coming in tonight . . . it is his birthday, and it might be nice if we were here when he arrives."

"You've planned a party for him tomorrow, that's enough," Philip came back, too quickly, clipping off the words.

"I just thought . . ." she began, but stopped when he pressed his temples with the fingertips of both hands, a sign that his headache was getting worse.

She held her own hands out, palms down. "Just look at all the dirt under my fingernails," she said in a teasing tone of voice, meant to restore the mood. "Now that was a problem I never had before you came along."

"I'd say that hardly offsets the problem you inherited," Philip answered glumly.

She pulled her chair close to the chaise and would have taken his hand in hers, had hers not been caked with mud. "Philip, please . . . I wish I could make you understand that I don't consider Dan to be a problem. Not for me, anyway . . . it's the two of you who need . . ."

"I almost forgot," Philip interrupted brusquely, "there's a letter from May in my coat pocket. It was in the mailbox here—I guess you didn't check. Why don't you read it while I close my eyes for a few minutes? You can tell me all her news while we get ready for the concert."

Karin looked at him, bit her lip and nodded. She felt a weight shift on her chest, press in on her. She cupped one hand under her breast, as if to relieve some pressure, knowing even as she did it that the pressure was not physical. Gingerly, not to get mud from her hands on his coat, she lifted the letter from his pocket, tore it open and took note of the sudden rush of comfort she felt, seeing the familiar handwriting.

September 14, 1971

Dear K,

I'm on a Pan Am flight to Japan, the first real chance I've had to write in a thousand years. I didn't realize my postcard habit would make all of you so crazy—even Faith is after me to give her "more than twenty-six words and a picture of Mt. Fuji." And as you know, from my last 4 A.M. (your time) call from New Guinea, I'm not all that good about figuring out time differences. So here's your letter, parts of which I expect you to share with the others.

Under ordinary circumstances right now I would be working like mad on a sheaf of reports delivered to me a few minutes before takeoff, to be studied en route so I know exactly what I am coming into. But the Japanese are nothing if not organized. All their reports arrived in plenty of time, so I don't have to review them on the plane at the last minute. Not only that, but I'll be met by a car, my bath will have been drawn, my favorite mineral water will be waiting, nicely cooled, in my room. At the office a young man named Miko will answer my every question, and we will proceed to the field where I will find everything in perfect working order. If only I could transfer Miko to the Philippines, where I must put up with a second cousin of Imelda Marcos, who gives new dimensions to the word 'inept.'

Even so, the real problem in the Philippines is not this Marcos flunky, but the fact that there is nobody at all on the project who has taken charge. I've discovered an interesting thing, working with so many different groups in so many countries—when the work is being done at all well, you can almost always trace it to one person who has taken charge. And almost never is that person the number one man. Miko, in Japan, is in fact the assistant to the director. In New Guinea, a fifty-year-old woman clerk is the one who sets the tone, who knows where everything is, who keeps all the rest of the staff heading in the right direction. And of course she hides it all very well! My first job was to discover who these main movers were, and to spend as much time as possible with them without jeopardizing their positions. If only I didn't have to waste so much time with the "superiors." I am not cut out for diplomacy, and of course in most of these countries being a woman does not help one bit. You will be pleased to know that I am called "the Dragon Lady" in certain quarters (echoes of Mt. Holyoke!). Did you know that Asians, for the most part, have a profound disdain for mixed races? When I challenge them on anything, I can see it in their faces—which are not at all inscrutable. There have been a few indirect complaints issued through channels, and Dr. Obregon shoots them down, which only goes to show how little they know if they think he is running this program.

The good doctor is happy to sit in Honolulu with his old dog at his feet and a stack of reports to ignore. Not long ago he happened to mention he had never played backgammon, so I gave him a set. The directions say that you can learn the game in half an hour but it takes a lifetime to learn the strategy. Well, I'm content to stick to the fundamentals but Obregon, of course, immediately became enthralled with strategy. No matter the time of day or the urgency of the work, I must play a game with him before he will do anything. And the funny thing, of course, is that I just plop along, moving the stones with cheerful abandon while you can almost hear his mind grinding away. It doesn't seem to matter to him that I am not really *playing*—at least not the way he is playing. He says that my unpredictability adds a certain piquant challenge to the game. It is amazing to me that he is able to play so well, because he is faltering in other areas.

You remember I told you I was puzzled about why a man of his age would want to leave his country and start all over in Hawaii, alone? I think now that when his wife died a year ago, the rest of the family gathered around and became suffocating. They harass him. Every now and then he will ask me to call one or the other and say he's out of town, but wanted them to know he got one letter or the other and to do whatever they think best.

I'm rattling on, I know. No rhyme or reason to this letter, I suppose what's on top of my mind is just sort of oozing out. I do have some news.

Sam showed up in Honolulu last week. I'd had messages from him a couple of times when he was passing through, on his way to or from Vietnam, but always before I'd been away. This time he caught me in town, and we had dinner together before his plane left, back to the front again.

The whole thing was a little surreal. Not a word was said about the way we parted last time, there was no hint that anything at all had gone wrong. He introduced me as May Reade, not Wing Mei-jin as I had asked, and said I was his 'Berkeley roommate,' purposely, I thought, not bothering to explain what our relationship had been. I did not contradict him, I think because I am still so disturbed about the defacement of the bathroom.

Those slick press corps boys in their standard-issue bush jackets play a wonderful game of "men-at-war." I had a terrible urge to deflate them, but I didn't. Sam is full of himself, but at the same time, I think I have never seen him happier. He even looks different—he is more relaxed and that has given him a kind of style he didn't have before. I've always thought he was terrifically good looking, but the anger seemed to keep him from being genuinely handsome. Now the anger is gone, and he cuts a very glamorous, even dashing figure. *Sam Nakamura, combat photographer.* The girls stop and stare, and one even asked, "Are you somebody important?" I thought it was funny, Sam didn't. Took me a while to figure out that what he wanted to answer was yes.

You will be pleased to know that he paid me back much of what he owed me. I tell you this only because I know it bothered you. I told him it wasn't necessary, but he insisted—so I guess it was necessary for him, as of course it always has been for you. Money. What a nuisance. But of course without it I could never afford to be doing the work I am doing. I don't even like to think about that. I do love this job, even with all the headaches. The other day someone in the office asked me how I liked being the "pulse-taker of the Ring of Fire?" Sometimes when I'm roaming around one of the volcanoes, I actually feel that way!

At mention of headaches Karin glanced at Philip. His eyes were closed and he was breathing regularly. *Good,* she thought, *he needs the sleep.* She turned back to the letter.

Sam told me quite a few harrowing war stories. He has been at the front, and has won a press photographers' award for his picture of a young marine, holding his dead friend in his arms and sobbing.

This last trip home, Sam said, he went to see Hayes's parents and was surprised that Mrs. Diehl was drinking less, not more, which is what he clearly expected after the awful jolt of Andy's death. She has, Sam said, thrown her considerable energies into refugee work. I think Sam wanted to question me about Hayes, but he didn't—and I was glad.

He would know from the Diehls that Hayes is in Paris working on some esoteric research project for the OECD—the Organization for Economic Cooperation and Development. I told you that, didn't I? The idea for the organization, according to Hayes, is to stimulate the economies of developing nations, mainly by collecting information. He says he's not sure he's going to help anybody, but he's pretty certain he won't hurt anyone either.

I've had several long letters from him. In his last he told me he isn't reading anything written after 1900, and to get him in the proper frame of mind he doesn't listen to any music written after that time, either. He said he lives in a damp little room on the third floor of a gray building, he and Proust and Beethoven, and that he always feels slightly mildewed. I've suggested he come to Hawaii to dry out, and he says that he thinks after all that sunshine I may need a little damp chill in my life. I could never, ever think of Hayes as a damp chill. I wish I could take time to fly to Paris. I would if I could!

Still no luck on my China visa front, as Kit will have told you. She is doing everything in her power, and with Kit that's a prodigious lot. I know she thought Kissinger's secret trip to China to set up a meeting with Nixon might help, but so far no. Then again, Kit is so firmly viewed as in the Kennedy camp it is no wonder she has made little headway with the Nixon people. She abhors the man, actually. I figure if she can't manage it, no one can, but I can't get her to accept that. She's scared I will do something "rash" and she's made me promise to give her a year. In the meantime, I am taking lessons in Mandarin so I can speak without accent, and learning Cantonese at the same time. I hope that by the time I can get into China, I will be fluent in both dialects. Sam thinks it might be better to go in through Thailand. He knows of some who have done it, he says. There's supposed to be a network of people who can help you get in, for a price. I don't mind the price, but I do mind trusting somebody with my life in return for money.

I had a good chat with Kit last month. She thinks she has finally convinced Faith to come over for a long visit. Kit thinks Faith will give in just to give Israel a chance to get to Hawaii. He stopped over

at Hickam once, at the end of World War II, and remembers it being
'paradise on earth.' Of course he barely got off the base, so he hasn't
seen anything.

My house on the Big Island is all ready for guests. I've had it
decorated with rattan furniture and bright island colors. You can
practically walk off the lanai and into the ocean, and I know you are
going to love it. I'm enclosing a mimeographed sheet which shows
my travel schedule for the next four months. Talk to Philip and
arrange a trip for one of the times when I'm in. You can stay on as
long as you like, of course. But I do want at least to see you for a
couple of days. There's too much you can't say in a letter or on the
telephone at four in the morning.

Love to Philip and Thea and Dan. I hope all goes well on your home
front. Don't know when I'll be California way again. You're going to
have to come to me—but I promise, you'll love Hawaii. Tell Philip
I know exactly what he's thinking: no culture in the Islands. Tell him
he can do without for a week or so, and if he can't I'll introduce him
to Auntie Abigail Penwell who can provide him with background for
several books.

All my love,
Mei

Karin folded the letter, put it back into its envelope and sat for a
time, studying her sleeping husband. In repose, the age lines around
his eyes were evident, and the skin under his chin sagged. She did
not want to wake him, did not want to go into the house, did not
want to go to the symphony. She did not, even, want to tell him
about May's letter. It wasn't that she had anything to hide, in other
circumstances she would have read it aloud, stopping to fill in details
for him, adding her own comments. *In other circumstances:* that was it.
Dan would be arriving in a few hours, and they would be gone and
that is what hurt. She wanted to be there when he arrived, to wish
him a happy birthday, to sit down and talk to him . . . Most of all,
she wanted Philip to be able to sit down and talk to him. When she
was alone she tried to imagine how the conversation would go.

Philip would say, "Okay, son, it's time we talked." Or maybe, "It's
time you talked and I listened."

And Dan would answer, "Okay, Dad. If you really will listen . . ."

And Philip would say, "I really will."

It seemed so easy, when she thought about it. So easy and so obvious, and it was only when Philip and Dan were in the same room that she could see how impossible it was. What was worse was her own position. It would have been tolerable if she could agree with Philip, if she could take his side, if they could have presented a united front. That was Philip's phrase—"united front."

"Wake up, sleepy head," she whispered. He opened his eyes and for a moment she saw in them a kind of panic and she knew he didn't know where he was.

"What?" he said, then "Oh," as he lay back to catch his breath. "I was having the damndest dream . . . Professor Offenbach was sitting next to me at the symphony, they were playing the Schubert and he was lecturing me on one of his crackpot theories . . . mad as a hatter, but nobody else seemed to notice. They all thought he was brilliant."

"I thought you were sleeping sweetly."

"Thanks to old Offenbach, no."

"Actually," she teased, "I think he sounds charming. Especially the aloha shirt. I think I'll get you one. May's insisting we come to Hawaii."

"I would not," he said, pinching her nose playfully, "be caught dead in an aloha shirt. But I'll happily entertain the idea of a Hawaii vacation. I'm beginning to think I need one."

"The headaches?"

"Yes. Including the one named Daniel. We'd better get moving or we'll be late."

It was almost midnight when they returned from the symphony, but all the lights were on and hard rock was pounding out of the house and spilling over into the streets.

"Daniel's home," Philip said angrily.

"Let me handle it," Karin pleaded. "You're so tired, why don't you just go on to bed and I'll talk to Dan."

"You mean let you run interference?"

"I guess so. Why not, if that's what you both need?"

"That's not what I need from you," he said tersely, moving quickly into the house, his face tight with anger.

Thea had strung balloons over the dining table and made a carrot cake with "17" spelled out in orange butter-cream icing. It was a small party, only Marge and Hank Fromberg and one of their boys, Grover, a schoolmate of Thea's.

The argument started much the way they always did, innocuously. The Fromberg boy happened to say, "Seventeen—only one more year until the big one."

And someone else said, "What can you do at eighteen that you couldn't at seventeen except vote?"

And Dan responded, "Join the marines."

What Philip said next didn't matter, it was the slightly raised pitch of his voice that was meant to warn, loud and clear, *don't push it.*

Dan countered with an under-the-breath mutter, some unintelligible provoking comment.

And then Philip: "Could I speak to you in my study, Daniel? Will you excuse us please?"

And then: Voices raised, muffled shouting.

And then: Philip returning to the table to apologize, his face dangerously dark.

They stayed at the table, all interest in the dinner gone, the balloons and the cake mocking. The door slammed, Dan was gone. Karin wanted to get up, to run after him, but when she put her napkin on the table and started to rise Philip put his hand over hers to stop her.

She sat down again, angry. She thought he might have let it go, this once. It was the boy's birthday. He was seventeen, only seventeen. She could not look at Philip because she knew he would see how angry she was, and then he would feel betrayed. She looked at Thea instead. The child's head was bowed, and her long, straight hair fell forward to expose the naked curve of her neck. Karin felt her throat go dry with fear. She had never seen anything quite so desperately vulnerable, nothing so exposed and unprotected and so terribly, terribly young, as the sweet pink skin of her stepdaughter's neck.

He will want to make love tonight, Karin thought. It was a pattern. He would know she was angry, would know she blamed him and he would reach for her. *No,* she resolved, *not this time.*

19

January 5, 1972

*R*ain makes my old joints ache, it's true. And it has been raining for six days running, great galloping sheets of the stuff, pounding down. The gutters on this poor little house are running over, sending solid waterfalls over the windowpanes.

Kit calls me everyday to ask, "Had enough?" She wants me to go to Hawaii. Israel is less direct, but not much. "Eighty degrees and sunshiny in Honolulu," he announces every morning when he arrives, subtle as a water buffalo, "says so right here in the *San Francisco Chronicle.*"

How can I tell them that I am afraid of the effort it will take . . . a five-hour flight, all my stupid physical problems, the need to avoid dehydration. My plumbing is as faulty as this old house's. If only we could both get brand-new gutters! I cannot go five hours without a trip to the bathroom, and I simply cannot negotiate those tiny airline toilets, certainly not with everybody watching. I haven't had the courage to make this embarrassing admission to Kit, but I am running out of excuses.

I lead a paper existence these days, working on the archive, receiving and answering letters. Kit breezes in several times a week, and we have dinner together every Friday night. Karin pops in now and then, but mostly we talk on the phone. I seldom get over to Berkeley any more; I have given up my work at the Peace Coalition office. The reason I gave was my advancing age (I will be eighty this year) and physical complications. The real reason was a kind of beat-down disaffection with this tortuous war in Vietnam. It has been going on so long, so very many boys have been killed, are being killed, and yet our leaders in Washington keep trying to convince us with hollow words. "Peace is at hand," Kissinger tells us, or one of the generals says, "We can see a light at the end of the tunnel," not knowing the French invented the phrase before they were defeated by Uncle Ho.

The flickering black and white television presence of Nixon, his jowls all aquiver, telling us that Kissinger has been negotiating secretly with the North Vietnamese. They try to cajole us along; we are told "American troop strength is down to 140,000 men." That is 140,000 more than I can bear to think of, risking their young lives . . . for what? The war goes on, but now it seems the majority of students at Berkeley are turning their backs on it. The papers report a "new mood" on campus, and the volunteers for the Peace Coalition confirm it. There is a decline in student activism: Young people are returning to their studies, are more concerned with jobs and careers. Fraternity rushing has reappeared on campus. I suppose you can't blame the young people, their protests seem to have come to so little. All the "standstill cease-fires" that haven't worked, the peace talks in Paris that drone on and on, the "productive discussions" and troop withdrawals and partial bombing halts and "limited" invasions. Nothing works. Perhaps the students are as worn down by the futility of it as I am.

Only Karin seems to have taken a new, feverish interest in the day-to-day progress of what is often referred to as "that dirty little war." But Karin has a reason. She is panic-stricken that it will not be over before Dan reaches his eighteenth birthday and can join the Marines. Karin does not want to join the ranks of the parents of those "only 140,000" troops left in Vietnam.

This is not what I set out to write; I must get on with it, before Israel comes for our morning workout. I am now required to do certain exercises every day. For a while, a physical therapist came to the house to put me through the paces. She was an officious young woman, given to remarks like "Now can we do this?" and "Now let's just try this," as if I were some three-year-old who hadn't an adequate grasp of the English language. I called her Miss Waterson. She called me "Faith." What made matters worse was that Israel insisted on watching.

Bless him. After she had gone through her whole repertoire twice, he announced that, if I would like, he would be glad to take over as my physical therapist. Oh I liked all right. And it has worked out wonderfully well. Israel is as good a companion as one could want. If I knelt by the side of the bed to give thanks at night, as my dear mother used to do, I would say, "Thank you Lord for bringing me Israel."

And the Lord would probably answer, "Then how can you deny this good man a trip to Hawaii?"

I'm beginning to sound like Phinney, I suppose because I had a letter from my son-in-law yesterday. Annie is giving them a rousing run for their money. She is sampling life with a passion; everything, all at once, seems to be Annie's motto. For a time she lived with a young man in a commune in upstate New York, but now she has become part of a women's direct action group. Annie's style has always been confrontational.

Phinney writes that he corresponds with a boyhood friend who has reached a position of prominence in the Geological Survey. This friend, Phinney says, has been keeping a close eye on the new data being published by Obregon-Mendonez on the Ring of Fire, and he says it is "of major consequence" and "critically important." Best of all, says Phinney, most of the papers are coauthored by one "Wing Mei-jin." Phinney took particular delight in informing his old friend that "Mr. Mei-jin" was our May.

This has been a week rich in correspondence. I heard from May in Sumatra, and Hayes in Paris, and I cannot but wonder if their twains will ever meet.

I hear the van out front. That will be Israel. In a few minutes he will be stamping in on the porch, shaking the rain out of his coat, singing out that it is 80 and the sun is shining in Honolulu.

We are going to Hawaii. Kit has chartered a corporate jet because, she says, she has so much to take over for May's new house. Kit happened to leave behind a pamphlet describing this airplane to me; on page three it says, "enlarged bathroom facilities available on some craft." I suppose I knew that sooner or later she would catch on, but it seems such an extravagance. Still, I have to agree with Kit, the light in Israel's eyes when he learned we were going is worth it. He has discovered a store in the Haight that sells ancient aloha shirts, the silky prewar kind decorated with palm trees and hula dancers and moonlight on the water. He is also learning to play the ukulele.

We will arrive the day after May returns from a month-long swing through the Southern Hemisphere. She has been working nonstop, she told Kit. She said she is glad we are coming, because if she doesn't take some time off she is going to drop.

We are here, in Hawaii. Correction. Kit and I are in Hawaii, Israel says he has died and gone to Heaven. Walking barefoot in the sand, he is just as happy as a clam. The chartered plane took us directly to the Big Island of Hawaii, where May has her house.

House is not quite the right term. It is more like a compound. May bought a stretch of property that surrounds a little beach. She had to have a road bulldozed in, part of it through an old lava flow, so we are quite isolated here. The beach itself is fringed with palm trees. The main house is not at all elaborate, but it is roomy, and the sea breezes stir through it all day long, making the heat quite comfortable. The living room and all of the bedrooms open onto a long lanai, or verandah, which is only a few steps from the beach. A smaller house is crammed with all kinds of special telephone and radio equipment, so May can be in touch with her office in Honolulu as well as the Volcano Observatory on the other side of the island. A young couple—Danny and his wife, Kuulei, have living quarters next to this "communications center." Danny is a big, strong boy who serves as a caretaker-guard on the property while his wife is a housekeeper. The third structure—set back into a grove of trees—is Abigail Penwell's little house which May had moved from the other side of the island. "My fingers wouldn't work over there no more," Abigail explained to me, "too wet, too cold. Time to come home to the Kona coast where it's warm all the time."

Abigail Penwell has provided this tropical outpost with a lively life of its own. Abigail has raised thirteen children, only three of which are her own, and they in turn have multiplied so that on any given day, at least two or three grandchildren or cousins or nieces will come to visit. A series of pickup trucks makes its way over the rough-cut road. There is always someone ready to run an errand, pull a fish out of the ocean for supper, or spend an afternoon. There is much to be said for the Polynesian way of life.

Except that we have been here for two days and still no May. She is stuck in Honolulu, trying to resolve some problem. Every few hours she calls, and Danny comes over to the main house to relay the message. The last one was: "I'll be there for dinner. Tell Kuulei to light the fire at six and have mai tais ready."

But she didn't arrive at six. Her young assistant, Clarence, appeared with a box of groceries May had asked him to bring over from Oahu, and to tell us not to wait up for her. He is a sweet boy, Clarence. "May feels really bad," he told us, dutifully. "There's a problem with the professor," he started to explain, but then he must have changed his mind because he left it at that, only shaking his head.

My first glimpse of May was at breakfast, and I was shocked. She is thin, thinner than I have ever seen her. All skin and bones and smoking now, that is something new. Her skin has lost its lovely glow, even her hair seems lank. Worst of all she looks so tired, so absolutely worn out.

We had breakfast together, the three of us, and afterwards May insisted on taking us on a tour of the place, though we had seen everything the day before. When we got to Abigail's little house, she said to May, "Where you been? Keeping your aunties waiting, that's no good."

"I know, I know," May said in a low voice.

"We have been doing just fine," I put in.

"Sure," Abigail came back, "you do fine, but look at her. All those bones sticking out." She pulled May to her, and against her girth May looked almost emaciated. "I told the boys to make a hukelau tonight. Fatten you up."

"Good," May tried to laugh, "I promise to stuff myself."

"You always do," Abigail told her, and then to me, "You come back Faith, have tea with me this afternoon. Let these young ones play."

Kit laughed. "How wonderful to be called a young one."

"Young is up here," Abigail told her, putting her hand on her head. "Up here you are young."

That afternoon I made my way over the path to Abigail's.

"So here you come," she said, "and now you know."

"Know what?"

"Know about May. Know about her boss."

"All I know is that May looks terrible—she looks worn out. I don't know anything about Dr. Obregon-Mendonez except what May has told us—I got the feeling he was a charming old gentleman."

"Hah!" Abigail snorted, fanning me in long, slow arcs with a woven fan that had "Jesus Loves You" printed on it, "He's one crazy old buggah, that's what he is. And she's letting him work her to death. Calm down, don't let your heartbeat run away. Now you know."

"Now I know," I agreed, "everything but why."

For some reason, that made Abigail laugh. She is a large woman, and she has a large laugh. She stood, hands on hips, and gave herself over to some inner merriment that escaped me altogether. When finally she had finished she sat down in a rocking chair and fanned herself. "You find out why," she told me, "you'll know plenty."

"But I don't think we'll get a chance to meet him."

"He'll be here," Abigail said, "a couple of days, and he'll be coming. Wait and you'll see."

She was right. Three days later, Obregon—as May called him—arrived with his old dog. The great doctor was not at all as I had imagined him to be.

From the moment he set foot on the veranda, he dominated the conversation. He has something to say on every subject—and assumes you will hang on to his every word.

Oh, he was charming I suppose. And attentive—particularly to Kit. At first I was surprised at the blatancy of his name-dropping, but then I realized he was probing to see the extent of Kit's influence. It is clear that he has a lordly opinion of himself.

Israel said he thought he was suffering from a "great man" complex. Well, he is a great man, I suppose. Certainly he is highly regarded for the work he has done. Kit calls him a "celebrity scientist." Somehow I prefer great men with a touch of humility.

"I know, I know," May began when we sat down to lunch on the verandah after the doctor's departure, "the last time Peter Rensaeller came out, and saw what the situation was, he was pretty upset. He all but came out and told Obregon that he was taking advantage of me. What Peter said to me was, 'The old man's got what he wants—

the lion's share of the credit for a project that is getting worldwide attention, without doing any of the work.' But that's not really fair, you know. Sure, he's resting on his laurels—but without those laurels we would never have gotten funding for this project. Never. And he has a body of magnificent work behind him, he deserves the credit."

"He did include your name on the reports, that was generous of him," I put in. Something in May's expression made me add, "How did that come about?"

"Peter insisted," May answered, reluctantly. "I think he is afraid I won't continue unless I get some credit."

"Did Peter have any problems convincing him?" Kit wanted to know.

May wrinkled her nose. "It was a long session, and Peter came out looking pretty grim, but somehow he managed to do it."

"Good for Peter!" I blurted.

"It *is* good for me," May came back, reaching for a cigarette, "I figure this project should be good for another year, possibly two. But good for Obregon, too," she said, defensively. Seeing the skeptical looks on our faces, she added, "Really, he isn't as bad as he seems. There are times when he is actually quite dear, but those times are getting rarer, I admit. And the work is adding some luster to his reputation. In many ways I'm really quite lucky, that I could take on all that I have. I'm pretty much running the whole thing, and it is turning out well—in fact, we're causing quite a stir in the field. Asking for my name on the reports could be seen, in some quarters, as quite arrogant. But Peter is backing me—you're right, because he knows the inside story, that Obregon can't perform. When the work here is established and I can go on, I figure I should be able to pick my next project."

"But you're working too hard, May," Kit said, her voice filled with concern. "You've lost weight, you look as if you have been ill."

"I caught some strange bug in the New Hebrides a couple of weeks back . . . nonstop dysentery and fever for a few days. I took to my bed for a while: Unfortunately, that bed was a sleeping bag thrown in a bamboo hut in the high-grass of Tanna Island. Not a great climate for recuperating. But now that you are here, I'm going to take time out—the next five days at least. Sans the good professor, I hope. There are times when he wears me down."

"Okay," Kit said, standing and taking a tough-guy stance that reminded me of Lauren Bacall, "now that Obregon is gone, I give the orders around here. You sit right where you are, Miss May. From this moment on, for the next five days at least, you are going to do absolutely nothing but eat and sleep and talk a little in between. We are going to wait on you, and you are going to let us. That includes running interference with the good Doctor. By the time I leave I want to see some meat on those bones and the glow back in your cheeks. Agreed?"

May took Kit's hand and pressed it to her cheek. "Agreed."

We plan our day around May. We take our breakfast under a spreading kiawe tree on the far side of the house, so she is not awakened by our voices. Israel puts me through my paces then, and tries to coax me into the water because he has a theory that the exercises will work better there. Abigail joins us then. She is teaching me how to plait pandana leaves into little baskets. We visit for a while, until May comes out and we watch her eat. She accuses us of counting the bites she takes, and of frowning when she reaches for a cigarette.

Late in the morning May and Kit go in for a swim, and sometimes others appear to go with them. Today Clarence came with a pretty little girl named Noelani who looks to be scarcely older than Thea. She brought me a lei of ginger she had made herself, placed it around my neck, kissed me on both cheeks, and smiled so prettily that I could feel my eyes filling with tears, I was so touched.

I watched them all walk into the water together, diving into the surf as it pounded in, looking for all the world like brown little seals cavorting in the blue sea. Oh, it is glorious here. I can see—no, I can feel—why May loves it. In the afternoons we stretch out on the chaises on the lanai and listen to May's stories from her travels.

Clarence has been much on her mind. It became obvious yesterday, when she told us about an adventure they had shared in Chile a few weeks ago. "I'm worried that I've misjudged Clarence," she began, carefully. "I thought he wanted to learn about volcanoes, to probe and discover and answer as many of the unanswered questions as he could. But I'm beginning to believe that isn't what Clarence really wants."

She shifted on her chair, put her hand under her hip as if to cushion it, and you could almost see her mind shift. "I don't know what would have happened if he hadn't been with me in Chile. We were in the field, heading into the mountains near Rio Bueno . . . it was right after Allende had been elected, and there is a lot of opposition to him there. We heard that some guerrilla units had been operating in the area we were going into, so we hired some bodyguards. A couple of people from the Red Cross needed to go into the area to check out some problems in a village that was on the way, so we went flying Red Cross flags, and up till that point everything was fine. It was when Clarence, the guards and I set off alone—and the terrain got steeper and the underbrush thicker—that things started getting dicey. It was fairly clear that the trail had been used. There was fresh dung from the animals and the guards began to get a little nervous, you could see by the way they were acting. You have to remember how macho Latin men are . . . if they begin to think that you might think they are cowardly, they have to show you they aren't. One tried to show me that night. He crawled into my tent and put his hands over my mouth, so I wouldn't yell out. He was trying to squirm around, to get on top of me, when somebody started pulling him from behind. It was Clarence, and he was furious . . . I guess the man had his pants undone, because Clarence pulled them down to his ankles and the guy went into a kind of crouch, and came up with a knife. By then, I'd scrambled in my sleeping bag and found my gun. I held it to that man's head and I heard myself say, 'Drop that knife or I'll blow your fucking head off.' My mouth was so dry with fear that I don't know how I got it out, but I did. He dropped the knife, but God! I'll never forget his eyes. He would have cut Clarence's heart out on the spot if I hadn't a gun to his head."

"Good lord, May," Kit exclaimed for all of us. "What happened?"

"The three of them were gone before we knew what was happening . . . they took one of the Land Rovers. We could hear them for miles. We just sat looking at each other for a while, then Clarence said, 'I didn't know you had a gun.' "

" 'It isn't loaded,' I told him, reaching in my sleeping bag for the bullets. 'I was afraid it might go off accidentally.'

"He started laughing then, but he loaded the gun and then he took a Red Cross flag he had swiped and put it on a stick and we went on up the mountain, alone."

"And I take it you weren't bothered?"

"No, both of us had the feeling we were being watched, but nobody did anything. Maybe they saw what happened, I don't know. Luckily, we got what we needed and we won't have to go back for a long time. Maybe Allende will get things under control by then."

"He's a Marxist," I asked, "how long do you think Nixon is going to let him last?"

"I don't know," May said, thoughtfully. "He was elected, that should be worth something. And some of his social reforms are badly needed. But there is powerful opposition . . . South American governments are so volatile. I've never known who to trust . . . The bodyguards we hired were recommended by the American Embassy people—they said they were reliable. That should tell you something. Thank God for Clarence."

"But you really need more help, don't you?" Kit asked.

"I've got Peter Rensaeller working on it. He is so pleased with how the program is going that he's hustled up funding for a new assistant. He'll be here in a couple of weeks, a young man from Berkeley, as a matter of fact. He's dropped out of the program there—it was pretty obvious to most of us who knew him that he really didn't have what it takes, and I guess he's finally faced up to it. He's a very mild fellow. I know I can work with him. If only he can get along with Obregon, things should be just peachy—all pressures will be off, and I'll be able to cut back to about a sixty-hour week."

Another day May told us about Marie-Claire Benoist. "Her name began cropping up in Hayes's letters about three months ago," she said. *"Marie-Claire* took him to the opening of a new film, or *Marie-Claire* is off to Brittany, on location. She seems to have something to do with filmmaking and she is the sister of someone in his office. That's all I know about her."

"But you wonder?" Kit said quietly.

May shrugged.

"Why can't you take time out, fly to Paris, say hello?"

"Why can't he take time out, fly to Hawaii, say hello?" she came back, an edge of very real anger in her voice.

"Have you tried to meet in the middle?" Kit wanted to know.

"Twice. He was in Bangkok last month, but I got held up in Japan. Before that, I missed him in Hong Kong."

"What was he doing there?" Kit suddenly asked.

"I'm not sure," May answered. "He is being rather evasive, but I think it probably has something to do with the girl his brother left behind . . . and their child." She paused then. "Maybe *Marie-Claire* will be able to tell me more. She's coming to the islands to scout locations for a documentary film on Vietnam. Hayes says he has given her my number."

Two days before the end of our idyll, Kit got an urgent call. Her presence was needed in Los Angeles for an important vote on one of the boards she served on. They had booked her a seat on the first plane out of Kona. She would have to leave at once.

"I'll be back for you whenever you're ready," she told me as she quickly threw some clothes into a suitcase, "But I have to be honest," she added, "I hope you will stay through the winter, at least. I think it will be good for you, I know it will be good for May, and I can't imagine that Israel will complain."

"Do you really think May needs another geriatric?" I asked.

"You heard Auntie Abigail—age is all in the head," Kit answered, tapping mine playfully.

20

That winter I kept a Hawaii journal; I sometimes thought it was the only way to distinguish one day from the next, such was the even rhythm as the waves washed the beaches, depositing a steady necklace of puka shells and cowries along the tide line.

Such an easy life it is: the sea and the sand and the soft clacking sound the palm fronds make as they are riffled by the trade winds. Israel, wearing nought but a pair of rather long, red and white flowered shorts, busies himself with projects. He is building a series of latticework trellises, and the bougainvillaea is already clamoring up. The colors are luminescent—bright red and purple and a delicious peach color, all of which are incandescent against the lava rock.

Abigail and I spend part of each day together. She is a marvelous storyteller. This island is filled with legends, and I believe she knows them all. The other afternoon I got my camera out and began to photograph her. She is at ease with the camera, it does not bother her one bit, which is unusual in one of her age. (Her age—our age! We are often so vain.) For the first time in a long time, I can hardly wait to get my film developed to see what I got on her. If it is as good as I think it is, that is, if I did the job I should have done, I think I will attempt a whole series and call it "The Hawaiians."

They come in so many different colors, the island people who have been here for generations. The other day Abigail introduced me to a blond, blue-eyed woman who traces her Hawaiian ancestry back to the time of Kamehameha, the king who ruled at about the same time that George Washington was rowing around on the Delaware. This woman explained to me that her great-great grandmother was a "Molokai lady" who had married "the Frenchman." She explained her pale coloring this way: "My family always seemed to marry the light-skinned Europeans." Her husband, a delightful man who works for one of the sugar companies, is quite dark, even though his "great-grandfather was a sailing man out of Gloucester, Massachusetts." Somehow, when I talk to Abigail and her friends, the past in this place seems so much more a part of the present than it does in our part of the country. Perhaps that is because a great many Californians came west because they wanted to leave all that behind. Most Hawaiians, at least those I have met, seem happy with their islands and have no wish ever to leave. We have had such fun, May and I, talking about what Phinney's reaction to this place will be. We will have a chance to find out early this summer, when the family is to gather here to celebrate my 80th year on this planet.

It is three weeks now since Kit left. May has been over every weekend. Dr. Obregon came once, just after the new assistant arrived. I think he was worried that May and Tim might be ganging up on him, and he wasn't going to let them out of his sight. His worries must have been quickly quelled; Tim is the mildest young man I think I've ever met, terribly anxious to please. He is skinny and slope-shouldered and wears his head at a peculiar angle, as if he is always considering something ponderous. He treats Obregon with the kind of respect the doctor clearly expects and needs. May says Tim is the sort of young man who takes direction much better than he is able to give it. All of which is to the good. May is not only relaxing, but filling out a bit on a steady diet of coconut milkshakes.

Karin and Philip and Thea came for the long presidents' weekend, and Karin has stayed on for a few days. May and Karin are at the beach this very moment, I watch them from the lanai. They are sitting at the edge of the water, where the waves can wash up on them, their heads are bent together, the dark and the light, and they talk. Words pour out of them, spilling over and lapping about each other, like some soothing balm. You can almost see them take strength from it. May seems softer, the tension is gone, she is more supple. And Karin, with her old friend at the edge of the ocean, seems quite different from the stylish young woman who arrived in a white linen suit, blue silk shirt with her hair pulled back into a sleek bun.

They spend their days in the briefest of bikinis, May's body long and sleek, Karin's soft and voluptuous—each wrapping a pareau around when they come in for lunch or dinner. I have never been much interested in photographing the female body until now, watching these two, but could I do it? Could I show, would I be able to capture on film, the love that exists between them, between women, that is not sexual but is sensual . . . full of trust and understanding? I think of my life's great friendships, most of them with women, and wonder why it is so hard to define the kind of exquisite intimacy that does not require sex. And wonder why my Annie, and her generation, in the name of women's liberation feel it necessary to tell us that all touching is sexual, and that denying it only reinforces our inhibitions. I know it is not true. I watch Karin and May, their heads close together and their words pouring gently over each other, and I am reassured.

And I see too that they are no longer girls, but women. We celebrated May's twenty-ninth birthday while Philip and Thea were here, with a luau on the beach. Clarence's father, Kimo, came early in the morning to make the imu, or pit, for the kalua pig. This is man's work, I am told, fathers and uncles and nephews and sons dig the imu and line it with stones, all the while drinking quantities of beer. A fire of kiawe wood is set, and after several hours, red hot stones are pulled from the imu and placed inside the pig, which has been gutted, dressed and salted. Ti leaves and banana stumps are piled on top of the fire and the pig, wrapped in chicken wire, is put on top of the moistened bed of greens and topped with more greens, wet burlap bags and a canvas that covers the whole thing. Dirt is thrown on top of the canvas, and the pig is left to cook all day long. Israel loves the ritual of it. He could hardly wait to get in there and lay the ti leaves and help put the hot stones into the yawning empty pig's cavity. Kimo, clearly the man in charge, says he thinks Israel must have been Hawaiian in an earlier life.

Clarence and his brothers played music at the luau, and some of the little girls danced the hulas they learn at school, and then some of the older women got up and danced. It is such lovely, graceful dancing—there is nothing in the least torrid about the Hawaiian hula.

271

It is, in fact, almost chaste, the hint of a body swaying inside the long muumuus, the arms and the hands telling the story so elegantly.

Abigail sat next to me at the luau, and I began to notice the younger women coming to her, one by one. Sometimes they would whisper a few words, more often they would only look at her expectantly. In her own good time she stood, and everyone seemed to be waiting for the moment.

She moved into the music slowly, beginning with a languid, swaying motion, her hands raised, fingers poised; and then her whole body seemed to merge with the music and the sea sounds and we sat, transfixed. If there is such a thing as timeless beauty, infinite grace, we were witnessing it. When she finished, the little girls gathered around her and she caressed them, and that too was part of the dance.

After a while, nothing would do but that May and Karin and Thea should dance. Thea needed coaxing, but in the end she did get up and her years of ballet lessons gave her a graceful presence. She is fifteen now, and not yet fully formed. There is still a long, lean child-look about her. Philip was sitting next to me through all of this, and enjoying it immensely. Thea has settled on the grass between her father and Karin, leaning, in turn, between them. And Karin and Philip exchange fond glances; I heard her say to him, "I knew you were going to love it."

March 18. Early each Monday morning May takes the short flight over to Honolulu where she stays during the week. She works until seven, sometimes eight, but last Thursday she returned early to the apartment she keeps on Beretania Street, to be there when Marie-Claire arrived.

May had rented the furnished apartment sight unseen, from a realtor who assured her she would absolutely adore it, that the last tenant had been an interior designer who had decorated it to perfection. She did not need perfection, May told the woman, all she needed was a comfortable place close to the office and convenient to the airport.

The rugs and the walls and most of the furniture are white: thick white carpeting everywhere, white linen walls, white silk sofas, fluffy white bedspreads and towels and draperies. Here and there are splashes of color: fuchsia and turquoise and coral, in silkscreened prints on the walls and pillows scattered about. Against the wall of glass that looks out over the city is a virtual forest of plants, many tall enough to touch the ceiling. All very chic, May supposed, but she felt as if she were staying in a hotel.

There is nothing in my Hawaii journal about May's meeting with Marie-Claire; it was a long time afterwards that May told me what happened.

She unpacked the groceries she had brought back to the apartment: eggs, a loaf of bread, orange juice, coffee. The refrigerator was bare. She emptied the remains of a quart of milk that had been there long enough to have soured, and wiped the sink clean. She checked the cupboards: instant coffee, cereal and a can of curry powder. She could not remember why she had bought the curry powder; she did not think she had ever actually cooked a meal in this place.

She filled a glass with ice, poured some orange juice over it and went into the living room. The carpet had been vacuumed that day, and her bare feet left prints. She caught a glimpse of herself in a mirrored wall: Sweet Jesus, she thought, me in a white dress in this great blinking white palace. She went into the bedroom, rummaged through the closet until she found a loose, olive-drab jumpsuit, climbed into it and felt better. She was tying the belt when the doorbell rang.

The voice on the intercom caused her to reach for a cigarette: "Is it Mei there?" the voice said. "I am Marie-Claire, Hayes's friend." Lilting French, very feminine. Damn, May thought, swallowing a sudden surge of anger, what the hell does Hayes think he's doing? She put the cold glass against her forehead, and told herself that it didn't matter, that she didn't care, as she pressed hard against the buzzer.

"How beautiful," the girl said, her eyes moving slowly about the apartment, "it is very modern, very splendid. Are you doing this yourself, the decorating?" She was small, precise, and very pretty. Dark curly hair, cropped short; a heart-shaped face, intelligent eyes. She was dressed simply, in cotton slacks and a tailored shirt, but she wore them with style. May noticed a small, antique locket that hung on a gold chain around Marie-Claire's neck, and wondered, unreasonably, if Hayes had given it to her. Suddenly she felt awkward in her rumpled overalls.

When they had settled on the balcony overlooking the city, May realized that she had meant to greet her guest in French. Now she knew she would not, that she would be safer in English. It was

Marie-Claire who brought up Hayes. "He has told me so much about you," she said in her soft, French accent. "I know you are great friends."

"Oh, well," was all May could bring herself to say. She did not want to talk about Hayes to this woman. She turned the subject away with, "But he didn't tell me much about what you are doing here—something to do with a documentary film?"

Marie-Claire nodded, took a small sip of juice, and explained, "I am doing advance work for a film on the Vietnam War. It is to be historical, going to the early French colonial history and through Dien Bien Phu, where we were defeated, you know. There will be many film clips from archives. They do that work now in Paris. We have a film crew in Vietnam, and I am here to see about two episodes: The young servicemen who are sent here on what is called R and R—rest and recreation—and where they meet with their families, before going back to the fighting. And a burial in the military cemetery here, the Punchbowl, I believe it is called."

"How did you happen to get involved with this particular film?" May asked, to keep the subject away from Hayes.

"You are like Hayes." Marie-Claire laughed. "Always asking the questions, keeping the other talking. I should like to know about you—I know you do fascinating work with the volcanoes, that much Hayes has told me."

That much Hayes has told me. So he didn't talk about her, she doesn't know. Her spirits lifted.

"I do," May answered, smiling back, "but right now it seems to me that since your time is limited, we'd better get down to business and make sure you get what you need. How can I help?"

That night they went to a military party on the beach at Fort DeRussy, arranged for servicemen and their families. The entertainment was pure tourist flash—Tahitian women dancers with their wildly swinging hips, and male fire dancers, all laced with erotic innuendo, and the audience cheered and whistled and wanted more. At the luau, May found herself next to a pale young girl from Tennessee who laughed too loudly and jarred the tiny baby sleeping in her arms. "He's seeing his daddy for the first time," the girl confided, and May smiled as she watched the big-boned boy put his finger in the baby's mouth for it to suck. Marie-Claire moved among the youngest of the servicemen and the women who had traveled here to meet them, wives and girlfriends, occasionally a mother or sister. May watched her smile and draw them out, then listen as if what they had to say was of tremendous importance. She wrote their names and made notes in a black leather notebook, and when she was finished she thanked them as if they had done her a great honor. She is charming, May thought. And bright, and she is in love with Hayes. About that, she was certain.

The next day May drove Marie-Claire to the National Memorial Cemetery of the Pacific and stood on the sloping sides of the crater of the ancient, long-extinct volcano, which now was the sacred repository of the bones of men killed in the world's wars. A long sweep of markers marched in painful symmetry down in the low, scooping bowl as dark sea birds turned and glided above, sliding in unison high on the wind. At the hour before noon, only a few living beings shared this place with the thousands of dead. A middle-aged couple stood, arms around each other, while a casket was lowered into the newly opened, red earth.

May and the French woman watched from a decent distance. A warm wind tore at them, blew their skirts hard against their legs and sent May's long hair blowing and tangling about her face.

May heard it, and did not know, at first, what it was. A soughing in the winds, she thought, and then she realized Marie-Claire was sobbing. She had her hand over her mouth, she was crying and she couldn't stop.

May led her to the car. They sat there, surrounded by the graves of soldiers, while Marie-Claire worked to regain control. She took a deep breath. "I am so sorry," she finally said, "it is so foolish of me. It has all been so long ago . . ."

"You don't have to explain," May told her, but she said that yes, she did. Her father had died at Dien Bien Phu. On March 15, 1954, the day after a major battle. He had been a colonel of artillery. It had been his responsibility to position the bases which would guard the garrison. When these were overrun by the advancing army of the Vietminh, he had pulled the pin out of a grenade and killed himself. "He said he was dishonored," Marie-Claire explained, wiping her nose. "You know how the French are about honor. The fact is, I suspect, that he thought himself to be invincible, and discovered he was not, and could not live with the shame of it."

"How old were you?" May asked.

"Seven. I scarcely knew him, he was gone so much of the time. I have only vague memories. That is why it is so stupid that I should break down like this. And quite unexpected! I think perhaps it was last night, those couples, so young. The little wives with their tiny babies, so sweet and simple and sad. It is such a terrible war, this one. That boy over there in the grave, that mother . . ." The couple was moving away from the grave now, their bodies bent in attitudes of grief.

Her chagrin was so genuine that May reached to touch her arm. "I was thirteen when my father died," she heard herself say. "I can still touch a place where it hurts." She put her hand under her breast and held it there.

Marie-Claire smiled through lashes tangled with tears, and May saw in her eyes the intimacy she had been trying to avoid.

"Hayes does not speak of himself, you see," she began, as if they had been talking about him, "I thought perhaps you could tell me . . . there is so much I want to know. How do you know him? He has never said if you . . ."

May caught herself; she had been thrown off guard, she struggled to regain control. She knew exactly what she was being asked, and was determined not to answer. "We were friends at the university," she began carefully, starting the motor and edging the car down the narrow road, "at Berkeley. I don't remember exactly how we met . . ." She felt Marie-Claire was about to interrupt, so she hurried on, "Oh yes I do, now. It was through Sam Nakamura—has Hayes ever mentioned Sam? No? Well, he and Sam had gone to high school together. Sam's in Vietnam now, as a combat photographer. Hayes hasn't mentioned him at all?"

Marie-Claire shook her head. "Hayes always makes a joke when I try to get him to talk about himself. He can be very amusing—that you know, of course. But very exasperating, too."

"Yes," May laughed, feeling suddenly light, elated. She knows nothing, she thought, Hayes has told her nothing about me, about us, about anything.

"I tell him he knows everything about me," Marie-Claire said, as if reading her mind, "while I know nothing about him, and I do not understand how he can expect us to go on in this unequal way, I tell him if he truly loves me, he will talk to me, but then he only makes jokes."

May had to tell herself to shift down to second, to first, to stop. Clutch in, brake on. Breathe. She felt as if all incoming messages had to be simplified; she could not do two things at once. She could only drive now, negotiate the curve onto Auwaiolimu Street. Shift down to first, shift up to second, third, figure out how much time they need to get to the airport to make Marie-Claire's flight home. To Paris, to Hayes. Merge onto the Lunalilo freeway. She could not think about anything else now. She could not even try to figure out what it meant: *if he truly loves me.*

May came to the Big Island that weekend, angry. I knew something had gone wrong by the way she climbed out of the truck and slammed the door behind her. Every motion of her body was explosive. Taking out a cigarette and lighting it was an exercise in fury. Her first words to Israel were, "Why didn't you finish the trellis before starting the gazebo?" And to me, "Nobody around here knows how to follow orders."

She could not sit for more than a few minutes at a time, could not stay with one project. She was like a lioness, stalking about, nervous and angry and ready to attack.

Clarence came in about midafternoon, trailing Noelani. They stood together on the lanai, shifting from one foot to the other in front of May, who was making an attempt to read what seemed to be a report. She did not ask them to sit, did not even look up for a few moments though she knew they were there.

"I—we—have some news, May," Clarence began uncertainly.

She looked up, unsmiling, waiting.

"We're going to get married, Noelani and me."

Still May said nothing, only looked at them, as if waiting for more.

"I wanted you to know first," Clarence said, dropping the "we" in his nervousness.

"What do you want me to say?" May came back, her voice clipped. "Congratulations? Okay, congratulations." She turned back to the report.

Noelani looked at Clarence, full of uncertainty. The boy stood there for a long moment, confusion and pain flashing across his face. He wanted desperately to say something, you could see that, but he could not find the words to break May's cold anger. Finally he turned and, with Noelani by the hand, walked away.

I watched them go, and ached for them.

May waited until she heard their truck rumble down the road, and then she exploded.

"Christ!" she said, flinging the report across the lanai, "He wants to get married! He comes whimpering in here, pulling that child behind him . . . throwing it all away . . ." All the fury that had been bottled inside her came bursting out. She stalked around the house, ranting and throwing things. Israel heard her and came in double time across the lawn. I waved him off.

When she had exhausted herself, she went into the room where I was staying and curled up on the bed. I followed, with one hand I smoothed the hair back from her wet face and with the other, I grasped her hand. She was crying; soft, wet sobs came choking out of her.

"I've lost him," she managed to say, her voice shaking so hard I had to strain to understand, "I waited too long and I've lost him."

I frowned. Whatever could she mean, "lost"? Then it came to me. Marie-Claire. Hayes. It was Hayes she had lost.

"Listen to me now," I said. "Listen carefully, my darling May. Clarence came here because he needs your permission . . . no, listen, I know you are not talking about Clarence, but I am. That's right, Clarence. Permission and approval, if possible. He needs to hear you say that it is all right to get on with his life, the way he chooses to lead it. You are important to him, and that means you have a certain power over him. What Clarence needs from you is what you need from your mother: a release."

She turned on the bed and looked at me, her eyes widening with the realization. After a few minutes she pulled herself to the edge of the bed and sat there, her face in her hands. And then, having reached a decision, she did not take time to wash her face, even, but climbed in the truck and roared off.

She found Clarence near the Volcano Observatory. He was alone, staring into the crater of Kilauea, his back a study in misery.

"I am sorry about what happened," she began, sitting next to him and looping her arm in his. "Clarence, I was angry when you came today, but not with you. I was angry with myself, for being stupid about something else—something that has nothing at all to do with you. If what you want is to marry Noelani, then I will be happy for both of you. Truly."

He looked at her, studied her face and saw what he wanted to see.

278

She put her arms around him, then, and he touched his face to her shoulder, so she would know the depth of his relief.

March 27. Everything has happened so fast. The phone call, saying that Sam was in town and would be coming out for the weekend with a couple of his friends. Their arrival: three of them, Sam and a misshapen Laotian man with no hair at all on his head, and a woman from Italy introduced as a war correspondent.

"Nicky's English isn't so good," he said, grabbing her by the arm and pulling her around. She had a sharp, hard little face and eyes that scanned us with obvious disinterest.

"Hi," she said, automatically.

Sam made a great show of greeting me. Perhaps he was glad to see me, I can't tell any more about Sam. When he joined me on the lanai and I tried to get him to talk about taking photographs at the front, he was strangely glib. But I am wrong to criticize. I can only believe that what he has seen is too painful to talk about, and of course his photographs speak for themselves.

Making conversation at dinner was laborious. Neither the Laotian nor the Italian woman made any effort to answer questions, nor did they volunteer. They concentrated on eating and drinking, and left May and Sam and me to carry on a desultory conversation. I excused myself as soon as I could.

The murmur of talk drifted along the lanai late into the night. I supposed the liquor had loosened their tongues, and was glad I had escaped to bed.

When I got up the next morning the living room was strewn with detailed maps of Burma, Thailand and Laos, with empty glasses and the two bottles of scotch Sam had brought along, also empty. A thick, pungent odor lingered in the room. When I opened the door leading to the lanai I found May, dozing on a chaise lounge, fully dressed, a beach towel pulled over her for warmth.

The others didn't leave their beds until after noon and then they left quickly to catch a plane. Sam, I noticed, shared a room with the Italian woman. They are gone now, and I have tried to find out what is going on but May is being evasive. When I asked her what she thinks of Sam, she had to think for a while. "He's changed," she said. "Maybe Nicky has something to do with that. I gather they work together . . . I'm glad he has found someone, but I'm not sure that she is . . ." She broke off, started again with another, more positive thought. "I'm impressed at how much Sam knows about Asia. He's been all through Thailand and Laos, he has contacts among the hill tribes, it really is fascinating to hear him talk about it . . ."

"He didn't have much to say at dinner," I interjected, rather too tartly.

"No, he didn't," she grinned. "I have a feeling the booze and the pot got him going . . . those folks live hard lives, judging by their consumption."

March 30. May called from Honolulu to say she has to go to Japan and that she isn't certain how long she will be gone. She wanted to know if I would be all right. I told her I thought it more appropriate for me to ask that question of her. This is not, I am almost certain, a routine trip. She was evasive. I considered asking Israel to fly over to Honolulu to talk to her, to try at least to find out what she is up to, but then I decided no, it wouldn't work. She is going to do what she is going to do, and I am afraid for her.

———————

Three weeks later, we had what as a kid I used to call a "cloudburst." It almost never rains on the Kona coast, but the afternoon Hayes called the heavens opened and long silver sheets of rain poured down and beat so hard on the roof that I had to strain to hear. "I'm in Hong Kong," Hayes shouted, his voice familiar even through the bluster of the rainstorm. "May wired me from Thailand to meet her here. She was supposed to arrive yesterday—do you know where she is?"

21

She chewed gently on the inside of her cheek and listed the things she was not going to think about. Hayes, and Marie-Claire. Faith, who would be wondering and worrying. Mad Obregon, God. He had flown into a fury when she told him she needed to be away for a couple of weeks, and wouldn't tell him why. Her mother, what would happen when . . . and Sam, she wasn't going to let herself think about whether or not he could do what he said he could do. She stood at the window of her hotel room watching a long-tailed boat make its way up the Chao Phraya, leaving a wake of brown water that lapped against the barge moored by the hotel's dock. She had been here two days, had been waiting two days, and it was too long. *Damn you Sam,* she thought, in spite of her pledge, *You had better not leave me hanging.*

She climbed into the shower, let the water stream over her and went over the plan again. She was to take a room at the Oriental Hotel in Bangkok and wait to be contacted by someone who would direct her to the people who would take her into China through Burma. Here she was, waiting, afraid to leave the room for fear she would miss the contact, feeling trapped. Anger rising, she got out of the shower, twisted her wet hair on top of her head and pulled on her bikini. Sam's people had better move their asses or she was going to turn around . . .

And do what? she asked herself as she strode through the corridor. Go back to the status quo with Obregon? Ignore Marie-Claire? Forget about her mother? She stepped through the double doors and ran point-blank into a wall of heat but it didn't even slow her down. She dumped her towel and keys on an empty chaise, kicked off her sandals and, almost without breaking stride, dived into the pool. The water pressing against her felt good, moving felt good. She swam the length of the pool underwater, surfaced for a gulp of air, swam back again. She did this twice more before climbing back out of the pool, her lungs aching.

When she reached for her towel, her keys clattered onto the tiles. Her vision was blurred, but she could see a note folded tightly and tied to the chain. With wet hands that would not work as fast as she wanted, she opened the paper and read: "You will be glad to go to Grand Palace this day at 3, see Jade Buddha. Sam says."

She buried her face in the towel, pretending to dry it, and when she looked up again a tall, blond man was standing in front of her, a drink in his hand.

"You swim well," he said in accented English. She dried her hair slowly, and wondered how he knew to speak English.

He repeated the remark in French. She did not smile, but she did not frown either. Her tone was careful: "Is there a reason I should be talking to you?"

"Ah, you do speak English. I thought you might like a drink. Dreadfully hot, this country, for an Austrian like me."

She managed a short, perfunctory laugh. Just a pickup, she thought, a standard line, it had happened to her enough times, she should have known. This thing with Sam was making her paranoid. "Thank you no," she said, "I'm meeting someone."

She sat on the carpet in front of the Jade Buddha, her legs tucked under her so her feet were pointing at no one—an important point of courtesy to the Thai, who were seated all around her. She had positioned herself in front of a fan, so the heat was not oppressive. The Jade Buddha sat, high above her, a small green figure in a glass case. Amazing, she thought, the power of religion here, as the man to her right bowed to the Buddha and rose to leave, smiling at her and whispering, "Samsas." She looked at him blankly, not knowing if he was speaking to her or to someone else, or if it were some kind of prayer. Confused, she looked away. "Samsas," he repeated, and she got it: Sam says.

Outside in the courtyard he handed her a note, pressed his palms together, fingertips up, and left. It was from Sam, and it was dated three days ago. "Sorry I couldn't wait, but I'll be here when you get back. Take a bus to Chiang Mai, check in at the Railway Hotel, then go to the Night Bazaar to a shop called Srisupan Gems. Ask for Phorn. He will make all arrangements. I'll be waiting for you in Bangkok when you get back. Happy trails."

She leaned against one of the mythological beasts that guarded the Chapel Royal and grimaced. Happy trails. Wrong, Sam. You've got it wrong.

She arrived in Chiang Mai in that gray period between sunset and dark. The evening air smelled of smoke and jasmine. She climbed into a pedicab, told the driver to take her to the night bazaar, and leaned back to try to get a sense of this northern town. It was the jumping-off spot for the Golden Triangle, where Thailand, Laos and Burma came together, and where the opium poppy was the largest cash crop. For all its notoriety, she thought, the town seemed prosaic. Even in the gathering dark, she could see shards of light glint off the golden stele of a monastery behind a high wall. She stopped at a food stall and pointed to the green coconuts piled in a bucket of ice. With a machete, the man sliced the top off one and, with great precision, placed a straw in it. Then he handed it to her with a flourish and a smile.

"Thank you," she said, pressing her palms together in a wai, before paying him. It was the right thing to do. The man broke into giggles, as the Thai tended to do, and insisted she sit on his chair to enjoy her drink.

She took two long, deep sips of the cold coconut water and then asked him to direct her to the Srisupan shop. He repeated the name twice before he began calling out wildly. Presently, a small boy appeared, and May understood that she was to follow him.

She had a hard time keeping up, as the child ducked between the stalls—dozens of them, set up every night in the broad wasteland only a few minutes from the heart of town. "Wait," she called out, but the child scurried ahead, she had simply to plow her way through the night throngs, muttering, "sorry, sorry."

Phorn was short and thick with a heavy smile perpetually in place. He wore an immaculate white knit golf shirt, shiny green trousers and dress shoes. "Oh yes," he said when she told him who she was. "Everything is quite okay." It was a phrase she would hear over and over again in weeks to come. That night she had no idea that it was applied as soothing balm, that all it meant was, "Everything is out of your hands."

When she came out of the Railway Hotel the next morning a small girl, about eight, approached her carrying a huge rattan tray. On it were stacked a dozen small woven cages; inside each were two tiny sparrows fluttering madly.

"Ten baht, madame," the girl said, holding out one of the little baskets in which the birds batted wildly.

May laughed. "Whatever would I do with them?" she said out loud. The girl's eyes were opaque; she did not understand. A pedicab driver standing nearby answered for her: "You set them free, madam. Make a wish and if they fly off together, your wish is granted."

"Ten baht," the girl repeated.

How perverse, May thought, to capture some poor creature for the pleasure of releasing it. While she was trying to open the cage she made her wish: *Hayes, to see Hayes.*

She stood, watching the birds fly off together, until tears stung her eyes. Suddenly she whirled and went back into the hotel, to the desk. Screw secrecy, screw Sam. On a sheet of paper she wrote: *Going to find my mother. Meet me in Hong Kong, Peninsula Hotel, April 20. Please.* With painstaking care, she printed his name and Paris address and gave the man at the desk fifty baht to send the telegram at once. He looked at the money, dissolved into a delighted fit of giggling, and got right to it.

For three days they traveled, first by jeep, then across a lake on a boat that sat so low in the water her feet were perpetually wet, through a forest on elephant back and finally, by foot. Her companions were Phorn, still in his golf shirt and shiny green pants, but now wearing bright blue Adidas running shoes, a woman of the Meo tribe with black teeth and matching cotton costume heavily embroidered in bright reds and yellows and with loops of silver weighing on her chest, and a wiry young man who was a mahout, or elephant handler.

Only Phorn spoke English, and not very well. She was never quite certain if he understood and didn't want to give her a straight answer, or if he simply did not understand. For this reason, most of the journey, for May, was spent in silence. She did not mind; the heat and the dust and the insects drained her of any but the most immediate concerns. Tiny mites worked their way under the moneybelt she wore, biting her until she had what looked like a red ring separating the top of her from the bottom. Her stomach was giving her trouble, in spite of the medicine she had brought along. She was as physically miserable as she had ever been, and she had to concentrate simply to keep going, to keep her equilibrium. The worst of it was, she had a feeling that things were going to get harder before they got easier. Occasionally, when she watched the Meo woman squatting in the dirt preparing their food . . . stuffing sticky rice in hollowed-out sections of sugarcane, wrapping it in leaves and roasting it deep in the fire . . . she would wonder what the woman could be thinking, how she felt about a strange English-speaking woman in an Abercrombie safari suit who could only sit and watch.

She did not know when they crossed the border into Burma; it must have happened on the third day. All that afternoon they had traveled by foot along a stony dry riverbed, a canopy of teak and bamboo shading them, the tangled jungle rising on either side. As the light began to lower, Phorn motioned for them to stop. At first she thought they were going to make camp, but logic told her it was too early. Instead, they waited.

After a while, May asked, "Do you suppose you could tell me why we are waiting—is someone going to meet us, and where we will be going now?"

"Oh yes, someone," Phorn answered with his usual set smile. "Everything is quite okay."

There were three of them, small and wiry men in oddly matched clothes—jeans, sneakers, army fatigues and floppy hats. They carried rifles and shotguns and led a string of sturdy little ponies, each carrying a heavy pack. One of the men, a cigarette dangling from his mouth, set to work. He took the pack off one of the ponies, and repositioned it. Meanwhile, the others had engaged Phorn in a furious conversation in a dialect she had never heard.

It was about her, she knew that. The men would look at her and glance away. They sat on their haunches under a giant teak tree, smoking and chattering. She lit a cigarette too, and filled her lungs with the harsh dry smoke. *This feels wrong,* she thought, and bit the inside of her cheek. *But I've gone too far to turn back.*

Phorn approached her. She made no move to meet him, instead, she took another long drag on the cigarette.

"Madam May," he said, "I am very sorry to say, these men say need more money."

"More money? Sam already paid them."

"Not so much enough. Very hard, getting men to take to China. Very hard time."

"Sam made all of the arrangements, they were paid in advance."

"Oh no, Madam, they say he pay not enough."

She sighed. "How much?"

"Two thousand U.S. dollars."

"Christ!" she blurted angrily, not knowing if she should be angry at Sam or if they were extorting more money from her. "Tell them two thousand dollars is all I have, and if they take that now I will be left with nothing," she lied. "Tell them they can have a thousand dollars now, and the rest when I return to Bangkok."

Phorn walked the few steps to the other camp, spoke rapidly for a few moments and then came back to say, "Give them fifteen hundred dollars, everything will be quite okay."

"Sure," she said, wanting to slap the stupid grin off his face, "sure it will. But tell them they are leaving me with nothing."

Phorn looked at her, for the first time not bothering to mask his disapproval. "Five hundred U.S. dollars is not nothing."

She leaned against the tree and closed her eyes. He was right. In this part of the world $500 U.S. was a fortune. And they could have demanded all of it, they could easily have taken it from her.

She continued the journey north with the Meo woman and one of the Burmese, an old man with a shock of white hair and enough English to explain that she was now in Kachin territory, and what she had just encountered was a caravan of jade smugglers on their way to the Thai border, that he was to deliver her to the Chinese who would then take her where she wanted to go in Yunnan Province.

"Who are these Chinese?" she said, then rephrased her question. "Why do the Chinese come to Burma?"

"To Kachin," he corrected her, "Here, is Kachin land. They come for jadeite."

"Ah," May said, beginning to understand. The Kachin tribes had always ruled the north of Burma, where the best jade mines were. The civil war continued, with the Kachin holding their own ground. But now even the Chinese were coming to them for the fine green jadeite mined in these mountains.

They walked for another day, at times picking through jungle so thick the old man had to cut a way with a machete. She could feel the sweat caking on her body; her shoulders ached and sharp pains shot up the back of her neck. Her mouth and throat were parched, even her eyes felt hot. She tried to loosen her shirt, her underpants began to bind her and she wished she could take them off altogether. She swung her backpack off and dragged it for a time, but then she put it back on when the woman—in her heavy black dress, carrying a load of pots and pans on her head—moved around her, to take the second position behind the old man.

"If I ever get out of this . . ." May was beginning to say to herself when they came into the clearing. Two small thatched huts, a rusted frame of what may once have been a jeep and several haystacks. She hoped she could make it as far as the water jar. At first she did not notice the small knot of men huddled in the shade cast by one of the huts.

Now it was the old man's turn to confer with one of the men who was, she could see now, Chinese. They spoke earnestly for a few minutes, then he turned and motioned her over. "This man say cannot go so far now," he said. "He say too much long they go, man no come."

Her legs gave out under her and she sat down hard, hitting her tailbone on the exposed root of a great tree. She wailed with pain. The old man came to squat beside her, his face registering concern. That was all she needed: she began to cry, short, soft sobs came gulping out of her.

The Chinese stood staring at her. The Meo woman busied herself picking something off her arms. The old Burmese man made soft cooing sounds.

"Okay," she said, rubbing her hand across her face and mixing the sweat and dirt in a large smear. She took a deep gulp. "Okay. Now ask him if he wants more money."

The old man looked puzzled, but he did as she asked.

"No," he said, "no money. Nothing. Can't go."

"Why?" she wailed. "Why can't we go?"

"Man no come," was the only way he could think to explain it.

"So I can't go on? I can't go to China and you can't even tell me why?"

The old man stood there, looking at her and shaking his head in sorrow. She felt numb. This can't be, she thought, *Sam was so sure,* Sam had made her believe. A sharp cramp ripped through her stomach and she bent forward, to ease the pain. *Sam was wrong, and I was wrong to believe him.* The sick, empty feeling of failure went through her like a wave.

She looked at the watch she had bought in Bangkok. In eight days Hayes would be in Hong Kong.

Or wouldn't be, either way.

There was time, at least, to get back.

Something dark seemed to hover and settle in her chest. *Her mother was just over those mountains, but it might as well be a million miles.* She lifted her eyes—they did not seem that formidable, not so high or wild as mountains she had crossed in the Pacific Rim. She put her hands on her head. *Why? Why couldn't she seem to do this thing, this one thing?* A small, hiccoughing sob broke out of her as she accepted her failure.

The old man took them back, until they met another smuggling caravan heading south, toward Thailand. The old man arranged for this one to take her for $200 U.S. By now she and the Meo woman had worked out a certain routine: for food, for water, for waiting while one or the other went into the bushes. The woman's foul odor no longer offended May; she suspected it was because she smelled as bad herself.

She was trudging mindlessly behind one of the ponies when it stumbled and fell. For a minute she had to balance, to keep from tumbling herself. Several of the men gathered around the beast, two of them taking off its load while the third helped it up again. May sank to the ground nearby, resting against a stand of bamboo. One of the men tossed the heavy bags from the pony's back to the ground beside her, and a brown rock about the size of a football fell out and rolled to her. She reached to touch it, turning it until she noticed a shiny square that had been cut and polished. Through this square she could see into the boulder: a deep green and, below that, a pure lavender color. It was jade, a huge chunk of it, to be sold in Chiang Mai. *God,* she thought, watching the man who stood guard, his rifle drawn. *How did Sam get mixed up in this?*

At that moment the guard called out sharply, and the other men grabbed their weapons and scattered to the edges of the caravan, the animals inside. May looked for the Meo woman, and found her crouching in the bushes, her eyes black with fear. She crawled in beside her and they sat silent for a time, only the ponies making an occasional shuddering sound. Then two of the men moved off, into thick underbrush on both sides of the riverbed. May closed her eyes and thought: It can't get any worse.

She had no idea who was hunting them, but she knew that someone was as they moved through the southern part of Burma. She could not sleep more than a few minutes at a time, she was exhausted, her body too tired to feel the aches and bites and cuts, her feet swollen and bruised and molding inside her walking boots. She could not slow down, she had to go when they went, stop when they stopped. She ate the rice the Meo woman cooked, and never questioned whatever else was in it—though she could make out bits of bamboo shoots and vegetables, she did not know what some of the other things were. Now it was simply a matter of lasting; she wasn't certain she had any control over her own body, she would go as far as she could and stop. That was all. And if that happened, she had no doubt that they would leave her behind, she meant nothing at all to them.

But they did not leave her behind. When she could not get up again after a rest period, they rearranged the loads the ponies were carrying and lifted her onto one of the small, hardy creatures. Her long legs almost touched the ground, and its backbone cut into her, but she didn't care, she was so glad not to have to take another step.

This time she knew when they reached the Thai border, because three men were waiting for them with elephants, to carry out the jade stones.

One of the men, with a soft face and eyes that fluttered said to her, "You know American Sam?"

She nodded.

"Come," he said, leading her to an elephant. The young mahout signaled the elephant to kneel, and put out his hand to help her climb on. The man handed her a small package. "This for Sam, you give it him."

As weary as she was, she could feel the fury rising in her. "No," she said, looking hard into his moving eyes.

"Yes," he answered, his hand increasing the pressure on her arm.

"No," she came back, her eyes beginning to smart at the pain. "No," she repeated through her teeth.

He jerked her aside, crashing into a thicket. He tore open her shirt and saw the moneybelt. His eyes fluttered even faster. She tried to cover her breasts with her hands, but he slapped them aside. He was not interested in her breasts, he was interested in the money belt. When he began to rip at it, she held her hands up and said, "Wait, I'll give it to you."

He waited as she unbuckled the belt; her fingers were stiff and swollen, she could hardly manage, but his fierce tugs pushed her on. His back to the others who were busy now loading the elephants, he flipped through the bills she had left. She knew there should be about $1,500.

He removed all of it, replaced it with the package she did not want and pulled the buckles so tight she could scarcely breathe. She said nothing, wanting only to get away from him, wanting only to get onto the elephant and out of Thailand as fast as she could, wanting only to be done with them all now, Sam most of all . . . Sam, who was using her as his personal drug runner. She was finished with Sam forever.

It took all the strength she had left not to slide off the elephant at the same time that she struggled to get the belt off. Her fingers were too swollen, too bruised. A knife, if she could get a knife and cut it off.

The sound came shrieking out of the forest, one sharp loud wail of warning, and then they were surrounded. On all sides, small hard men with menacing faces holding automatic weapons on them.

In Bangkok she was taken to the jail on Mahachai Street. There she was given a shower and a set of cotton pajamas. Her watch was taken from her on the day she was to have met Hayes in Hong Kong, if Hayes had gone to Hong Kong. Probably he had not, probably he was with Marie-Claire in France right now. Even if the telegram had reached him, even if the boy in the hotel had sent it. She sat on the floor in the corner of the room where it was dry, opposite the hole that was the toilet, and stared at the things that had drowned in the damp corner: great flat black bugs, clots of hair, dirty strips of rag. She lifted her eyes to the barred window near the ceiling. Dust motes danced in the sunlight that filtered down, and mixed with the sounds that drifted in, people talking, laughing, calling to each other. The sour smell of rotting vegetables rose from outside. She could hear the splash of water and guessed that the jail was next to one of the city's old klongs.

"In Thailand, only fifteen years for drug smuggling," one of the young police guards had told her, adding, "Very good for you, other places give you death."

She had asked them, each time they brought her in to be questioned, to call the American Embassy. "American?" they would say skeptically, and she would explain again that her passport was in a safe deposit box at the Oriental Hotel, that the key was in the money belt they had taken off her. They had not answered, had looked at her with blank expressions and asked her questions she could not answer about where she had been and whom she had been with.

She did not give them Sam's name, she didn't know why. She told them there was a man named Phorn she had met at the night bazaar in Chiang Mai, but they did not ask the name of his shop, and she did not offer it. Then they put her in the room with the wet floor, and brought her good food which she would eat and then throw up, and she would spend the night curled in a knot on the floor, her stomach churning.

On the morning of the third day she was led down two flights of stairs and into a room with a table, two chairs and on the wall a picture of the King and Queen. She was sitting, staring at the royal couple, when the American walked in. He was young and brisk, and wore a starched light blue shirt, and striped tie, a tan Panama suit and well-polished shoes. "Miss Wing, is it?" he began in distinct American accents, the annoyance seeping out in nasal tones. "Looks like you've got yourself into some trouble, miss."

She took a deep enough breath to marshal all of her strength, she stood to face him and when she spoke it was with all the authority she could command: "My name is Wing, yes. Dr. Wing Mei-jin. What is yours?" She scarcely gave him time to answer. "All right Mr. Stanson, here is what you need to do. First you tell your ambassador that he is to contact Mrs. Katherine McCord at her San Francisco headquarters at once. If you don't know who she is, he will. He is to tell her my situation here, and that the drugs found on me were put there against my will—only minutes before the police arrested me. I had no intention of passing them on to anybody, I intended to throw them away as soon as I possibly could. Most important," she looked him hard in the eyes so he could see the determination, "I need to be out of here, I need to be in Hong Kong today."

He stepped back and stared, not knowing what to make of her.

She stepped toward him, bearing down. "I promise you, if you don't get onto this, and now, the State Department is going to be very unhappy with you. All you have to do is get word to Kit . . . Mrs. McCord."

"I know the name," he answered, defensively.

"Good," May said, using the brisk tone he had abandoned, "then you know my aunt—and guardian—knows how to make things happen."

He looked at the floor, and ran his hands through his hair. When he looked up again, his expression was one of sweet wonder. "I'll get right on it," he said.

22

She sat in the back of the taxi, the thick Asian heat pressing in on her, the food she had tried to eat on the plane churning angrily in her stomach. The driver swerved and pitched, darting into every opening, wasting energy. The traffic was too dense to move more than a few feet at a time.

I could get there faster on foot, she thought, it can't be more than a few blocks. She looked at the perpetual movement of the crowds that surged along Nathan Road. For a moment it seemed hopeless, she could not survive out there, she would not be able to walk, her legs would not move. A sharp pain shot through her stomach, as if to warn her. She put her hands over the thin, gray fabric of the pajamas they had issued her that morning when they released her from prison. She clutched the purse the man from the embassy had given her; it held her passport, three thousand Hong Kong dollars and a new American Express card. Kit had arranged that. Kit had also arranged a hotel for her in Bangkok and a later flight to Hong Kong, but she had not wanted to wait. She had made so many mistakes, she could not make another, and she had caught the first flight out. *She was so close, so very close now.* The taxi passed Peking Road.

"Here," she called to the driver in Cantonese, "Let me out here."

He turned to give her a dark, angry look. "Peninsula Hotel not yet," he answered, lurching forward so she could not open the door.

May reminded herself how she must look in the cheap gray pajamas and the long, peasant's braid down her back. She could feel lice crawling on her scalp, but she was too weary to scratch. *Would they allow her into the Peninsula?* She couldn't worry about that now, she had to get there first and she wasn't sure that her legs would carry her.

She waved money in the cab driver's face and he pulled to a stop, causing an explosion of car horns to add to the noise and confusion. She stepped out into the street, almost losing her balance as she tried to walk against the tide of people surging in upon her.

Steamy gusts of heat blew at her, rising from the pavement, making it hard to breathe. It began to seem as if she could not put her feet down in the right places, the sidewalk was moving up to meet them. *Faster,* she told herself *almost there.* The looming gray building came into sight and she heard herself make a small, whimpering sound. *Not far now, not far now, keep moving, don't stop.* It had been like this for so long, so long. Swimming upstream, struggling to get here, be here, and always something to hold her back. Suddenly at Middle Road the wave seemed to reverse itself and the crowd carried her across the street. She blinked to force back the darkness that was moving into her peripheral vision.

She entered by a side door, and for a moment simply stood leaning against a pillar, reveling in the cool English calm of this great colonial hulk of a hotel, breathing in the sweet, clean air. She moved carefully, one hand on the wall for support. Had people taken notice, they might have thought she was blind. She reached the edge of the lobby, grasped the back of a Morris chair. *She could not make it across the great expanse of the lobby.* She was going to fall, her knees were giving way. She eased herself into the chair. Whatever else she knew at that moment, she knew for certain that she would not be able to get up without help.

She leaned back in the great, soft chair and closed her eyes. When she opened them again, she saw him. On the far side of the lobby, sitting at a small table reading a newspaper. *It can't be,* she told herself. *You are hallucinating.* But it could be, it was. Hayes. Here, waiting for her. He had been waiting for four days, he had not left. He was here, only this great, marble lobby of the Peninsula Hotel separated them. She tried to get up but could not. If he left now, there would be nothing she could do about it. She felt the sour taste of panic rising in her throat. Her mouth was too dry to call out. He was beyond her reach.

He looked up, his eyes scanned the lobby, a man who had been waiting so long he had ceased to expect. He lifted the cup and took a sip, his eyes still moving mechanically about the room. He glanced past the place where she was sitting, as if she were invisible.

A bellboy was walking toward her. *He is going to throw me out,* May thought, panicked. She clutched her purse to her chest and held on to it, hard. It was the only motion she could make, the only thing she could think to do to defend herself. She felt as if she were in a dream, trying to scream and no sound would come out.

Hayes put his cup down slowly. He was staring. He stood, not certain . . . and then he started toward her, determined now, looking at her so steadily that he did not see the bellboy, did not see that they were about to collide. The boy went tumbling, but Hayes did not break stride. His eyes were on her and he had one hand out, as if he were coming downcourt in a basketball game, with only the goal in mind. He knew. He knew and he was coming and she could stop now, she had done it.

She took the hands he held out to her and let him lift her, and then her arms were around him, her cheek pressed into his chest and they stood, holding hard together.

"Can you walk if I help you?" he asked.

They went slowly, Hayes holding her so tightly that her feet scarcely touched the floor. There were those in the lobby who watched, and perhaps wondered about the tall American and the slender Chinese woman who appeared to be ill, her face pressed into the man's shoulder and her eyes closed.

She lay in the bath and he washed her, carefully cleaning the bites that covered her body, unbraiding her hair and soaping it carefully with a strong, green liquid he had had to send out for. His shirt and khaki pants were splashed wet, but he seemed not to notice. May lay back in the warmth of the water and tried to get her thoughts in order, so she could say what she needed to say.

"I didn't think you would be here," she tried, "I thought I'd never find you."

"Shh," he told her, "no talk, not yet. We'll get you washed up and medicated—looks like half the insect population of Thailand took a bite out of you—then you will sleep, and then we'll talk. You'll tell me everything . . . I won't leave, I promise."

"You promise?" she repeated wearily, her eyes half closed in the warm comfort of the bath, of his hands holding her.

"I promise," he said, caressing her cheek.

"I do have to admit," he went on, "I had a small problem recognizing you in your little gray pajama ensemble . . . which, by the way, has been donated to the incinerator. Too many tiny little crawling animals managed to hitch a ride on this trimmed-down body of yours . . ."

"I look awful," she moaned.

"Not possible," he answered, lifting her gently and rubbing her dry, his hands caressing her through the towel.

She leaned into him as he wrapped her in an oversized terry bathrobe. "This is your complete wardrobe for the moment," he said, lifting her and carrying her into the room. Instead of putting her in the bed he had turned down, he sat on the sofa, May cradled in his arms. She lifted her face solemnly and he touched his lips to hers, carefully.

"You need to sleep," he said, and she could feel his breath against her skin. "I need to get some medicine for those bites, and some clothes for your body. So . . . I'm going to tuck you in, and you are going to sleep, and when you wake you will eat and then we will talk."

Still he did not get up, but sat holding her. Long, wet strands of her hair brushed against his face and he did not try to remove them. Not until he heard the soft patterns of her sleep breathing did he carry her to the bed.

When he was smoothing the covers she opened her eyes and said, "Come in with me."

"Not now," he told her, and with his forefinger traced her lips.

When she awakened the first time, it was twilight. He helped her to the bathroom, then back to bed where she went instantly to sleep again. The next time she opened her eyes it was dark with only the streetlights filtering into the room. All was quiet, but she knew he was there, and then she made him out, sitting in a chair, watching her.

"Welcome to the world of the living," he said, turning a light on low. "You've had a solid twelve hours of sleep. Now for some food, and you may survive."

"Twelve hours," she groaned, and then, "I'm ravenous," pulling herself up in the bed so that the robe fell open.

"And naked," he added, "but I'm about to remedy both those conditions."

He called room service, then poured her a stiff scotch which she sipped, slowly, while he showed her the clothes he had bought while she slept.

"The woman in the Chanel boutique assured me this size fits all," he said, holding up a pink silk dress that was all soft folds.

She could not take her eyes from his face. "I cannot believe I'm here," she finally said, "I cannot believe you are here with me."

He touched his glass to hers: "Here's to Hong Kong," he said.

She wanted to add, "And to us," but she did not dare.

He watched her eat, sipping his scotch as she drank hot soup and then worked her way through a plate of Chinese noodles. When she had finished and had washed her face with a hot towel, she said, "All right."

"All right?" he asked.

"Time to talk. The Moment of Truth. Q and A. Everything you always wanted to know about the jails in Thailand and were afraid to ask." She hesitated, her voice suddenly wavering, "And what I need to know about Marie-Claire."

He was sitting on the bed across from her, his hands clasped between his legs, a look on his face she could not decipher. She did not know what he was thinking, and suddenly she felt afraid. She needed to stand, to make certain she could move on her own. She pulled herself up, swayed, he rose to catch her, his hands slipping under the robe. He pulled her hard to him.

She could feel the air around them expand, enclose, hold. It broke over them, in great gulps, their mouths moving and searching and their bodies straining for each other.

"Want me," she could not keep herself from crying, "please, please want me."

"I have never wanted anyone more than I want you, right now," he said in short angry bursts, as he touched a place she had not known existed, and cried out for the joy of it; it was as if he could not help himself, as if he were committing to her body a confession he could no longer contain.

For three days they lived in their own rhythms. They rose at first light, and walked. The first day a fine mist hung over Hong Kong harbor, a single ferry moved across the bay, leaving a sharply defined wake. They walked, and watched the city come to life along with the practitioners of tai chi in the small green parkways along the waterfront, their ritual movements scarcely stirring the warm morning air. They sat watching the freighters and container ships and cruise liners and, skittering in between, the sampans and walla-wallas that filled Hong Kong harbor. They walked to the Star Ferry terminal and climbed aboard one of the little green and white ferries and crossed over to Hong Kong Island and back again, on the second-class deck of the *Meridian Star,* the *Celestial Star,* the *Night Star.* They walked the narrow back streets of the old part of the city, pausing at shops that sold rhinoceros horn and hundred-year-old eggs and birds in cages. That day large, dark clouds hovered over the city, and the promise of rain was strong but still they walked. When it came lashing down on them, they dashed for cover into a temple called Man Mo and had their fortunes told as they breathed in the thick incense. The priest gave them a piece of yellow paper filled with Chinese characters. May translated: *"It is a time to plant new trees, which will put down new roots, and bear fruit."*
The rain stopped and the steam of the afternoon heat sent them back to the cool of the hotel, where they made love and slept, and made love again, and talked.

He told her about his search for the Vietnamese woman Le Tien An, and her child—Andy's child, who would be almost two years old by now. How he had gone to Saigon, and had been turned away by her family, but had learned that the child had been born. A son, he said, Andy has a son.
She told him how it had been, when the Thai troops had surrounded them at the border. She explained how they had found the heroin on her, how Sam had used her. How he had promised to be in Bangkok when she returned—she realized, now, to pick up the heroin. He must have planned it all along, must have known she wouldn't be able to get into China . . ."I was so stupid," she said, "I

wanted to believe, and Sam seemed so sure of himself. I thought it was my last chance, that if I didn't see her and get it settled . . . you, we . . . would never . . ." She caught herself, took a deep breath. "From the beginning I knew there was a chance that I might fail to get into China through Burma, the terrain is difficult and there are all sorts of unknowns—but I felt certain Sam would never betray me . . ."

Hayes paced the room, anger flashing on his face. "The bastard," he spat out, "the filthy bastard."

"I guess I worked a lot of my anger out while I was sitting in that prison cell, watching insects crawling around the walls. I have no feeling left for him, none at all, except maybe disgust."

They talked about Sam for a time, about his anger at the Diehls, his anger at the world, and how it had consumed him.

Hayes told her about his work at the headquarters of the OECD in the Chateau de la Muette in the western part of Paris, and rattled off all the acronyms as he might a child's ABCs: DAC and NIC, The Organization for Economic Cooperation and Development, The Development Assistance Committee and the Newly Industrialized Countries. His own work was with DAC, his special field of study Sub-Saharan Africa, an area with problems so vast, he said, it is going to require an enormous effort in the coming decade on the part of the rich nations of the world.

And when she asked, Hayes answered: "Yes, it feels right. I know now what I can do, and what I can't, and both of those things were important for me to find out."

They rode the tram to Victorian Peak to watch the lights come on over Hong Kong harbor, and ate long noodles and *lo han* vegetables at the *dai pai dong,* or street stalls, and drank Iron Buddha tea.

They lived in the present, and only talked selectively about the past. He told her that Eli was in Libya, that he had married a Palestinian woman who was in the university there, an act which had complicated both their lives but which seemed to have preserved Eli's sanity.

Late in the afternoon of the third day, they lay in bed together, with all that had not been said pushing hard between them. Hayes sat up. May ran her hand lightly along the spine of his back. She forced herself to say, "There is so little time left."

He ran his hands through his hair. "My flight is at eleven, we should be moving."

She took a deep breath: "I have to know. Please, Hayes. Now."

He turned, and she saw that he couldn't trust himself to speak.

So May said it: "I have to know about Marie-Claire. I know she loves you. I have to know if you love her."

"What you have to know," he said, almost angrily, "is that I love you, more than anyone. Anyone."

"But she thinks . . ."

"She knows," he said, his mouth tight, "I called her the day you came, while you were sleeping, and she already knew. I didn't have to say it."

"Then say it to me," May pushed, "what you would have said to her, if she hadn't already known."

He got out of bed, pulled on his pants, poured a drink for himself and did not look at her.

"That I was sorry, that I had never wanted to cause her any pain, that . . . I was sorry."

May pulled the sheets around her, and huddled in the depression that was descending upon her. Hayes was leaving, was returning to France. She wouldn't see him for how long, how long . . . he was returning and he would not say he didn't love Marie-Claire, would not say what it was he felt for her. A kind of panic moved into her throat, "I need to know, Hayes," she began in a pleading voice.

He turned now and said very calmly, "I don't want to talk about Marie-Claire, and there's no need. Please try to understand, May. I could never marry anyone else, not when I feel this way about you."

"Marry?" she blurted. "I didn't know you wanted to be married, I didn't think you were ready . . ." She burst into tears, and let them stream down her face.

"May, listen to me . . . can you do that? Listen?" He spoke in a slow, measured way. "There are things about you, about your life, that are complicating . . . the way you work, for one thing. Your ambition, and you are ambitious. I've never been sure that I'd be able to hold you. On top of that there's the bloody Hunt fortune . . . I know what an albatross that kind of money can be. My father became a banker so he could manage my mother's family money, and that's a fraction of what you are worth."

"It isn't that much of a problem . . ." she began, but he stopped her.

"Wake up, May. You haven't had to deal with it because Kit is doing it for you. Kit knows very well what you are refusing to see—that money is power, whether you want it or not. Kit hasn't been afraid to use that power, but I don't know what's going to happen when you're faced with it—what I do know is that I don't want to be in the position of taking over from Kit."

She smiled, she couldn't help it. "And I had you figured for a fortune-hunter," she said, wryly.

He brought her a robe, held it out for her and, when she lifted her hair, he could not resist bending to kiss her on the neck. "I only need to think about you and the juices start flowing," he said. "You are the most exciting woman I've ever known, and I don't think I can live without you. I've just got to get used to the idea that it isn't going to be any kind of an ordinary life."

"Is ordinary what you want?" she asked. "No, wait, don't answer that. Instead, tell me what you mean by ordinary?"

He grinned, reached for her hand. "Going to bed in the same bed together at night, waking up together in the morning, having break-fast in a kitchen that belongs to a place we share, making love, having children, fixing peanut butter sandwiches . . ."

She looked at him, wide-eyed. "And you don't think I want that too?"

It was his turn to look serious. "There are so many complications, May. This thing about your mother needs to be resolved before we can begin to be together, we both know that. And it scares the hell out of me to think you might try another crazy scheme. If I'm the reason that you went off half-cocked into Thailand, then I'll tell you this, I'll wait for you forever, if I have to . . . but I want you to promise me you won't try to go into China illegally again."

"Wait. Before I make any promises, let's get back to my question. What makes you think my career would be more important than my husband, and where did you get the idea that I wouldn't want a family? I just don't understand. You never asked me, remember— you were the one who went off to France to find out how you fit into this world, after all the turmoil in Africa and the South and Berkeley. I didn't try to stop you because I had some questions to answer of my own. But there was never any question in my mind, I always knew I wanted to spend my life with you. I never subjected you to the kind of cold scrutiny you seem to have subjected me to . . ." She didn't finish the sentence, but started on another tack, "Did you think Marie-Claire would make a better wife? That life with her would be less complicated, is that it?"

His face went cold; he began, methodically, to dress. May went into the bathroom, showered, and when she came out he was packing.

She put on a beige silk suit she had bought that morning, slipped into sandals, brushed her hair and all the while the silence grew, swelling, filling the room, pressing against her rib cage. She could feel time pulling against them; rushing to empty. She looked at his back and wanted to touch him, but she could not.

"Where should we have dinner?" he asked in a stranger's voice.

"It doesn't matter," she heard herself say, *"I don't care."* The words exploded inside of her. She felt herself disintegrating, tiny black spots moved across her field of vision. "Oh my God, Hayes," she cried, "I do care. I care terribly. I was so frightened when I thought I'd lost you, when I thought you wouldn't be here, but you were. You came and you waited for me and I love you, oh God Hayes, I love you . . . I should not have. . . ."

He held her quietly, rubbing her back thoughtfully. "We'll work it out," he said. "Somehow, we will make it work."

23

Fall 1972

A splinter of sunlight pierced the thin layer of my eyelid and lodged there, sending sharp, insistent messages into the dark center of my brain, needling me awake. Resisting, I moved my head on the pillow but the sunlight tracked me. It was no good; I was not to be allowed to rise easily to wakefulness. I opened my eyes and saw the problem—a rip in the old green window shade. It had always been temperamental and the girls—two of Annie's school pals who stayed in the cottage while I was away—were too young to be patient with this crochety old place. I suppose one must have given the shade too hard a tug and tore it. Why haven't I noticed it before? Of course! The sun had to move into place. It was the first good thought of the morning, the idea of the sun working its way around the heavens to get at me. I will have to add the shade to my list of things for Israel to fix.

"This old place is too idiosyncratic to loan out," Israel said to me after the first round of repairs. (He is studying the dictionary again, building his vocabulary.) I told him that as far as I was concerned, he was the resident expert on eccentricities. He wasn't about to be sidetracked into semantics, and grumbled, "Why didn't you just leave those rambunctious young ladies a list of things not to do?"

"Because," I explained, "the list would have been so long they would have thought me an intolerably fastidious old fussbudget, besides which you can't say on a list just exactly how to jiggle the handle on the toilet to keep it from running all day, or precisely how to lift the screen door and push it out ever so gently so it opens easily."

Still he fusses and fumes. His lumbago has returned, he complains that the fog makes his joints ache. He complains. The problem with Israel is he didn't want to come home.

It is no good lying here thinking; Karin and Thea will be along in no time. They promised to stop by before Thea's lesson. The family has been traveling so I've seen them only twice over the summer. Greece, Italy, Spain. I should say Philip, Karin and Thea have been traveling. Dan did not go with them, he went to summer school. I suspect that Karin's coming here today has something to do with Dan.

Thea bounded in, long arms waving in free, floating movements: "Look, look," she said, dangling a card too close to my eyes for me to be able to read it. "It's my driver's license," she chanted. "The temporary one they give you right after you pass the test. You are looking at a certified California driver!" Karin stood behind her, hands clasped behind her back, delighted.

"Who would ever have thought it?" I teased. "That is quite a wonderful achievement."

Thea was dancing around the cottage, her long, slender legs threading their way perfectly through the small empty spaces like a butterfly, a graceful burst of delight. She came to rest behind Karin, her arms folded on her stepmother's shoulders. "And guess who is going to drive me to pick up my friend Amanda and then go on to our dance lesson? Guess!"

"I could never imagine," I pretended.

"Me! Yours truly. Thea Ward, licensed California vehicle driver."

"Sweetie," Karin began, "I'm not sure if . . ."

"You promised," Thea came back, holding Karin very tight from behind, as if to fortify her resolve. "You said I could at least drive from Aunt Faith's to my lesson and back, and Amanda's is on the way. You did say I could . . ."

"I thought I said 'maybe' . . ."

"No 'maybes,' " Thea said, giving Karin a quick kiss before releasing her, pirouetting perfectly, then breezing out the door. "I'll come straight back. No detours, two hours longest, not to worry . . ." and she was off.

Karin sank back in a chair and grinned at me. "She is so pleased with herself," she said, "getting a driver's license really is a rite of passage for today's kids."

She took a deep breath, and I could almost see the happy mood begin to dissipate.

"Let's sit out on the back deck," I suggested, "we have to make some good use of this sunshine while we've got it, and you can admire my dahlias."

"Sunshine and dahlias," she said, and for a moment I thought she had something more to add, but she hadn't. She lay back on the big redwood chaise, closed her eyes and told me May had called her at eight that morning, from Paris.

"Hayes has been offered a position with the State Department," she told me.

It caught me by surprise, which must have shown because Karin said, "I know. I wouldn't have thought it, either, he has been on the other side for so long."

"What does May think about it?"

"May has always been determined to be apolitical, you know that—because of her father, what it did to him. What is important to her is that Hayes come to terms with himself, that he has a clear idea of what he wants to do. She says he feels he hasn't been able to accomplish anything outside of the power structure, and that events seem to be pushing him to work from within. Or at least to give it a try. May is pretty certain he is going to take it, and that is fine with her because what she wants is to make a life with him. She did say that Washington is a good place for her to be, too. She thinks she can finish her part of the Ring of Fire project by June if she works her tail off. In the meantime, with Hayes in Washington they can meet halfway in San Francisco, instead of these incredibly long flights all over the world."

Karin smiled. "It's so wonderful to hear the happiness in her voice," she said, her own voice catching. "For a while, I thought this obsession with finding her mother was going to take precedence over everything—"

"I don't think she's given up the idea," I said, "but the fiasco in

Thailand frightened her enough to make her want to go in legally. The problem is, the Chinese don't seem to want to give her a visa. Kit thinks they must have her name on a list somewhere, that possibly they know about her connection to Wing Soong and they don't like the idea that one of the heroes of the revolution has a granddaughter who is a U.S. citizen."

"I tried to warn her about Sam," Karin said, her mouth turning down with disdain, "I honestly believe he wanted to hurt her—don't try to defend him, Faith. Maybe it wasn't conscious, but I think he has this rage in him and somehow, it all got focused on May. And it's unforgivable, really!"

"I wasn't going to . . ." I began, when the phone rang. It was Philip, for Karin.

The phone was just inside the kitchen, so I could not avoid hearing her end of the conversation. "Yes," Karin said, "I did." And then, "It is only a few blocks, and I thought . . ." Her back hunched, she leaned against the wall. "She is a good driver, Philip, you said so yourself . . ." She straightened, rubbed the small of her back as if it pained her. "I'm sorry, yes. I know. I shouldn't have, you're right, letting her drive for the first time in San Francisco probably was poor judgment. It's just that she wanted so badly . . . I know, I shouldn't be swayed into taking risks. I'm sorry to have upset you . . . yes, well, I know it's her safety that concerns you . . . Shall I call you as soon as she gets back, so you don't worry?" He must have been mollified, because her voice became relaxed: "Sure," she said, "take my extra set. I left them on the bed table in my room."

She walked to the edge of the deck to examine my dahlias. "They are so outrageously beautiful," she said, "my dahlias are puny next to these." And then, defensively, "It's not how it sounds, Faith. Philip has so much on his mind—he's having trouble sleeping, he's up most nights reading or working on his new book, and he worries that it keeps me awake. So sometimes I sleep in the extra room. Poor Philip, when it isn't insomnia it's headaches, he's working so hard and he's so upset about Dan that he's tightening his grip on Thea."

She did not turn around. "Dan was eighteen last week," she finally said, "and I'm almost certain he's coming home today to tell his dad that he is going to join the Marines."

The silky fabric of her blouse stretched tight across her shoulder blades. "Philip thought Dan would spend this year finishing high school. It is going to come as quite a shock to him to learn that the kid has managed to get enough credits to graduate early. At least, that's what I suspect. I figured that was his idea when he decided to go to summer school."

"And you haven't told Philip?"

She shook her head. "We can't talk about Dan anymore. What it seems to come down to is Philip telling me to 'stay out of this, it's not your problem.' It's okay for me to love them, I'm just not supposed to share in the responsibility. He was more surprised than angry, I think—that I would have made the decision to let Thea drive. I don't know what he'd do if Thea gets in an accident today and is hurt. As it is, with Dan and Philip I feel caught in the middle and bruised by both sides. And neither one of them can be made to see what the other feels or wants. Dan can be a royal pain . . . he's so gung ho you would think he'd invented the Halls of Montezuma. And Philip's just as bad, in a much more articulate way. He can listen all day long to one of his students, but he can't hear a thing his son is saying. To tell you the truth, I wanted to get out of the house today. I've got a feeling Dan is coming home to square off with his dad, and I'd just as soon not be there when they decide to slug it out." She paused, added wistfully, "Kids put a terrific strain on a marriage, don't they?"

"I can't think of a parent who wouldn't agree with that," I told her.

They were sitting opposite each other in the living room when Karin and Thea returned. Philip leaned forward, turning the pages on a small file of papers placed precisely in front of him on the coffee table. Daniel slouched on the couch, his arms flung wide. Thea started rummaging in her handbag, to show her brother her license, then she saw her father's face and checked herself. "I'll catch you later," she called out to her brother, "I've got to get going on your cake." Karin tried to follow Thea to the kitchen, but Philip called her back.

They've waited for me, she thought. They didn't want to start the war without me.

"What do you think of this?" Philip asked, nodding toward the papers.

"I don't know what 'this' is," Karin came back, on guard.

"Daniel's school records. He has given himself an eighteenth birthday present. He has managed to finish high school a full year early. Isn't that a surprise?" he asked, caustically.

"No, it isn't," she answered, looking at him steadily. "Usually people who choose to go to summer school do it for a reason."

"I see," Philip said, his lips pursed. "I suppose then I'm the only one who didn't know."

Karin was silent. Dan watched, sprawling in an awkward attempt to look at ease, waiting for the first blow.

Philip delivered it. "So you want to go to war, is that it? The marines are going to make a man out of you, is that what you think? They'll give you a gun and take you someplace far away from home where you can kill a bunch of foreigners, and you'll come back to waving flags and a hero's welcome, is that what you have in mind?"

Dan's eyes narrowed, as if some bright light had been shined in them. "I see nothing wrong in fighting for my country. The American Way may sound corny to you, but not everybody thinks the way you think. I love my country and I believe in it, and I'm ready to go . . ."

"Dan," Karin broke in, her anguish spilling over, "don't you think the Vietnamese boys love their country? You wouldn't be fighting for the American Way in Vietnam. You would be fighting Vietnamese boys who feel they are defending their own country against you—an outsider. That is a civil war, and there is a question of morality."

"That's enough Karin," Philip broke in sternly, "don't try to talk to Daniel about morality. He's got that all figured out. Reason doesn't work with Private Daniel Ward here," he taunted.

"At least Karin talks to me, at least she gives a damn what happens to me."

"Listen . . ." she began as calmly as she could, but she could see by the vein that was standing out in sharp relief on Philip's forehead that he was not going to be calmed.

"Karin, I think you'd better just keep out of this . . ."

"Oh right," Dan said, standing and flailing his arms about his body as if he were engaged in some sort of awkward warmup exercise. "You bully everybody else in this house, so why not bully Karin? She tries her damndest to please you, but that's not good enough, is it? My mother tried her damnedest, too, and she couldn't quite cut the mustard either, could she? Nobody can please the famous Dr. Ward."

"We're not talking about your mother and we aren't talking about Karin," Philip said, struggling to keep calm. "Don't try to provoke me, Daniel. What we're talking about is your joining the Marine Corps. I'm against it. And I intend to do everything in my power to keep you from doing something that you are going to regret. And you will regret it, mark my word. You will."

"There's nothing you can do," Dan came back, but his denial lacked conviction. Karin knew he thought his father might be able to stop him. Dan lashed out, "The truth is, you got yourself a deferment so you wouldn't have to go to the Second World War, and one coward is all we can afford per family."

He hit a nerve so raw that even Dan seemed shocked by the ferocity of Philip's counterattack. Suddenly they were shouting, standing chin to chin, blasting each other with sounds of echoing anger, furious and fatal. Karin watched, beaten back, unable to take her eyes from Philip's face, which was a mottled red.

Thea came screaming out of the kitchen and flung herself at her father; she began beating him on the chest with her fists. "Stop it, stop it, stop it" she shrieked, repeating the words hysterically until they were but a whisper. While Philip and Karin struggled to quiet her, Dan slipped out of the house. Karin heard him start his car, heard it rumble off down the street and she thought: We've lost him, he's gone forever.

She did not know if she had been sleeping; she thought so but she could not be sure. She felt the sudden, sick surge, the raw, aching memory and then she knew she had been asleep but that something had wakened her.

She heard it. A sound, not loud. Soft, wrong. She listened, straining to place it so she could dismiss it and escape back into sleep. But no. There it was again. An animal noise, muffled and grotesque. She sat up, waited at the edge of her bed, listening. She walked into the hall, to the door of Philip's room and listened. Standing there in her nightgown, in the chill, she began to tremble. Carefully, she pushed open the door. The noise grew louder. She switched on the light. Philip was collapsed sideways on the bed, his mouth open, the hideous sound blowing from his mouth and nose.

The call came at six in the morning. I will never know how I knew, but I knew. It was Kit, and it was bad news. My fear was such that I could just barely rasp out a "hello" to let her know I was on the line and listening.

"I'm at Alta Bates Hospital with Karin," she told me. "Philip has had a stroke. A massive stroke." She waited to give it time to sink in. "They don't know anything yet, a whole team of doctors is with him now—it's going to take time to assess the damage. He is paralyzed, Faith. It doesn't look good."

Frank Egon got out of his old Ford Falcon, walked around to open the barbed wire fence, drove through and stopped again to close it behind him. He squinted up at the sky. Clear, bright blue, only a few wisps of clouds over the mountains. He should be able to make it into Cat Canyon by eleven. If he was wrong, and Dan wasn't there, he could be back at the school for his three o'clock class. And if he was right, well . . . to hell with the three o'clock class. Murray could take it. He realized he should have left him a note. But he hadn't wanted to leave a note, he didn't want them to know, he just wanted to find the kid and this was the last place he could think to look. Cat Canyon. Dan was the one who had said that if he was an outlaw, that was where he'd go to hide. After that, the boys used to tease him about "heading out for Cat Canyon."

It was a longshot, Egon knew. But it had been more than a week with no word and the kid had to be somewhere.

The blue plume of smoke was visible from the top of the trail, and he knew he had been right. Scrambling up a rise, he saw him sitting by the edge of the stream, tossing rocks in the water.

Hands cupped around his mouth, he shouted, "Hey, Ward."

Dan turned and looked at him without surprise.

"I hope you've got some coffee going, boy," Egon told him when he was within talking distance. "I just double-timed it up this frigging mountain."

Dan rummaged in his pack, found a packet of instant coffee and handed it to him.

Egon squatted by the fire, poured hot water into the tin cup Dan had given him, taking his time.

"Your folks have been trying to find you," he started.

Dan's eyes flared and he stood up to be prepared, as if he might bolt. "If my dad sent you here to talk to me, forget it."

"No, no, it wasn't him. It's not that . . . Your stepmother's been calling me, she's pretty upset." He paused then, looking directly at the boy. "Dan," he said, using his given name for the first time, "I'm bringing bad news, I want you to prepare yourself."

Dan frowned.

"There's been a kind of accident. Your father is in the hospital." He decided to give it to him straight, all at once. "He's had a stroke and he's paralyzed, he's going to live, but it's pretty bad. Do you understand what I'm saying?" The flashes of pure, clear pain and confusion that flickered across the boy's face made the older man put the coffee cup down and stand, at the ready.

"Careful, boy," he said, staring Dan hard in the eyes. "Hold on to it. Don't lose it."

Dan blinked and managed to slide a frozen expression over his face, to hide the one Egon had seen.

"What happened?" Dan asked, his voice clamped even.

"Your stepmother has been calling me regular . . . She thought you'd probably turn up at the school, so she wanted me to be able to give you all the details." He did not tell Dan that Karin had been terrified that he might hear about his father from a newscast or the paper, that he might blame himself and do himself damage. That was why she wanted him to find Dan. She thought he could handle it. He wasn't so sure. "You ready to listen to me now? You want a few minutes to get used to the idea?"

Dan said, "Go ahead."

"He has what the medics call locked-in syndrome. He is awake and he understands everything that's going on, but he can't move and he can't speak. In other words, he is fully conscious. The doctors say it is a rare kind of stroke that he had." Egon pulled a crumpled piece of paper from his pocket, smoothed it and read, "Most strokes take place in the cerebrum. Your father's was in the area called the pons, the brain stem—it's the pathway from the brain to the body. The pons is so badly damaged that it can't relay the messages from the brain to his body. Since the visual and auditory pathways are higher up, they weren't injured. So while nearly all voluntary movement is paralyzed, he can still see and hear perfectly well and his thoughts, sensations and involuntary movements are normal."

"You mean he's trapped?" Dan said, horror on his face. "Jesus God, he's trapped inside his body."

Egon looked at him carefully, and continued in the tone of voice he used in the classroom.

"If the damage had been a few centimeters lower, it would have affected the regions of the brain that control blood pressure, the heart, breathing . . . and he would have been dead. If it had been one centimeter higher, in those parts that control thought and sensory perception, he would be comatose. That's what usually happens. But in your father's case, the stroke acted to disconnect the brain from the body. Your father can blink his eyes, and that's a beginning. The doctors won't really know the extent of the damage for a few weeks. It's possible he might get some movement back."

Dan sat looking at the ground. "When did it happen?" he finally asked.

Egon stared at him until he lifted his eyes.

"The night you left."

Dan blinked, trying to absorb this new piece of information.

"The fight," he finally said, "his face was all red."

"The doctors said it had been coming on for a long time. He was being treated for high blood pressure, but he didn't want anyone to know. Your stepmother didn't even know. She is worried that you might blame yourself, and she says to tell you that you shouldn't. Looking back, she says, she can see the signs . . . and most of them were when you were in school. She said to tell you . . ." Egon paused, then went on, stiffly, ". . . that she loves you, and she wishes you could come home now even if you don't stay very long. She says she and your sister could use your support."

He had said it all, more words of emotion than he had spoken at any one time to anybody for longer than he could remember . . . Korea, probably. That's what it reminded him of, men at war. Out here in the mountains, pine trees all around and the stillness and knowing there was death out there, behind that pretty tree-humped ridge, and pain and boys you weren't ever going to see again. The wind shifted and blew the fire smoke in his eyes, making them smart.

"Let's break camp, Ward," he said. "I've got a three o'clock, and you need a shower and a shave before you head up there to help your family."

He was relieved to see the boy had submitted to orders. He wasn't sure what he would have done if he had cut and run.

24

The sweet, spicy smell of carnations caught in her throat as she passed the flower shop in the lobby, and for a moment she thought she was going to throw up. She hurried on to the elevators. "Good morning, Mrs. Ward," one of the nurses called out to her, "I've been setting my watch by you all these months, what do you mean being late this morning?"

Karin wanted to laugh but she couldn't, laughing would bring her too close to tears. The elevator doors opened. She looked in; it was empty. She stood, staring, until the doors closed again. A man in a white coat came to wait beside her. He was reading a medical report and did not look up. The doors opened again, he waited for her to get on. "Going up?" he finally said, and when she shook her head he went in and was back to his report when the doors closed.

"I wondered where you were," Marge Fromberg whispered, as Karin entered the room, "I've read the entire *New York Times* but I'm not sure how much Philip heard—he closed his eyes about fifteen minutes ago. I think my fine, droning delivery may have put him to sleep—or maybe it was the story about the Watergate burglars."

Outside, in the hallway, Marge asked, "How did it go at school this morning?"

"I don't know what's happening, Marge," she answered, and was surprised to hear her voice quaver. "Thea hasn't been to school for the past week. I don't know what she's been doing all day long. And I don't know what's wrong with me, either. I stood downstairs like an automaton just now and let three elevators go by before I could get on one." The worried look on Marge's face made her cough, as if to pull herself together. "Thanks for coming over early, good friend," Karin said in what she hoped was a normal tone of voice. "I'd better go in—Philip's going to wonder if something's wrong."

Marge put her arms around her and held her for a long moment. "You're going to have to take some time for yourself, dear heart. You really are."

Karin felt the anger rising, but she swallowed it. She could not explode at Marge as she had at May. "How about you?" May kept saying. "You're pushing it too hard, I'm worried about you."

"Well don't," she had screamed into the telephone yesterday. "It's not me lying in that rotten hospital bed, day after day, all these months, trapped inside a body that won't work . . . I'm not the one you should be feeling sorry for, for Christ's sake."

As soon as she leaned over the bed, he opened his eyes.

"Were you playing 'possum?" she asked in what she hoped was a light tone.

He blinked once. Yes.

"Marge is dear, but I think you would rather have me?"

Two blinks. "No? Is that the truth?"

Two blinks. "Ah," she said, "you had me going for a minute there, you tease." She looked into his eyes and wondered if she would ever get accustomed to it: those living eyes in a body that was so totally still. In the beginning she had thought she should be able to read his eyes, to understand what he was feeling by looking into them. She knew now that she could not. Only those few times when his eyes had filled with tears did she have any idea what he was feeling. She took a tissue and dabbed at a bit of dribble that had slipped out the side of his mouth.

"Did Miss Parnell go through the morning drill with you?" she asked.

No.

"No? Damn! She promised she would do it first thing. You can't trust anybody . . ." She felt the anger flash through her and she took a deep breath to bring it under control. Anger was counterproductive. Her stomach fluttered; she stood very straight, put her hand over his.

"Okay, let's get on with it then. I'll try to zip through the list as fast as possible. Okay?"

One blink. "Okay." (Why, she wondered, did she feel he was angry with her?)

"Are you in pain? Yes. Okay, let's localize. Is it in your feet? No. Your lower legs? Yes."

It took ten minutes to discover that his lower right calf had been cramping, that it had been going on all night and that it was driving him crazy. She had asked him that: Is it driving you crazy? And he had answered with a fluttering of his eyelids, which was answer in itself.

The last question was always: "Are you comfortable now?" Sometimes it took an hour to get there. Karin hadn't realized how much she had come to dread the routine until yesterday, when nurse Parnell had said she would do it—there had been such a flood of relief. She bit her lip, realizing that the anger she had felt was not so much for the discomfort it had caused Philip as it was her own disappointment.

"Okay," Karin made herself say, pulling her chair up close to the bed. "You will want to know what I found out at Thea's school this morning. You know I was meeting with Mrs. Rourke, the principal— and she had already talked to all of Thea's teachers, and she had asked the school psychologist to sit in. They are concerned about Thea's behavior, too. I decided to wait until this morning to tell Thea I was going to her school, and when I did she just flatly refused to go at all. Marge is going over to the house now, she said she has been wanting to spend some time with Thea and this would be a good morning for her."

She rubbed his hand, and went on: "I know how sensitive you are to your girl, and I know you have seen how tense she has been . . . after coming to see you every day for so long, then suddenly not coming this past week. You have been worried, haven't you?"

Philip blinked once, his eyes steady on her face.

"I knew you would be. The school psychologist gave me the name of a psychiatrist—a woman who treats adolescents, mainly. I'm going to talk to her tomorrow, if it's all right with you. Just to ask her advice, at this point . . . is that all right?"

He didn't answer for a time; then he did blink yes.

"If you object . . ." Karin began, but was interrupted by a young nurse who came in apologizing: "Mrs. Ward, I'm so sorry I'm late," she said. "There was an emergency on five, and two of their nurses are out and I had to cover . . ."

"It's all right," Karin said, "Everything is under control here."

Turning to Philip, the nurse asked, "Are you okay? Is there anything I can do for you?"

He blinked once, waited, and then once again.

"I read that as a yes and a yes rather than a delayed no. I'm getting good, right?" the girl laughed.

Philip blinked once again. It took her six questions to discover that his bed was wet.

When the nurse left and Karin came back into the room she apologized, "I'm sorry, I should have asked you if there was anything else I could do to make you comfortable—I usually do, but this morning I'm so out of whack . . ."

He blinked once. Yes. He understood. Her eyes filled with tears.

"I am sorry," she said again, wiping her eyes with the back of her hand. "Sometimes I sit here and look at you, and I want so badly to hear your voice, to get your advice, to know what you are thinking. Then I feel so awful, thinking about what I want to hear, when I can only imagine how grim this is for you. Okay. I can hear you telling me now, 'Get on with it, girl,' so I'll get on with the family news. I want to tell you about Dan, too. He's called every single day since he got out of basic training. He said they didn't throw anything at him that came close to being rough enough. That sounds like bravado, but it isn't, really. I just think it is how he is coping with what has happened to you. He'll be getting leave soon and he's coming home. I'm glad because I think he'll be able to comfort Thea. I know you don't remember much about those first days after it happened," she went on, "but I'm not sure either Thea or I could have managed without Dan. I was surprised, I have to admit, at how steady he was."

"Test time," an aide called out, knocking and walking through the door at the same moment. "We have to take Dr. Ward to X ray for a scan. It'll be a couple of hours—if you're going out, you might want to call before you come back."

As she bent to kiss Philip goodbye, a wave of dizziness swept over her. She straightened and concentrated on keeping her balance.

"Are you all right, Mrs. Ward?" the attendant asked.

"I'm fine," Karin told him, "I've been feeling a little woozy—I hope it's not the flu."

"Plenty of that around here," he answered, as he wheeled Philip out of the room.

She had to hold herself back, not to run through the lobby. She covered her mouth as she passed the flower shop to avoid the sweet, funereal smell of carnations. Outside, she held on to a post while she took in several large gulps of air; if I had to go back inside right now, she thought, *I could not do it.*

The music was loud enough to hear from the front door. The Who, Karin thought. That means she's at home. As she put her key in the lock, Marge opened the door from the inside.

"I can't find her," she said, "I got here about ten minutes ago, and I've been looking . . ."

Karin switched off Thea's stereo and the house seemed to swell with the silence. The women stood, listening. A tree limb brushed against the window; the wind was rising, it was going to rain. Karin began to tremble.

"Stay here," Marge said, "I'm going to make a more thorough sweep."

Karin could hear Marge as she entered each room . . . the spare room first (she would see that Karin slept there), then Dan's. She heard the closet door squeak open and close again. On down the hallway, into the master bedroom. Philip's room. Then Marge's voice, loud, calling: "Karin, come!"

Thea was huddled in a corner of Philip's big closet, her face just visible between the folds of his suitpants. Her expression was blank, empty, lost. A long thin wail escaped into the awful silence. *Thea is screaming,* Karin thought, until she felt the sound ripping out of her own throat. Thea crouched motionless, clutching to her chest an old leather case, and Karin knew exactly what was in it: Philip's father's straight razor.

Israel's arm was hurting him, I could tell by the way he favored it when he lifted my chair through the doorway. I pretended not to notice. I hadn't wanted to ask him to take me to Karin's, it was drizzling out and cold, and I knew he wasn't up to it but I also knew it would have angered him if I had asked anybody else.

On the drive over the bridge he had said to me, "I just keep thinking of how they were that night at the big party Mrs. McCord gave them down at Wildwood. And in Hawaii, at the luau on the beach. That poor sweet little girl . . ." I did not know if he meant Karin or Thea, and I did not want to interrupt to ask. There was a certain comfort in the low, biblical roll of his voice: *"For the mountains will I take up a weeping and wailing, and for the habitations of the wilderness a lamentation."*

Kit was already there, and Marge and Hank. Thea sat in a corner of the sofa, a quilt over her knees as if she were an invalid. She waved weakly to me, and managed a smile when Israel called out in one long breath, "Hello over there in the corner little Miss Thea Ward, registered California driver, when we going to the drag races darlin'?"

I took one look at Karin and I wanted to cry. Her eyes were rimmed in red. I reached for her hand and could not help but see her poor fingernails, bitten so deeply beneath the quick that they were bloody. "Dear child," I blurted, "you have got to have some relief."

"Exactly right," Hank Fromberg said, putting his arm around her firmly and leading her over to the sofa to sit next to Thea. "And that's what we're here to talk about, Karin . . . and Thea. Both of you need a respite . . . no, listen to me first Karin. May wants the two of you to come to Hawaii to stay with her for a little while. There is a very fine private school in Honolulu, Punahou, and we've talked to some people we know there, the Browns, their daughter Lynne is going there—you remember Lynne, Thea. She'll be happy to have you go to classes with her while you're there, if you want to."

Thea was looking at Hank intently, as if everything he was saying was of tremendous interest. He asked, "What do you think? Does that sound like a plausible idea, Thea? Going to Hawaii for a while?"

"Wait," Karin tried to cut in, "I don't see how . . ."

Thea began to cry then; she lowered her chin to her chest and sobbed quietly. "Darling," Karin said to her, "please, don't cry. Tell me, do you want to go to Hawaii?"

The child said nothing.

"Yes?" Karin prompted. "Would it help to get away for a bit?"

"I can't go back," Thea said, her voice rising with the threat of hysteria, "I can't see Daddy like that any more. I can't."

"All right," Karin said, petting her to quiet her down, "all right honey, you don't have to go, we'll figure it out."

Kit had been quiet all this while, but now she broke in, "We've all talked about this, Karin and Thea. Behind your backs, I'm afraid, because we are worried. We think that you should go to Hawaii together. I know it is hard to leave, but let me tell you something. Marge and I had a talk with the psychologist at the hospital today. He thinks that Philip is so overwhelmed with the need to deal with his family that he can't deal with what is going on within himself. He even believes that Philip might feel a sense of relief, if he knew you were someplace where you were getting some rest.

"There are therapists who could be brought in to work with him. And I will be able to help. As a matter of fact, I dropped by the hospital this afternoon, after Marge called, to take him a book about Morse code. I remembered Philip saying that he knew it once, and today when I asked him if he would like a refresher course he said yes. So that would be something I could work with him on while you are away. And you could take a copy with you, so when you get back you'll know it too.

"One more thing. I know you go in every afternoon, Karin, so I knew Philip would be wondering where you were today. I told him that Thea wasn't feeling well, and you had asked me to come and explain why you couldn't be there. I asked him if it upset him, not having you there, and he made the signal for 'no.' Obviously, he wanted me to explore that answer, and I tried to. I asked several different questions, but it was only when I said, 'Are you worried that Thea and Karin are pushing themselves too hard?' that he said 'yes.' What both of you have to remember is that he loves you, and that he is quite capable of being enormously worried about the effect his illness is having on you."

"Yes," Marge chimed in, "and that is the very best reason for you to go . . . don't you see? He will have a chance to think about himself if he knows that you are all right."

"Karin?" Thea asked in a tiny voice.

"Do you want to go, darling?" Karin asked.

"Yes," Thea said. "If it will help Daddy."

Karin looked at me. "Tell me what to do, Faith," she said.

"I can't tell you what to do, child," I answered, "but I do believe that if you ask Philip, and he says 'yes' he wants you to go, then you should go. You know we will keep close watch over him for you."

On the way home that night, Israel said rather wistfully, "I hope they go. I do believe Hawaii is a balm for the sorrowing soul. They could restore themselves there. If I had my druthers . . ."

"You don't need to finish," I told him, "I know where you'd be right now, if you had your druthers."

"You are right, lady Faith. Back in those blue Pacific islands." The rest of the way home he sang me songs that Kimo and the others had taught him, all about palm trees swaying and silver moons shining and the pretty wahines on the beach at Waikiki.

Kit came bustling into the hospital room, balancing a cup of coffee and a croissant—"my breakfast," she explained to Philip—with a tote bag filled with books and papers.

"Sorry I'm late but May called this morning just as I was heading for the door, and she wanted to *talk.* She's the one who usually speaks in shorthand because she is in such a rush, but not this morning. Which is well and good, because she had lots to tell me about Thea and Karin and I took notes, so I could remember it all."

She stopped, turned and looked at him, took a deep breath, smiled widely and said, "Good morning."

Philip blinked once. "Yes," she echoed him.

"All right," she went on, "I'm going to slow down for a moment, have my breakfast and tell you all the news. Then we can get down to the business of the day. But first, have they made you comfortable? Yes, good."

She smiled again. "I'm going to have to get used to the sound of my own voice, I suppose. And of being alone with you. Hank said you asked that your visitors be limited, is that right? Yes. Well, that makes sense, if we're going to get any work done.

"The news from Hawaii now. At the end of the first week, May says that Thea seems much like her old self, though she still gets weepy when she talks about you. She has had one session with a psychiatrist who has had quite a lot of experience with adolescent trauma, and Thea said she would like to continue seeing him. May is more worried about Karin. She says she sleeps too much, and seems lethargic. But she has stopped biting her fingernails, which May takes as a sign that she is calming down. They are staying at May's apartment in Honolulu, and Karin is talking about coming back at the end of the week. May says it doesn't do to try to push her right now, but she thinks it is going to take longer for both of them to settle down and get their balance. May knows somebody who has a modest little house to sublet which is up in the hills in the Makiki Heights section

320

of Honolulu, within walking distance of Punahou School, and it looks like they may move up there tomorrow. Yesterday Thea went to class with the little friend of the Frombergs, and she liked it so much she wants to sit in next week, too. The school is tough to get into, but we've squared it with them—don't ask me how, I don't want to have to tell you." She looked at him, grimaced and said: "Oh to hell with it, you know anyway. May did a little endowing . . . but she can afford it, believe me." She laughed, and added, "I hope you think that's funny."

She paused to sip her coffee and looked at him over the cup; his eyes were fixed on her face. She thought, "He is still such a fine-looking man." Then she smiled and said it out loud. "I'm telling you this because it suddenly occurred to me that it would be wonderful if we could just tap into each other's minds, and forgo the words. And then I thought, why not try to do that, as much as I can, by telling you my thoughts. Not doctored, not edited for any particular consumption, just as they are—unvarnished, sometimes unlovely, but as true as I can make them."

He blinked once. Yes.

"Are you sure?" she asked, and he blinked again.

"This could be an interesting experiment," she told him, adding, "or it could be a disaster. I've never allowed anyone into my thoughts before." She took a sharp breath, remembering. "Oh my God," she said, staring at him, "that's what you accused me of—when you were thirty-one and I was forty-one, all those years ago—you said I would never allow you all the way into my mind, my thoughts."

He closed his eyes, and opened them again slowly.

"You were wrong, Philip . . . I am letting you in, now. A little late perhaps—but not too late, I hope. I am sixty-nine now, so you would be fifty-nine. The difference in our ages was terrifying to me then, and it's terrifying to me now. But now, I think, I can face it. And part of the reason . . . to be cruelly honest . . . is because of what's happened to you."

She leaned close, put her hand over his. "Nobody knows for sure how much you are going to be able to do for yourself. There are some hopeful signs, the doctors say. You know that much. What you don't know is that how well you recover has a great deal to do with how much you want to recover. You're going to live another fifteen years or more, but how well you live is something else."

She stopped, turned her back on him and looked out the window.

Then she turned back, resolve in her face, and said, "I have to tell you that I take a certain comfort in not knowing if what I am about to say is going to embarrass you. But here it is. I can't tell you why, Philip, but the prospect of working with you, of helping you get back as much mobility, as much speech, as you possibly can, excites me tremendously. If only I could crawl inside of you right now and turn on all the switches that say 'Go, Kit! Do it! I'll work with you as hard as I can!' I would, because *I* want it so much. I have been feeling so tired with my life, Philip. This may sound melodramatic, but I think you could be my salvation. This is the first real challenge I've felt for a very long time . . . this is so hard, not knowing what you are thinking about any of this . . . I'll try to explain—Philip, it wasn't right for us all those years ago. We didn't make a mistake, it could not have worked, not then . . . you had too much to do, and I was never any good at tagging along, you know that. I didn't do a very good job of explaining it at the time, I know I hurt you . . . but I have so much feeling for you left over from that time. It surprised me, too, truly it did." She paused to wipe her eyes and said, "I'm sorry."

He blinked his eyes, twice. *No.*

She smiled, put her hand over his again and said, "You're right. I'm not sorry."

25

-- ▭ ▭ ▭ --

They ran, one in front of the other along the sun-splotched path that paralleled the beach. May, tall and dark, in the lead and Karin, small and blond, behind. They ran in rhythm to each other, their strides measured. The only sound they made was the pull of their breathing, and the crunch of dry seed pods under their running shoes.

Finally Karin called, "Time-out. The banyan tree."

May pulled up under the vast, spreading tree, grabbing on to one of the dangling roots that dropped from the branches and swaying with it. "You're getting there," she said as Karin collapsed in the leafy shade.

"I certainly hope so," Karin answered, pulling off the headband she had been wearing so that her hair sprang out. "It's all frizzy—that's what this climate does to me."

"Makes you frizzy? Looks to me like you're reverting to hippie-hood."

"And you're reverting to sado-masochism, making me run every day . . . besides, I never looked like a hippie."

"Correction. You never smelled like a hippie."

"That's because I hate patchouli oil." Karin laughed.

May considered her, and said, "God, it's good to hear you laugh again."

323

"Well, if I may return the compliment, I have to say it is good to see you looking so happy, and I don't think it is totally from the sheer enjoyment you get from torturing me in these exercise outings."

"Right you are. It's because I had my Wednesday morning Hayes fix—about an hour ago. The aura lasts about half a day, then I go into withdrawal, wanting him so badly my teeth ache. Not to mention other tender parts. It's so crazy, K—all those months without him, and now it's pure agony if I don't talk to him every day. His voice is enough to turn me on."

"How much longer till you wind up the program here?"

May sighed. "Obregon isn't making it easy. He acts as if I'm deserting the ship. I think he would like for it to go on forever—and why not? He gets the lion's share of the credit while Tim and I do all the work. But the bulk of the work is in place. It's actually become pretty boring—luckily, Tim doesn't think so. But I am definitely going to be done by June, that's the one thing I am certain about. This morning Hayes talked about setting the date. We want to keep it simple—maybe a small ceremony in one of the little churches on the Big Island. What do you think?"

"I think that would be perfect . . ."

"And you will be my witness. That's as much as we've planned."

They walked slowly to the car, talking about May's plans, May's future. "It's so strange how everything has fallen into place," she said. "After Hong Kong, it just seemed as if all the obstacles were surmountable." She laughed. "I didn't make it over the Burma Road, but that fiasco somehow made everything between Hayes and me possible. Wouldn't Sam hate that? If being together means I have to go to Timbuktu, then that's where I'll go. Hayes thinks we can find a place where both of us can work. Wherever we end up, being together is the important thing."

Karin's face was soft with reflected pleasure. She listened, nodded, asked questions. When they reached May's car they opened the doors and rolled down the windows. They faced each other over the top of the car, waiting for it to cool. Suddenly May blurted: "You just look so sad, I, I wish . . ." She could not say what she wished.

Karin rested her chin on her arms and thought. "You asked me to be your witness. Now you be mine. Help me do what I should do."

"*Should* is a worrisome word."

Karin ignored the remark. "Thea's doctor says she is doing very well. He doesn't feel she was seriously suicidal. The thing is, we've been here almost three weeks and every time I try to talk to her about going back, she turns me off. She has been going to school every day with Lynne, but now she is doing the homework, which means she no longer thinks of herself as a visitor. And she is talking about taking a dance class—with a woman who teaches at the University of Hawaii. There's even a boy who likes her . . . and this weekend she is planning to go off on a senior class trip. It's making me very nervous—we need to get back."

"Need?" May said, "What do you *want* to do?"

Karin slapped her hand, hard, on the hot top of the car. "Can't you hear me? What I want has nothing at all to do with it. What I want is not the issue and never was. We can't all go around doing what we want to do."

The look on May's face made her say, "Oh, I don't mean you, May—I'm talking about myself. I've been doing what I want to do instead of what I should be doing. Philip is my husband and my place is with him but I don't know what to do about Thea."

They drove in silence for a time. "What does Kit have to say about Philip's progress?" May asked, changing tactics.

"That he 'said' his first word in code. Steak. Seems he is starving for real food. The therapists are working with him every day, and now it looks as if the damage may not be as devastating as they thought. The important thing is that Philip seems to be up to the effort. Kit says he always wants to work longer than any of them, that his resiliency is amazing them all."

May worded her next question carefully, keeping her eyes on the winding road. "Before Philip's accident, how were things between you?"

"Why do you ask?"

"I don't know, just a feeling."

Karin nodded and pressed her lips together. "Okay, you asked, I'll tell you. The marriage was a mistake, my mistake. I was charmed by Philip, but I wasn't in love with him and I never figured out how to be his wife, the one he wanted. The role was too much for me— except where Dan and Thea were concerned. I love them, I couldn't possibly leave them. But I didn't love Philip, and the strain of the charade was becoming unbearable."

May waited awhile before asking, "What do you think about Kit's role in his rehabilitation?"

Karin cradled her head in her hand, as if she were very tired. "You

don't have to tiptoe around. I know about Philip and Kit," she said.
"I found some old photos in a foot locker in the basement a long time
ago, I think Philip must have forgotten about them. It was only a
couple of snapshots, really—from the 1940s, I think. They looked so
young. It was fairly clear that they were more than just casual ac-
quaintances."

"You never asked Philip about it?"

Karin shook her head. "I figured Kit would have told you, and that
you would have warned me if you thought it mattered."

"You trusted me that much?"

"Yes. And Philip and Kit, too."

"And now?"

"Now? I don't know why Kit is doing what she's doing—if you are
suggesting she might still feel something for Philip, I don't think so.
She might feel she owes me something, or Philip. I think it is more
likely that she simply wants to help, that it is a challenge, as she says.
To be honest, it really doesn't matter. The only thing I know for
certain is that I am Philip's wife, and because of that I should be there
to help him if I can."

May hesitated, then said it. "And if you can't?"

Karin didn't answer at once. She finally said, "I've been such a
disappointment to him, you know . . . before it happened I wasn't
even sleeping with him, except when he asked and then he quit
asking . . . and I was . . . relieved. I don't really know what happened.
He was so hopeful, so sure when he married me, and I thought
. . . but somehow whatever Philip wanted didn't happen, and there
was the trouble with Dan . . ."

"Things were going wrong with Dan long before you came into the
picture, K. I'm not going to let you flog yourself about that."

"I know, but you see," she bit her lip, "Philip expected me to be
his wife first, and the mother of his children second. The truth is,
almost from the beginning I cared more about being their mother
than I cared about being his wife. And I'm still doing it—I'm here
because I'm worried sick about Thea . . . and it isn't right, May. It
really isn't. Philip deserves better from me." She was close to tears.

"Okay," May told her, "listen. I have an idea. You said Thea was
going away this weekend on a class trip. Why don't you use the time
to fly back home and see Philip? I'll cover for you with Thea on
Monday, and you can come back on Tuesday."

"I don't know . . . I mean, I didn't think we would be staying so
long—and I don't know about going without Thea."

"Face it, K. Thea isn't ready yet, and you are going to get more and more tense, the longer you're away. This way you can at least explain to Philip what's happening with Thea, and you can get an idea of how he's doing."

May stopped in front of the steep drive that led down to the little house where Karin and Thea were staying. "I think you're right," Karin said as she got out, "I will make a quick trip back. But right now I'd better go in and see who belongs to that nifty little sports car in the drive."

He was sprawled on the swing on the lanai, and Karin knew at once he was Alex Hollowell, who had been voted, Thea told her, "senior class heartbreak." Karin could see why. He had a tight, graceful body, his jeans outlined his slim hips and his shirt was unbuttoned to allow a glimpse of the hard muscle coil of his chest. His face was almost beautiful. Had it not been for the eyebrows, which almost met, he would have been too pretty to be acceptable. He looked at her and she knew the look. Instinctively, she lifted the bag she was carrying to her chest.

"Here she is," Thea called out, her voice artificially high as she introduced them.

"Alex has promised to take me to see Sunset Beach—the waves are supposed to be perfect today, and all the great surfers will be out . . ."

A wave of apprehension washed over Karin: "When, you mean now?"

The look on Thea's face was a warning. "I've been wanting to go there . . ." she started, reprovingly.

"I just want to know how far it is," Karin said, directing the question to Alex, "and if you'll be back before . . ." She had been about to say "dark," but she managed to catch herself, and said "by dinnertime."

Alex answered for her: "I'll have her back by seven, Mrs. Ward, that's a promise." He smiled winningly. Karin wondered how long he'd been using his charm to get what he wanted.

"I still need to know how far it is," she told him, "because I don't want you racing that sports car over mountain roads to make it back on time."

When they left, Thea was pouting because the trip to Sunset Beach had been postponed. They were going over to the local beach, to see who was there. Alex's smile was intact, but Karin could see that he was not pleased.

327

. . .

That night Thea ate her dinner in angry silence, her eyes on her plate. Karin made several attempts to break through, but Thea was having none of it. Finally, Karin sighed and said, "Look, honey, I know I am being very protective and I'm sorry, if that makes things hard for you but . . . well, we don't really know Alex that well . . ."

"What do you want to know about him?" she came back, suddenly combative. In short, hot bursts she recited, "We're the strangers here—his family has been in Hawaii forever. Both his parents graduated from Punahou. He's an only child. His mother died last year in a boating accident—we have that much in common, both our mothers are dead. His father owns a boatyard and works all the time. They aren't rich and they aren't poor either. The reason he can afford a sports car is that his father let him trade in his mom's Cadillac. He doesn't make terrific grades, but he's terrifically smart. He likes me, but I don't know how long that is going to last if you keep quizzing him every time we go out." Her eyes flashed as she finished, but Karin could see that the anger had spent itself.

"Is Alex going on the trip this weekend?" she asked.

Thea frowned in disappointment. "No, he'd already made other plans . . . he said if he had known I would be going . . . but it was too late to change."

"While you're away this weekend," Karin began, so that Thea would know at once that she was not expected to go with her, "I thought I would make a quick trip back to California, to see how your dad is doing."

Karin saw the panic rising in the girl's eyes: "When will you be back?" was her first question. Her anger over Alex was gone, Karin noticed. Then, plaintively, "You will come back, won't you?"

"Yes," Karin said, caressing her hair, "I'll be back on Tuesday. May said she'll be here Sunday night when you return, to stay with you."

"That isn't necessary," Thea told her, "I can stay with Lynne. I mean, I know how busy May is and all . . ."

"All right," Karin agreed. "You understand why I need to go back?"

Thea nodded, her eyes closed as if to hold back her own misery.

"Thea, dear," Karin went on, "listen to me now. I don't want you to go with me, because we need to be very careful—you and I—about not upsetting your dad's new therapy. He is working very hard, and it is possible that if he sees how worried we are about him, that could upset him so he isn't able to work. In a way you could say he needs you to be here, to try to carry on your own life in as happy a way as possible. So I am going back mostly to see what will be best for your dad. Do you understand?"

She nodded to signal that she did, but she kept her eyes lowered so Karin could not see how relieved she was, to be told she didn't have to go.

When Karin arrived, Kit was sitting in the chair at the foot of Philip's bed, reading out loud from *The New York Times,* yet another analysis of Nixon's firing of Cox in the Watergate affair. Karin stood at the door and the words *run . . . now* flashed into her mind before she could choke them off.

Kit looked up, saw her and smiled. "Here she is," she said to Philip. Then she rose to embrace Karin, and quickly gathered her things to leave.

Karin wanted to ask her not to go, not to leave them alone. "I'll see you later, Kit," she said instead, and moved to Philip's bedside.

"Hello, dear," were her first words. She took his hand in hers and added, "Your errant wife has returned. I needed to see for myself this wonderful progress I hear you're making."

He blinked, but she didn't know what it meant. "Let me give you all the news from Hawaii," she heard herself say, hating the false-hearty tone of her voice. "Thea . . ." she began, and talked at length about how well she was doing. When she had exhausted the news of Thea, she talked about Dan for a time, and even fished his last two letters out of her handbag, to read to him.

All the while she was aware of his eyes on her, watching. What does he see? she wondered. What is he thinking?

She did not know how long she could bear having him watch her.

Karin kicked off her sandals, took off the linen suit she had traveled in and sprawled on the thick carpeting. The sterile white of May's Honolulu apartment made her think of the hospital, so she closed her eyes. She was dozing when May came in.

"I needed to talk to you," Karin said, "but first I have to call Thea to tell her I'm back . . ."

"Thea's having dinner at Lynne's," May answered. "They were going to bring her here at eight so we could pick you up at the airport. You came back early. How come?"

"How come," Karin said, taking a deep breath. "That's what I need to talk to you about. I don't really know *how come* anything."

"Do you want a drink?" May asked.

"No," Karin answered, "though sometimes I think it would be grand to get gloriously drunk and stay that way."

"No you don't."

"No, I don't."

Karin pulled herself up and rested her back against a chair. A small gold locket fell in the tender spot between her breasts. May saw it and smiled. It had been her first gift to Karin, the year they had met in school. "You still wear the locket?" she said.

Karin lifted it out, caressed it tenderly between her fingers. "Philip used to say that some people have security blankets, but I had my security charm."

"Well, if 'security' means permanence, then Philip was right."

"Philip was often right."

May lowered herself onto the rug and reached for Karin's hand. "Tell me about him."

Karin pressed her lips hard together. "Philip," she said, "is making truly remarkable progress. Kit has organized a whole battalion of therapists, and a few stalwart friends like Marge and Faith, to work with him. The communication system they have set up is amazing. And while he looks much the same—he remains paralyzed—he seems different, too. I think because there are ways now that he can make his wishes known—he isn't so isolated."

She put her head back on the chair and closed her eyes. "I haven't been sleeping—I can feel it in the pit of my stomach."

"What are his wishes?" May asked. "Did you talk to Kit?"

"Kit was at the hospital when I arrived, then I didn't see her again until Faith's on Sunday afternoon. That's when Hank Fromberg takes his stint with Philip. It was so strange, May—to be with Faith and Kit and feel . . . awkward. So much was being left unsaid. The three of us spent several hours together, and for the first half of that time the talk was trivial . . . just small talk. Oh, they wanted to know about Thea and how she was doing, and Dan, of course. Faith told me all about Israel and his 'lumbago'—whatever that is—and how a friend of hers went over to check on him and was distressed to find him living in a tiny, one-room apartment with only a hot plate to cook on. Kit was doing what you used to call her 'vanishing' routine, where she manages to make you think she is taking part, but she really has withdrawn."

May interrupted. "I've only talked to her twice in the last few weeks, and both those times she wanted me to talk about you and Thea, come to think of it. She answered my questions as perfunctorily as possible. Still, there was something in her voice . . ."

"Exactly," Karin answered. "It's how she looks that gives her away. She is just . . . the only word I can think to describe it is 'luminous' . . . she looks absolutely wonderful, you would never guess that she was sixty-nine, she looks ten years younger. But wait, I'm getting ahead of myself. Anyway, I guess Faith figured out that I was about to go crazy with all the avoiding, so she said something very sweet and gentle, I don't remember her words exactly, but something like, 'Karin, dear, tell us what you need to know.'"

Karin stood, stretched, then leaned over to touch her toes, as if she could not sit still with the memory. She straightened, clasped her hands in front of her, and went on. I said, 'I need to know what I can do to help Philip.' No one said anything, there was this long silence— I think Faith was waiting for Kit to speak up, and she didn't, so I decided to dive in. 'And I need to know if all you are doing is for me, Kit. Or is it for Philip?'

"Then something very strange happened. Kit's eyes flooded with tears. She wasn't really crying, but the tears just started streaming down her cheeks. And stranger yet, she didn't try to turn away. I always carry a linen handkerchief—you know that old habit—so I got up to give it to her, and instead she took my hand and clung to it. She was sitting on one of Faith's old settees . . . I sat down next to her and put my arms around her and we held each other.

"After that," she went on, "all the barriers were down, it was as if one group of women had been replaced by another, and the three of us were old friends again, and we could really talk. I'm not sure that Kit knows why she is working so hard to help Philip. She says it is a tremendous challenge, and that it makes her feel as if she has a purpose again. I envy her, May . . . wanting to do it, I mean. I really do." Karin's voice cracked, and she began to cry, softly. The telephone rang, as if to announce a time-out, and May sprang up to answer it.

"Yes," she said into the receiver, "I was just about to call you. Karin caught an earlier flight. Yes, everything is okay with your dad, she'll tell you all about it later. No, that won't work." A long silence, then, and with steel in her voice she said, "No. They don't have to bring you here, we'll pick you up in a while. Just sit tight and wait."

"Was that Thea? Is something wrong?" Karin wanted to know.

"We'll talk about Thea when you've finished telling me about Kit."

Karin frowned, but did as May said. "Well, Philip's rehabilitation has become something of an obsession with her, that's the first thing. It took me awhile to catch on, but she has pushed everything else in her life aside, to concentrate on him. She is at the hospital almost every day. In the beginning I'm sure it was to give me some relief. But then it became a challenge, and when Philip began to respond, she said, she had a feeling of great *reward*—that was her word."

It was May's turn to frown. "Did you tell her what you know?"

"You mean that they were lovers once? No, I didn't, any more than I would tell her that Philip and I were never truly lovers. That's in the past, done."

"And . . . ?"

"What I discovered is that Philip wants me to concentrate on Thea . . . what he said, using Morse code, was that he would be 'forever grateful' to me if I helped his children, so he could put all his energy into his recovery."

"Do you think he meant it?"

"Yes. Yes, I'm sure he did. What I'm not sure of is why. If he thinks I would be acting only out of a sense of duty, he would hate that. I don't know. I just know there is nothing more for me to do there, right now. I went in to see him this morning, very briefly, on the way to the airport. I interrupted his first session with a physical therapist, and I got the oddest feeling that he was annoyed at the interruption. That may not have been true, of course. There is an atmosphere in the room of work underway, people in and out all the time—it's a major production, really. You could title it, 'The Reclamation of Philip Ward.' I don't mean to sound cynical. Really, the feeling is very hopeful. I give Kit good marks."

May's stomach growled. "I skipped lunch," she said, in explanation. "Let me stick some frozen dinners in the oven. Chicken divan, how does that sound?"

"Terrible," Karin answered, "why don't we call out for Chinese?"

May ran her forefinger down the list she kept taped to the wall next to the telephone and placed the order.

"You were saying that you didn't mean to sound cynical," May reminded her, "but you did . . . a little. Or did I misunderstand?"

Karin struggled with the chopsticks, trying to pick up a square of barbecued pork. "I feel . . . impotent. I mean, when it comes right down to it, the best thing I can do for Philip is to stay out of his way. Oh, everybody—Kit particularly—works overtime to make it seem right to me. Because they know I don't have this driving passion to do what Kit is doing . . . they may even know that before Thea and I left, I had to force myself just to enter the hospital. It's as if I can't seem to come up with the right feelings, or reactions, or something. I'm disoriented—I don't know what I'm supposed to do . . . except I'm not supposed to be dismissed, am I?"

"You're not being dismissed, and you're not running away. Thea and Dan are big responsibilities. They're still very young, and your work is cut out for you—it's not going to be easy sailing, you know."

"I guess I can't put it off any longer—tell me about Thea," Karin said wearily.

"Last night I called Lynne's house about nine, just to check to make sure the girls got back okay from the outing. Lynne was there, but Thea wasn't. She had never made plans to stay overnight. I drove right up to the house and found Thea there with the kid who has the green sports car. Alex? They were snuggled up together on the lanai, in a cloud of cannabis."

"Damn!" Karin exploded. "That bastard Alex!"

"Maybe," May came back, "but Thea was the one who lied to you."

Karin ignored the remark to ask, "What did you do?"

"I didn't want the kid to drive home stoned, so I made him call his father, and the guy was up there in about ten minutes and packed him off. Didn't have much to say, but he did the job—told the kid to get in his car and wait for him, he didn't even have to raise his voice. Then he apologized to me and Thea, though I'm not sure Thea heard, she was so out of it. I brought her here and put her to bed, and she is very contrite. She asked me if I felt I had to tell you, and I said yes. She is probably on pins and needles right now, wondering how you are going to react."

Karin was holding her head in her hands. "I guess you're right. I do have my work cut out for me."

"And you're on your own, Philip can't back you up."

"He never really did," Karin answered. "Did I tell you Dan will be coming through in a couple of weeks? He called on Saturday to say he got his orders. He's being posted to the embassy in Saigon. I thought sure he wouldn't have to go at all, now that the war is over."

"The war will be over when there aren't any more American military in Vietnam," May said.

The telephone rang again. "That's Thea," May said, "she can't stand it another minute."

Karin cleared her throat, picked up the phone and answered in a voice with a studied distance. "Yes, we were about to come get you . . . yes, she did . . . not so much angry as disappointed, I think, but we'll talk about it later . . . I hope so, but I guess that is something we'll have to work on . . . yes, in about twenty minutes."

She came back to the living room, smiling wanly. "You were right. She is very contrite, and very worried—and very sincere, I think. But I'm not sure just how smitten she is with this Hollowell kid."

"You sound so old-fashioned, K."

Karin started clearing the food cartons from the sink. "Maybe that is my problem," she answered. "My marriage was a mistake, but saying it doesn't exempt me from my responsibility to Philip. He is still my husband, and he is helpless, and while Kit's great passion to help put him back together again is a wonderful help right now, I'm sure her commitment has its limits. I can't allow myself to forget that someday soon I am going to have to go back and take charge—and I should. It's my job. Philip would have done it for me."

"If you had decided to . . ." May started, then stopped and shook her head. "Forget I said that."

"Said what?" Karin answered. "If I had divorced Philip before this happened, would I still feel so responsible?"

"And so guilty?" May added.

Karin slipped into her sandals and began to gather her things. "I would have done whatever Thea and Dan needed me to do."

"Isn't that what you are doing?" May asked. "Isn't that what Philip has asked you to do?"

"Yes, but," Karin said as they climbed into May's car, "the difference is I hadn't made a break before the accident, and now I never can . . . and live with myself. I'm Philip's wife for life, and nothing is going to change that."

"Nothing sounds pretty hopeless."

"We make choices, May. I made one and it turned out to be a mistake, but that doesn't mean I can walk away from it."

"Some people do," May answered. "My mother did."

"And look at the pain her choice gave you," Karin answered.

26

April Fool's Day, 1973, May scrawled in the journal, *I hope my starting on this date is not prophetic.*

She was in a small stateroom on the river boat *Nam Shan,* one hour out of Hong Kong on her way to Macao on the China Coast.

She wrote: "I am keeping this notebook as a record. For Hayes and Kit, in case. And for Faith, for the archive. I do not mean to sound cataclysmic, it's just that I left in something of a hurry and without letting anyone but Karin know—though by now she will have called Hayes and Kit with my messages."

She nibbled on her pencil, thinking, and then began to write again. "I have real confidence in the Hong Kong people who are helping me. Kit put me on to them a couple of years ago, and they have been working to set this up since the Thailand fiasco. I will not name any names, or give any clues to their identities here, in case."

"In case," she repeated out loud. It was possible that something could happen. But they had all been so careful, so much attention had been paid to detail. She scribbled, "If all goes according to plan, I should go into China through Macao's Barrier Gate on April 6 and be back out again on Friday, the 13th. I am operating on the theory that the days between April Fool's and Friday the 13th will be lucky."

She closed the journal and made her way to the deck, to breathe in the Orient. There was, she thought, nothing in the world quite like it, the sweet smoky smell and steam rising.

A heavy mist hung over the shores as the *Nam Shan,* flying the British flag, approached that point where the brown silt from the Pearl Estuary meets the waters of the South China Sea. The line of demarcation was almost pencil sharp, the water was so still. From the upper deck she could make out, even in the mist, the hills of Macao. Beyond them lay China.

An Englishman, reporting to his wife from behind the pages of the *South China Morning Post,* read, "The last American troops left Vietnam yesterday. Today, all remaining American prisoners of war will be released in Hanoi." Then he offered, "The Yanks finally decided to cut and run—serves them right, arrogant bastards."

When his wife attempted to shush him, he came out from behind the paper long enough to scan the deck and announce, "No Yanks here, why are you making all those dreadful squawking noises?"

May felt an urge to correct him, but she held herself back. It was just as well, she thought. It showed she was passing already, if only in the mind of a smug, middle-aged British couple. She thought instead of the report from Vietnam. Hayes would be even more worried now about Andy's child and his mother, and she wasn't making matters any easier for him by choosing this time to smuggle herself into China. Karin's mind would be on Vietnam, too. Dan Ward would soon be on his way to Saigon to serve as a marine guard. It is all so strange, she thought, how so many threads of their lives seem to be coming together here, in Asia.

As the docks at Macao hove into sight, the boat took a long, slow dip and May's stomach rose and fell with it. Her heart began to race. She held hard to the railing and faced into the stiff, hot breeze to try to catch her breath. She did not recognize her own anxiety, did not realize her body was reacting to the fear that had been buried in her for most of her life.

She was to make her way to the old Bella Vista hotel, register as Kwan Da-yong, and wait to be contacted. The mist that was turning into a light rain seemed to be conspiring to set the stage.

She tried to imagine how it would be, meeting the woman who had deserted her, the mother who had lived for so long inside of her. She tried to set the scene, predict the dialogue. "I'm the daughter you left behind," she would say, "I'm the one you walked away from, and never bothered to look back." And her mother would say . . . She could never get that far, never imagine even how she would look or what the sound of her voice would be. She could only see herself standing there, in the middle of an empty room—it was always empty—saying, "I am the daughter you left behind . . ."

The Bella Vista, a rambling old colonial hotel set into the hills high above the Praia Grande Bay, had been in a state of decline for several decades. From the end of the Second World War until 1950 it had served as a NAAFI for British soldiers. It was all pillared splendor and faded grandeur from another century, now quite shabby except for the wonderful views from the balconies. Aside from two meals on the verandah, where a warm breeze was blowing, May stayed in her room, waiting.

In a drawer she found a faded booklet that detailed the history of the hotel. It included a poem called "Macao" written by a young English cadet named Jollye, who had stopped at the hotel for a time, the booklet reported, before being posted to Malaya where he was killed in a jungle ambush in the 1950s. She scanned the poem:

> *An alien city rimmed by shallow seas*
> *And purple islands, at the world extreme . . .*

At the world extreme. She sat propped against the iron headboard of the bed and a cramp in her neck caused her to shift. *At the world extreme.* She looked out over the calm sea, watched as a junk made its way slowly across her field of vision. When she could no longer see it, she turned back to the poem.

> *The yellow hour of twilight that recedes . . .*
> *The slow sad songs girls sing . . .*

She stood, stretched, squinted into the light. Once more she glanced down at the poem and caught a closing phrase:

". . . a woman I loved too much . . ."

A woman loved too much. She wondered if it was an Asian woman he had loved too much, or one he had left behind in Britain.

How can you love a woman you have never known, she wondered. The thought stopped her. Is that what she expected? For her mother to love her? Did she think it was an automatic response, motherly love? That once you had it, it never went away? Was she going to China to meet her mother and collect what was coming to her—all that stored-up love? No! Absolutely not. If that was what she was expecting, she should turn right around and go home and hug Kit and crawl into bed with Hayes and make her own babies, and hold them tight and love them hard and never let them doubt, not for a minute. You can't store up love, you have to use it.

So what did she expect? she asked herself. Why was she going to find her mother? She knew why. To shed some light on the dark place that had existed within her for so long, simply to see the woman and understand that she was just that—a woman, a human being, no goddess with superhuman qualities. Not the golden creature who still appeared in her dreams, beckoning her to come with her.

She had always believed that when the dreams stopped, she would be free of her mother. But they had not stopped.

She wanted Hayes to be with her, she wanted him so much it was all she could do to keep herself from going down to the lobby and putting in a call to tell him where she was. That was the hardest part, cutting herself off from Hayes for even a few days. The letter she mailed that morning would reach him when she was already inside. There was no turning back . . . she had come this far, everything was in place, she could not waver.

The waiter brought her a note with the bottled water she had ordered. She was to go to Luis ca Moes Square at four that afternoon and walk through the old Protestant cemetery.

She couldn't fathom why they would choose to meet in a cemetery. Maybe in a ghoulish way they wanted her to feel at home. It was Western inside the walled garden—old and beautiful, spacious and ornate with the heavily carved old stones and frangipani bushes spilling flowers over the green, grassy graves. She was standing before the stone of Fidella Bridges, beloved daughter of James B. and Sarah A. Endicott, who was born in Macao on August 21, 1853 and died on September 15, 1859. She was thinking sweet little Fidella, poor James and poor Sarah. Sacred to the Memory of. The man— Chinese, short, wearing black trousers and a gray short-sleeved shirt—came walking rather blithely down the stairs that led into the cemetery and headed straight for her. There was nothing secretive about the meeting. He smiled broadly and said she should call him "Joe" and that everything was set, that tomorrow she would meet her Chinese "family." He told her the family numbers seven or eight— depending on who works on any given day—and comes through the Barrier Gate every morning at seven to work in the fields around

Macao. They go back through before eight at night, when the gate closes. She was to join the family in the fields tomorrow and work with them for three days so she could study their gestures, their dialect, and learn how a peasant girl should act. If she was a good student, she would be allowed to go into China with them on the evening of day four.

Every joint in her body ached, she felt as if her back was permanently deformed and she knew she had no vocation for hard physical labor. Coming back to her room at the finish of the third day in the fields, she attempted to write in her journal. "The family," she began, "has taken me under its wing. I have learned the proper way to spread night soil, the proper way to pull weeds, the proper way to tie my apron, the proper way to hold my chopsticks. Proper for a young peasant woman from Wanchi. I work without a hat to get as dark as possible, and without gloves to toughen my hands. I also know how to answer if I am asked to produce my identification certificate from the Revolutionary Committee for my county. It is a pretty good forgery. I suppose some of Dad's old nemeses would say that makes me a card-carrying commie. We go in after work tomorrow. Tonight I must sew my stash of gold and silver coins, and some pieces of jade, into the gray pajamas I will be wearing. There is also a money belt, in which I have gold taels. To pay and to bribe, if it becomes necessary. I will be able to carry only a small knapsack to hold some clean rags. I am expecting my period. Tampax is not allowed. Welcome to the dark ages. I am too tired to write any more."

At seven on the evening before she was to go in, Joe took her to the temple of Yuan Yin to pray for a safe journey. She found herself looking into the goddess's smooth face and whispering, "Please bring me home safely to those I love." Joe gave a few last-minute admonishments and made her go over the route and all the landmarks he had insisted she memorize before he returned her to the family. Before he left, he smiled and said, "Until we meet again," in the peculiar brand of English he spoke.

They approached the Barrier Gate a few minutes before eight, just at closing so the guards would be thinking about their dinners and not pay so much attention to the last-minute rush of workers returning to China. Because of her height, she rode in the cart. She lifted her eyes as they approached the old archway that marked the border.

Across the top was enscribed: *A Patria Honrai Que A Patria Vos Contempla.*
As the cart rolled toward the Chinese border officials, her heart was
pounding so hard she was certain it could be heard above all the
chatter and noise the family was making.

A large, conical hat shielded her face and her eyes were trained on
her lap. She had her hands in the folds of her apron so the blisters
could not be seen. In a moment it would be her turn. She began to
breathe through her mouth; she was sure every move she made could
be heard. The silence was broken by the wild flapping of a red-brown
chicken that had got loose, setting off a cacophony of voices, calling
and screeching. In the periphery of her vision she could see feathers
flying, and behind them the drab green uniform of the officials, and
a high-pitched voice filled with authority, shouting. As the feathers
floated lazily to earth and the noise calmed, the guards waved the
family through. In the confusion, they had not asked questions. Her
teeth were clenched so tightly that her jaws ached. She gave herself
up to the lurching of the wagon, allowed the crunching noise of the
wheels to enter her bones. Her ears rang with the aftermath of fear.

China was dark, quiet, vast. After less than an hour the lurching
cart stopped at the dirt road where she was to leave the family. They
had been paid by Joe. When she offered more, the father refused,
smiling but determined. The girl who had braided her hair giggled
and pressed her hand in goodbye, and she had an awful urge to shout,
"Don't go." She did not. The first rule Joe laid down was "Follow the
plan and do exactly as you are told." And then he had said, gently,
"If you do not, you could hurt all of us who want to help you."

It was dark now, but the moon was full and so bright she could
easily follow the road. She walked some distance—a kilometer, Joe
had said—until she came to a small harbor with several dozen sampans, just where he had said they would be. It took three tries before
she found one that would be heading upriver in the morning, and
would take her on. A large old woman with short, bowed legs said,
"Climb aboard, climb aboard" almost before she could finish telling
her where she wanted to go. Soon she discovered why. The woman
lived on the boat with a son who looked to be about fifty and was
mute, whether by choice or not May could not say. He simply did
not talk, and the poor old soul was starved for company.

That night the cicadas' song echoed over the water, loud and shrill
and throbbing. May had been given a pallet in the corner of the boat
under the roof, and a pot of very hot green tea. From this perch she

could smell the mud, smell the night. Brown and green and gray, the colors of China. She was not afraid.

Almost at first light, as the son poled the boat from the nest of sampans, the old woman started talking. She talked compulsively as she made their morning gruel. She could not stop: stories of her girlhood, of her father and her mother, stories from another time. It was why she took her on, May realized. She was a fresh ear to hear all the old stories. It was why, she supposed, the son had so thoroughly tuned out. The woman gave May some nets to mend, but when she saw the blisters on her hands she took the nets away and brought out some White Flower Medicated Oil and rubbed it into her palms, murmuring, "so young, so young." It was the only glimmer of interest the old woman showed in May. Not once did she ask her any questions.

May left the sampan at midday and walked for perhaps an hour along an empty country road. She wished she could have brought a watch; it was terrible, not knowing the time. The only people she saw close-up were two men sitting on their haunches near a flame tree. The colors struck her as outrageous—the orange-red of the tree against a field of brown and green, the tight brown muscles of the men's bare legs, sculpted by years in the fields. She could not let her eyes wander, so intent was she on spotting the hut that would be standing alone in the middle of a field of Chinese cabbage. When finally it appeared, she felt relieved enough to lift her eyes and look out over the green fields which merged in the distance with low hills. Dust and manure and the smell of green things growing filled her nose and mouth and eyes. A water buffalo moved slowly across a field, straining at its harness. She could feel slow beads of sweat slipping between her breasts, the prickly dampness of the money belt around her waist. She sat on a stump and fished two gold coins out of a pant cuff. That is what Joe had said it would cost.

The short, squat man who had been sitting outside the shack greeted her with, "Have you eaten, Sister?" She knew it was a standard greeting, what the Chinese say instead of "How are you?" and the answer is supposed to be "yes." But the only thing she had had to eat that day was a watery gruel with a few bits of oily fish on top, and she was starved.

"I have, yes," she told him, "but if you have some food, I would be grateful for a small portion." He looked at her and cocked his head, as if she were some new species of animal, and went to the back of the shack where a small fire was going. In a few minutes she was eating huge black mushrooms and greens she could not identify, cooked in a great black wok and served on top of a bowl of rice. She lifted the bowl to her mouth and shoveled the food in. It was all she could do to remember the proper way to hold her chopsticks, she was so hungry.

As soon as she finished, the man ushered her inside the shack where two bicycles were waiting. She offered him the two gold coins, but he took only one. She was puzzled, but there was something about the methodical way he took the coin that told her not to offer more. They set off right away, pedaling along a narrow roadway that struck out through the field, then they veered off onto a smaller road. After an hour or more, when she was beginning to think her legs might fall off, they stopped to have warm tea from a Thermos he had in his kit, and moon cakes. An artist or a photographer might have thought it a charming scene, peasants taking tea and cakes under a lychee tree. The charm escaped May. Her cotton slacks and shirt were wet with sweat, and her period had started, right on schedule.

Eight days after her arrival in Macao, May found herself spending the night in a small farmhouse on the edge of a village in south China. They had arrived after dark, and she had climbed a ladder to a loft where she slept among rough sacks of what smelled like grain. She had a new traveling companion, Xue Lian, a woman May guessed to be in her early thirties who had a smooth, round Mongolian face and who exuded competence and good humor.

As they were settling in for the night, Xue thrust her feet into a roost of sleeping chickens, causing an uproar of outraged clucking. "Quiet down little babies," she crooned to them, "Xue Lian's big feet did not mean to enter your dreams."

As soon as May opened her eyes the next morning, Xue was there with a bowl of warm water so she could wash up. "Hurry down," she whispered, "I have fixed our morning meal." May climbed back down the ladder, stepping onto the hard-packed dirt floor of the main room. There was not enough light to see well, but she thought several bundles in the far corners, under the loft, must be sleeping bodies.

She breathed in the fresh, cool air of the compound and shook the dust out of her clothes. Smoke was rising from the roof of the cooking room. Xue Lian came out carrying a black kettle filled with gruel, and another pot containing rice with more of the ubiquitous giant black mushrooms and greens. They ate in the gray predawn light, sitting on their haunches outside of the cook house. May started to speak, but Xue Lian shook her head, motioning to her to be silent and eat.

They pushed hard that morning, traveling along a dusty country road so rutted that they often had to walk the bicycles. Once they passed a young woman shepherding a gaggle of geese. She carried a long wand and prodded the birds along, and all May could think of were the old pictures in a Mother Goose book she had as a child. Softly, under her breath, she began to hum, "Mary Had a Little Lamb." Xue Lian turned, smiling, and began to hum it too. The two women crossed a great field, humming the old nursery rhyme as loud as they could, and when they were finished they began to laugh.

"Where did you learn that song?" May wanted to know.

"Some missionaries taught my mother, my mother taught me," Xue Lian said proudly. "I used to sing it to the children, but no more. Not since Western influences have been discouraged."

"Then you are a teacher?"

"Once I was. In nursery school, I think you say."

"And now?"

A broad smile grew into an irrepressible laugh. "Now I guide travel tours for American ladies." She pushed far enough ahead, then, to make talk impossible.

Usually they skirted the villages, but now they were headed directly into one, a very old place surrounded by a brick wall, streaked black with age. Clustered at the road leading in was a group of young men in uniform and behind them, at the gate, two older men who were checking identification cards. May glanced anxiously at her companion who said, "Be calm, do as you were told." She tried to remember what Joe had said to say when they asked for her card, she tried to remember her alias, but she couldn't. Her mind was utterly blank.

She almost lost her balance when she got into the queue to present her card. Xue's hand shot out to steady her bicycle. Her underarms felt prickly, a sweat bee buzzed around her neck but she did not dare free a hand to brush it away. Xue was next in line, then it would be May's turn. She concentrated on breathing deeply, on swallowing the rising panic when an old man came running toward them shouting something incomprehensible. A dozen villagers rushed up to him, older people mostly, pushing in front of Xue and May, surrounding the man and the officials, and soon everyone was shouting and gesturing.

She felt a tug on her sleeve. Xue was moving ahead, through the gate, and May knew she should follow. She started slowly, keeping her eyes on Xue, who was entering the gate . . . only a few steps more and she would be safe.

"Stop. You there." He meant May, she could feel it in her back.

"What is your name?" he asked.

"Kwan Da-yong," May was amazed to hear herself answer in a voice she scarcely recognized, as she handed over her card.

He examined it carefully, holding it close to his eyes. Then he looked at her and frowned. "What business have you here?" he asked, holding the card up between them.

She reached for it with her hand open, so he could see the single piece of jade that was nestled in her palm.

At this moment the other official extricated himself from the hubbub and approached them. *This is it,* she thought, *you're caught on illegal entry . . . spying, probably . . . forged papers, bribing an official, it's all over.* She forced herself not to look to see if Xue Lian had fled.

With the dexterity of a magician, the official lifted the jade from her palm with his middle fingers and pocketed it, while handing back her card from the Revolutionary Committee. "Just another student," he said, waving her through.

Xue Lian was waiting around the first turn. "He took a bribe," May said, her voice quavering.

Xue shrugged and said, "If the troubles we have just been through have taught us anything, it is that greed is inevitably part of the human condition."

They went down narrow streets, turning right and left and right again until May was lost. The buildings were close together, crowded along the narrow lane so she saw only the doorways, was aware only that the buildings were old and high, of stone that was black with age. She turned into a narrow doorway in a house that was dark and smelled as if animals were kept there. She was led up a steep flight of wooden stairs to a room that was empty, except for a table covered with a blue and white flowered cloth, and two elaborately carved chairs that she guessed had been salvaged from some grand place.

Her companion smiled enigmatically, and said she should wait and not to go near the window, and then she left. Ten minutes passed, to May it seemed an hour. This was not her mother's town, she knew that. It would be another day, possibly two, before they reached the remote village where her mother lived. This stop had not been on the schedule. *Do exactly what you are told to do,* Joe had said, but this wasn't Macao and she had no idea what was happening. What if someone had turned her over to the authorities? But if that had happened, she asked herself, what would she be doing in a home?

She heard someone enter below, a door pushed firmly shut, slow and shuffling steps. She stood, pressed against the wall, hardly daring to breathe. The window was the only way out. She wanted to run over to it, to see if she could climb out. *Stay away from the window. Do exactly as you are told.* It was too late, she was committed to trust them. She had no choice.

Voices rose from below: Xue Lian's, laughing, and another. Then someone was climbing the stairs, slowly. The head appeared; it was bigger than the body. At first she thought it was a boy, a dwarf. Its twisted body seemed to sidestep into the room, moving with difficulty. She turned to face it.

"Wing Mei-jin," it said in a voice so feather soft it seemed to float across the room to her, and then in a very old-fashioned, stilted English: "Do not be afraid, my child. I am Tsiao Jie. My father—your grandfather—had the name for me 'China Rose.' I should like to present myself to you as your aunt."

She smiled, a big, open, glorious smile that spilled over into her eyes. May felt something come loose inside her which began to roll around, making her feel giddy. "You," she said, with a laugh on the verge of becoming a cry, "it is you."

"Yes," Tsiao Jie laughed too, a wonderfully sweet laugh. "Have I surprised you, dear one?"

They spoke in Mandarin for the speed, because there was so little time and so much to say. Tsiao Jie told May about her grandfather, about her father when he came to China. She said that it had been her most precious wish someday to see May, to touch her face and tell her how proud her grandfather would have been. "He loved beautiful women, you see," she said, her eyes sparkling with wit, "and you are so beautiful. I see now why Chou said we must hide your face."

Chou. Pronounced "Joe." Of course. The English he spoke was Tsiao Jie's English—May's grandfather's English.

345

"Is Chou your friend?" May asked. "How much did you have to do with bringing me here?"

"There is no time to talk of such things," was her answer, but May knew. Tsiao Jie had put herself in jeopardy to help her. She had engineered the journey, and the people who were helping May were doing it for her aunt, for China Rose.

"Have you talked with . . . my mother?" May asked.

Her face, which was the most alive face May had ever seen, became sad. "I have seen Ch'ing-Ling twice," she answered, and May knew the words had been rehearsed. "Once when your father was still alive, again just after his death. Then I was sent far away, to the North, and I have not seen her again."

"Does she know I am coming?"

"No," Rose answered simply, "I feared that if she did, she might not agree to see you."

"She may run from me, even now."

"Yes. It is possible that you will be disappointed."

May's answer came without hesitation. "It won't matter, Aunt Rose. If I had to leave now, it would be all right—seeing you, talking to you, being here. It's as if I've found a part of my past that has been missing. I'll always remember how it was, being here today with you."

Rose took her hand and squeezed it so hard it would have hurt, had May been able to feel pain. "I'm going to come back to China," May said. "I'm going to come back with Hayes, so that you can meet him. And Kit. We will have a family reunion. China can't keep me out forever."

May watched her great eyes fill with tears; she laid her cheek next to the tiny woman's, and found it soft and smooth. Then Rose's hands pressed gently on her arms as she said, "Go now to meet your mother, and then go back to your betrothed and live in happiness and peace, and when you come back to China, bring me also a grandniece. Or a nephew, or one of each."

That afternoon May pedaled her bicycle for four hours over rough country roads. She could have gone on forever.

They slept under a thatch of ironwood trees not far from a stream with duck pens. May lay awake, filled with a kind of elation. She listened to the ducks scrabble, and went over and over everything Rose had said to her. She had tried so long to imagine what it would be like, meeting her mother, but she had not thought about Rose.

China Rose. Dad's half sister, those same wonderful eyes—his eyes!—in that poor little twisted body.

May knew that her grandmother had been crippled. Grandfather had been tall and straight, like her father, but he had loved two crippled women . . . Rose's mother, she would have liked to ask about her. There was so much she wanted to know.

Realizing that Xue Lian must be a follower of her aunt's, she asked, "What can you tell me about her?"

Xue answered, laughing, "She has greatness, your aunt. There is nothing we would not do for her."

"We?" May asked.

"Those of us who have the honor to know her, to be at her service. There are many."

"How many?"

"That you must ask your auntie—when you come to see her through the front door." She laughed hard, as if she had made some wonderful joke. "Your Mr. Nixon," she ventured, "he is opening the door to China, you will be back."

May tried to tell her why he wasn't "her" Mr. Nixon, tried to explain why he was probably going to be tossed out on his ear over a scandal called Watergate, but Xue could not understand. As far as she was concerned, Nixon is a great man simply for having come to rap on China's closed door.

That morning, the first karst formations came into view, strange mountains rising in the morning mist. May felt as if she had entered an ancient Chinese scroll, pedaling through green fields as the karsts came closer and closer. She watched the sun reach its apex and tried to think what time it would be in Washington, but she could not. Washington was another world, another time. When the sun was at an oblique angle, they arrived at the River Li.

"We rest now, and let the river be our feet," Xue Lian said as they waited on the river bank. Soon a raft made of giant bamboo poles pulled up, and they maneuvered to get their bicycles onto it.

For more than two hours they floated down the river, the karst formations rising majestically on every side and into the distance. This was the China of May's imagination: delicate in its complexity, light reflecting off the water, giant stands of bamboo casting tender shadows. Here and there villagers harvested weeds from the river's bottom or fished. Cormorants stood motionless on a sandbar, children played alongside the river as their mothers washed clothes and spread them on the rocks to dry. This was life along the River Li, represented on the ancient scrolls, China of a thousand dreams, the poet's China. She could understand why Madame Mao did not want foreign visitors to come to this place, to disturb the old ways, to bring change. And she could see why her mother would have chosen to live here, in the calm of a village on this winding river at the edge of time.

She sat cross-legged on the raft, one hand holding on to her bicycle to steady it, and felt as if she could drift forever down the River Li.

The village was like several others they had passed—a high, dun-colored wall behind which nestled several compounds. Children played along the riverbank, clamored over the boats that were tied there. The raft bumped to a stop on the stony quay, and a small boy jumped out to steady it so the two women could disembark with their bicycles. May stretched to make the jump from the raft to the slippery rocks, dragging her bicycle with her. She lost her footing and fell, the bicycle crashing down upon her, metal tearing into the flesh of her leg.

"Owww," Xue Lian cried out for her as she came to her aid, "It hurts."

May tried to smile as she pulled herself upright. A young boy jumped to help. She limped up the quay, allowing the boy to guide the bicycle for her, and sat down on a low wall. The cut was bleeding profusely. Xue Lian knelt to look at it, clucking.

"Here," May said, taking one of the clean rags out of her sack, "wrap this around it."

Xue worked efficiently, pressing the cut to stop the bleeding.

"Good we go to see the doctor," she said.

"Here?" May asked. "Is this the village?"

The other woman nodded, not smiling now. "It is not far, can you walk?"

The searing pain in her leg could not compete with the fear rising in May's throat. She rose, and for an instant thought she might faint. She took a deep breath.

"Lean on me," Xue Lian said. "The clinic is there, down that road."

As the women hobbled off, the villagers began to gather to follow them. Strangers seldom came here, they were something new to see, and one was bleeding. They pointed and chattered. You could see the dark blood spreading on the rag tied around her leg. By the time they reached the small white building marked with a red cross, some twenty people had gathered to follow and watch.

One old man offered, "The doctor is not there."

A reprieve. The tightness in May's chest seemed to subside.

"Where is she?" Xue Lian asked.

"In another village," the man answered, waving his arm vaguely in the direction of the river.

"When will she be back?"

The man shrugged, he had said all he could say. A woman pushed forward, taking over. "Babies sick there, she gives medicines. Back before dark."

Xue Lian looked at May. "Let's go inside and stop the bleeding. You can wait there while I find us some food."

May did as she was told. She seemed to have lost the ability to think for herself. Whatever happened now would be determined by forces she could not control. She could only wait as she had waited on the raft, floating down the river. Xue Lian lifted the latch on the clinic and pushed the door open. They stepped into a single large room with a wood floor and whitewashed walls. Xue guided May to a wooden chair, and she sat patiently while the other woman found soap and water to wash out the cut. The villagers watched from the open door, but none crossed the high threshold.

"The doctor," Xue Lian said to May in lowered tones, "must have very strict rules. Look how clean and neat this place is, compared to the village."

As if given permission, May looked around the room, studying the place where her mother lived and worked. It was a large and airy room. In the front section were two tables, one which might serve as a surgery, and a narrow bed. Medical supplies and instruments were neatly categorized in a glass-front cabinet set against one wall. In another were Chinese herbal medicines.

At the rear of the room was her living space—a platform for sleeping, a soft chair, a chest with a photograph on top. May was torn by a wish to see the photograph, and a rush of guilt that she was invading another's privacy.

"Perhaps I should not have come in," she remarked.

Xue Lian looked surprised. "You are hurt, you must see the doctor."

May lowered her voice. "I am the doctor's daughter, she may not want to see me."

"Even so," Xue said, smiling to take the sting out of what she was about to say, "she must see you as a patient before we can leave." She considered May, then asked, "Can I leave you to find us something to eat?"

Xue closed the door behind her, removing May from the scrutiny of the villagers. She sat back in the chair and concentrated on her breathing, Karin's trick. When you feel the anxiety rising, Karin would say, all you have to do is think about your breathing and you can control the panic. After a while May managed to stand and, by holding on to the chair and the tables, make her way to the back of the room, to the chest with the photograph on it.

It was a snapshot of a young boy, perhaps twelve. He was straddling a bicycle, both hands on the handlebars, looking gravely into the camera. The picture was yellowed around the edges. May guessed it to be ten or fifteen years old.

She lowered herself onto the sleeping platform, needing to rest a moment before returning to the patient's chair. She would not want her mother to find her here, in her living space. Except, May thought, looking around her, there is so little that seems personal. A flowered apron hanging on a nail on the wall, a dish with a small round of soap. She lifted the soap to smell it, but there was no perfume to it.

Xue Lian returned carrying two bowls. The smell of the food made May go weak. She was, she realized, ravenous. "Rice and vegetables and fish," Xue said, putting down the bowls so she could help May back to the chair.

"Are the villagers still out there?" May wanted to know.

"No, they've moved down to the riverfront. I think they will meet the doctor, to tell her you are here," Xue said as she scooped the last bits of rice out of her bowl with her fingers. That accomplished, she took May's empty bowl and said, "Now I go to the house of the family who shared their food with us. When you are ready to go, send one of the children for me."

At the door she hesitated. "We must leave at dawn. It would not be wise to stay longer."

May nodded and whispered, "Yes."

When the door closed behind Xue, May felt the blood rush to her head. She was here, in her mother's house, waiting. Always waiting. Then she knew. Her mother would not return, May was not going to see her, she would never meet her mother. She could feel the certainty of it flooding through her body, into her arms and legs and toes. She was not meant to meet her mother, it was over. An awful sadness took possession of her, transferred into a lethargy. She had done all she could do, she had reached her mother's house, the place she had been all these years. But she was not here, she would not be here.

May felt the warm tears roll into her mouth, she licked them with her tongue and tasted the salt. She began to cry, small sobs that eased into quiet little catching cries. She moved from the chair to the narrow bed, wrapped her arms around herself for comfort, pulled her knees up to her chest and allowed herself to escape into the deep, mindless cloud of sleep.

She heard it around the purple edges of consciousness, sounds. Musical, low, hushed. She tried to push it back, away from her. She did not want to hear it, did not want to be brought back.

The sounds persisted. She could not deny them but she did not know what they were, she did not know where she was. People were talking softly, very softly. She did not open her eyes, she tried to move back into sleep, she did not want to rise to the surface.

The chill moved up her arms, into her teeth. She clamped them shut tight. The sounds were voices, there were voices in the room. She began to shiver and could not stop.

"Ah," the voice said, "my new patient from the North awakens, and she is chilled."

May opened her eyes to look into the face of a woman who was observing her with humor in her eyes. "I am told you went to war with your bicycle," the woman said, pulling a thick comforter over May. "As soon as I finish lancing Mrs. Chen's boil, we will have a look at your war wounds." She smiled and turned back before May could say anything.

She is here. The words rang up May's spine, into her stomach, into the small nerve endings of her fingers. In this room, standing there, her mother. Liao Ch'ing-Ling. May closed her eyes and forced them open again. To see her, she had to see her.

Her body was slender under the dark cotton pajamas she wore, her hair was cropped short and was streaked with gray. But the face . . . May's eyes were riveted to the face, absorbed now in her work . . . the high cheek bones, the wide-set eyes, the delicate smoothness. Her mother's beauty had not been erased by time, only softened. She wore dark-rimmed glasses and as she tilted her head back, May could see they magnified her eyes. She bit hard on the inside of her mouth to keep from crying out. *Dear God,* she wanted to pray, *help me.*

Quickly, with hands that were sure, the doctor removed the bloody rag and looked at the cut. "Not so bad," she said, in the reassuring tones of one who had looked at many cuts, and then repeated, "Not so bad, we'll just clean it out some more and I think you will be fine. Did the part of the bicycle that cut you have rust on it?" She looked at May for the answer.

May could not think what to say, all thoughts were gone from her head. She lay there, blinking her eyes, her mind spinning, words rolling around in her head. She had to say something, so she blurted in the Mandarin taught her by her father: "I had a tetanus shot before I left."

The doctor moved back a step and stared at her, confusion and suspicion written on her face. She asked, carefully, "Who are you?"

"You are Liao Ch'ing-Ling," May said, and then she whispered. "I am Wing Mei-jin."

Her mother stood as if facing into the wind, arms out to steady herself. She was staring at May, looking at her as if searching for someone, something . . . and then she lifted one arm and moved it across her eyes, as if to shield them from the light.

May was the light, and she was blinding her. Ch'ing-Ling began to move backwards, away from her.

"I had to see you," May said, sitting up. "I can't stay long, only a few hours, but I had to see you." She heard the pleading in her voice. She had promised herself she would not plead, but she could not stop. It had happened, they were alone in the room, and she had to finish it, to see it through. She could not let her leave.

"Please talk to me," she begged. "You are my mother. I have only to look at you to know that. You left me behind thirty years ago, in San Francisco, and I have to know why. I promise, if you tell me I'll leave and never bother you again. But I can't continue . . . I have to know."

Ch'ing-Ling clenched her hands tightly together and tried to speak. Nothing would come out. She walked toward the door and for a moment May feared she would walk out, walk away from her again. But all she did was open the door, say a few words to a small boy who waited outside, and come back in again, latching the door from the inside.

Those few actions gave her time to regain control. She stood very straight in the middle of the room, regal, May thought, in spite of the surroundings. She bowed her head slightly, as if she were about to say something.

May waited. The silence began to gather. "Why did you say I was from the North?" May finally asked, to break the growing awkwardness.

"I am told your traveling companion is from the North," she answered in a halting voice, "and your height. But now I understand . . . the height . . . your father . . ."

"Thank you," May said simply, "for admitting that you are my mother."

Ch'ing-Ling moved to take a seat on a small bench, sitting with her back very straight. Her eyes did not leave May's. They sat facing each other, in the manner of a doctor and patient, hands folded. May looked at her mother's hands. They were long and slim and strong, the nails short and blunt. They said nothing, only waited, as if words were rationed. The gulf between them was too great, May thought. They could never bridge it, it was wrong to have come.

"I gave you life," Ch'ing-Ling said in choked tones, "but I am not your mother. Sister Kit is your mother. I left you with the old Aunties and with Sister Kit, who wanted you as much as any mother could want." Her eyes did not waver, they held May's.

All the questions that had formed in May's mind rang hollow. She stared at her mother's face, into the dark intelligence of her eyes, and closed her own not to witness the pain and the hurt. "Why did you leave me?" she tried, knowing it was the wrong question, knowing it would not provide the flash of light that would fill the dark place inside of her.

Ch'ing-Ling stared as if searching for some manifestation of May's illness, of the fever that burned inside her.

"Reasons are often not what they seem," she began. "You will understand that someday, when you have lived long enough to look back on your life. You will consider the decisions you made, actions you took, and know that the reasons you gave were not the true reasons." A long shaft of last light entered the window and splintered on the gleaming steel instruments, sending flares of light dancing about them.

The silence gathered. Ch'ing-Ling seemed to draw into herself, so concentrated was her thought. May knew she must wait. She folded her hands in her lap and watched the splinters of light move about the room.

When Ch'ing-Ling spoke again, her voice seemed almost to echo in the room, and though it was a small voice it carried to the far corners, to the stainless steel containers that held surgical equipment, to the boxes piled against one wall that held her patients' records.

Thirty years of records, in this one room. May looked at the peg on the wall, saw the flowered apron, and felt the weight of the years her mother had spent in this place.

"The Taoist Lao Tsu believed that words were not forms of reality, but symbols only, which always must misrepresent the true, or inner, reality. Words alone can only confuse us. They can never penetrate the essence, they can only warp the reality. But you say I must find the words to tell you, and if that is what I must do, you must first understand how unsatisfactory these words will be. And you must attempt to hear *beyond* the words, to grasp the reality. Do you know this?"

May answered with a quotation: "Let the hearing turn inward and let it not be interfered with by the intellect or intelligence."

Ch'ing-Ling did not smile, but her mouth relaxed: "Even Confucius, at times, agreed with the Taoists. Well then," she went on, "how much do you know?"

May was cautious. "I know that you felt homesick, I know that my father was not faithful."

"Yes," she sighed, "I longed for my family and China, and your father had dishonored me. Reasons enough to leave, my family accepted those reasons. I did not tell them there was a child, but if I had they would have thought my judgment correct, leaving the child with the aunts, for this was not a child that would have been welcomed in China. This was not a Chinese child. Yes?"

I nodded.

She paused then, deep in thought, searching for the words . . . the symbols . . . that would take May into her mind, her reality.

"Coming back was failure. The war was over, my family left Shanghai, left China to follow Chiang to Taiwan. They left at night with their gold bars and their jade, and I did not go with them. If I had gone, it would all have been for nothing, can you understand that?"

She paused, out of breath, as if they had been walking together and now she was waiting for May to catch up. May could not take her eyes from her mother's face; the mask was gone, all the pain was there and it was terrible to see. Pain and disappointment and hurt, buried for all those years.

"I have ripped away her protection," May thought, "she has had this great wound, and whatever healing there has been, I have come along and opened it up all over again." A wave of remorse washed over her. She began to shiver, her teeth to chatter.

Ch'ing-Ling rose, walked to a cupboard and pulled out a thick padded jacket which she brought to put around her shoulders.

"Put it on," she said, and as May pulled it around her shoulders their hands touched. In a voice that vibrated with warmth, Ch'ing-Ling said, "You are cold, these hills are filled with chill." And then, in the same mesmerizing voice she went on, "In China there are legends. Many legends. Those books on that wall are filled with parables and stories and koans. The rabbit in the moon, pounding the elixir of life, there are many legends about the rabbit in the moon. Once, I took a very small sip of the elixir, and found myself in the place the Chinese call the Land of the Golden Mountain, but I did not drink deeply enough to climb the mountain. I had no bravery in me, and no forgiveness, not then. I longed for the safety of my family, and fled to them, and found that safety to be illusory.

"And so I came here, to this town which is so poor that no medical doctor would ever want to stay, so the authorities do not disturb me. For thirty years I have worked among these people, they are glad to have me." For the first time she smiled, and May caught a glimmer of her beauty. "My patients pay me in eggs and geese and sometimes coins, and it is enough. I have no wish to leave."

"Your family, do you ever hear from them?"

The muscles in her face tightened. "I have no family. I was never brave enough to have a child. That was my great failure. I could not keep you and infect you with my unhappiness. You have come here looking for your mother, but your mother is not here. You are Sister Kit's child. I have always believed this, and take comfort in it."

She waited, gave me time, but when I did not speak she went on:

"It is my habit," she said, "on the nights of the full moon to look for the rabbit, and when I see it I think: *Mei-jin, Sister Kit's child in America, I hope you have found the elixir, and drink of it in great gulps.* Now I look at you, now I see.*" Her face was filled with yearning, with the need for May to see, to know.

May searched her mother's face so she would not forget. "All my life," she began, searching for the right words, "I have had you here, inside of me." She placed her hand over her heart. "But it has not been a good feeling," she went on, "I was angry with you for leaving me."

Ch'ing-Ling bent her head, and for a moment May thought she

was crying. To ease the situation, she moved to the dresser to get the photo. "Who is the boy?" she asked.

Her mother took the picture, studied it as if she had not seen it before. "Only a boy," she finally said. "A poor boy with a damaged spine. His parents were dead, and all of his family, in the war. I tried to cure him, but he died."

Something in her voice caused May to murmur with sympathy.

"I know why he died, the medical reasons," Ch'ing-Ling went on, "but I do not know why he had to die."

"Did you love him?" May asked.

"Yes," Ch'ing-Ling whispered, "as I loved you, but it did not help him, and it did not help you."

May stood, shaken. Nothing was as she had imagined, nothing. "Can I have some tea?" she asked, giving her mother a task to take her mind off the pain.

They drank tea and talked in low, earnest voices. When it grew too dark to see, Ch'ing-Ling lit a lantern and they put it between them and drank more tea and talked through the night. She answered May's questions with the studied thoroughness of a doctor who knows her patient's needs. She told a story of struggle, and privation and pain, and she made May understand that she had finally found a kind of peace in the small village clinic. When May's questions began to lag, she asked some of her own.

For May, it was as if a long thirst was finally quenched. She wanted to talk about herself, to tell her about Faith and Sara, about her break with Kit and their reconciliation. She told her about Karin and Hayes and about her work with volcanoes. The light outside the window had worked its way through several shades of gray when she spoke, at last, about her father.

"When he died," she said, "I thought I was loose in the world, that there was no one to hold on to. I dreamed of you every night. In my dream you held your arms out to me, and motioned me to follow you."

In the lantern light she could see her mother's eyes fill with tears. May reached to put her hand on her arm, and felt the frailness under the thin stuff of her blouse.

As the early morning moved into the room, it illuminated two women sitting together, their heads bowed as if in prayer.

27

The telephone rang and Kit lunged for it, almost knocking over the pitcher of water next to Philip's bed.

"She's out, she's safe," Karin shouted over the long distance line. "Hayes just called me from Macao. He was waiting when she came through the gate this morning and he says that everything is fine, that aside from being terribly tired May is wonderful."

"She's all right?" Kit repeated, wanting to be reassured. "Everything is all right?"

"Right as rain. I didn't talk to May, but I could hear her in the background and Hayes was almost giddy."

"Did he say anything about what happened, did May get to see her mother?"

"Yes. He said it is quite a story and he's going to stop off in San Francisco for a few hours on his way back to Washington to tell you about it. May kept a journal, and he's bringing it to you. The only other thing he said was to give you a message from May—to tell you that she loves you very much."

Tears choked her. She had to strain to say, "Thank God it's over."

To give Kit time, Karin filled the silence with chatter. May and Hayes would be staying in Hong Kong for two days, then she will spend some time in Japan, winding up her work there. Hayes will make a quick official trip to Vietnam before coming back—he said to say it would be about a week before he makes it to San Francisco, he would let her know. Thea was doing just fine, they were looking forward to Dan's coming through week after next, on his way to his first duty post in Saigon. They hoped Philip was doing well . . ."

"He's doing remarkably well," Kit said, regaining her composure. "The doctors can't believe the progress he is making. Everyone is working very hard, Philip hardest of all. He's right here—would you like to speak to him?"

"No," Karin came back, too quickly, "I mean, please, just tell him we are thinking about him. I hope he enjoys the 'daily news' we've been sending. It's probably a little boring for the readers, listening to all the everyday details of our lives—it was Thea's idea to write something every day, and send it off each Monday."

"It's a great idea. Philip says it makes him feel a part of your lives. He told me this morning to let you know that he thinks you are making the right decisions about Thea's school work. He doesn't want to influence her too much, but he would very much like to see her go to Stanford next year even if that means staying on at Punahou to go to summer school. He thought you might like to consider getting her a math tutor to help with the calculus. But he says the decision is yours, because you are right there and know all the variables."

"Good grief, Kit!" Karin laughed, "He must be getting well—that sounds just like Philip!"

Kit put the receiver back in its cradle carefully, letting her hands linger on it for a few moments before she turned and stepped into Philip's field of vision. She took his hand in both of hers and held it while she repeated Hayes's message.

"I think my darling May found what she was looking for," Kit said, "I do believe she is free now."

She felt the tears rolling down her face, felt them fall onto her hands, watched them merge and roll into the crevices between her hand and his. Then she stood motionless, holding her breath.

"Philip?" she said. "My God, Philip. Was that you?" One blink. Yes. And again, his hand pressing hers, stronger now.

"Oh, dear God," she cried out, "Philip, your hand. You moved your hand."

She was laughing then, and crying, all of the morning's emotion came streaming out of her as she stood, holding his hand, feeling as if her world was expanding in great, glorious bursts, feeling as if she had been waiting all her life for this one exquisite moment.

———————

Karin sat at the kitchen table, brushing crumbs from a package of Pepperidge Farm peanut butter cookies into separate little mounds on the table cloth. She was thinking that the time had come to take stock. Now that May's odyssey was over. Now that Philip was progressing with Kit's help. Now that Thea had got her balance and soon would be able to walk on her own. Now that Dan had found his niche. Now that everybody she loved best in the world was in place, what about Karin? Where did she fit in the grand scheme of things?

She walked out to the lanai and squinted in the morning light. The whole of Honolulu lay beneath her, high rises glinting in the distance, planes coasting across the sky toward the airport, a vast and silent panorama. Nowhere, she thought, I fit nowhere. She leaned far over the railing, looking down into the treetops on the steep hillside below. *A "Be Still" tree,* the woman who rented her the house had called them. *They say it was because you had to be still while walking the horses through them.* She wished she could be still; she wanted to feel calm again, peaceful. Useful. In place. *What does it mean, "in place"?* She wasn't sure. Kit had taken over, for now. Rising to the challenge, pure Kit. But decisions would have to be made for the long term. She did not like to think about the long term.

The day lay before her, flaccid and empty. She would have to get out of the house, away from the telephone. The wait for Hayes's call had exhausted her, the wait and the dread. She had tried to prepare herself, had told herself, 'Something is going to go wrong,' so it wouldn't be such a shock. But nothing had gone wrong . . . best now not to tempt the gods, best to get out. Still, she did not move because she did not know where she would go. Yesterday she had spent the better part of the day roaming the Ala Moana shopping mall, losing herself in the maze of cheap shops and food stalls that smelled of carmel corn and rancid oil and teriyaki chicken. She had bought a toaster oven that she did not need and did not want because an overweight salesman had spent so much time describing how it worked. All because of the telephone, of the bad news she knew was coming.

The phone rang. She turned to look at it, startled and afraid. What is happening to me, she thought, when the ringing of a telephone terrifies me?

The woman's voice on the line was hesitant. "I'm calling from the carnival committee—you know about the Punahou school carnival next week?"

Karin laughed with relief. "I've heard of nothing but the carnival for days . . . Thea's working in the ring-toss booth. Is there anything I can do to help?"

"Oh, if only you would," the woman blurted, rushing into a complicated explanation of how the chairman of the fine arts booth had broken her hip and was in the hospital, how it was an especially important job because the banks and several businesses always make large art purchases at the carnival, to benefit the school. How she hoped Karin could see why they would need someone who knows something about art to take over, which wasn't going to be easy at the last minute. But then they heard that Karin had a degree in art history, and she would be absolutely saving their lives if she would agree to take over the job. Even if it means doing what they know is impossible—becoming familiar with the local artists and the works they were donating, all before the weekend.

Within the hour Karin was on her way downtown with a list of artists and local galleries. At dinner that night, Thea said, "You did all that in one afternoon? You don't waste time, do you?"

"It's awful, having time to waste . . . it's the worst thing that can happen to you," Karin answered. "I needed something to do, and this is perfect. Tomorrow I'm covering the museums and the Art Institute. I'll at least have a notion of what's going on in the local art scene."

Thea concentrated on cutting her asparagus spears. "You should probably see the art collection at Alex's house. That was his mother's thing—art. She was a docent at the Art Academy, stuff like that. She bought from local artists when they were just starting out. Alex says her collection is worth a lot now."

"I thought you weren't seeing Alex," Karin answered, working to keep her voice even.

"I'm not seeing him," Thea shot back. "I do talk to him—or is that not allowed?"

Karin looked at her. She did not want a struggle, not tonight. "Freedom of speech—a constitutional right, isn't it?" she tried to joke.

.   .   .

360

She arrived at the school grounds early and made her way along the midway with its food and skill booths to the arts and crafts section. The art booth had been set up next to one that sold leis. She stopped to look at the exquisite, small circlets of fresh flowers. One of the ladies told her, "These are haku leis—that means 'head'—try this one on, the pink plumeria matches your dress perfectly."

She was wearing a traditional Mexican festival dress of soft white cotton, the bodice lavishly embroidered in shades of pink and rose. She positioned the lei on her head, looked in the mirror and thought: May's right, I've reverted to flower-childhood. She laughed; the woman in the booth joined her, saying, "You look like a Botticelli angel—it's perfect."

She was organizing the canvases, and didn't notice him until he coughed and said, "I'm here to help."

He was not tall, but he had the look of a large man, perhaps because of the way he stood—very erect, his feet firmly planted on the ground, or because his face and arms were bronzed by the sun and that made them seem, somehow, powerful.

"I'm Karin Ward," she said, her hand out to him, "I'm pinch-hitting for Mrs. Purvis."

He lowered his head and rubbed the back of his neck in a gesture at once awkward and appealing. "That means you're Thea Ward's mother?" he said.

"Her stepmother."

"It was my son who behaved badly at your house. I'm Paul Hollowell. I should have called you . . ."

A woman in a flowered muumuu sailed by, calling out, "Paul, you came! Exactly what I needed—a miracle! Introduce yourselves and I'll be back in a few minutes."

"Who was that?" Karin asked.

"Jeannie Bremer—she's in charge of this thing. I'm sorry but I don't know the first thing about art—you're going to have to give me my orders."

Karin thought about Philip and Dan, and now Paul Hollowell and Alex, and wondered again how fathers and sons could be such opposites.

By the time Jeannie Bremer came back they had hung the best of the oils, and had organized the watercolors and sketches and lithos. "This is amazing," the woman burbled, "just absolutely amazing, what a team the two of you make . . . why have you avoided us all these years, Paul? If we had known what a dynamo you were . . ."

"Whoa, Jeannie," he said, "slow down. I'm just doing what Karin tells me to do."

"Well, keep telling him Karin," the woman said, "you're doing good, guys," waving her arms like a cheerleader before breezing away again, clipboard held high.

"I guess it takes that kind of energy to fund-raise successfully," Karin said, trying to keep a straight face. "I gather you've never done it before?"

He was working to pry a nail out of a casing, and didn't say anything for a while. She started to turn away when he spoke. "My wife died last year. She used to organize this booth. I thought I should try to help out . . ."

She started to tell him that she was sorry about his wife, but a balding man in a fluorescent Hawaiian shirt was standing in front of the booth, hands on hips, surveying them. "I don't believe my eyes," he said in a high-pitched voice, "the great Paul Hollowell . . . can it be? Will wonders never cease?"

"What say, Jimmy?" he answered laconically, his attention on the nail he was pounding.

Jimmy wasn't deterred. "You always were a lucky son of a bitch," he said. "Who's this gorgeous blonde and why have you been hiding her?"

When he left, Karin waited a bit before asking, "What makes you the 'great' Paul Hollowell?"

"Jimmy's an ass," he answered, "one of those guys who graduated from Yale but never got out of high school." The conversation was interrupted by their first customer of the day, a man from the Bank of Hawaii who bought, in businesslike fashion, four large oils and several lithographs.

For the next two hours the booth was crowded with buyers. She fielded questions and took their money while he packaged and carried. During one short lull, he went for Chinese food. They sat on packing crates to eat, but he was unable to take more than a few bites before some old school friend saw him and stopped to talk.

Thea came by with Alex, his hand casually positioned on the small of her back in a carefully choreographed show of possession. "How nice to see you working with my father," Alex said, all polished politeness. "You've probably discovered that he's a connoisseur of boats, not art."

Karin answered with what she hoped was a frosty smile. "As a matter of fact, I haven't." Seeing the father and son together, she was struck again by their differences: Alex, dark and lithe and, Karin couldn't help but think, deceptive, and the father, fair and solid, measured. Turning to Thea, she said, "You'd better get going if you're to make your lesson on time. I'll pick you up at the Y at four."

Smiling, Alex grabbed Thea by the hand and pulled her away. Paul Hollowell said, "Do you want me to make him stay away from her?"

She looked to see if he was serious.

"No," she said, "I can't do that."

"I didn't ask you to do it. I will."

A woman who had been browsing gave them a dark look and, in a voice filled with exasperation said, "Do you suppose I could get somebody to help me?"

"Let's talk later," Karin told him, "our relief was supposed to be here ten minutes ago."

Twenty minutes later two women appeared, arms full of purchases, chattering and talking in concert: "Paul, we're late—how terrible to do this to you of all people. But we've been buying out the place . . . look." They dismissed Karin with easy smiles, and insisted Paul look at gifts they had bought their husbands and sons. Karin busied herself with customers, and watched from the periphery. They have him cornered, she thought, this man has eluded them, and now they are closing in.

If she didn't mind walking a little, he said, he knew of a place where they could talk without being interrupted. She followed his lead, slowing when someone would call out to him in case he should want to stop and talk. He shrugged them off awkwardly—Philip would have done it with style, Karin thought, but Paul Hollowell didn't have that kind of easy grace. Words did not come easily to him. Still, she noticed, none of the people he brushed off seemed either surprised or offended.

They settled on a bench hidden in a small grove of trees on the edge of the campus. "What is this?" she asked, opening the paper bag he had bought from one of the booths.

"Hot malasadas—a kind of Portuguese donut. These aren't the best I've ever had—the best are made by an old guy who has a hole-in-the-wall down by my boatyard."

She bit carefully into the deep-fried confection, chewed and smiled.

"Okay?" he asked, grinning when she nodded. They sipped coffee and ate the malasadas, concentrating on them until he brushed his hands together and said, "I think we should talk about the kids. Alex and Thea. When I said I'd tell Alex to stay away from her if you want me to, I meant it. He shouldn't have been at your house that night, and he shouldn't have given her pacalolo."

"Pacalolo?"

"It means 'crazy weed'—marijuana."

She nodded. A flower petal brushed her face as it fell and she remembered she was wearing the head lei. Reaching to take it off, it became tangled in her hair. He lifted his hand as if to help her, but pulled it back without touching her. To cover his embarrassment, she asked: "Did you and your wife both go to school here?"

"We graduated in the class of '51," he answered. "Ancient history."

Her mind went blank. She knew there was something she had to say, but it wouldn't come to her. She took a sip of coffee to cover up, to give him time to fill the silence. He said nothing. He was, she guessed, the sort of man who lived easy in silence.

"I'm sorry about your wife," she finally said. "It must be difficult."

He looked at her. "For you, too. Alex told me you lost your husband."

She stared at him. "Is that what Thea told Alex?"

It was his turn to look perplexed. "Yes, I guess she must have. He said it was a stroke . . ."

"Thea's father is not dead," she said, firmly, "he is paralyzed—but he is not dead." And then she blurted, "If you are wondering what the hell I'm doing here when my husband is lying paralyzed in a hospital in California, all I can tell you is I am wondering the same thing myself."

He looked at the ground. "I'm sorry," she went on, sitting up straight to pull herself together. "You wanted to know if I want you to forbid your son to see Thea. The answer is no. The reason I'm here in the Islands is because of Thea . . . she was beginning to have very serious emotional problems. She wanted—and her psychiatrist felt she needed—some distance from her father, geographical as well as emotional. She is having a very shaky time of it . . . her mother died two years ago, of cancer, and now her father is badly hurt . . . It's about as much as one young girl can handle. She needed to get away, and there didn't seem to be much I could do but come with . . ." She stopped, pressed her lips together hard. "No," she said, "that's not true. Both of us needed to get away. It was getting to be too much for me, too, and my husband said we should go. There are people who are taking care of him, who know how to help him better than I can . . ."

"Are there any other kids, besides Thea?" he asked.

She swallowed, nodded. "Yes. A boy, Dan. He's just eighteen—in the Marine Corps. He'll be coming through next week on his way to Vietnam."

"Good for him," he said. "And good for you, that he's missed the hot war."

She looked at him steadily. "We didn't want him to go to Vietnam at all, and we didn't want him to join the marines at age eighteen."

"Why not?"

She put her hand on her head, attempted a grin. "You were a marine?"

"When I was nineteen. Served in Korea. What is it you're worried about?"

She straightened her back, tried to think. "Mostly, I'm just worried. He and his father don't get along. That makes Thea and me his main supports, and both of us are pretty wobbly right now . . ."

He was clenching and unclenching his fist, as if his fingers were stiff. "The marines might be a good place for him, then. I know it sounds pretty corny, but there really is a sense of . . . a feeling of . . ."

"Esprit?" she tried to help him. "Comradeship?"

"I guess that's about it," he said. "That must sound pretty simple-minded, with all the antiwar feeling, the talk about Vietnam being a 'bad' war. The thing is, all wars are bad, but that doesn't make the men who fight them bad."

It was a long speech for him, she knew that. "You're right about that, of course," she said, "I didn't think we should ever have been in Vietnam. I mourn all the men who died there, and I'm thankful that my Dan won't have to go into combat."

"Your Dan?" he asked.

"Yes. In a way he is mine . . ."

Carefully: "You can't be old enough to be his mother."

Simply: "No. I'm thirty-one, but I feel like his mother. I love him, and I worry about him, and I don't know what to do to help him or Thea . . ." She tried to think. "What scares me is that Thea would tell Alex that her father is dead. Her therapist said . . ." She looked up, saw him struggling to understand, looked down again and went on, "You see, she is very, very fragile now, emotionally, and I have to be careful not to push her too hard. If you forbid him to see her, she will know it came from me, and that will make things worse. Your son is very appealing to the girls, you know—and Thea's never really had a boyfriend. She's overwhelmed by it all—I wish she weren't, because I'm not sure of him. I'm sorry to say that to you, I know he's your son."

"I'm not sure of him either," he surprised her by answering, "that's why I'm here today. It's why I've taken his car away from him for a month, and I'm making him work regular hours at the boat shop. He doesn't like it, but he's doing it."

She looked at her watch and stood. "I've got to pick up Thea. The time got away from me."

She left abruptly, parting with words that embarrassed her as soon as they were out of her mouth: "Thank you for introducing me to the ecstasy of hot malasadas."

She found a parking place almost in front of the Y, which was unexpected. Thea wouldn't be out of her lesson for fifteen minutes, more likely twenty; it was too hot to stay in the car. She crossed the street to Iolani Palace, the parklike grounds had become one of her favorite haunts.

Paul Hollowell was on her mind. She thought about her parting words and flinched. Someone else might have thought she was coming on to him, but he had only nodded, there had been no quick rejoinder, no quick picking up on the obvious sexual overtones. The grass was wet and overgrown around the little bandstand; her sandals were wet, bits of grass flecked on her feet. Two middle-aged women wearing tourist tags on their dresses approached. Another time she would have struck up a conversation. Now she moved away before they were within speaking distance and walked toward the deep shade of a great tree on the opposite lawn, where she stopped before a small hillock enclosed by a low wrought iron fence, a royal grave she had never noticed before. "Kapu" the sign on the fence said, the Hawaiian word for forbidden, taboo, banned. She thought: It is kapu to tread on this land where kings lie buried. It is kapu to disturb the sleep of the dead. It is kapu to break your marriage vows. She had promised *for better or for worse, in sickness and in health* and she had broken the promise and she would be punished, she had to be punished.

A hot wind rustled through the thick leaves that sheltered the graves, and suddenly she felt afraid—for herself, and for Thea. *Thea is fine,* she reassured herself as she hurried back in a quick walk-run, cutting across the great lawn, perspiring in the afternoon heat. She reached the gate across from the YWCA in time to see Thea emerge from a car and run into the building. The driver of the car was Alex Hollowell.

Karin pulled back, out of sight. The heat seemed to close in. She leaned against the post, made herself breathe deeply to calm down. By the time Thea emerged from the Y, Karin was double-parked in front of the building, waiting for her.

"Have you been here long?" Thea asked, breathlessly. Her face was flushed, her eyes bright.

"Not long," Karin answered.

It wasn't until after dinner, when Karin got up to make herself a cup of instant coffee, that Thea asked, "What do you think of Alex's dad?"

Karin took her time. "I think he is very . . . nice, very solid and . . . square."

Thea giggled.

"I'm not mocking him, Thea. Square isn't necessarily bad."

"But he is *square,* Karin. A true straight-arrow. You should hear the things he does."

"You mean the things he is making Alex do? Like working in his boat shop?"

Thea sulked. "He doesn't care about Alex. He only cares about boats and sailing."

Karin sat down across from Thea, stirred her coffee. "I didn't get that impression. He was working at the carnival today because he is trying to be a good father."

"Well it's a little late, don't you think?" Thea came back sharply, echoing Alex's anger. "You can't try to be a good father, you just are. I guess I'm spoiled, because my father really was a good father."

"*Is,* dear," Karin corrected her, "your father *is* a good father."

Thea's expression froze. "It's just that . . ." she began, stumbling, "he can't speak . . . he was so eloquent and now he can't . . ."

"He may not be able to speak yet," Karin told her, "but he can communicate. They've devised this special machine with electrodes that . . ."

367

"Stop it," Thea raised her voice, putting her hands over her ears, "I don't want to hear about any machine . . . it's horrible, horrible . . ."

Karin moved to put her arms around her, to calm her. "All right, dear, it's all right. We won't talk about it, not now."

"I'm going out with Alex again," Thea blurted. Karin flinched, understanding that Thea was pressing an advantage.

"Maybe we could talk about that later, too," she said.

"No," Thea answered, committing herself, "I want to talk about it now. I didn't go to my dance lesson, I was with Alex. I lied to you and I don't want to, I can't lie to you. Please, Karin, please trust me and say it's all right for me to see him again."

Karin stirred her coffee. "I'm glad you told me, Thea. I do trust you—it's Alex I don't really trust . . . and it's not just the pot or the fact that he was driving today when he wasn't supposed to be. Let me try to explain." She paused, paced a few times around the room. "I think you probably know that it wouldn't have been possible to be a student at Berkeley in these past years without coming into contact with a joint or two . . ." Thea met her eyes, nodded. "I'm not of that generation that believes that a few tokes leads to heroin addiction." They managed to laugh a little. "But I also know, from experience, that a person who is going through a hard time emotionally can go a little crazy if she gets hold of some powerful stuff . . . strong pot, or one of the mind-bending drugs. Do you know anything about them?"

Thea gave her a "Do you think I'm a baby?" look, and Karin answered by stroking her hair.

"Okay," Karin went on, "I'm asking you not to do any experimenting at all right now. *Nada.* Things have been tough for you these past months."

"The shrink says I'm doing well, considering," Thea spoke up. "He says if I wasn't doing so well I wouldn't be working so hard to make good grades, and getting everything lined up for Stanford."

"That's right," Karin told her, approvingly, "and I'm so proud of you I could pop. But please, try to understand. I don't think Alex is a good person for you to be with . . . I think he's on a fast track, and I know he messes around with dope."

"He doesn't 'mess around with dope,' " Thea said, her voice petulant. "Besides, you met his dad, I don't know if he told you about the rules he made, or how well Alex has kept them. I think he deserves another chance."

Karin relented. "You have a point. I suppose . . . if you promise me you won't try anything again—not even pot, I'll go along with your seeing Alex."

Thea wrapped her arms around Karin's neck and hugged her, saying, "Thank you, thank you, I love you," then almost ran into the wall in her hurry to get to the telephone.

Karin walked to the lanai, looked out over the city. The lights were coming on, she could see Waikiki glittering against the purple of the night sky. *Don't pull the strings too tight,* Thea's therapist had told her, but he didn't say how tight was too tight. Karin sighed. She would have to find something to occupy her, now that the carnival was over. Otherwise she was going to go bananas, worrying.

"You look wonderful," she said, squeezing his hand across the table, "Just . . . wonderful."

"So do you," Dan told her. "What are you doing out here, besides babysitting Thea?"

"What am I doing?" Karin repeated. "If you mean how often do I get to have dinner beachside at the Royal Hawaiian with a handsome young marine, the answer is not nearly often enough."

The tight grin broadened into a smile. "Ah, there it is," she said, "now you look like my Danny." She saw she had embarrassed him, so she rushed on. "You want to know what I do, okay—lately I've been spending quite a lot of time learning about Hawaiian lore at the Bishop Museum, which is a wonderful place. And I've been trying to make myself knowledgeable on the subject of contemporary Hawaiian art. Does that answer your question?"

The setting sun was casting long, silver-pink shadows on the ocean. They watched a lone surfer catch the crest of a wave and ride it in, sending out flickers of light as he moved across the cool pink froth. "God," he said, "this has got to be the most beautiful place on earth . . . Mr. Egon said it was, and he was right."

"Is that why you wanted to come here to dinner?" she asked, allowing herself a small smile. "Mr. Egon suggested the Royal Hawaiian?"

"No . . . yes, I mean, he talked about it a lot. About coming here at sunset, and the rest of us, we always said if we ever got here . . ."

"I'm glad we did. It is a beautiful place, looking down Waikiki beach, yet out of the tourist crush."

"And elegant," Dan added, "I think even Dad would like it. He may get here, too, you know. I spent the last couple of days with him—with them, I should say. I get the feeling Mrs. McCord is there a lot. Aunt Faith told me that as soon as Dad was able to move his hands, they've been in overdrive—teams, hell, whole platoons—of people doing all these things. Physical therapists work on his muscles, keeping the joints moving. Speech therapists now . . . I talked to the doctors, and they said that it looks for certain like he'll regain some use of his voluntary muscles. They think he'll be able to talk again, but they don't know how much . . . so he may sound funny, and he probably won't be able to walk, which means a wheelchair. It's going to be a long, long haul, any way you look at it."

Karin nodded. It had been explained to her, in detail. Kit made sure she knew everything that was going on. Well, almost everything, she thought.

The waiter delivered their entrees and Dan pushed himself back from the table so he could look at it. "Food," he said.

Karin laughed. "Yes, I think so."

"I mean real food," he answered, moving his face directly over the plate so he could breathe it in. "Ahhhh," he murmured, "heaven."

"Thea felt so badly about not being able to join us for dinner that she made you a special dessert. Wait till you see it," she told him. "Then you'll know what heaven, tropical style, is."

"You mean she's graduated from carrot cake?" he asked, taking his first big bite of steak.

"I can only tell you this much—it has papaya and pineapple and coconut in it, and orchids floating on top, and you will never be the same again after you've had some."

"Sounds like sex," Dan said, glancing up mischievously to see if he had shocked her.

"I'm not even going to respond to that," she told him, making a show of stifling a smile, "other than to say I wonder what else they've taught you in the Marines."

"What they've taught me," he said, suddenly serious, "is that a human being is as strong as he wants to be, that with the help of his buddies he can accomplish whatever he sets out to accomplish."

The light was gone now, only the tops of the waves gleamed white in the moonlight as they broke. They watched the froth wash up on the beach, causing those few people still walking along the edge of the water to scurry. The waiter lifted the hurricane lamp to light the candle, asked if everything was all right and Dan answered solemnly, "Everything is just fine, thank you." He said to Karin, "Dad taught me some things, even if I didn't know it . . . like how to answer a waiter."

"I'll bet your Dad taught you a lot of things, and I think you have probably taught him a thing or two as well. He must have felt proud of you—seeing you like this, so . . . solid."

He poured the last of the split of wine they had shared into her glass. "He said he was . . . through that little machine he uses that translates from Morse code. Here, let me show you." He fished in his wallet and took out a piece of typing paper which had been carefully folded. On it was written: "I was wrong and you were right. You make a helluva Marine."

Karin pressed the paper to her lips and closed her eyes. "Oh Danny," was all she could think to say. She knew that Philip didn't believe he had been wrong, but he could say it for his son. Thank you, Philip, she thought.

"I've been wondering about Mrs. McCord," Dan said, "I mean, why is she doing all this for Dad? I know she's mongo rich, and I know she's a really good friend of you and May. But it seems, well . . . strange."

"You're right, it would seem strange, I guess, if you didn't know Kit. Partly she's doing it for me. She's been like a fairy godmother to me, I respect her and care for her as much as if she were my . . . well, my 'real' mother."

"I can relate to that," he answered.

A wave of warmth washed over her. "Good," she said, "I'm glad."

"Mrs. McCord said you were coming back for a visit pretty soon."

"As soon as May returns from Japan, to stay with Thea. Then we'll be going back for good in September, when Thea goes off to college."

Dan finished the last of his steak, pushed back his chair and pulled a small cigar out of his pocket, making a show of lighting it, and took a long puff. "I don't know," he said, leaning back in his chair. "If I was you, I think I'd just hang out here on this beach for the rest of my life."

"Tell you what, fella," she came back, "when you come back from Vietnam, no matter where I am, I'll meet you here at sunset, for dinner."

"You got yourself a date, lady," he answered, holding her chair out for her.

. . .

Alex's car was in the driveway when they came back, that was the first thing that was wrong. Thea was supposed to have been at an honors banquet, and Alex was not invited. The carport lights were out, that was the second thing. Thea was expecting them, she should have turned the lights on.

"Something's wrong," she said, holding tightly to Dan's arm as they hurried down the steep drive. "Listen."

It was a strange sound, muffled, bleating. A warm wind blew against her face. She shivered. Then a scream broke the surface calm, long and sustained. Dan broke loose, slammed through the back door, running toward the scream. Karin stumbled, something tore at her leg, she pulled herself up, arrived inside in time to see Dan struggling to pull Thea off the railing, onto the lanai. Alex was clinging to her legs, his head down as if to ward off her blows. She was biting and kicking and screaming at them, her eyes wild.

"It's me, Thea," Dan shouted at her. "Look, I'm here, it's okay, it's me, Daniel." He had her now, clamped safely in his arms. "Let go," he told Alex, but Alex seemed not to hear. "I said let her go," Dan repeated.

"Daniel?" Thea said in a thin, high voice. "Daniel?"

"I'm here," he told her, "Karin's here. You're safe now."

Karin pulled her into her arms while Dan tried to extricate Alex. "Let go of her," he shouted into his ear. "We've got her now, we'll take care of her."

Alex tightened his grip. "You son of a bitch let go or I'm going to rip your goddamned arm off," Dan said. A loud, brittle crack sounded, and a wail. "Goddamn you," Dan said, kicking him away, "I'm going to break every fucking bone in your fucking body . . ."

Thea stiffened, screamed one long, thin note that seemed to shatter the darkness and then she slumped in Karin's arms.

"Dan," Karin ordered sharply, "bring her here, inside. Sit here with her, on the sofa."

He did as she told him, holding his sister firmly and stroking her arm, talking quietly to her to calm her, while Karin knelt beside Alex.

He was rolled into a ball in a corner of the lanai, clutching his arm and whimpering.

"What did you give her?" Karin demanded, her voice urgent. "I want to know exactly what you gave her."

He tried to look at her but his eyes wouldn't focus. "Hurts," was all he could say, "arm . . . hurts."

"Acid," Dan said, not varying the tone of his voice so he would not set Thea off again. "He's loaded on something else, but I'm pretty sure he's given her LSD. She freaked."

Karin didn't ask him how he knew, it was all she could do to keep her hands steady so she could dial Paul Hollowell's number.

28

The cottage is filled with ribbons and shredded bits of packing material and tissue paper—we are awash in a sea of tissue paper, pink and white and silver, packed in and about all of the wedding gifts that we are to take with us. Annie has packed our dresses, even, in tissue paper, so they won't wrinkle. My blue lace, her 'slinky green' as she calls it, a brazen, backless creation that will doubtless set her poor mother to grinding her teeth. Annie has moved in with me, for "the duration," as she puts it.

May and Hayes are to be married this coming Saturday, in a weather-worn little green and white church that sits all alone above the sea not far from May's place, and looks as if it might have been plucked off the coast of Maine, steeple and all. It is a New England church, built by sailing men out of Gloucester and New Bedford and Nantucket, high and narrow and straight, with polished pews made of koa wood and tall gothic windows tilted open to catch the sea breeze. Nowhere else in the Islands can you see the historical juxtaposition so clearly as in the churches built by the stern, New England missionaries and attended by the soft, lyric Hawaiians. It is Abigail's church. One of her myriad nephews built a ramp so I could go to services with her. After the ceremony there will be a luau at the compound, on the grassy enclosure next to the beach.

. . .

Yesterday, I read again May's journal from China. "It is over now," she wrote from Hong Kong. "With the help of my two extraordinary aunts—Rose in China, Kit in America—I have learned who I am.

"I am Wing Mei-jin, I am May Reade, and soon I will be May Reade Diehl. One person, American and Chinese, at peace with herself.

"That is what is so wonderful—this great calmness that has invaded my body, as if suddenly I am possessed. Hayes says that he can tell the difference. He says that if someone could X-ray my soul, the dark spots would be gone.

"It was not just discovering that the woman who gave me life is very human, and very good, and never meant me harm. It was meeting Rose, and being drawn into her magnetic circle, it was traveling through China with Xue Lian, who told me when she left that she will always be my friend, even if we should never meet again. And it was seeing Hayes standing there, waiting outside the Barrier Gate in Macao when I came out of China. I knew then, when I saw him towering above everybody else, squinting to try to get a glimpse of me, and not recognizing me at all, sitting in the Family's cart. No barriers are left for me, I know where I belong—with Hayes, with my family back home. And someday soon, I hope, Rose will be part of that family.

"I am not certain that Liao Ch'ing-Ling ever will be, I think that seeing me again might be too painful for her. She has spent so many years forcing her life into narrow channels, I think she will not allow herself to open up again. It does not hurt me to say that. All the mystery is gone, I know what she looks like and how she lives and something of how she thinks. All the blanks are filled in. She leads such a simple life in her little village, her only pleasures are her books.

"It was so strange, hearing her version of what happened all those years ago. She was not at all easy on herself, there was no trace of self-pity. I think that is what affected me so, that still lovely woman reciting hardships that were beyond belief, yet not expecting any sympathy. Her life has been so sad, so filled with failed choices. She made me understand that she did not leave me by choice, but by necessity. Poor woman, poor mother. And once I felt that surge of sorrow—for her, not for myself—I knew it was settled in me.

"Before I left that morning she made gruel and tea for us and said, 'We will take it in the garden.' In the back of her little clinic was a small walled garden, and in it was a mimosa tree. I could not believe my eyes when I saw it, I have dreamed so often of my mother sitting under a mimosa that I actually wondered if I might be hallucinating. To prove it really was there I broke off some leaves and put them in my pocket, and now I am tucking them in the pages of this journal."

I touched the small spray of dried mimosa leaves and smiled to myself, thinking of May. We leave day after tomorrow for her wedding, "we" being Annie and me, Kit, Phinney, Emilie and Amos, the Diehls, Mrs. Nakamura. And Israel. May remembered that Israel is an ordained minister, and asked him to perform the ceremony, bless her. These past months Israel has been what he calls "poorly," he has lost a great deal of weight but his voice can still rise to great lofty, ringing-from-the-rafters heights. He tells me he is going to tie that righteous knot so everlastingly tight they will never be able to undo it, and I believe him, I do. Annie is at his place right now, helping him pack. She is the only one he will accept help from . . . Em couldn't believe it, when I told her. But then, Emilie was convinced it wouldn't work—my asking Annie to come live with me for a while, to help out.

Kit has chartered a plane, a good idea in view of the sheer quantity of *things* we are taking.

The sweet, celebratory scent of carnations and roses and star jasmine is in the air—my garden is bountiful this year—and I have this peculiar sense that the curtain is about to rise, the show is about to begin.

That is foolish, of course. The show has been going on full-tilt for several months, it's just that all the action has been off my stage. I've been sitting here, in my old sunlit cottage, petting the cat and hearing about all the momentous events secondhand.

Kit spends most of her time across town at Children's Hospital, where Philip has been moved to give him better access to the rehabilitation teams at the University of California medical school. Kit and Karin decided that Philip should not know about Thea's setback two months ago, when she had to spend several days in the hospital after a misadventure with drugs. The child seems to be fine now, but she hasn't wanted Karin to leave her, not even for a short visit to the mainland.

My last conversation with Karin was notable not so much for what she said, as for an echoing kind of sadness I could hear in her voice. I could not tell her that Kit had confided to me that Philip was

relieved she would not be coming to the mainland, that he is filled
with a kind of self-recrimination about Karin. He knows how miserable his accident has made her life, he says, but he hasn't the energy
to try to sort out what he should do about it. He acknowledges, too,
that he needs her to care for Thea and to maintain touch with Dan.

Philip is in a wheelchair and he is beginning to make sounds that
approximate words. When Annie finally talked Israel into letting her
take the van and me out solo, our first outing was to the hospital to
see Philip.

I was flabbergasted. Now that he can manage a small smile, he
looks more like . . . Philip. His old self. Oh, a bit older, I admit. His
hair is very much grayer. (Annie thinks he used to dye it.) Kit has
had many of his books brought over from the house, and his desk
and a lovely old walnut tea table, so it looks more like a study than
a hospital room. We had tea together, Earl Grey served from an
antique Queen Anne service he acquired in England some years back.
Kit poured.

"Faith," Annie hollers from the bathroom (we have been on a
first-name basis since she was three), "could you wheel on in here
and hand me the shampoo? I got into the shower without it."

I wheel on in, I hand her the shampoo, she rewards me by flicking
me with a fingertip spray of water.

"Incorrigible," I tell her.

"Just like me darlin' old grand-mum," she comes back, gurgling
with laughter, spraying water every which way.

Emilie had told me I would be sorry, that Annie moves in and
makes a place her own, scatters her belongings like leaves in the
autumn, turns the volume up full blast, is bossy and loud and generally obstreperous.

It is true, Annie's like that. But I am not sorry. From the day she
walked in, heaved her giant duffle bag in the corner and shouted,
"She has arrived," I have not been sorry. She is a tall girl, and solid,
with masses of red hair which is curly to begin with, and with a
permanent is electric curly. That's what you notice first: This great
aureole of red hair, glowing in the light. Then the tattered jeans and
cowboy boots with rundown heels, the wrinkled denim shirts embroidered with sunflowers and the orange suede jacket, fringed all
over, bought for five dollars cash from some down-and-out country
singer.

My granddaughter, who is twenty-one now, walks into my cottage emitting sparks . . . electrons . . . pure energy. The air all but crackles, the music begins, she laughs a big, bubbling laugh and I know I am alive.

I needed Annie, and I think she needs me, too.

The "updated plan" (Annie's label) is for her to enter San Francisco State's theater program in September.

But first, Hawaii and the wedding.

FMG: Notes, Reade family file, box 16

On Thursday, June 7, in this good year of our Lord 1973, Hayes and May, Karin and Thea were waiting for us on the tarmac of little K'eahole Airport. Those marvelous soft Hawaiian tradewinds tossed us together in one big tangle of arms and embraces, ruffling our hair as Thea and Karin lifted flower leis over our heads and kissed us on both cheeks, island fashion, in a wash of fragrance.

Hayes stood, looking for all the world like the young Charles Lindbergh, the hero of my youth, except not quite so bashful, not quite so shy. And May, holding tight to his hand, looked as all brides should look—radiant. Hayes bent to kiss Mrs. Nakamura on the cheek as May looped her arm through Israel's and whispered something that made him fight to keep the tears from his eyes. (He cries so easily these days.)

I was moved almost to tears myself when I saw Kit take Karin's face between her hands, and the two women came together with an affection made stronger by adversity. I watched Amos, very much the college man, lose no time moving around the periphery of our group to speak to Thea, and I watched the lights go on in her face when she saw my grandson again.

"Round 'em up," Phinney shouted.

"Move 'em out," Annie bellowed, and our wagon train started on down the road.

Friday morning, June 8

I am staying with Abigail in her little house. We rise early, she and I, before any of the others are up, and have our coffee at the picnic table under the kiawe tree.

"Have you brought him home to die?" she asked me.

I could not speak, so I nodded.

"Does he know?" she asked.

"He knows," I was able to say, "but he doesn't want the others to know, not until after the wedding."

"Israel," she said, "the promised land."

"To Israel," I said, "this is the promised land."

"And so it is," she answered me, "and so you will stay with him here, until God calls him."

Friday afternoon, June 8

May is to wear Hayes's mother's wedding dress. It is ivory satin and cut in the style of the thirties, on the bias, soft and clinging. Marylee Diehl is beside herself with pleasure. She walks around the house, bourbon and soda in hand, calls everyone "hon," has an opinion on everything, is terribly anxious to please. She talks about everything, that is, except her other son. That pain lodges within her, inconsolable.

Hayes's father will be his best man, in Andy's place. There has been a refreshing minimum of planning for this wedding. May and Hayes are taking the attitude that everything will fall into place without a lot of fuss. The wedding is to be at four o'clock—the minister of the little country church asked only that we close the door when we leave. Two of Abigail's daughters asked if they could decorate the church and May said, "That will be wonderful." Kimo and Clarence are preparing the pit for the kalua pig right now. Israel is with them, talking and laughing and hanging on to a beer bottle, just as if he could still drink.

Hayes and his father have gone with Kimo into Kailua to meet the fishing fleet and buy ono and mahi mahi and several other kinds of fish for dinner tonight, and the luau tomorrow. Thea and Amos volunteered to drive to the other side of the island to buy fresh vegetables—a good excuse to be off together, though when I mentioned this to Emilie she told me I was imagining things. Annie and Karin are attempting to bake a wedding cake. Annie found a picture of a spectacular-looking marzipan cake in a magazine and insisted it should be her contribution to the wedding effort. Never mind that she has never baked anything in her life. Emilie took one look at the picture in the book and the three pages of directions, threw up her hands and joined May and Kit and Marylee, who were starting out on a hike that will take them along the old trail that follows the sea.

Now I am going to pull back the beautiful red and white quilt that covers the narrow bed in my little room in Abigail's house and take a nap. I tell you, it is wonderful—knowing they are all here, moving and milling about, those I love most in the world, and that they will be here when I wake.

Saturday, June 9

She came down the aisle on Phinney's arm, her face lifted, luminous with light and love. She smiled at Hayes all the way, and we smiled back, all of us, in love with her and their happiness.

Israel's face, gaunt and gray, became beatific; his voice rose, gained momentum until it resonated to the rafters and carried out the high windows to the ocean beyond, great moving tones that echoed his Baptist childhood, the wonderful words of the King James Version of the Bible.

"We gather today in the sight of God . . ."

"I do," Hayes answered, firmly.

"I do," May sang out with perfect clarity.

And then the joyous release of the processional and we were all outside, circling the newlyweds. I looked at May, tucked inside Hayes's arm, her head turned for a moment into his shoulder, and prayed a short prayer that Porter and Sara and Lena be watching us this day.

Sunday, June 10

May and Hayes left last evening to catch a midnight flight for New York, then on to honeymoon at Kit's place in the south of France. Kit left this morning, after an early breakfast with Karin. They sat, their elbows propped on one of the long tables set up for the luau, and spoke in low, urgent tones that did not carry. Kit looked into her coffee cup and nodded; Karin lifted her hands and asked a question Kit could not answer.

Thea starts summer school classes tomorrow, so she and Karin will be leaving tonight. Amos was going to spend a couple of days with us here—he had been keen to explore Volcanoes National Park—but he and Annie have decided to go over to Honolulu with Karin and

Thea to sample the night life. Amos talked Annie into going. Em is sure it was the other way around. She does not want to see how smitten her son is with Thea.

In another week everybody will be gone, except for Israel and Annie and me. We are here, as Annie says, "for as long as God says." I am beginning to see of what firm stuff my granddaughter is made.

29

Hayes coughed.

"Are you catching cold?" May asked.

"Would I catch cold on our honeymoon?" he laughed, pulling her to him to kiss her, keeping one eye on the road.

"Let's get there fast and go straight to bed, just in case," she teased.

"Good idea," he answered, moving his hand up the cool flesh of her thighs.

They arrived at Kit's house in St. Paul-du-Vence in midafternoon, but they did not go directly to bed. The housekeeper was waiting for them, there was information to be exchanged, directions to give. They would not require a cook, they would not require a maid. Madame Reneaux understood perfectly.

"The French do understand," May said as she undressed.

"How do you know that?" Hayes answered, helping to remove her underpants.

"No time for explanations," she said, pulling him into bed with her. "I can't wait."

She nuzzled her head into the crook of his neck and asked, "Who would know to send a wedding gift here?"

"Umm," he answered, drowsing.

"Madame Reneaux said it arrived yesterday. The package in the front hall. Who would know to send it here?"

"Umm," he muttered again, so she would know he was listening even if his eyes were closed.

"I think I have to go see," she told him, sitting up.

"Curiosity killed the cat," he answered, pulling her back on top of him, his hand pressing her into him so she could feel him rising.

She giggled.

"You laugh," he said, moving into her, "I've got me a wife and I plan to love her."

They moved into the rhythm with fresh energy, as if they hadn't made love a few minutes before, as if it were the first time, looking into each other's eyes, she arching over him so he could cup her breasts in his hands.

When she woke he was sitting on the edge of the bed, holding an object in his hand for her to see, and his eyes were grave.

"What is it?" she asked, pushing away the tangle of her hair.

"A totem. An African family tree, this one is carved from a solid piece of mahogany—an exceptionally fine piece of native art. It's called the Tree of Life."

"Eli?" she said.

He read the card: "Glad you moved off the bench, brother. Love to your bride. Want to see you both."

"How did he know?" she asked, smiling and wondering why Hayes wasn't.

"I suppose he figured it out, from my note."

"I didn't know you kept in touch."

"I didn't want you to know. The less you know the better, in fact."

"You know that won't work, not with Eli," she came back, annoyed. "We went through all that."

"I deposit money for him every two months in a Swiss bank account."

Now May looked shocked. "Your money?" she asked.

It was Hayes's turn to be surprised. "Of course my money. What did you think? That I was acting as a conduit for some Panther supporters?"

"No, not really," she said, "I just mean . . . well, I thought with the State Department appointment . . ."

"Right," he said, his hands tracing over the bodies on the carving,

384

faces and backs and legs, intertwined to form a tree, smooth ebony faces. "It's risky business, but I couldn't leave him stranded, either."

"What happened to the money we gave him when he left?"

"It went to the people who smuggled him out. When he contacted me the first time, he was broke."

"The first time . . . have there been other times?"

"Only once. When he got married, he let me know."

"How?"

"I was in Paris, I got a phone call telling me . . . not from Eli, from someone else. They also asked for more money. Later I got a note from Eli through the mail. He said marriage complicated his life, but that it had saved his sanity. That was about it, except to thank me for the money."

May touched the totem, moved her fingers along the smooth flat back of a boy, clinging to the tree. "So you sent it," she said, a statement, then asked, "But how did you get messages to him?"

"Through the mail. I have an address in Libya. In fact, the only message I've ever sent him was that you and I were going to be married. I knew there was some risk involved, but I thought it would be minimal—and I did want him to know."

"You remember I asked if there was any way we could let him know," May reminded him, pulling a silk robe around her.

"I remember," he said. "What I don't know, and would like to, is how he knew we would be here. How he knew about this place at all."

May was walking into the bathroom, but she stopped short, turned and looked at him. "You didn't tell him?"

He shook his head, and watched her face as she tried to come to grips with the puzzle.

She spoke slowly. "I'm trying to remember if I ever said anything about Kit's place in St. Paul-du-Vence. Maybe I did. Do you remember when I first told you about it?"

"I've been trying . . . I can't get it clear. It seems to me there was a conversation about the summer you went to Greece, to study the volcano at Thera. Karin was supposed to have gone with you and Kit to the house in France, but Karin backed out . . . something like that."

"I remember talking about it to Sam, but I can't be certain we ever did when Eli was around. And frankly, I'm not sure it was the kind of thing we would have talked about to Eli. Not after Sam accused us of being jet-setters."

They sat in silence for a while, thinking. "Somebody could have done some research," May finally offered.

"I know," Hayes said, a grim set to his mouth. He caressed her shoulder, but it was an absentminded caress. Their seclusion had been violated.

Honeysuckle vines grew heavy on the stone walls of the garden, sending out waves of fragrance into the early summer evening. They sat side by side on an old bench, watching the birds feed on small clouds of insects that were lit by the waning light, waiting.

May was wearing a white dress that gleamed against the green of the garden. They touched fingertips, and smiled and did not break the silence.

The ring of the telephone ended their waiting.

"Speaking," Hayes said, pulling May to him and turning the receiver so she could hear too.

"Mr. Diehl," a woman's voice said in heavily accented English, "your friend is very looking forward to seeing you and wife. He asks if you and she can meet him at a place on the border with Spain tomorrow evening?"

"I understand that my friend has asked you to make this call for him," Hayes said in a firm voice, "but I will need to talk to my friend myself, to make the arrangements."

There was a long pause. "That will be difficult," the voice said.

Hayes did not answer.

"Stay where you are," the voice ordered, "he will call within an hour."

They sat at the long table in the kitchen, eating cheese and fruit and a cold asparagus soup May had discovered in the cooler, along with a fresh baguette. Hayes started to open a bottle of wine, then stopped and looked at May. "None for me," she said, "not yet." He put the bottle back. Their celebration had been interrupted, now they needed to think clearly.

"Whoever the woman is, she's giving the orders," Hayes said. "She didn't have to ask anybody's permission, she said he would call."

"Why didn't he call in the first place? Did he think our line would be tapped?"

"No. I don't know why—logistics maybe. He can't move as easily as she, is my guess."

She concentrated on cutting a slice of cheese. Hayes sat down, picked up a small piece of baguette, put it down again, got up and paced.

The ring of the telephone stopped him in his tracks.

A familiar smile spread over Hayes's face, so she knew it was Eli on the other end of the line.

"Yes," Hayes said, "she's right here."

May called out, "Hello old buddy!"

Though an echo on the line seemed to indicate it was a long distance call, Eli seemed not to be in any hurry. "Tell me about the wedding," he said. "Who all came? Karin was there, right? And Sam and Israel?"

"Karin was, not Sam. Israel was the preacher."

Eli laughed. "Good for Israel. How about Rags? Did he make it?"

Hayes frowned. "Afraid not, couldn't make it," he said.

"Well that's too bad, I know he would've wanted to be there. Just like me. But let's talk about us now. Do you think you could drive to the Spanish border—a little place called Cerbere tomorrow evening? I surely am homesick to see you, Bro," he added. He started to give directions then, but Hayes interrupted.

"Listen, friend, as much as I want to see you I have to say it doesn't look too probable. May's not feeling too well—she's running a fever and we think she may have a recurrence of a bug she picked up in Fiji. She's going to see a doctor tomorrow. Anyway you look at it, she won't feel up to it for tomorrow evening. Maybe we could make it day after tomorrow, if the doctor says it's okay."

Static filled the line, and for a long minute neither could make themselves heard. Hayes shouted, "Are you still there?" and a voice shouted back, "Can you come by yourself?"

"I don't want to leave her," Hayes said, but the connection had broken.

May took the receiver from Hayes and returned it to its place. His face had gone stone gray, stunned.

"What is it?" May asked. "Tell me."

"Rags Wegman."

"Yes?" she prodded.

"Eli asked if Rags was at the wedding. Rags was a civil rights worker Eli and I knew in Mississippi in the summer of 1961. He was arrested and thrown into jail, all his ribs were broken. We got him out, and two days later we found him hanging from a rafter in his cabin. He left behind a note that said, 'It isn't worth it. We will never be free.' It haunted Eli, that message."

"And you think that's the message he was sending you now?"

"He was telling us not to come, that something is wrong."

"What do you think?"

"I think it's probably a kidnap attempt. If they know about this house, they know about Kit. She could afford a hefty ransom."

May stumbled when she said, "Eli knows about the *Paris Match* article, where I was named one of the ten richest women in America."

"That's why they were willing to let me come on my own. Two would have been better than one, but they figured you would come through for me."

"Don't say it, Hayes. Don't tell me my money is already making problems for us."

"I'm not going to say that, wife," he told her, smoothing her hair back from her face. "It's not your money that is making problems for us. It's Eli. Our friend." The last word was uttered with an edge of bitterness.

"What now?" May asked.

"They know where we are, May. Right now they want us to come to them because it will be safer for them that way. But if they begin to think we aren't going to come, they might come for us. We're at risk, and I think I have to get in touch with someone I know in Paris. He works in some sort of deep-secret agency that deals with terrorists."

"But it is an agency of the French government?"

"Yes."

"So it is likely they will know about it in Washington?"

"I'm not sure. The French don't like to share very much, and this is a good friend—Jacques Benoist."

"Marie-Claire's brother?"

Hayes nodded, watching her.

She sighed, looking at him. "What will happen to Eli?"

"Eli warned us, remember?"

She put her hand on his shoulder, and said, "Make the call."

They sat in the darkened sitting room that gave a view of the walkway that led to the house, waiting.

"Is this how you planned to spend our honeymoon?" Hayes asked.

She tried to laugh. "Do you realize how much we've been through together? I don't remember anything ever going smoothly. If you wanted smooth, you should have . . ." She stopped herself, and he squeezed her hand for it.

"I don't want smooth," he said, "but I do want safe. I put us in jeopardy by sending Eli that letter."

"We don't know that Eli was part of any kidnapping attempt. We don't even know for sure about the attempt."

"He might not have been part of it, but he was the instrument. There is no way we can absolve him of that, May. And I promise you, there was going to be some kind of plan to extort money."

At that moment a man approached the gate. In the shadows they could only see that he was alone, that he was wearing a light jacket of some sort and took long, quick strides so he was at the door almost before they could move to the hallway. "I am Jean-Claude," the man said in husky French.

They spoke in the kitchen, situated in the center of the house, without windows. "Benoist sent me." You are to move about the village in a normal way, doing what you would ordinarily do," he told them. "But first you must call this number and say exactly where you are going and what route you will take. If you get another of the calls, you must put them off, give them excuses but do not say you will not come. Pretend instead that you want to, it is only madame's malaise that keeps you away. You will let us know, immediately, if there is another call and what exactly is said. Am I clear? Do you have questions?"

"Can you tell me," Hayes asked, "if Eli Barnes's name is on any of your lists?"

"No, Monsieur Diehl, I cannot," Jean-Claude said.

"Could you tell us if he was not?" May added.

He shrugged, apologetically.

The call came late in the afternoon. "Your friend hopes your wife is feeling better now that she has seen the doctor," the same female voice said, this time with a surfeit of good will. "He is very much hoping you can come to see him this evening, or tomorrow. Will that be possible?" Hayes could imagine her gums pulled tight over her lips in a cobra smile.

"I'm afraid the doctor says my wife cannot travel today or tomorrow, he thinks she can come with me on the following day. Will my friend still be able to meet us?"

"Your friend is beginning to think perhaps that you do not wish to meet him, that you are making excuses."

"My friend would never believe that," Hayes said. "We have been as close as brothers."

"Then you must come to your brother, today. He has asked to see you, you should not deny your brother."

"I am sorry, I cannot leave my wife. Tomorrow . . ."

"Remember," the voice spat, all pretense of charm gone, "we delivered the Tree of Life. You should remember that we know where you are."

Hayes stood holding the phone, the line was dead.

"Call Jean-Claude," May told him, then added with sudden fear, "Quickly."

At precisely 3:11 the next afternoon May was standing in the foyer, resetting her watch when the phone rang and a voice ordered in rapid-fire French, "Go to the wine vault and stay there, move!"

Hayes pushed her ahead of him down the stairs, they were pulling back the heavy door when they heard the three shots ring out in rapid succession. "Stay in there," he told her, shoving her in.

He reached the top of the stairs, slammed open the door and ran point-blank into a man with a gun.

"Jean-Claude," he said with relief.

"You don't follow orders well, do you?" the Frenchman answered, drily. "We got both of them, one is dead. Our men are exploding the bomb in your garden right now."

The explosion brought May crashing out of the wine cellar. "It's over," Hayes called to her.

They stood staring at the smoldering hole the bomb had blown in the middle of Kit's garden. Bits of honeysuckle and columbine and a few stray rose petals marked the scene.

"Jacques said they've identified the two men who planted the bomb. The dead one was Mahmoud el-Asmar, the one that's in the hospital here is Abu ben Sharif. He's the brother of Sofia."

"Who is she?" May asked.

"Eli's wife."

30

She knew she was driving too fast for the winding road. She heard the bags of groceries shift and tip over in the trunk but she didn't care. She was late, it was getting close to noon and Thea didn't like to come home to an empty house.

The hurry was for nothing. Thea wasn't home.

Karin put the groceries away, opened a can of tuna and began to mince celery, very fine, to put in it. She glanced at the clock; Thea had been out of class for an hour, she had never been this late.

She dried her hands and called the Browns, no answer. She walked out to the lanai, shielded her eyes and looked down at the path that Thea would take if she had walked. But she would not have walked, she never did. One of her friends always drove her home. She went into Thea's room and found the little book decorated with pictures of yellow and blue balloons which held her telephone numbers. She was not at the Robinsons and no one answered at the Yungs. Karin let the phone ring eight times, ten. Her hand was shaking when she gave up, her heart seemed to be skipping beats.

Something had gone wrong, she could feel it.

She turned the pages of the book slowly. E, F, G, H. Alex Hollowell. Thea had drawn little stars around his name and outlined his address in red and blue pen. Ferdinand Street, Manoa. Karin lifted the phone, her hand poised over the dial, then she put it down again.

. . .

It was a big frame house, hidden in a grove of kiawe trees. A small Japanese woman opened the door and motioned her into the dark, cool interior. Karin looked at the woman's feet. She was wearing old felt slippers. Somebody else had worn slippers like that, but she couldn't remember who. And now, for an instant, she couldn't remember what she was doing here.

"Alex," she blurted, "is he here?"

The woman stepped back, wary. "Alex is away."

"Can you tell me where he is?" she pressed. "I'm Thea Ward's stepmother, and I don't seem to be able to find her . . . I thought maybe . . ."

The woman's face arranged itself into a mask of disapproval. "I can't tell you nothing about that. You have to talk to his father at the boatyard."

"Thank you," Karin said feebly as the woman shuffled back into the cool dimness of the house.

Karin knew the turnoff to Sand Island and she had no trouble finding the cafe with a crude, handmade sign that said, "Hot Malasadas." The owner, a large man in an undershirt that failed to cover his stomach, gave her directions. From a pay phone that perched at a precarious angle, as if it had been nudged by one of the trucks that rumbled along the industrial avenue, she called her house and let it ring twenty times before giving up.

Paul Hollowell saw her before she saw him. He was perched on the spreader of the mast of a large sailboat, and he watched her walk toward him—tentatively, as if she might turn back. He called out to her, moving into the open so she could see him.

"I'm sorry . . ." she began, and then laughed, embarrassed at having started that way. "I mean," she began again, "I'm sorry to interrupt you at work . . ." She could feel herself flush, and wondered why she was doing this . . . Thea was probably at home right now, waiting for her. She lifted her hand in the air . . . it had been a mistake to come here, a silly mistake . . .

"What can I do for you?" he smiled, swinging easily off the boat.

"I can't seem to locate Thea, and I thought she might be with Alex. Your housekeeper said I'd have to ask you."

He frowned. "Didn't Sadame tell you Alex was at my cousin's, working in the pineapple fields?"

She shook her head.

"I guess she wouldn't," he added. "She's mad at me for sending him away. I apologize for her."

"No," Karin said, in a voice that sounded feeble, "it's all right . . . Thea's probably just out with a girlfriend and forgot . . . I didn't mean to . . . it was silly of me . . ."

He was already moving, his hand on her elbow, guiding her through sliding glass doors into an office. "If you'll just wait a minute while I tell the secretary, I'll help you find her."

She started to object, then stopped herself. He hadn't said, "I'll help you look," he had said, "I'll help you find." She needed help, she knew that. If she didn't find Thea, and soon, she was going to shatter, she knew that too.

"I really shouldn't bother you with this," was what she finally said, her phrasing formal, her voice precariously close to breaking, "but I would very much appreciate your help."

"We'll check your house," he answered, holding the door to his car for her, "in case she came and went out again. She might have left a note."

It sounded reasonable. Yes, that was it. There would be a note waiting for her, all of this would be for nothing, she was sure of it.

They checked the refrigerator, but there was nothing under the Minnie Mouse magnet where a note would have been. She looked on the gleaming koa wood dining table and on the coffee table and on Thea's dresser. All were empty, terribly empty. A T-shirt had been tossed on the bed; had it been there before? She was trying to remember when he called to her from the kitchen.

He was kneeling on the floor in front of the refrigerator, grinning, holding a note out to her.

"You've got a cross-draft blowing in here—I found it under the fridge."

The note said: "Dear wonderful Karin, we're going to Janie's house to get some help with calculus from her jerky (but brilliant) brother, then I've been invited to spend the night and go with her family tomorrow to Kaneohe Bay. Could you call Mrs. C to say it's okay? Love ya, T." All of the i's were dotted with little o's.

Karin sank against the cabinets, relief flooding through her. "Oh God," she laughed, "I feel so ludicrous."

He squinted up, smiling now. "I wish my problems with my kid could be solved that easily." He pushed himself up, and for a long

minute they stood awkwardly, each waiting for the other to say
something, then both spoke at once.

"Maybe you might . . ." he began, just as she said, "Can I at least
offer you a tuna fish sandwich?"

They laughed then. "Yes," he said, "except, I thought maybe
. . . when you came to the boatyard just now, I wasn't really working,
I was getting ready to take my cutter out to try a new jib. What would
you think about packing a couple of sandwiches and coming along?"

She hesitated, and he misunderstood.

"But you probably have plans . . ." he said.

"No," she came back, "no, I haven't. Really, there's nothing . . . I
was just thinking how strange it feels, and how nice really, that Thea
wants to spend the night at a friend's. She hasn't wanted to be
anywhere but here since . . . since . . ."

"Since Alex gave her acid," he finished, dully.

She swallowed. "Yes, since then. I'll have to call and tell her it's
fine, then it will only take me a few minutes to put a lunch together.
I think I'd love to go sailing."

It was Paul Hollowell's turn to look surprised. "Point me to the
tuna fish and I'll make the sandwiches while you make your call."

She pulled on white shorts and rummaged in her dresser until she
came across a soft, turquoise blouse with gold threads running
through.

"Good," he said when she came into the kitchen. She didn't know
if he meant the way she looked, or that she had taken so little time
or simply that he was glad she was going. She smiled to herself. It
was an old blouse, one Philip had thought gaudy. She didn't know
what had made her keep it, much less put it on today.

"How much do you know about sailing?" Paul asked as he guided
the boat out of the harbor.

"Very little," she answered, "almost nothing." She thought about
asking if that was a problem, but didn't. As soon as they had stepped
onto the boat, words had begun to seem superfluous, she didn't know
why. She positioned herself against the cabin, out of the way, and
watched as he raised the sails and the wind caught in them and they
were moving, free of the shore and heading out to sea. On land he
seemed solid, almost awkward, but here, on his own deck, he moved
with the grace of a gymnast.

"This is perfect," she called to him, but the breeze caught her words and mingled them with the crackling of the sails and finally, spilled them out over the turquoise blue of the water which matched, almost, the blue of her blouse.

They ate their tuna sandwiches, shared a beer, and exchanged a few words. She asked him about the boat.

"It's a cutter," he said, pulling it a little closer to the wind, "thirty-six feet, built so I could handle her myself on the open ocean. She may not be as fast as some of these modern sleds, but then I don't need a crew the size of the city of New York to sail her."

"You don't like racing?"

He took a swig of beer, peered into the sky as if he were making some calculations and said, absently, "I've done my share." Then he added, "It's really calm—ordinarily we would have run into some fairly stiff winds by now . . . we're going to have to go out a ways into the channel."

"Fine with me," she answered, tilting her face back to catch the sun, "I could stay out here all day."

She opened her eyes in time to catch him glancing away. To cover his embarrassment, she asked, "If you aren't that interested in racing, what is it that you love about it—about sailing?"

After thinking for a while, he said, "This—being out here, the freedom I guess . . . the quiet. I don't remember seeing it as quiet as it is today, but we'll be moving into the Kaiwi Channel and it will get rougher."

"That's what you want?"

He grinned. "For a while, enough to see how the jib is setting. I just wanted to warn you not to worry."

"I'm not worried," she said, turning over to feel the warmth of the sun on her back and the smooth, rolling motion of the boat under her belly. She had no idea how long she lay like that, listening to the soft thud and hiss of the water as the boat cut neatly through it. She felt the ocean lift her, rock her, cradle her. Now and then she opened her eyes and looked at Paul Hollowell until he looked back and smiled.

She must have been dozing, because his words startled her. "Rough water coming up," he said, tossing her a sweatshirt. "The winds are rising fast too . . . I've got her on a close reach, so we'll be moving, you might want to sit down here, next to the cabin where it's protected." She moved down, responding to the tension she felt building in him, and to the waves which were rising now, spraying over the deck.

395

She felt a hard slap as the cutter nosed into a wave; the boat heeled sharply. She held hard to the railing and tried to swallow the surge of fear that rose in her. Then she looked at Paul Hollowell's face, and the fear subsided. His boat was doing what it was supposed to be doing. She was certain he had everything under control.

"Just a few minutes more and we'll turn back," he shouted over the ocean rush and spray. His T-shirt was plastered against his chest, outlining the hard edge of his muscles. She pulled her legs up to her chin and let the excitement fill her, as the spray danced off her face and they moved with the wind, like the wind, fast and furiously through the deep blue water, through the froth of whitecaps, running silently.

He was standing, ready to change course, to turn back, when it happened. The boat pitched off one wave and was caught by another, hitting soundly. The crack was loud, wrong. She looked up, saw a long thin sliver of light where the boom had cracked and parted.

Oh God, she thought, a sour panic rising in her mouth. The thought rushed like blood to her head—what should I do? My God, what *could* I do? As if in answer, Paul shouted, "Hold this," indicating the wheel. "Right there, steady." She wanted to say no, I can't, please don't ask me, no. The boat hesitated, lurched ahead with the gaping crack in the boom. Terrified, she took the wheel and felt the awful lurch and thrust of the boat under her hands, pulling against her like some great, struggling animal.

Paul dived below deck, vanished. A sharp spray of water caught her in the face, took her breath. She concentrated on the wheel, on holding it just there, where he had said. He reappeared with a coiled line in his hand. The boat dipped and pitched, the waves were getting bigger, wilder now. She felt a sob escape as the fear washed through her with the full force of the sea, drenching her. Holding tight to the wheel she watched as he let the mainsail out, it luffed, flapped in the wind. Then he was up on the rail, balancing crazily—like a drunk on a high wire as the sea tossed under him, madly up and down. He was reaching for the end of the boom. He was going to fall, she knew it. He was not holding on, but trying to thread the line through a ring in the sail. He was reaching for the boom, balancing . . . he missed it, as they fell into a trough and lurched, sickeningly. *Oh God, dear God don't let him fall.* But he had to fall, he had to, anyone could see that he would have to. She could feel nothing but the fear, nothing, and then she realized what he was doing. Wrapping the line, around and around, threading it through a ring in the sail, standing above the sea and the foam and the angry rush of water, holding on to nothing, balancing in the bright sea light.

And then he was next to her, taking the wheel, his hand pressed tight against her arm to let her know it was over, and she sank to the floor and sat there, clutching her breasts in her hands to keep her chest from exploding.

He leaned over and shouted into her ear, "I've got it tied down, but we can't go back—we're going to run downwind to get into the lee of Molokai, things will quiet down there." She felt the fear draining out of her, to be replaced by a feeling of profound weakness. She glanced up at his face, and could see that he was angry. She began to sob quietly, her shoulders shaking in small spasms that she could not control.

It was as he had said it would be. After three quarters of an hour the sea became quiet. She pulled herself to a sunny place against the cabin, and lay open to the sun so it could soothe and comfort and dry her.

"Look," he finally said in a voice that sounded hoarse. She did look at him then, and was surprised to see exhaustion and misery in his face. He said with a barely curbed anger, "I don't seem to be able to do anything right . . . for you, I mean. The damned boom splitting, forcing you to take over the wheel . . . scaring you to death . . . I never would have had this happen . . ."

Her teeth began to chatter. He reached into a canvas bag, pulled out a sweater and tried, awkwardly, to help her put it on without touching her.

She dropped her head between her knees. When she looked up at him again, she was smiling. "I was so scared," she said in a tremulous voice, "horribly scared. Were you?"

He ran his free hand through his hair. "When I had time to think about it, yes. And mad too, I guess . . . that it happened at all." He waited a few minutes, then added, "There's something else. We can't go back now, not through those rough seas with the cracked boom. The fix I've made is only temporary, but I've got everything on board to do it right—that means putting in at a protected harbor. There's nothing on Molokai, so I'm going to run downwind and head for Lanai."

"What does that mean?" she asked.

He cleared his throat. "I'm afraid it means staying overnight."

He bit his lip. "I didn't plan for this . . . you don't have to worry that . . ." he began.

"I'm not worried now," she cut in sharply, knowing what he meant and feeling angry that he felt he had to say it. She knew, of course; she knew what he wouldn't try, wouldn't let himself try even if he wanted to. *Even if she wanted to,* she admitted, feeling a flush of anger at herself now. Reminding herself, *You could have drowned, he could have drowned, your husband is alive and he is hurt and you are not with him, others are taking care of him while you are alone in the Pacific Ocean, taking your pleasure. Wanting to be here, with this man, Oh God. You are not dutiful, not loving, and you have no right, none* . . . STOP, she told herself, and taking a deep breath said, "It's all right, I know it can't be helped, and Thea is away for the night, I don't have to worry about her . . ."

"I have a radio," Paul said, "I'll alert my office, and if you want they can call . . ."

"No," she said quickly, then more softly, "it won't be necessary. Thea will be fine and we'll be back . . . when?"

"By noon if we leave at first light . . . I really am sorry, Karin."

She could not remember if he had ever said her name before.

They sailed in silence for an hour or more, as the sun began to finish its wide arc, turning the boat, the sea, the world into a burnished brightness. "There it is," he finally said, pointing to the cliffs that rose steep and green, from the ocean. Finally she could make out a small cove with an arc of white beach tucked into the base of the cliffs.

"It looks deserted," she said.

"It is," he told her. "There aren't any roads on this side of the island, no way to get into this beach except by boat—and we're the only boat in sight."

"Have you been here before?" she asked.

"I guess I've put into most of these coves, one time or another. My dad liked to sail, my mother too." He grinned. "She was a better sailor than he was, at least that's what he always used to say."

"Have you been here with Alex?"

She wished she could take the question back.

He busied himself with the lines. "Alex isn't big on sailing," he answered evenly, managing to keep any trace of disappointment out of his voice. "Would you mind taking the wheel again when we come in? Just hold it here, into the wind, so I can get the anchor ready."

She laughed and took the wheel, surprised that she really didn't mind.

When the anchor was set and the sails were down she helped him fold and bag the mainsail so he could work on the boom. He went below decks and came back with a cordless drill, some epoxy and some brass screws, all of which he lay out neatly in a tray. She watched, fascinated with the precise way he set about repairing the split in the wood, with his concentration.

She finally broke the silence by asking, "How long will it take—and is there anything I can do?"

He looked up, as if he had forgotten something. "No," he answered slowly, thinking. "I've got to set the screws and glue it—it'll take about an hour. This would probably be a good time to take a swim, if you want."

The water was glowing gold and turquoise. She could see small schools of bright fish gliding under the surface, and suddenly it seemed like exactly the right thing to do. She sat on the edge, dangling her feet and legs in the water and waited for the chill to wear off, for the temperature to be perfect. When that happened, she slipped out of her blouse and shorts, and over the side, gasping as the water grasped her bare breasts.

She swam in careful little circles, not wanting to venture far from the boat. She was not a strong swimmer, and not entirely easy in the full swell of the sea. She turned on her back, looking up into the billowing clouds; she closed her eyes and lay there, arms out and back arched . . . when she opened them again he was looking at her. Quickly, she flipped over. The next time she looked, his back was to her and he was working.

He did not turn back again until she had dressed and spoke to him.

"I didn't mean to embarrass you," she said, "it just seemed so isolated and perfect, like it was meant for skinny-dipping. Sometimes I forget myself . . ."

"I'm afraid I'm not . . ." he began, giving the last twists to a brass screw in the boom.

She interrupted, "After today, I don't really think you could be afraid of anything. I'm the one who is afraid. Of everything, lately. I spend most of my days in dread. Except for this afternoon," she laughed, "when I was genuinely terrified for what seemed like a lifetime but was probably what . . . five minutes? Ten? How long did it take you to thread that rope through the grommet on the sail?"

He grinned. "Line. On board, a rope is always a line."

She went on, "What I am trying to say is that I've been feeling a kind of dread and it's just . . . deadening. Until now, with just the ocean and the boat and all this . . . emptiness. Here, now, it all seems so simple."

"That's my problem, I think," he said, caressing the varnished surface of the boom, "I spend so much time out here, I've kind of lost touch . . ."

"Lost touch," she repeated, as if it were the title of some mysterious game she had played once, "Yes, I know that."

"I keep a stock of food on board, some packaged soups and freeze-dried vegetables . . ."

"Do you have a fishing pole?" she asked.

"Two," was his answer.

It had been building, the magnetic field, the charged atmosphere. She thought that if she could listen hard enough, she would be able to hear a crackling, an electric awareness. Each moved carefully, not to come too close. He cleaned the fish. As she reached for it, their fingers brushed and both of them pulled back, as if burned. They ate at a tiny table in the galley. If she moved even half an inch, her knees would touch his. She made an effort not to move.

It was deep twilight when they finished. She watched as he cleaned each pan and utensil and returned it to its proper place. Here, in this small world, he could keep everything in meticulous order.

"Let's have coffee on deck," he said, his back to her. "You can bring up the foam pad from one of the bunks to sit on—I'll sleep topside tonight anyway, you can have the cabin."

She tilted her head back to watch the stars appear in the vast sky. "I'd forgotten how bright they are out here in the middle of the Pacific."

"Your husband's an astronomer," he said, handing her a cup. It was a statement of fact, a reminder—to himself? for her?

"He was, yes. Oh God, Thea's been using the past tense and now I'm doing it too. Yes, he is an astronomer, though I can't imagine he will ever be able to teach again. I can't imagine anything, to be honest with you."

To be honest with you. It was just a phrase, a cliché, words to fill in when you could think of nothing else to say. She could not see him clearly, but she heard the change in his voice and she knew it was because she had said, "to be honest with you."

"When my wife died last year," he began in a voice she had not heard before, low and earnest, "there was no warning. None. It just happened, she left home one morning that was just like every other morning, and she never came back."

"I believe Thea told me it was a boating accident?" Karin asked.

"That's the hell of it," he answered bitterly. "It was an accident I could have prevented."

Surprised, she looked up and he explained, "I guess that was why I was so mad at myself today, that I had put you at risk."

"We were really in trouble today?"

"We came pretty close," he said, looking out over the water.

"Your wife's accident, how . . ."

She could hear him breathing. She waited. Soon, in a halting voice that allowed long pauses between clusters of words, he began in a way that made Karin think he had never tried to explain it before. "She was taking a bunch of first-grade kids on a whale watching outing. She belonged to a lot of charitable groups. It was the kind of thing they did, working with kids in some of the poor neighborhoods. She didn't tell me she was going, or if she did I have no memory of it. But I think she didn't because I would have asked what boat they had chartered and I sure as hell wouldn't have let them go on the one they took. The guy was trouble, everybody knew that. Everybody but Helen."

Karin let the silence gather. Finally he went on, "It should never have happened, the guy running the boat just didn't know what he was doing. They ran into some big swells, and he panicked. A wave washed over them, and two of the kids were swept overboard. They had on lifejackets, but Helen didn't—she was a strong swimmer. She was trying to reach one of the kids and the boat shifted. She went in and was pulled under the boat. By the time they fished the kids out, Helen was gone. They found her body later that day, there was a bad cut on her head.

He paused, a long four-count, and picked up again. "The thing is, we didn't talk to each other. It seemed like we did, but I can't remember now what we said, all that time. All I know is that we got to the place where she didn't bother to tell me that she'd be on the water that day. And I didn't always tell her, either, when I was going out. She didn't like to sail all that much, and I didn't like the functions she . . ."

He stopped, let the words trail off and for a moment Karin thought he was through. He picked up again: "I can't remember what we talked about. I'd known her all my life, we went to school together, we got married when I got out of the Marines and all that time we were talking, we had to be, and now I can't remember any of it. What was said. I lay awake at night and try to pull out a whole conversation, but I can't. Not one. Not in all those years together."

The air was warm but she felt a chill. She took a sip of the hot coffee and held it in her mouth.

"Sometimes I think if I could remember," he went on, "then I would feel something else . . . because . . . when I go home at night, Sadame lets me in, just like she always has, and I sit down and eat dinner. Alex isn't there much, and that's not different either. I thought Alex and Helen talked, it seemed like they must have, but when I asked him he said no, only about school, what was happening, what he wanted for dinner, things like that. I thought maybe he knew something I didn't, something we should have been saying, but he doesn't want to talk to me . . . It seems like something should have changed, that it's wrong for everything to seem . . . the same. I don't know what we talked about at dinner, but it doesn't seem to matter, I mean, it doesn't seem any different. Except she isn't there."

She could see the outline of his face in the starlight. "Do you mean you feel numb, that you haven't been able to accept her absence?"

"No," he said, and waited. "No, I think I was the one who was absent. I think I left a long time ago, I think we seemed to be married, to be living together . . . we ate at the same table, we slept in the same bed . . . but if I'd been there, I should be able to remember what she said, what she looked like when she was a girl, I should feel some terrible loss . . ." his voice cracked with misery, "I think I must have left a long time ago, and . . . I don't know where I've been."

The words collided in her brain. *Lost, you've been lost, we've been lost . . . wandering, looking, lost . . .* She could not speak, no word was enough. Her fingertips touched the back of his hand. He looked at her hand on his, looked at her, not knowing, not certain. She moved into his arms, was clinging hard to him. She found his mouth, felt the catch in his body, moved into him. They gave themselves to the heat and the pull and the inevitability of it, the sea gathered them in, rocking them together, letting the hot flush rise.

Her ears rang with wanting, her head filled with light, exploded with color. She rose to meet him, and she cried out and heard her voice echo over the water and come to rest on the shore, with the waves that lapped rhythmically on the way to the silver place where their worlds met.

When she could speak she said, "Now I know."

He pressed his mouth into the place behind her ear and murmured, "Yes."

When the sun was still behind the mountain and the light was a cool morning gold, they slipped into the ocean together, their flesh white in the clear water. He touched her face, kissed her, moved his hands to her breasts. There was no denying now, they gave themselves to the sexual field that enveloped them, reveled in it, gloried in it. She wrapped her legs around him and took a deep breath and pulled him under with her. They swam to the beach, letting the waves wash them to the shore where they walked, touching, holding. As the sun reached the beach she lay back on the warm sand and felt herself opening, like a flower, like a morning glory. He lay on top of her, entered her, they rocked together as the waves washed in. A wild rhythm overtook them, carried them. They fell into the sand and laughed and came together as the sea seemed to rise, tempting them, caressing them.

As they sailed out of the cove he said, "I want to be with you. Whenever I can, however I can."

She smiled and touched his face and moved her hand close on his stomach as she said, very simply, "I have a husband."

Then she leaned into him and refused to think of anything but the long, sweet swell of the sea and the touch of the man who had given her what she thought she could never have.

31

K it was early, but Philip was already at the typewriter when she
arrived.

"I hope that's the outline for the new novel—your agent called
again yesterday, he's pushing hard. . . ." She touched his shoulder as
she leaned over to see what he had written.

Karin, he had typed, *It is time we talked.*

She sat in a chair facing him.

"That's why I'm early," she said, "Karin called this morning. She
is flying in tomorrow. Thea has agreed to let Annie come stay with
her for a few days . . . Karin sounded, well, distraught. She said she
didn't know what she was doing, staying away for so long . . . she
kept apologizing to me for not doing what she called 'her share.'
There just wasn't any calming her, Philip. I think she has to come,
for her own peace of mind. She talked about getting the Berkeley
house ready for your return, arranging to have a carpenter build
wheelchair ramps so you can get around. She is going on the assump-
tion that when you leave the hospital next month you'll go home,
and she'll be taking care of you. I didn't say anything to her, or try
to dissuade her from coming. I didn't think I should."

She waited for his answer. Laboriously, he placed his hands on the
keyboard and typed: *You were right. Better in person. Harder but better.*

"What will you say to her?"

He typed: *Groan*

"I know," Kit said, "I've been rehearsing speeches myself. I can't bear to hurt her, and in the long run I know, from what you've told me, that what we have planned will be better for her, too. She has been so wonderful with Thea, but it doesn't seem to have assuaged her guilt about you."

His hands moved slowly over the keyboard: *Are you worried what people will say?*

She took his hand, held it between both of hers: "I'm only worried about Karin and your children. I can count on May and Faith and Emilie's family to understand. The rest of the world can go to hell."

Philip typed: *At the Malibu we shut them out.*

"No," she said, vehemently, "that's not why we're going to the ranch. We're going there to be together, to work together. I don't want to shut the world out, I just thought it would be a wonderful place for you to write and for me to remove myself from most of my business responsibilities."

His mouth twitched in the flickering movement she knew to be a smile. *Got you going,* he typed.

She laughed. "You did. Sometimes I think I should have left you trapped in that elegant body, sometimes I think I've unleashed a monster."

Too late . . . now Karin, he typed.

"Yes, we must talk about Karin," she sighed.

"What is a 'bouquet garni'?" Hayes wanted to know.

"Haven't the foggiest," May said. "Check *The Joy of Cooking,* or maybe Julia Child. If they don't know it probably doesn't matter."

"Like your style," he said, rubbing his hands on the front of his apron, on which was printed in large letters: "Kiss the Cook", and pulling her to him.

"No, no, you've got it wrong," she laughed, "I'm supposed to kiss the cook, and you're the cook . . . and the bechamel sauce is burning."

He reached for a whisk and began to stir. "I'll never make a Washington hostess."

"Oh yes we will," she told him, bumping him playfully with her hip. "You told your boss we were going to cook and we are. Come look at my table when you can—it's gorgeous."

"Next time we send out for Chinese," he muttered.

"Next time we send out for a cook," she answered, tiptoeing to bite him on the ear.

In bed that night he pulled her close and said, "You were good tonight."

"You mean when I dropped the pickled mushrooms on the floor?"

"That too." He shifted so he could hold her in his arms. "But mainly I meant, you were just easy and nice and made them feel comfortable."

She burrowed in, rubbing her cheek against his chest. "What were they expecting?"

"That's just it—they didn't know what to expect. Washington runs on rumors, and I think the rumors had you down as this exotic wild-woman who chases volcanoes, who is rich as sin, and is the sole progeny of Porter Reade. His name still evokes strong emotions in this town as you might have noticed. Weren't you a little surprised when old Jameson did that little testimonial about how your father's position on China has finally been vindicated?"

She was content to lie in his arms. She turned her face so she could kiss his chest, and answered, "You know, it doesn't matter any more, what they say. I loved my father, and I've forgiven him. I've forgiven my mother, too. They both made such sad mistakes . . . and I feel sorry that things weren't different for them, but it isn't churning around inside me anymore."

"I know," he said, and the way he said it made her ask what was wrong.

"Your talking about forgiveness, I guess. Eli. I haven't forgiven him and I don't know if I ever can. It's funny." he said, and fell silent, thinking.

She closed her eyes, but the tensions in him would not let her drift off to sleep. "It isn't funny," she prompted.

"No, it isn't." He sat up, turned on the light. She plumped the pillow behind her so she could lean against the headboard. It was coming now; he had been unable to talk about Eli, and now he could.

He got up, began to pace. "He violated it," he said, "our friendship . . . he betrayed everything we believed in."

She pulled the sheet over her bare arms and waited.

"I could always talk to Eli, about everything. And one thing we talked about, from the beginning, was our friendship, what it was supposed to be. He had very specific ideas, you know . . . it was important to him that we understood, each of us . . . that we play by the rules. He had no use for what he called the you make me feel good I make you feel good school of friendship. He thought being a friend was a responsibility, that each of you had a larger commitment to the common good. These weren't new ideas, Aristotle and Cicero had written about them. You were supposed to enjoy each other's company, and you were supposed to be useful to each other. But there was a moral commitment there, too. By holding each other to that moral imperative, you would create a better society . . . he believed, we believed that that kind of friendship was at the very heart of the society we wanted to build."

She ached for him. "And you feel he betrayed you," she said.

Hayes was at the window, looking down at the shadows thrown by the street lamp shining through the full leaves of the sycamore tree. With his back to her he said, "Maybe I failed him, I don't know. I'm sure he thinks my signing on with the State Department is a form of betrayal. What I do know is that he has thrown in with people who believe terrorism is an answer, and I can't accept that."

"Still, he warned us," she said.

He slapped his hand hard against the wall. "It was Eli who put us in jeopardy in the first place. The fact that he wouldn't go through with it doesn't mean he won't the next time, when the victim is someone he doesn't know. He's gone underground, May. I can't stay neutral, I've got to oppose him, and I wanted you to know the reason."

When he turned around she saw that his face was wet.

It was almost light before she felt him sigh and relax, and she could allow herself to slip into sleep beside him.

"What do you hear from May?" Kit asked, playing for time.

Karin concentrated on the tea bag she was dipping in the mug of hot water. A few drops sloshed onto the white Formica of the cafeteria table and she blotted them, absentmindedly, with a paper napkin.

"You know about the offer she got from the Geological Survey? But I don't think she's going to go back to work for a while. She's having too nice a time being Hayes's wife."

"I think so too," Kit said. "His mother called yesterday to tell me that May wants to work with her to find Andy's child. That whole situation seems almost made to order for May."

"What do you mean?" Karin asked. Kit could tell by her eyes that she was too weary, and probably too disturbed about her own situation, to make the connections, so she explained: "The child is Asian American, like May. There is a war, a cultural division between the families . . . and a boy who will grow up not knowing much about his father, in this case—not knowing if he wanted him, if he deserted him, what the father's family was all about."

Karin nodded, dully. "May did tell me they would like to resolve the question of Andy's son before they start a family of their own."

Kit coughed to clear her throat. She felt a quivering on the inside and wondered if it would show in her voice. "I wanted to talk to you before you saw Philip," she began, "to warn you a bit. I think you are going to be surprised . . ." She stopped, tried to organize her thoughts. "He has made quite wonderful strides. He can type fairly well now, so you can have a conversation of sorts—though he tends to leave out a lot and you have to fill in the spaces. It's going to take months, and a lot of work, to teach him to speak again but we believe it is possible."

Karin began to put her things together, she wanted to see him now, to get on with it. Kit could hear the beating of her own heart hot in her ears.

"What I wanted to tell you," she said, rushing now, "is that I hope you know how deeply I care for you."

She watched Karin walk away, her shoulder bag carried like a burden, weighing her down. Kit had meant to warn her, to prepare her. She had wanted to make it easier for Karin and for Philip, and she had not known how. Nor did she know what to expect from Karin. But she had gone too far now to turn back, it was all set in motion.

He was dressed and waiting, sitting with the typewriter positioned so she could read what he wrote without having to stand behind him.

He waited while she went through the formalities: The chaste kiss on the cheek, the slow, sad smile into his eyes, the messages of love from Thea, from Faith. How well Annie and Thea got along, how she felt Thea was finally ready to come back to enroll at Stanford next month. She began her apology then, starting by saying, "I feel I have let you down . . ."

He stopped her by beginning to type.

Wait, he wrote, *Please.*

She watched his hands crawl over the keyboard, watched each letter as it appeared on the paper: *In Sept. I go to Malibu ranch with Kit. She wants. I want.*

"I don't understand," Karin said, as if to herself. "Do you mean you are going for a visit?"

He typed: *To live.*

"To live," she whispered, and stared at him. She could not take it in, could not fathom what it meant. Kit and Philip, going to the ranch together. To live, he said. She sat back in the chair and felt as if she were about to fly apart, all the molecules of her body to float off into space. A wave of nausea threatened to move into her throat. She closed her eyes to stop it and the room began spinning. When she opened her eyes he was watching her and she wanted to scream.

Instead she forced her throat to open, her voice to say, "Tell me what you want me to do."

Slowly, he typed. *Care for Thea, Dan. Care for you. Divorce me.*

She tried to think and couldn't. "I don't know what to say," she began, "I'm sorry, I know our marriage has not been . . . I haven't . . ."

NO he typed, all in caps, *DEAR KARIN, NOT YOU. NEVER YOU.* Then he added, *My fault, total. Long story. Tell one day when you come Malibu.*

She took his hand then and let the sobs wrench out of her. "I'm so sorry, Philip," she said, "I wish it had all been different."

She felt his hand press hers and looked up. A small flickering of muscles moved his lips in a grotesque smile. "I'll go find Kit," was all she could think to say.

She lay back on the great pink moire pillows in Kit's guest room, a cool towel on her head and tried to sip from the ginger ale Kit had brought to settle her stomach.

"I feel better now," she said. "Not so dizzy."

Kit stood in the doorway in an attitude of uncertainty.

"Come talk to me, please," Karin said.

She looked so miserable Kit wanted to put her arms around her to comfort her, but she could not. Not this time.

"I don't understand, Kit. Can you explain to me what is happening?"

Kit sat in a small chair next to the bed, and tried to think how to start.

"I don't understand either, Karin. I wish I did. The way things happen, it is so strange . . . life is strange. When you and Philip married it seemed so right to all of us, and I believe in many ways it was right. I'm not certain what would have happened to Thea and Dan if you hadn't married their father. But you did marry him, and because of that those children have a chance for a happy, whole life now. Philip knows that as well as any of us. And I believe you and Philip were good for each other for a time, too. Just as Philip and I were once good for each other—for a very brief time. I didn't allow a relationship with Philip then because I knew it wouldn't last. It was wonderful, but ephemeral, and that is all it could have been at that time in our lives. But . . . and this is the hard part to explain . . . when Philip and I came together again, after his accident, it was as if . . ." she hesitated, her neck flushed, ". . . as if finally, it was time for us. Out of both our needs—mine as desperate as his, if truth be told— this, well, wonderful sweetness emerged. I so love being with him, K. The age difference doesn't seem to matter any more."

She leaned forward, reached for Karin's hand, "Ever since Connor died, Karin, I have carried this loneliness around inside of me. And now it's gone. Philip says he has much the same feelings. We didn't plan for this to happen, darling, but it did."

Karin looked confused, as if she still didn't understand. "I'm not sure . . ." she began, "I thought maybe you were doing it for me . . . so I wouldn't feel so guilty . . ."

Kit shook her head. "No, as much as I love you, I promise you I am not doing it for you. I am doing it for me, and for Philip. But I hope . . ." she hesitated again, "I hope with all my heart that it is right for you, that you can finally feel released from any obligation."

"When Philip said I should divorce him, he wants it for himself?"

Kit nodded, and asked, "Does that hurt?"

Karin managed a tremulous smile; she seemed to be taking stock. "No. No it doesn't. I don't know what I feel, Kit. It's so . . . new."

"Darling," Kit said, moving to sit next to her on the bed, "we want so for you to be happy, to feel free. Because in a way, we can't until you do. Does that sound selfish?"

Karin shook her head. "It's just so . . . strange . . . all these months, I've been walking around feeling that I should be doing something I couldn't bring myself to do. And now that feeling is gone, but I don't have anything to put in its place. I don't feel free, not yet, Kit. Maybe it takes awhile. I just feel kind of . . . stunned."

"Stay here a few days, let's talk—the three of us. We can make it right, together. I know it, K, I just feel it!"

Karin had never known Kit to be so animated, so intense. Her cheeks were blazing. Karin said, "I'll call to see if it's okay with Thea."

Occasionally now, when Israel spoke, he was continuing a dialogue from his childhood with people no longer alive. He talked to his mother about going out to collect coal along the railroad tracks— would he get to pull the wagon? he wanted to know. And he talked to someone named Odell who had been at Ft. Benning, Georgia with him, and who had never understood. "Let me explain," Israel would plead, "don't turn your back on me, please let me explain."

He floated in and out of a morphine fog, now and then rising to the surface of consciousness. His body grew frail, but his great voice was not diminished. He would sing the old hymns, beginning in a low, slow mode, "I was sinking deep in sin, / Far from the peaceful shore. / Very deeply stained within, / Sinking to rise no more." And then his great, booming bass would move into the almost rollicking chorus, "Love lifted me, / Love lifted me, when nothing else would help, / Love lifted me!" Abigail would join in sometimes, she had learned all the old Protestant hymns in the mission school, or any of the children who wandered on and off the lanai, where he spent most of each day.

On the day after Annie returned from Honolulu, he opened his eyes, saw her sitting beside him and said in a perfectly reasonable voice, "If I had it all to do over again, I'd work in a bakery so I could breathe in the smell of warm bread all day long, all day long."

Annie laughed. "I just popped two loaves into the oven—you missed me baking your daily bread, didn't you, sweet man?"

"My mama used to bake bread," he rambled on. "I'd go to the back door of the house where she worked, and she'd let me into the kitchen, her black arms'd be all dusted with white flour, and she'd give me a little piece of bread right out of the oven, and sometimes she'd pile applesauce on it, with cinnamon sprinkled on top."

He closed his eyes. She thought he had drifted off again when he asked, "Where'd you go?"

Annie soothed his forehead with a damp washcloth. "I stayed with Thea while Karin was in California. I was only supposed to be away three days, but Karin needed to stay on a while longer, and she wasn't feeling well when she came back so I kept her company for another day."

Annie was troubled about Karin and didn't want Israel to know so she picked up the morning *Honolulu Register.* "There's a wonderful story in the paper today," she said, "why don't I read it to you?"

"Don't read," Israel said, closing his eyes, "tell me the story. I like it best when you tell me your stories."

"Once upon a time, three days ago," she began, softly, and watched for the smile that flickered weakly, "on an island called Kauai there lived an eagle. Just one, a great golden eagle that soared among the peaks and into the deep valleys of the Waimea Canyon, which the Hawaiians like to call their Grand Canyon, a place so spectacularly beautiful that tourists by the hordes make the long, winding journey into the mountains to look at it.

"Nobody knew how this eagle came to be in the Hawaiian Islands—certainly there had never been one before—or even when it came. Some thought it might have been blown far off its course by a storm, others figured it must have come by boat and been set free. But anyone who knew anything about eagles knew that it should not be here, because eagles are fiercely familial . . . they mate for life, raising a family is what they do with their spare time.

"Our lonely eagle was first spotted by one of the helicopter pilots who take people into the valley on tours. This pilot thought the eagle was the most beautiful thing he had ever seen, with its great wingspan, its ability to soar high and glide low, to dive and scan the deepest crevices on the wild valleys. Sometimes, the pilot said, the eagle would glide alongside his helicopter, and the two would do a kind of precision flying. The pilot said that when this happened, he felt like he had wings.

"This went on for quite awhile, the eagle would hear the helicopter and come to meet it, and they would fly along together. When he could, the pilot went up by himself so they could fly freely together, without having to worry about passengers.

"It was good business, flying people into the valley, and very quickly there were three and four different services sending copters into the valley, and pretty soon the sky was full of them, and the eagle was not happy. Not at all.

"The eagle no longer flew alongside, but began to drop from above in a sudden dive and the pilot became worried that it would become entangled in his rotors. Twice he had to effect sudden maneuvers to miss the bird. Gradually it began to dawn on him: the eagle is fighting for his territory, he sees the helicopters as invaders. So the pilot went around to all of the helicopter services in Kauai, and warned them about the eagle, and asked them to give it plenty of room and to watch out for it.

"Three days ago the pilot was just entering the main branch of the canyon when he saw the eagle ahead of him, hovering directly above a Ranger, he saw the eagle go into a steep dive and attack the helicopter."

She stopped, leaned toward Israel to look into his face. She could tell by his breathing that he had slipped away into sleep, so she whispered, "And that was the end of the beautiful eagle."

The bad news did not come over the telephone, as Karin had always believed it would. It was delivered by a man in a uniform, with a bright row of ribbons emblazoned over his heart.

It was the middle of the afternoon and she was lying on Thea's bed, thinking about October light, the slight difference she sensed, a subtle haze that perhaps existed only in her mind, remembrance of other autumns in other places. Since Thea had left for Stanford, she had spent a good part of each day in this room. There was a good breeze, and she could look up toward the mountain. When it rained she could see clouds of water waft by. It pleased her to lie in Thea's narrow bed, to look at the pale yellow walls, empty now of the jumble of posters and signs and pictures.

She looked out the window and saw him, limping down the steep driveway. A serviceman, she thought. Probably he is lost, she thought. He needs directions. She knew she should get up, should go to meet him, should let him know where she was. She had been napping, she supposed, otherwise why would her legs feel so heavy? A lassitude had overtaken her these past days. She had promised to call Annie. She should do that, Annie was worried about her. But first, the man in the driveway, the directions.

He stood on the other side of the screened door, his hat tucked under his arm and said, "Mrs. Ward?"

He was looking at her yet not looking at her. It was, she thought, as if he were saying the Pledge of Allegiance. He had memorized his speech. "It is my sad duty to inform you that your son, marine Private Daniel Ward . . ."

She felt the medals on his chest rip into the flesh of her forearms, but still she pounded on him, screaming, "No. There is no war, no. No. No, you are wrong, wrong."

The next thing she remembered was Paul Hollowell striding into the house, his strong arms around her, holding her steady in the storm that had broken over her.

She had not seen him since the morning she left him at the sailboat, two months before. He was here, now, because the man in the uniform had found his name and two phone numbers on a piece of paper by her bed. She had written them out two days before, when she learned she was pregnant with his child.

Daniel Ward died on October 11, 1973, when the South Vietnamese army helicopter in which he was a passenger came under fire near Dalat, exploded and crashed, killing all aboard. He had been acting as escort to one of the ambassador's aides, who had been sent on a fact-finding tour of the area north of Saigon. A small story went out over the news wires, naming the aide and adding, "his Marine escort was also killed in the crash."

He was buried in the military cemetery in Punchbowl. Philip could not make the trip, and Kit—worried at how he was taking this latest blow—stayed with him. Neither could Faith leave Israel, his cogent moments were few now, the end was near. May was on a flight to Hawaii two hours after receiving the news. Hayes followed the next day. The Diehls came with Thea.

Kit, always thoughtful, wired air tickets to Phinney and Emilie, but Amos came in Phinney's place. "It's a hard time for Phinney to get away," Emilie explained. Throughout those long, hard days Amos stayed close to Thea, holding tight to her hand at the cemetery.

Marge and Hank Fromberg flew over, and some of Thea's friends from Punahou came to the graveside services. They stood in the full sun, a warm wind snapping the flags that flew; the sound of taps echoed around the ancient volcanic bowl, and drifted out to sea. The flag was folded, precisely, and placed in the hands of Karin and Thea, who stood close together to receive it.

Everything about Karin became more tenuous. She walked

through the house as if dazed, she couldn't think what to do next. Often, May had to stifle the urge to put her hand out to steady her.

"Can you talk to me about Dan?" May asked when they were alone in Karin's bedroom, and the words echoed in her memory. *"Can you talk to me about Andy?"* It was too much, she thought. Too much pain, too much death, too much hurt.

Karin shook her head, and the tears squeezed out of her eyes. "Not yet," May said the words for her, cradling her friend in her arms. "Not yet, dear one."

Paul Hollowell came to the cemetery and then to the house to pay his respects. May watched him walk up to the door, watched Karin cross the room to meet him, watched how they stood next to each other.

"Of course he's in love with her," Hayes said. "Who wouldn't be? She's a beautiful woman, even now when she's full of grief. There's something almost translucent about her, have you noticed?"

"I've noticed," May said. "Were you?"

"Were I what?"

"In love with Karin."

"Of course."

"I mean it."

"I probably would have been, if you hadn't got in the way."

With a sudden passion that caught them offguard, May said, "Sometimes I think about the day you found out about Andy, about all the times we might have missed each other, and it frightens me so much I can hardly breathe. Don't leave me, Hayes, not ever."

"Not ever," he whispered into her neck, then he pulled back to look her in the face, holding tight to her still. His mind was working, she could see.

"Come with me to Saigon," he said. "Help me try to talk Le Tien An into meeting us, and letting us see the boy. Maybe together we can do it—God knows, something has to move her, and soon. Then I'll go on to my rendezvous in the Philippines and you can come back this way and spend a couple of days, before we head home together."

She looked at Karin, who was standing in a group with Paul Hollowell, Thea and Amos. Paul Hollowell, May noticed, was looking at Karin as if he were stifling the urge to steady her, too. Karin's eyes seemed not quite to focus, as if she were looking at something in the distance.

"I thought Karin might need me," she told him, "but maybe . . ."

"Ask her," Hayes said, "if she wants you here, you should stay—it was just an idea, a sudden urge."

Two days after everyone else had left, Annie intercepted the postman as he made his way along Makiki Heights. She slipped the letter into the deep pocket of her loose dress, and left it there for several hours while she tried to think how to tell Karin.

The conversation at dinner was desultory. The usually ebullient Annie was quiet, distracted. Afterwards, Karin would not let her launch into the dishes, but insisted they take their tea out to the lanai.

"You'd better tell me what's up," Karin said when they were seated, she in the chaise and Annie in a chair. "I can't remember the last time you were in such a deep blue funk. It's not your color, love."

"You're right," Annie said, "I have a letter from Daniel in my pocket, and I can't decide how to tell you or what to do with it."

Karin clasped her hands protectively over her stomach and said: "I think I want you to read it to me, but give me a few minutes to get ready."

Annie opened the letter, unfolded a lined page of notebook paper filled with small, tight handwriting, written with ballpoint pen that left thick smudges down the page.

Saigon, September 28, 1973

Dear Karin:

I've been trying to figure out what to say to you ever since I got the letter from Dad three days ago. To tell you the truth, it's you I've been thinking about mostly, what this is going to do to you and what you are thinking. Maybe you remember I told you it seemed sort of strange, Mrs. McCord and Dad being together so much and all. Dad says they were pretty good friends a long time ago, and that they have renewed that friendship. It seems like, from what he says, Mrs. McCord feels pretty good about being able to help him, he's pretty sure about that. He also said that he thinks the world of you, and he wants you to be happy.

I wish I could ask you to wait for me to catch up, and then I'd ask you to marry me and then we (I) could live happily ever after. (A little joke, ha. Or maybe only half a joke.)

If you want my opinion, marrying you was the only smart thing Dad ever did. I don't know if Thea or me would have made it without you, knowing you were pulling for us. So what I want to say is this—you'll always be important to me, even if we aren't related anymore. And I guess there's something else I want to tell you, because I think maybe it could help you now, too.

You remember when I joined the Corps I was in bad shape, figuring what happened to Dad was my fault. The fight and all. I pushed myself pretty hard physically, and that was okay for a while, but then I started feeling pretty awful and, well, I won't go into all the details but finally this guy I'd met from Georgia, a real cracker, told me I ought to go see the chaplain and, to make a long story short, I did. I talked to him a long time, and I told him I felt like I'd been carrying this 200-pound pack up a mountain, and I just couldn't carry it any more. I felt like I wanted to lie down and go to sleep forever. Then the strangest thing happened. He was just this nice little guy, but when he started talking his voice sounded like it was coming to me from outer space, and what he said was that God had sent his son to suffer for me, and that if I would believe in him, my burden would be eased. I can't tell you how it happened, or why, but that changed my whole life. I prayed, and this heavy thing was lifted off of me. I suppose this may sound strange to you, I know it would to Dad, he doesn't much believe in religion, which is why I've never told him.

It's been raining here pretty much ever since I arrived. Everyone says the VC are getting ready to make their move and we'll see some real fireworks as soon as the ground dries out a little. They've been hitting storage facilities and small airfields and other little stuff all summer long. It's kind of a creepy place, you know. Some of the guys who have been here before, on other tours of duty talk this "you should've been here when . . ." bullshit, almost like they liked it better when the VC were offing our guys. I guess you think I'm getting cynical, huh? Well, maybe I am. I still think the Corps is great, and I'm proud to be a member, but it just seems to me like this little piece of the world is not worth 58,000 American lives, which is what somebody told me is the dead count.

Don't mean to sound morbid. Had a long letter from Thea, and I guess you've had some long talks with her from what she said. It was kind of funny (not really), but you've been worried about her for so long, and now she's worried about you. Thea said something to me that she didn't say to you. That was, that she couldn't stand to think of you spending your future taking care of Dad. I'm telling you because I feel that way too. Thea told me about the offer you got to run a gallery for some artists. Are you sure you want to stay on in the islands? It is kind of nice, thinking of you there. Don't forget our date, beachside at the Royal Hawaiian, sipping a mai tai. Whenever I start getting homesick, I just think of that day . . . and the sun setting all pink and blue on Waikiki beach.

In the meantime, write me when you can because out here we live for the mail call.

Love,
Danny

Paul Hollowell had been waiting in the lobby for half an hour. She had said it was important to be there by sunset and he had given himself plenty of time to stop at the florists to pick up a ginger lei. He walked across the lobby to meet her, carrying the flowers awkwardly, like a boy on prom night. He lifted them over her head and brushed her cheek with his lips, formally. She was wearing a dress of blue cotton gauze, very full, her hair was loose about her shoulders and she smelled of lilacs.

"Thank you," Karin said, "for the flowers and for coming. There is something I have to tell you and I wanted to do it here, for a reason. I'll explain."

He took her hand and they walked toward the oceanfront terrace, her high-heeled sandals making clicking sounds on the polished tile of the Royal Hawaiian's promenade.

"We sat at this table," she told him, "and Danny insisted we have mai tais."

"Would you like one now?"

She shook her head. "No. I don't drink now. But please, go ahead."

"Big waves tonight," he said, looking out to sea at the line of surfers waiting to catch the next big wave.

"The night we were here, the sun had turned the water a wonderful shade of pink. Dan said it was as close to heaven as he'd ever been . . ." her voice cracked and she stopped.

"He is in heaven now," Paul said, a simple statement of fact, "and maybe it is like this—all these shades of pink and blue playing on the water."

She could only stare at him. "Do you believe that?" she asked.

"Yes," he said, "Yes, I do."

She leaned toward him over the table. "I'm not trying to keep you in suspense . . . about why I asked you here . . ." she began.

"When you're ready," he answered, "no hurry. I know how your son must have felt, being here with you. I feel happy just sitting here right now."

"We had a date. I told him I'd meet him here, when he came back. It was important."

She turned to look down the beach, watched as a small figure far out beyond the breaking waves stood and caught one, moving before the swift cutting curl of the wave, gliding and sliding in the trough, staying ahead of the water that glimmered blue in the silken light. He seemed to ride forever, defying the forces. Karin and Paul watched, holding their breath as the surfer continued to elude the wave, choosing his time, his place, to dip into the pink-silver sea.

She looked at him and said, "I brought you here to tell you that I am going to have your baby."

He stared at her. Then a slow, sweet smile moved over his face, his eyes came to life with a kind of wild delight. He reached for her hand, took it in both of his and bent to touch her fingers.

"We have to talk," she told him.

"Yes," he answered, solemnly, "we will talk, every day of our lives. I promise you that, Karin." He looked down the beach as the lights began to blink on. "God," he exclaimed under his breath, "I didn't know it was possible to feel this way."

"It isn't going to be easy," she warned him. "There are all sorts of problems. I'm not sure when we can be together."

"We're already together," he said, "the rest is details."

32

*T*he plane descended into the saffron air that lay like dirty gauze over the city, and they landed at Tan Son Nhut at midday. May was blinded by the glare of light on the tarmac. With her free hand she groped for her sunglasses, lost somewhere in the bottom of her handbag. She gave up the search when Hayes's hand on her arm hurried her into the terminal, and concentrated on threading her way through the crowd that pressed against them inside the building, everyone pushing for position.

"Is it always so chaotic?" she gasped, but Hayes was too intent on getting them through immigration to answer.

Outside, waiting for a bus, she stood in the noise and the heat and tried to make sense of the scene. She was in Vietnam, the country that had weighed so heavily on their hearts these past years, and she expected to feel something, but the shouting and the confusion and the heat stifled all feeling. The bus, gray and battered, pulled up in a cloud of exhaust fumes. The windows were open, but covered by grates. "So no one can lob in a grenade," Hayes explained. This is a country at war, she told herself. None of the old rules apply.

As they drove through the French part of the city, she studied the pastel Colonial architecture from the nineteenth and twentieth centuries, the broad leafy plantain trees that cast the streets in deep shade. She knew that once it must have been lovely, but now it was not. Heat and a sense of exhaustion permeated the scene. The buildings, the roads, the people, even the trees, everything seemed to be in a state of dazed exhaustion. As if all energy had been drained from the country, as if all that was left was a sense of desolation, a loss of faith that was utter, complete.

Hayes broke the silence. "The French like to say they don't colonize, they civilize. But this is not a civilized place, all you see now are the remnants of culture. It's changed, even, since I was here six months ago."

"The gas fumes are making my throat raw," May told him. "Is it always like this?"

"A lot of the vehicles use a mix of oil and gas, so you get a constant smell of burned hydrocarbons."

The taxi jolted to a halt at the Caravelle Hotel on Tu Do Street, in the middle of Saigon. Heat did not usually trouble May, but in combination with the gas fumes and the smoke that seemed to pervade the city, her head ached and her eyes burned.

When they were in their room, May sprawled across the bed, her arm over her eyes to shut out the light. Hayes rummaged in his shaving kit and came up with two aspirins which she took without waiting for the bottled water to be sent up. "Aggrrh," she said, trying to swallow. "I can't stand the taste of aspirin."

Hayes opened a bottle of bourbon he had brought as a gift or a bribe, and gave her a sip.

She lay back on the bed, feeling as exhausted as the city. "Why don't you take a nap while I go meet the Corsican?" he suggested, his hand pressed gently to her head. "I'll call you around six—it should be cooler then, we can meet for drinks if you feel up to it. If the guy turns out to be helpful, I could invite him to join us."

"The one who was in the French Army, and stayed on?"

"His name is Gerard Levasseur and he seems to be connected to most of the principals in this city. I'm hoping he knows Le Tien An's father, or someone who has influence with the family, who will intercede for us."

The two men sat at a table on the terrace of the Continental Palace Hotel and watched May approach. She could feel their eyes on her, could read the approval in their faces. She had showered and changed into a cool white two-piece dress that was loose against her body, and had pulled her hair back from her face and caught it up with lapis combs.

"My wife," Hayes said, rising to present her with the pride of possession, and the other, a man in his late fifties bent low over her hand, glancing briefly at Hayes in approval.

"Gin and tonics all around?" Hayes asked, as they rearranged themselves to accommodate May.

"Gerard was telling me about the changes he's seen in Saigon over the past ten years," Hayes said to May.

"Please go on," May prompted.

Gerard paused to looked around him at the scattering of people who had gathered on the terrace. "Once, you would have heard laughter and easy conversation in this place . . . people greeting each other as they met for an early evening drink. The sounds were soft, lyric—many of the people speak a mix of Vietnamese and French, a language we called matisse. Very soft and singing. The city still had a French character in those days, the whores were not so aggressive. They did not accost you on the street and demand, 'G.I. you buy me one Saigon tea.' "

"And tell you 'G.I. you number ten,' if you don't," Hayes put in.

"What does that mean, number ten?" May wanted to know.

"Very bad," Gerard answered. "It means you are very bad for not wanting to spend money on them." He went on, "I would say it was about 1965, when the Americans began to come in numbers, when the change began. Now the voices of the city are shrill, crass. If you will excuse me for saying so, I believe that the Vietnamese and the Americans have brought out the worst in each other. Saigon has become a cruel place, a city of buyers and sellers, and everything is for sale."

They sat for a time, looking out onto the street in the dimming light, and May fought to shake off the feeling of lethargy that had hovered over her since their arrival.

"How about dinner in Cholon?" Hayes asked.

"If you like steamed crab claws, there's a place called 'Diamond,' that attracts a mix of Westerners, Chinese and Vietnamese," Gerard offered. "It is noisy, but the food is good." He shifted in his chair and leaned toward Hayes. "Do you happen to know the fellow over there, with the long dirty blond hair and the flowered shirt?"

Hayes glanced, shook his head.

"He came in soon after we arrived and he's been watching you ever since. I must be getting Saigon fever—all the time suspicious. It's a dreadful way to live, but there seems to be no alternative, not in these times." He sighed. "But this is my home, France would be foreign territory after all these years."

"What would happen," May began carefully, "If the North Vietnamese should take over . . ."

"My dear," the man laughed, "you mean, *when* they take over. The only ones who doubt it are the poor naive souls who also think you Yanks would never let it happen."

"An's father," Hayes broke in, "what does he believe?"

"Ah," the Corsican answered, "an interesting question. A linguist and a scholar, he is from an ancient family. I have known these men. They think they are above politics, living in their walled villas, certain they are immune. An's father believes he *is* Vietnam. Even now, with everything crumbling around him, he cannot accept the inevitable."

"Will he leave?"

"No."

"Will he allow An and the boy to leave?"

"I believe," he began, and stopped himself. "I cannot be certain, but I believe that it will be her decision."

"Then there is a chance?"

"It would be a terrible decision for a dutiful daughter to make, you understand that?"

May felt a long, slow ache gather in her chest. She did understand, and she wished that she and Hayes did not have to be the ones to force An to make that decision.

Hayes answered, "Yes, and I also understand that it is a hard decision for a dutiful mother, when the child's life could be at stake."

May closed her eyes, pressed the cold glass against her temple. The image of her mother, sitting under the mimosa, entered her mind. A difficult decision, oh yes.

"Are you all right?" Hayes asked.

She opened her eyes and smiled. "Actually, I'm hungry," she said, wanting to leave.

They walked over to Nguyen Hue Boulevard, passing hawker stalls that sold flowers and noodle soup and black market cigarettes, walking in the street because Hayes was too tall to fit under the hawkers' canopies.

"The Aussie with the dirty hair is following us," Gerard said.

May glanced back just as the man ducked into a stall. "How do you know he's Australian?" she asked.

"The way he walks, that loose-boned stride. Also," he said, grinning as if caught out, "I've heard about that one. Name's Galt. A bad hat, I'm afraid."

"A bad hat?" May laughed, and decided that she liked Gerard.

They crowded into one of the small, blue and yellow Renault taxis which took them into the Chinese section of the city, called Cholon. The streets were narrow, the movement more intense. Music blared from the shops on the street level, a mix of Chinese and popular. On the floors above, in the family quarters, children looked out from shuttered windows.

As she climbed out of the taxi, May glanced up and was tempted to wave at a small boy whose eyes met hers. A motorized rickshaw passed so closely it brushed her arm, scuffing the skin. Hayes pulled her close, rubbed her arm. "Evil goddamned place," he muttered.

They took a table in the back, away from the door, so they did not see the man called Galt enter. He waited until they were midway through their meal to make his way through the crowd to their table. He stood behind May.

Her stomach turned at the raw smell of him. She put down her chopsticks.

"You the bloke they call the Big Deal?" he asked.

Hayes shot May a don't-say-anything glance and answered, "Who wants to know?"

"Old mate of yours," the man said with a show of teeth.

"What's his name?" Hayes came back.

"Sam, his name is Sam," the Aussie answered, as if Hayes were a little slow, and handed him a piece of rumpled paper.

She watched Hayes's face. It didn't change in the slightest, but he shifted in his chair, leaning forward, so she knew he was on guard.

They had half expected the contact. Andy's son had become an obsession with Hayes's mother, and Mrs. Nakamura was her confidante. It was natural that Sam's mother would try to enlist the efforts of her son.

What she did not know, and Hayes would not tell her, was that her son hadn't worked as a photographer for more than a year, that the journalists in Saigon had nothing good to say about him, that nobody seemed to know or to care where he was, except for those who had loaned him money.

May did not want to find him, did not want to see him again after Bangkok. She could not think of Sam without remembering the smell of the jail on Mahachai Street.

The note, in Sam's distinctive hand, said: "I can help you get Andy's kid. Galt will show you the way."

Hayes stood, motioning May and Gerard to stay. "I don't know what Sam is up to, but I think I'd better find out."

"I'm going with you," May said.

"I believe," Gerard broke in, "that we should all go." They knew by the way he said it that it was more than a suggestion.

Galt led the way, on foot, through narrow alleys flanked by concrete apartment buildings streaked with black and mossy with mildew. They walked single file, Galt first, then Hayes followed by May, Gerard bringing up the rear. May stepped around piles of detritus pushed against the buildings, and began to feel the terror of Vietnam. It edged slowly up her spine, cold and dark. She felt as she had once felt around a campfire in a mountain wilderness, as if something wild were there, waiting, in the darkness just outside the circle of light. She watched a sweat spot spread on the back of Hayes's blue cotton shirt, and knew he was feeling it too.

"Careful, there," Gerard said, his arm quickly guiding her clear of a man without legs, sitting on a wheeled platform. "Too many of those boys around," the Corsican muttered, sad and angry.

Galt turned into a doorway that smelled of urine and rotting fish. Hayes held tight to her hand as they climbed the narrow stairs. Though they were going up, May had the sensation of entering a rat hole.

The air seemed to thicken with the sickly sweet smell of smoke. May strained to see. Slowly, the room came into focus. On his haunches in front of a low table was Sam, hair long, eyes dull. It was not the Sam she remembered, this Sam was emaciated, spent. She felt horror, bitter in her mouth, then the sour taste of revulsion. Hayes held hard to her hand. As he acknowledged Sam, his voice steady and remote, she managed to pull her eyes from Sam's face and look about the room.

A short, thin-thighed girl in a short skirt and grotesquely made-up face, her small breasts pushed together into a cleavage, stared back at her, fury in her eyes. The distinct, fetid smell of a dirty diaper wafted toward them, just as a baby's wail filled the air. No one seemed to notice. As May's eyes became accustomed to the gloom, she noticed another young woman sitting on a mat in the far corner, staring into space.

Opium. The word formed full in her mind. Of course, that's what had happened to Sam. Another casualty of Vietnam, in spite of himself.

Hayes was speaking. "You said you had information about Andy's boy. Are you going to give it to me?"

Sam blinked up at him. "I've got what you want," he said. "Sit down."

"We didn't come for a social visit, Sam," Hayes told him. "If you have some information, give it to me."

Sam looked past them as if they did not exist, into the thick air, the face that had been beautiful, gaunt now and wasted. May looked at him and tried to remember the other Sam, before Bangkok, the Sam who had been her friend.

"It's not information he's got," the Aussie spoke out impatiently, "he's got the kid. And if you want him, all we need to do is establish a price, mate."

Hayes lunged at Sam, grabbed him by the throat and the Aussie, caught off guard, hesitated just long enough to allow May and the Corsican to get between them. Hayes's face was dark with fury; she knew he wanted to strangle Sam. Galt flashed a long knife and snarled, "You want to see the kid alive, mate, you'd better ease off."

The woman in the miniskirt crouched, her teeth bared. Hayes had surprised them, thrown them off guard. May stepped toward Sam. She wanted to slap him hard across the face, she wanted to feel the sting of it on her hand, she wanted to hurt him. "How much?" she said.

"One million U.S. dollars," Sam told her, his eyes squinting shut.

"You always were full of shit," she spat out, disdain thick in her mouth for the Aussie's benefit. "What did you tell your friend here, that I was loaded with money? Well, he's wrong," she said, turning to Galt, ignoring Sam.

"I've got five thousand dollars with me, and you can have it right now. Sam was lying if he told you I had more. I might be able to get a couple thousand extra from my relatives in the States, but if you hold out for that you run a very large risk of being pulled in on kidnapping charges. You and your smart friend here," she finished.

"Eight thousand," Sam said, petulance creeping into his tone, but Galt made a motion that silenced him.

She caught Hayes's glance, and repeated, "All I have is five."

"If you push for more," Hayes put in, "it will mean having money telegraphed in. That will mean more risk than you can afford, I promise you, mate."

Sam closed his eyes.

"Done," Galt said. "Give me the dollars."

"The boy first," Hayes demanded.

The Aussie nodded to the girl, and she darted down a back stair. As they waited, the fetid smell of the room closed in on May. She pressed her face into Hayes's shirt. "Where is the money?" he whispered.

"Money belt," she whispered back.

He slipped his hands under her loose blouse and unbuckled it, whispering, "How did you know?"

"I didn't, I just felt . . ." It was not until that moment that she realized she had expected someone to ask for money. Gerard's words echoed in her ears—buyers and sellers, and everything is for sale. Even a small boy, half Vietnamese, half American. Sam could even sell Andy's son.

The girl led the child in, pushed him forward. He was small, his eyes were large and dark, but there was something about the shape of his mouth, the lift of his chin that was like his father. May looked at Hayes and remembered the night he had learned about Andy's death, and it was all she could do to stifle her tears. She dropped to her knees, her arms out to the child, and said in French, "Come to me, little one, and we will take you back to your mama."

His chin quivered, but he stepped forward and stood before her. She wanted to put her arms around him, to scoop him up and get him out of that dreadful place, but she knew it could frighten him. Instead, she said to the child, pointing to Hayes, "This big man will help us get to your mama's. You must trust him. He will not harm you."

The child looked from her face to Hayes's, and May followed his glance and saw tears filling her husband's eyes. In that instant, she understood why he had needed to find the child, Andy's son, now Hayes's to watch over.

Gerard spoke quietly, so the others could not hear. "Make a show of turning the money over to me. Then take the boy and leave quickly. A taxi should be waiting for you—I told the driver he would be paid double. Take the child to the French Embassy and wait for me. I'll hold off here long enough for you to get away, then I'll join you."

When May began to protest, he took her hand and pressed it to his belt. She felt the hard outlines of a pistol under his shirt.

The taxi was waiting. Quickly, they pushed into the back seat and were threading through the mean streets of Cholon with the child wedged safely between them.

May bent close to ask, "What is your name?"

"Le Minh Hao," he answered, with a small, catching sob that quickly escalated into hiccoughs.

"Don't be frightened, son," Hayes said in French, "You are safe now. You will be with your mama very soon." They could feel his sobs subsiding and soon his dark head fell against May's arm. He was sleeping.

"Poor little guy, he must be exhausted," Hayes said, his own voice weary.

"Thank God for Gerard," May answered.

"We needed a Gerard, right here and right now," Hayes answered, "It is good to know there are a few decent men left in the world."

Hayes's credentials got them into the French Embassy, and they were left sitting in an anteroom until someone could be found, as an aide put it, "to address their problem."

Hao began to cry for his mother.

"We have to let her know he's all right," May said in English. "She must be frantic with worry."

"But if we call directly," Hayes answered, "we won't be allowed to speak to her, to explain what happened, and it is possible that she may think we had something to do with the kidnap. If she believes that, she will never let us help her. She has to understand that we had nothing to do with this."

May bent to place her cheek against the child's, and tried to reassure him. "Soon, little one," she murmured. "We have to talk to your mama on the telephone, and she will come here with your grandpapa, or maybe they will ask us to take you home, because we are your friends." She rummaged in her bag and found a pack of chewing gum, which she held out to him. His small hands carefully removed one stick from the pack, he put it in his mouth and looked up at her, smiling.

"Ah," she said, beaming back at him, "what a nice smile you have, little Hao."

"And what a good wife you are, Wing Mei-jin," Hayes put in.

"Mei-jin," Hao said, looking at her timidly.

"And this is your uncle," she said, "Your Uncle Hayes."

"Hayes," the boy repeated, testing the word, then he pointed to himself, "Hao."

"Yes," Hayes said lifting the child to his lap, "our names sound alike, I've noticed too."

Gerard pushed through the door in a stream of rapidfire French aimed at the aide, who was following him. "Sorry to keep you waiting," he said. "Our man Galt insisted on counting out the money, and his arithmetic is sadly lacking. Unfortunately, your acquaintance was in no condition to help, and the girls only know piastres. Follow me, please," he directed, almost without breaking stride.

Hayes lifted the boy in his arms and they climbed the stairs to a spacious second-floor office where a man with thin, graying hair listened attentively as Gerard explained the situation.

"And you would like me to act as an intermediary?" he said.

"If you would be so kind," Gerard answered with the slight lilt of sarcasm old friends use with each other. Very quickly, May and Hayes chimed in to say how grateful they would be as well, and it was settled.

"My venerated friend," the ambassador began when An's father came on the line, "I have here before me in my office your grandson, quite well and healthy, and the good people who have rescued him." He gave a brief account of what had happened, emphasizing Hayes's determination to return the child.

The ambassador told them, "He has asked that you bring the boy to his villa. He has agreed to allow his daughter to speak to you in his presence."

May and Hayes exchanged glances, May's more triumphant than Hayes's.

The Le family lived in a walled villa on Nguyen Dinh Chieu Street near the diplomatic quarter. Driving down the tree-lined street, May noticed shadows swooping in and out of the trees, flickering in the street lights.

"Bats," Hayes told her. "They live in the plantain trees." May shuddered.

A servant was waiting at the gate. He held it open long enough for them to hurry through, then bolted it with a loud scraping. They followed him along a path that led to the house.

An's formidable father waited for them. A small, fragile man with the eyes of a hawk, he ushered them into a dimly lit courtyard. At that moment, Hao's mother rushed to her son, her cry hanging in the night air.

She held the boy close to her, her eyes closed as if in prayer. Then she opened them and saw Hayes and wavered. Her beauty was soft and luminous and complex.

The child was turned over to an amah. Hayes stood, bowed, and spoke in French.

"We beg your forgiveness," he began, addressing the mother but including her father. "Hooligans who learned we wished to see you took your child. Our first concern was to return the child safely to you, so we did as they asked. Hao was frightened, but he was not harmed. He is a brave little boy. We are very sorry that this should have happened. I should never wish harm to come to the child of my brother, or to the mother of his child. Nor would my wife, whom I would like to present to you."

May bowed, lowering her eyes before the father's piercing glance. "You are Chinese," he said, in ragged Mandarin.

"My mother is Chinese," she responded, in properly low tones. "My father was an American. Like your grandson, I am a child of two cultures."

He turned his back on her. She understood the disdain Southeast Asians feel for the Chinese, for mixed races even more. There was nothing she could say to him.

Le Tien An bowed to May. "Thank you for returning my son. It was kind of you, and I am grateful with all my heart." She turned to Hayes, then, and said, "Thank you, the brother of my son's father. I have received your messages, and those of your mother in California, and I must say to you that it is the wish of my father and my mother to stay in this land where our family has lived for many generations. Elder Brother died in the war with Japan, Second Brother was killed while serving with the French forces and Youngest Brother left one year ago and we have not heard from him. I am all that is left to my parents. They have accepted my son, Hao. They revere our country and can never leave, nor can I leave them."

"We believe Saigon will fall," Hayes began, a pleading note in his voice, "and we feel certain that the son of an American soldier will face great hardships under a Communist regime, as will his mother and her family. All we wish is to ensure your safety, to try to make certain my brother's family is spared unnecessary suffering. In a letter written only days before his death, my brother asked me to care for his family. He wished to bring you to our country. I loved and honored my brother, and I am pledged to do this for him. If you do not wish to come to America, perhaps you would consider France . . ."

The old man stood, anger rising. Hayes saw it and finished, rapidly, handing An one of his cards, "This is very important. All you have to do is to let me know and I will arrange everything. We want you to know that you can trust us, that we honor you and . . ."

The father stepped in front of his daughter, his small legs spread, and slapped the card to the earth. "Enough," he said with a flourish in English. "You leave. Now."

"Please, sister . . ." May tried, reaching out to An, but the old man and his servant intervened, pushing at them.

"I'll be back," Hayes called to An as they left.

The ceiling fan rasped as it turned, stirring the heat above them. They lay on their backs in the bed, trying not to listen to the fan, wanting and needing to sleep. They were exhausted from the long flight, drained by the encounter with Sam, with their meeting with Hao and An. It was too much to grasp, she could feel the tension in the muscles in her chest, her arms. She shook her hands to try to loosen them.

"Are you all right?" Hayes wanted to know.

"If I could just stop thinking, I would be. Everything keeps whirling in my head."

"Sam," he said.

"Yes Sam—my God, Hayes, I thought Bangkok was as bad as it could get, but this . . . stealing Andy's boy, what could bring him to this venality? And Hao and An, and her father, and Gerard and the ambassador, why would they help us?"

The fan made several grinding rotations while she thought, and when she spoke again, she started in mid-sentence, ". . . in Hawaii that last time, when he talked me into going into China through Burma, I knew something had changed with Sam—he was doing a lot of dope, for one thing. Bells should have gone off in my head when they came to my house, after only two hours in the Islands, with a stash of Maui pot. Sam was already stoned, and later on he got a little drunk too. Faith tried to warn me that something was off, but I wanted so much to believe he could do what he said he could do. Then, it never occurred to me that he was capable of betrayal. And now, this—it is evil, truly evil." Her voice slipped away into the heat.

Hayes laid his hand lightly on her thigh, a comforting touch. "I wanted to kill him," he said, "I've never felt that way before, I didn't think I could. Jesus. But it's the truth, May."

"I think he won't live long," she answered. "He's been eaten from within, like wormwood . . . it's been this long process, all the resentment and anger and envy. But why your family? He seemed to focus so intensely on your family . . ."

"And you," Hayes said, "he shifted part of his rage to you."

She thought about that. "Sam brought us together. It's strange, but I remember thinking once, at the beginning, that it was purposeful— I'm not certain why, but I think he meant to set up some sort of tension among the three of us . . . as if he was using me to get at you. I don't know, this doesn't make sense, but I think he wanted to be you . . ."

". . . No, he wanted to destroy me, and he's come too damned close . . . first, sending you into Burma, and now this with Andy's boy."

"I don't know," she said, "it doesn't seem to me that he's capable of revenge any more . . . he's too burned out. I get the feeling it's survival of a sort now. He saw a chance to make money to support his habit, that's all. I don't think it mattered who we were, and that's even more frightening . . . betrayal of that magnitude, I mean. I just don't think he's capable of feeling."

"Or that's what he wants us to think, to get himself off the hook. 'It's the drug talking, man. Can't help myself.' Bull. He can help himself, and he's doing it by extortion and blackmail and kidnapping. He should be locked up for all those reasons. Hao and An are my first priorities."

"Sam is going to destroy himself, Hayes. Faith tried to warn me. She sensed the struggle going on inside of him long ago. That last time we saw Sam, she told me she thought he was losing. She helped him get a start in photography because she felt he was an artist at heart, and she thought that somehow that art might turn out to be his salvation. In Hawaii, she knew it wasn't going to be enough. I didn't listen to her because I couldn't, not then. I was afraid if I waited any longer, I'd risk losing you. Again, you, me and Sam."

For a moment she thought Hayes had drifted off to sleep. "Honey?" she asked, quietly.

"Yes," he answered, so she knew he was thinking. He took his time; the room filled with the sound of the fan as it rasped through the warm air. "So you're saying Sam's whole life has been an act of self-destruction? That the only way he could live with it was to direct his self-hatred somewhere else, and my family was it?"

"Something like that. Love and hate all mixed up."

"Maybe. I know people become unhinged over here. It's not hard to see why . . . our motives are so goddamned mixed. Remember Gerard's remark about Vietnamese and Americans bringing out the worst in each other? Sam proves his point. If he weren't so dangerous, I might be able to dismiss him. But he knows about Hao now, and things are so goddamned volatile here, I've got to do something about Sam."

"You don't think he'll just nod off into oblivion?" she whispered.

"I can't take that chance. And there's Galt, too. Hao and An are too important."

Her stomach rumbled. She put her hand on it, felt the sticky dampness of her flesh. A faint light filtered into the room from the street, casting shadows on the wall. She thought about the bats in the plaintain trees and shuddered. In Hong Kong, Hayes had talked about her money and the complications it would bring to their lives. She felt a sharp cramp in her stomach. The faint light that filtered in from the street was enough to guide her to the bathroom. She poured herself a spoonful of Pepto Bismol, drank it with a shudder and thought, Hayes was right. First Eli, now Sam. Flesh for money. Her money was the draw. For a moment she thought she was going to retch. She felt dizzy, her skin was cold and clammy to the touch. She forced herself to drink two more spoonfuls, and drank some of the bottled water.

When she returned to bed he asked, drowsily, "Okay, babe?"

"Yes," she whispered, "go back to sleep." She wanted to say how sad it made her, how sorry she was. She lay her head close to his, and listened to his sleep breathing, in rhythm to the turning of the fan. Sleep, when it came to her, was troubled.

When they woke it was full light, the ceiling fan had ceased to revolve, and the air pressed heavily on them, as if their bodies had to carry the burden of the pressure of this country.

Before sunset that day, Sam Nakamura was on one flight out of Saigon, Galt was on another. The South Vietnamese functionaries who escorted them to the planes made it clear that if either attempted to reenter the country, he would be imprisoned. Sam left with only a navy blue nylon flight bag, in which he carried all of his worldly possessions—two or three changes of underwear, several shirts, a shaving kit and fifteen rolls of unprocessed, uncaptioned film. His cameras were gone, he could not remember when he sold them, or how much Mud they had bought. Mud. Asian Mud. Opium. He was rolling in it now, he was up to his neck in mud and it soothed and comforted him. Words sang in his head. *I am the kingdom and the glory, come unto me, come into the mud, sink into the mud.* He wondered how it would feel, when finally he slipped under, into the cool, cool dark.

When the cabin attendant reached for the blue nylon bag to stow it above his seat, he had to stifle the urge to grab it back, to hold tight to it, to feel through the cloth the canisters of film, wherein lay his security, his Mud.

Hayes was shaving when the first call came through. "Get your body back here on the double, boy-o," Davis in the deputy director's office shouted over the bad connection. "You are being summoned to the Presence. Your star is definitely in the ascendency. The word is, big things are in store, buddy."

"What does it mean?" May wanted to know.

Hayes grinned. "Hard to say. I hope it means my radical background is going to be less of a stumbling block. Since Congress has overridden Nixon's veto of the law limiting the president's right to wage war, the writing is pretty much on the wall—for him, and for Vietnam."

"All the more reason to get Hao out," she said.

"All the more reason," he repeated, grim.

The second call was from Karin, in Honolulu. "Israel is gone," she said, her voice hollow with grief.

May felt the tears slide down her face, the salt taste of them in the damp heat. A blotch fell onto her silk slip, leaving a wet mark. Hayes sat next to her on the bed, touched the wet place with his fingertip as if he could absorb some of her grief. "It is all so hard," she cried, and he had no answer except to hold her and rock her in his arms.

They left without seeing An or Hao. None of their calls were answered, and when they stopped by the house on Nguyen Dinh Chieu Street on their way to the airport, the servant said no one was there, that everyone had gone, that they should leave and not come back. They stood in the dusty street, under the plantain trees, and May thought about the bats and felt the futility of it. "How do we make them understand?" she said, knowing he had no answer.

That same day Hayes returned to Washington for his command appearance, while May returned to Hawaii for yet another funeral.

On the long flight over the Pacific she thought about Israel, and about Andy and Dan and Vietnam, and about Eli and Sam, and lost battles. Her stomach felt tight from sleeplessness and grief and the strange, unsettling spell cast over her by Vietnam. She drifted into a troubled sleep, filled with the choking smell of burning trees from which bats escaped, and a child's scream for help. Struggling out of the dream, she wakened to the bright glare of a moonset. She opened her eyes to the white-silver light, to the full moon shining over the empty sea, and she blinked and saw it, as clear as day: The rabbit in the moon.

May wants me to stay on but I cannot. Now that Israel is gone . . . buried in Punchbowl, not far from Daniel Ward . . . it is time for me to go home.

"Why?" Annie and Karin ask me, why when you love it so here where the weather is warm and the sky is forever blue and your bones don't ache all the time?

"Because," I tell them stubbornly, "I have to go home." How can I explain the hold that old cottage has on me? It is silly, of course, to be so attached to a collection of old boards, many of which have had to be replaced in the sixty years I have lived there. How to tell them what comfort there is in knowing every inch of a place, of being able to run one's fingertips over a soft redwood window ledge which bears the imprint of Emilie's baby teeth?

Emilie. I want to be closer to my daughter. And my granddaughter needs to return to the mainland and get on with her life.

I need to finish my work on the archive, to get it ready to pass along to the next caretaker. Kit writes from the Malibu that she will have time, now, to go over the work I have done and decide, with my help, who is to succeed me. She hopes I am in no great hurry.

I am in no great hurry, but I am eighty-one. My candle burns low, at times the light is not bright. I must use a magnifying glass to read. Old age is such a bloody nuisance! Annie threatens to become my eyes and my ears, and I must be diligent not to let her become indispensable. She is such a big, robust, generous girl, but she blows with the wind. She has talent and energy to spare, but little ambition, I think. "Big girl, big heart," Abigail said of her, approvingly, but then she had added, "She better watch out, that one, before she gives it all away."

I didn't need to ask Abigail what she meant by "it." There are always boys who hang around, hankering after Annie. Sometimes, late at night, I can hear them laughing and singing out by the beach. Her voice is a firm, steady contralto, Annie's candle is strong and bright and burns at both ends, and she flings herself into the storm, lighting the way for everyone. That is what distresses Emilie, of course. That her girl cannot take what she calls "any of the ordinary precautions." Even when she knows that Annie is neither ordinary nor cautious, and can never be.

So it is settled; we are going home, and I am going to concentrate on the "May Papers," as I call them.

After the funeral, Karin and her Paul came back to the Big Island with us for a few days. Abigail welcomed him like a lost son, they have so many family connections. He is a quiet man, there is no small talk in him. I believe he is responsible for the new calm I sense in Karin. He may not have much to say, but his eyes follow her with such unabashed love that I take heart.

She is carrying his child. Annie suspected, but said nothing. (I was relieved to learn that Annie is capable of knowing when to say nothing.) Karin talks happily about the baby, and Paul smiles when she does.

"She's already married," Annie jibed when I brought it up. "Who needs two husbands? Or even one for that matter?" I shot her what was meant to be a black look and she burst out laughing. Still and all, Kit has told me that divorce proceedings are underway. She and Philip tried every which way to make a large settlement in Karin's favor, but Karin would have none of it. She begged Kit to understand why she could not take any settlement, and Kit did understand.

Four well-known island artists are opening a cooperative gallery in Honolulu and they have asked Karin to manage it for them. She likes the idea, she says, her hand placed protectively over her belly. She is not showing yet, but you can tell that she can hardly wait.

Kit wants to know what I think of Paul Hollowell. I will tell her the truth, that he loves Karin as she is, and I think he is the constant she has always sought.

Annie, of course, tells me what she thinks—even when I'd rather not know. Annie thinks he turns Karin on in a way other men never have, that's what Annie thinks. I didn't ask her how she knows, but I suppose she'll tell me that too, one day.

I cannot escape from Sam; he has invaded my thoughts since May told me what happened in Saigon. I search my memory for clues, thinking back to the early days in Berkeley, when May and Karin and Sam were a trio. Sam. I think I have never known a soul so ill at ease with itself. I had prayed that his passion for photography might prove his salvation.

It did not. Sam is lost. Consumed by a savage resentment, a fatal belief in himself as victim.

Is that it? Is that the answer? That we become what we most passionately believe ourselves to be?

And my thoughts are filled, too, with my dear friend Israel, who died on a soft day when the trade winds rustled, ever so gently, the palm fronds of the trees off the lanai.

"Just look at those clouds scudding by," he had said to Annie and me. "Just look at that chariot up there, ready for to carry me home." He had managed a little coughing laugh to show how indomitable the will, and then he closed his eyes forever.

I am going home, to my cottage in San Francisco, to wait, as Abigail puts it, for the next song to begin.

EPILOGUE

——⫘⫘⫘——

May 1975

The world watched, with fascination and with horror, as the North Vietnamese closed in on Saigon in the last days of April, 1975. Television took us inside the American embassy and out onto the streets so that we could see, could feel the frenzy, the panic, the fear of those last hours. Cameras panned in on lines of people, running in the engine backwash to climb into planes.

Images of violence had been relayed on the nightly television for all the long years of this war. But this was chaos; what was seen on the television screen that night was apocalypse.

As time was running out, Le Tien An had sent the message, "Help us." Hayes was in Beirut, and could get only as far as Bangkok. But May was in Japan attending an earthquake symposium, and she was able to talk her way onto one of the last flights into Tan Son Nhut.

"Duck and run like hell," the *Time* correspondent told her as they reached the tarmac. She clutched her flight bag to her chest and ran. It was a long distance, they were in the open . . . the wind blew smoke into her eyes, her lungs burned from the effort but she did not stop. A thunderous explosion seemed to burst all around them. "Don't stop," someone yelled, "Fuel dump . . . go!"

She slumped against the terminal building. The muscles in her legs began to twitch painfully. "Oh God," she whispered to herself. "How am I going to do this?"

"Hey lady, what the hell you doing? Move your ass out of here," a G.I. yelled at her, just as another loud, booming explosion sounded in the distance. "Come on," a man with cameras hanging around his neck shouted, grabbing her by the arm, and pulling her through an opening in the barbed wire fence.

She had learned the hard facts from some of the newsmen who had been on the flight: 16 North Vietnamese divisions now surrounded the city; that was 140,000 men. Saigon's defenders numbered 60,000—if they didn't break and run as they had in Da Nang, two weeks before. Then it would be sheer horror, American marines faced with the prospect of shooting South Vietnamese to protect Americans. Inside the terminal it was a madhouse, noise and heat and long lines of people talking, shouting.

"Screw customs," the photographer said, diving into what seemed a solid line of bodies. She clutched at his jacket and followed, her elbows close to her body to move through the choking mass, not looking at the faces, pushing back the hands that seemed to clutch at her.

Outside, she leaned against a pole and said, "This is hellish." The photographer told her, sardonically, "The best is yet to come."

A rolling crash sounded from a distance. She didn't know if it was an explosion or thunder, thick black clouds were boiling in the sky, lit by flashes of lightning. The first thunderstorm of the monsoon season was brewing. Barbed wire and piles of old tires and dusty trucks and buses were everywhere. The fast-rising storm winds blew dirt and rattled the corrugated metal that lined the passageway out to the street.

All routine was gone from the city and in the midst of the rising storm you could feel the fear. One of the old gray buses she remembered rolled up, packed so tightly that people came tumbling out in a burst, and hit the ground running—as if they expected a plane to be waiting.

She climbed on, flung herself into a seat next to the window so she could breathe through the open grates. As they rolled down the long drive, she squinted to keep the dirt from flying into her eyes. Her face burned tight. A few large splats of rain splintered and sprayed, and she turned her face to them. She wanted it to rain, wanted the heavens to open and cleanse this burning place, wanted water to wash down the fires, to calm the terror, the panic.

Stay calm, she told herself. You have a job to do. For Hayes, for Hao. For An.

The bus paused long enough for her to jump out about a block from the hotel. She ran as if she were fleeing from something other than the hard, driving rain that had begun to fall. By the time she reached the hotel, her shirt was clinging wet to her body, her hair dripped with rain. An American wearing an olive-drab undershirt and smoking a long, brown cigarette stood behind the desk, trying to work a walkie-talkie.

"Is there a room?" May asked.

He glanced up for a minute, then waved the cigarette in the direction of the stairs. "Help self," he said, "they're all open." As she was walking toward the stairs, he called after her, "Did you just come in from Tan Son Nhut? Is it still open?"

"It was half an hour ago," she said.

The man walked around the counter and stood, studying her. "Why did you come?"

"I need to get some people out. Vietnamese. Any suggestions?"

"Sure. I'd suggest you get them over to the embassy as fast as you can. The shit's really hitting the fan now—they'll be shuttling the rest of us out by helicopter. I'd say you'd better hurry."

May went up to her room, placed a call to the embassy and asked for the political officer, who knew Hayes.

After a long wait, she got through to him and he repeated what the American at the desk had said, adding that they should use the back gate, the one on Hong Thap Tu.

Now to get Le Tien An and the child.

"I need a car," she said to the American at the desk. He opened a drawer, pulled out some keys and said, "Here, take the black Citroën parked out back. Its owner left yesterday."

"I can't do this," she told herself as she put the key in the ignition. "I don't know where I'm going, I don't know how to get there, this is crazy, it is never going to work." She backed the car, slowly, down the alleyway. The monsoon shower had ended, the air was somewhat cleaner and steam was rising.

Aside from a few trucks and some bicycles, the streets were almost clear. To May's amazement, she remembered the way to Le Tien An's house almost perfectly, taking only one wrong turn which, miraculously, led to the street she was looking for. She felt a sudden surge of elation. They would be packed and waiting, she would drive the Citroën to the embassy, it was going to happen after all. She rang the bell and stood, looking at the trees, wondering if the bats were inside or if they, too, had fled. She rang again, making the bell sound as loud as she could, and after a few long moments heard the familiar scraping of the lock. An old man looked out at her, his face filled with confusion. "Not here, all gone," he repeated.

May screamed at him. "Let me in, An told me to come. Open this door." She would not be turned away, not again. She pushed the door hard and almost sent the old servant sprawling. A young girl stood behind him, in the shadows of the garden.

"Where have they gone?" May demanded in French.

They shook their heads. No French, she thought, so she said the names, slowly. Le Tien An? Le Minh Hao?

The woman looked at May as if she were trying to remember something, and then her face changed. She ran into the house, motioning for May to follow. Inside, she pointed to the telephone and to a number written on a pad.

May dialed, listened for the series of small whirring and clicking noises that told her the automatic telephone system was still working, and bit her lip until the phone started to ring.

It rang four times, five. *Be there,* she whispered, drumming her fingertips on the top of the desk. Six times, seven. They weren't going to answer, she had lost again.

"Hello?" It was a woman's voice, not An's.

Then An was on the line, blurting out all that had happened . . . her father had been taken by two men with guns, she had fled with her mother and the child to a friend's home, they had been afraid to answer the telephone and afraid not to answer. She didn't know what to do, everything was coming apart, she couldn't find out where they had taken her father, the police didn't know, nobody knew.

May spoke with as much calm as she could muster. "You must take your mother and your son and leave with me. There is no more time."

"My father," she said, "my mother will not go without my father."

"You must convince her. An, you and Hao could be in danger— we're not certain you will be able to protect him, and once the North Vietnamese take over, we won't be able to help you."

May could feel the terrible pressure of the choice An had to make. Her own stomach tightened.

"There is so little time left, An. I am sorry, I am so very sorry but you must come, for your son's sake. For Andy's sake." She heard a short, sharp cry on the other end of the line, and a burst of static which told her they would be cut off. "Quick," May shouted, "Meet me at the American Embassy at the back gate, on Hong Thap Tu. If you come quickly, I can get you in."

It was deep twilight now, the streets were wet and shiny and now and then bursts of light made them glisten with color. Streets that were once alive with people and bicycles and food stalls were now deserted, except for an occasional furtive figure, hurrying. The noise of the day had subsided, though it almost seemed that she was hearing white sound, the calm before the storm. She drove as fast as she could, now and then having to swerve to miss a vehicle that had been abandoned, or that had run out of gas or had simply quit. An and Hao would be there, somehow she would get them in the back gate, they would leave tonight. That is how it would have to be, she could not imagine any other ending to this day.

She was driving down a tree-lined boulevard when a large burst of light seemed to hover from above and then there was a roaring noise. She looked up to see a helicopter descending, its beams lighting the street with a garish white light. *It has to happen now,* she told herself, as she turned the corner and saw the mob that had gathered at the back gate of the American Embassy.

She watched, transfixed, as the crowd, packed tight, surged forward. How could she possibly work her way up to the gate? And if she got up there now, and inside, how could she find An and Hao when they arrived?

Above her, a helicopter hovered and swung sideways, moving slowly forward, and came to roost on the embassy roof. They were going to have to fight their way through the gates, and then they were going to have to make it to the top of the stairs and onto one of those helicopters. How many more would there be, she wondered. *Help me,* she said, as if Hayes could hear her.

She looked at her watch. It had been twenty minutes. She left the keys in the car and began to make her way to a point where she could scan the crowd. It seemed to be multiplying, young men were climbing the walls of the embassy, and in the flashes of light she could see them silhouetted against the barbed wire. She was caught in a wild surge, pressed forward. She could feel her heart pumping, could feel a hot burning under her arms. A blast of wind from the helicopter, hovering over the crowd, blew her hair into her face. She pulled it back with her free hand so she could scan the crowd. An, Hao, they had to be behind her.

"Please," she shouted, pleading, "I need to go back," but no one heard, or cared.

Out of nowhere, it seemed to May, a camera crew was behind her and wedged her in as they moved forward. She had no choice but to go with them.

"Mei-jin," she thought she heard. "Mei-jin!" She pushed herself up, stretched to see. An, it was An who was screaming at her.

May shouted at the camera crew to help her, at the same time lunging backwards until her muscles sent flashing pains, her arms reaching out to An. "Help me get to her," May begged them. The sound man tugged at the cameraman's sleeve, pointed to An and Hao, then to May. They stopped their forward movement, and began to swing the camera back and forth, first at May and then back to An, who was holding Hao above her head, making a path through the packed humanity.

"Help me," May screamed, pulling hard at the arm of the camera-man. They followed her, like a phalanx, the cameras going.

"Take my hand," May shouted, reaching for An.

An was holding the boy above her head, he was crying. "Take him, take him," she screamed at May.

The crowd surged again, pulling them apart, but a man in the crowd passed the child over his head to May. She reached, felt her hands under his arms as the full glare of the television lights caught them.

"You bastards," May screeched at the crew. "Stop that and help me get that woman."

When she looked again, An had been swept to the side, she was out of reach. Holding the child firmly in one hand, May pushed away the camera, wanting to shield him from its awful glare.

"An," she screamed into the crowd.

"I cannot go," the child's mother screamed back, "I cannot go."

The embassy gates opened to allow eight Marines through. At first May thought they were coming to rescue her. Then she saw they were heading toward the camera crew. She held the child to her, tightly. She could feel him tremble.

The camera swung away from May to a point behind them. A young Vietnamese pointed an M-1 rifle at the approaching Marines. May froze in place, she was locked in, she could not move. "Get him," shouted one of the Marines, a tall black man, and another marine lunged at the man with the weapon. In the turmoil, the television cameraman went down. The weapon was wrested from the Vietnamese, and May watched as a Marine picked up the camera and smashed it to the ground.

As the black marine pushed his way back, she grabbed at his sleeve. "Help us," she said. "I'm American."

They were inside the gate, looking out, but she could not see An in the crush of Vietnamese pleading and begging to be allowed in. A helicopter hovered, lowered itself into the compound. Hao wrapped his small arms so tightly around her neck that she could not breathe.

"Little brother," May managed to gasp, "I will take care of you until your mama comes back. Shh, shh little one." She held tight to him, aching for his loss, breathing the awful pain of it. Her arms and her back hurt, but she could not think of that. The roar from the sky assaulted her senses. It was as if the bats, grown enormous, had come out of the trees and were roaring inside her head.

A light rain began to fall. She ran for cover, stumbling through a clutch of Vietnamese who cursed and kicked at her.

"Chinoise," one of them spat in disgust.

"American," she screamed at them, her anger bursting through. "I'm American."

She felt a hand on her arm, an insistent voice close to her ear. "Mrs. Diehl," he said, "it's okay, come with me." He tried to relieve her of Hao, but the child screamed and she said, "No, it's all right."

"Hayes is pretty frantic," the young political officer said, "I'll try to get a line through to him. And we have to get you on a helicopter pretty fast now. It's coming down to the line."

"All these people," May said, looking about her at the swarms in the embassy compound, "will they all get out?"

He pretended not to hear her question. May knew the answer, and suddenly she felt her cheeks glow hot with shame.

———————————

Marylee called to tell me that Hayes and May would be bringing the boy home, that Andy's son would be staying with the Diehls in

Burlingame. Her excitement was contagious. "Faith," she said, the words spilling out and over themselves. "Can you believe what May did? Did you ever think . . . they are in Bangkok for a few days, the child needs to be checked by a doctor, and May and Hayes are trying to find out what has happened to An. May told me to call you . . . she knew you would be worried," Marylee sputtered, adding, "Andy's son. My grandchild. Bless May, going in like she did . . . I cannot believe it, I simply cannot."

Marylee is totally immersed in the refugee program. The Diehls have a Vietnamese family living with them—a mother and father and two children, twins, a boy and a girl who are a year older than Hao.

"It's pretty chaotic down there," May laughed, when I asked how it was in the Diehl household. "Marylee is making a major effort to learn Vietnamese, and her pronunciation must be pretty funny because she has them all in stitches. How are the Nakamuras taking all of the uproar?"

May frowned. "Not well, I'm afraid. The whole thing with Sam . . . missing now, for two years. They are convinced he was captured by the Viet Cong and is in a camp somewhere. They still think he was on some kind of secret combat assignment."

"They must have asked Hayes to help them?" I probed.

May shook her head, sadly. "Oh yes, and he has very dutifully gone through the proper departments, and the last record they have is of Sam leaving Saigon on a World Airways flight in October of 1973, en route to Oakland, with stops in Manila and Honolulu. He never went through U.S. Customs."

"So," I said.

"So," May shrugged. "It is terrible for them, the Nakamuras, but it would be worse, we think, if they knew the truth. And in some ways it comes out the same—Sam is lost."

May had planned to return to Washington with Hayes, but when she told Hao she would be leaving he burst into tears, so they decided she should stay on until he became more accustomed to the Diehls, and was not afraid.

"As much as we might wish he were, he is not our child, he is An's," May told Hayes. "As long as a child has a parent who loves him and wants him, our job is to reunite them. We've got to get her out of there, to bring his whole family out if we can, and if they want to come. Then we can be Hao's godparents, his loving aunt and uncle."

"And what if we can't get her out?" Hayes wanted to know.

"We must," is all May could say.

———

May stayed on for a month, and part of that time she spent with me, going over all the details of that last day in Saigon and, though she laughed at the idea of it, helping me bring the "May Papers" up to date.

For lunch she fixed us little sandwiches of nut bread and cream cheese and Lapsang Souchong tea and we went through all the old papers, making notes and sorting. It was at one of these working lunches that I remembered the two men who had come to question me on the day Saigon was falling.

I was angry with myself for having forgotten. "They said it was only a routine background check," I told her, lamely.

"As it happens," May interrupted, "that is exactly what it was. I'm not supposed to tell anybody," she went on, grinning, "but you're as good a secret keeper as I know. The most curious thing has happened, Faith. Suddenly, all sorts of strange things have come together . . . Daddy has become a sort of hero in Washington. The revisionists' view is that what he wrote about the Chinese Communists was correct, after all. And suddenly my name—as his daughter—turns up on a small list of people who are invited to visit China as the personal guests of Chou En-lai, and we are told that it is because he respected my father as 'a friend of China.' I suspect the Chinese know about Grandfather. If nothing else, my name should have tipped them off. Or maybe Rose told them, she has been moving up in the hierarchy. Whatever the reason, the State Department seems to think that Hayes and I will be assets in Beijing, at the new embassy. If all goes well, Hayes will be posted there.

"Does he want it?" I asked.

She grinned. "He's studying Mandarin night and day. Calls to practice with me every night. Does that answer your question?"

"And you? Do you want it too?"

She hesitated. Then smiled, slowly. "It would have been a lot easier to say 'yes' before Hao appeared on the scene. But yes, I do want it.

Very much. It will be wonderful to be both Chinese and American, and in a position that could have real influence in bringing the two countries together. And of course I'll get to see Rose."

"And your mother?

"Yes," she said, drawing out the word so you knew there were qualifiers, "but only if I can make her life happier. I don't want to disturb her equilibrium."

I was not sure I could speak. I reached across the table for her hand. "Darling May," I told her, and my voice failed me, cracking to a whisper. She understood, finally she understood something of the failure of love, and found it in her heart to forgive, and then to go beyond that to give.

It was a long time before I could speak; finally I asked, "And Hao?"

She hesitated, thinking. "Marylee isn't drinking, not at all any-more. Of course, she talks twice as much. Hao calls her 'Grandmother Talk-talk'—he's got a funny little sense of humor. But he is taking to her, and she is his grandmother. He stays in his father's old room . . . all of Andy's high school pictures are on the wall. I think he is in a good place to wait for his mother . . . it's better that he stay with the Diehls, here on this coast where there are so many Vietnamese. Better for Hao, and for us—as much as I want him, and as much as Hayes wants him. To be honest with you, I am more than a little distressed by these people who want to bring all the babies out of Vietnam, to give them 'new parents' here. I think that when those babies have parents who want them, who would keep them if they could, we should be working to help them stay together, not taking their children from them on the guise of giving them the 'good life in America.' Hao loves his mother. He can't understand why she gave him to me that night. He doubts her love. Kit helped me, and I intend to help Hao and An. I am going to bring them together, if she survives this awful time."

Thea and Amos are to be married at Wildwood on Christmas Day, in front of a bank of red poinsettias. Thea is nineteen. Kit was nineteen when she was first married in the drawing room of Wild-wood, two days before Christmas in 1922. "I have had two wonder-fully happy marriages," Kit said to me. "One early in life and one late, one at Wildwood and one at the Malibu."

Thea settled on Wildwood for the ceremony because it is near

Stanford, and many of her friends. So the clan will gather once more, before they are all scattered by the winds.

We have much to celebrate. Philip's new book will be out in December, and in January, Hayes and May leave to take up a post in Beijing.

Karin and Paul and the baby, Katie (Katherine Faith is her full name) will come for the wedding. Paul's son, Alex, will stay behind to take care of the boatyard. "He says he is tired of sowing wild oats, that he wants to settle down with something as steady as the sea," Karin wrote me some time back, but she did not sound convinced. Karin is also bringing along an exhibit which includes a series of my photographs, called "The Hawaiians," which is to be shown in a local gallery.

Annie will fly in for the wedding, but she can only stay the day. After two years of playing minor roles in touring companies, she has hit what she calls the "semibigtime" in a new repertory theater in Cleveland. She is playing the role of the wife in a play based on James Agee's "A Death in the Family."

Annie is to be the maid of honor, Phinney will be his son's best man. Philip says he would never miss "rolling down the aisle" to give his daughter away, and Kit is ecstatic with the joining of the families. Hao is to be the ring bearer, though he has told Thea, whom he calls "Big Sister," that he is much too old to wear short pants.

Only Emilie is not entirely happy about the marriage. They are too young, she says, Thea should have finished school, Amos still has a long haul in graduate school. Thea is not emotionally stable, she adds, she will weigh Amos down.

I want to say to her that none of us is emotionally stable, that all of us weigh down those we love. I want to tell her that the one thing old age does not blunt is our feelings, that to the end of our days we ache for those we love when they are hurt, no matter they are five or fifty. We cut ourselves, and our children bleed and bear the scars.

These last nights, in the hour before sleep, I find myself remembering my mother. Snatches of songs she used to sing as she sewed and rocked . . . *In the sweet by and by* and *Shall we gather by the river.* The night nurse wakened me last night, she said I was crying in my sleep and she wanted to give me another pill, "to ease the pain," she said. I could only shake my head and try to hurry back to the dream she had interrupted. There was a parade down Market Street on a lovely, bright blue afternoon, bunting on the buildings and brass bands and music and everyone was there, all my old friends, long dead, laughing and strutting as the band played . . . May was there as a little girl holding Sara's hand and not far behind, May as a grown woman walking, arms abreast, with Karin and Hayes and Sam and Eli and Israel, all smiling. Phinney was wearing an Alpine hat, with Amos and Annie on his shoulders and Emilie shouting, 'Come march with us, Mother.' I jumped out of my wheelchair and ran to meet them, twirling and stepping high as the brass band played and the happiness swirled about me, and I was filled with the perfect knowledge that it was right, all of it was right, and that the parade would never end.

AUTHOR'S NOTE

When I came to the end of my first novel, *Hers the Kingdom,* I knew I wasn't done with the Reade family. Or, more precisely, they weren't quite done with me. What I did not know was that the baby born at the end of that book would become the main character in this one. In between I did a novel called *A Time Between,* in which several characters from *Kingdom* appeared, almost uninvited. (Just as Faith, from *A Time Between,* became the narrator of this book.) Diane Reverand has been the editor on all of my novels; I think she must be as caught up with the Reades and their friends as I am, because when I told her what I had in mind for this book her immediate response was something like, "Of course." In the long months it took to research and write *Gift of the Golden Mountain,* Diane and my literary agent, Claire Smith, would look in on me now and then, say a few encouraging words, cheer me on. Working with them has been part of the pleasure of doing this book, and I am more grateful than I can say to those two nice, smart, thoughtful women.

There are others I must thank. It amazes me how generous people are, how quick to help. I suppose you can expect it of friends (I did, and none of them failed me) but now and then an acquaintance would go out of his or her way to get a bit of information for me, or put me on the right track. I sat next to Dr. Peter Strykers at a dinner party, and happened to mention to him a medical problem I was dealing with in the book. The next day he phoned me with precisely the information I needed.

I knew our good family friend Karsten Prager was much too busy to take time out to read my Saigon chapters, but I asked him anyway. Karsten had been in Vietnam as a correspondent for *Time* and has strong feelings about that place, that war. He is *Time*'s international editor now, but he managed to read my chapters on a plane, then made the time to talk to me at length about his impressions of Saigon.

Tim Knowles is a lawyer friend whose grand passion is sailing. Tim painstakingly went over that part of the book which deals with sailing, his charts of Hawaiian waters spread out on my kitchen table.

My friend Suna Kanga, a journalist who lives in Singapore, set out with me to explore Hong Kong and Macao and the south of China. Then, a few months later, she went with me to Thailand. It was sweet, polite, determined Suna who got us to the jail on Mahachai Road in Bangkok.

Two other dear friends, Ingrid Schultheis and Carol Kirk, were generous to a fault with their time and energy—Ingrid did library research, Carol did whatever needed doing, and both offered unflagging encouragement all along the way.

In the Chicago area, my helpers were my college friend Jane Pritchett Bailey and her friend, Joan Lincke.

In Hawaii, Janet Sanborn was a wonderful source of information. We sat and talked on the lanai of her little house perched high in Makiki Heights, overlooking all of Honolulu, and I knew I would have to borrow the setting for the book. Expatriate Hawaiians Pete and Lynda Sanborn, now of California, never lost patience with me when I would call them—as I frequently did—for some bit of information. Nancy Maxwell of Honolulu was also a great help.

I ran into Dr. George Moore of the U.S. Geological Survey on the Hawaiian island of Lanai, where he was doing field research. He agreed to help me with my research on volcanoes, and was as good as his word. The folks at the Volcanoes National Park, and at the Volcano Observatory on the Big Island of Hawaii were a great help as well.

Dr. Bonnie Hardwick, head of the Manuscripts Division, Bancroft Library at U.C. Berkeley, took the time to explain the responsibilities of an archivist.

Carolyn Wakeman has a deep and abiding affection for the Chinese, having taught English literature in their schools. She was kind enough to go over several chapters for me.

In Los Angeles, our longtime friend Doug Ring, that fine barrister, has my heartfelt thanks for all of his good help.

So many others helped out: Ray Colvig of the University of California Public Information Office; Michael Moynihan, Head, OECD Publications and Information Center; Sara Brown and Jackie Fridell McKinley; Janice Eng, Susanne Robbins, Ruth Limtiaco, Barbara Sheehan, the Hong Kong Tourist Association; Bob Candiotti and Singapore Airlines; The Singapore Tourist Promotion Board; National Tourism Administration, People's Republic of China; The Tourism Authority of Thailand; Thai Airways International; and the Macao Tourist Information Bureau. If I have left anyone out, I am truly sorry.

I've saved for last the people who deserve a large blue ribbon (or maybe a purple heart) for bravery, patience and good humor—my photojournalist husband, Ted, who read the manuscript in progress and offered the kind of sound advice I've learned to listen to; my son Mark, twenty, and my daughter Maria, eighteen. They are good guys, and I appreciate them.

ABOUT THE AUTHOR

SHIRLEY STRESHINSKY is the author of the widely acclaimed novels *Hers the Kingdom* and *A Time Between*. Her articles have appeared in *Travel & Leisure, Redbook, Glamour, McCall's,* and many other publications. She lives in northern California with her husband and two children.